Don't Let Me Die In Disneyland

The 3-D Life Of Eddie Loperena

J.A. Marzán

Published by Open Books

Copyright © 2018 by J.A. Marzán

ISBN-13: 978-1948598026

For Silvina

DON'T LET ME DIE IN DISNEYLAND

Don't let me die in Disneyland,
where camera-posed
under Donald Duck's hug
and canopy beak
children don't see
a cloud pirate ship
of black cotton candy,
where sniffing me Pluto
picks up no scent,
and Goofy's too smart
to trip on a speed bump
he knows is just me.

Don't let me die in Disneyland,
where buckskin Crocket
aims his supremacy
at infantry-uniformed
Mexican clowns,
where home from the mine
Snow White's seven dwarfs
all claim to be Dopey
and dance around Hi Ho!
as off to death I go.

Don't let me die in Disneyland,
where Jiminy Cricket
chirps not at all
and Pinocchio's nose
stays thimble small
despite his big lie
I never was there,
Lost Boy who lost

every happy thought,
who fell from his flight
to Never Never Land
and had to grow up.

Don't let me die in Disneyland,
where in gunpowder night
fireworks awe
blooms to illumine
Cinderella Castle
but not the crossbones
of a black hull,
its treasure my corpse,
unseen above Main Street
as in Grand Master tux,
a trumpet for scepter,
Mickey Mouse leads
The American Parade.

—Eduardo Loperena, Class of '73, published in
All the Above, Smith Wesson College

PART ONE

MAIN STREET, U.S.A.,

1987

Chapter 1

...Graziela simply had to see Pirates of the Caribbean just then, at almost noon in that August heat. So we roasted on the zigzag line to the shade of Lafitte's Landing, her mood rotten as it had been all that morning, finally changing the second we boarded the production-line boat. Cheery down the Louisiana bayou, she lip-synched the recorded "Ho-Ho-Ho." Clown pirate scenes produced chuckles, not a predictable wisecrack like "the darker ones looked South Bronxy." As we approached the movie-set Spanish-Main port city, gazing up in awe at the replica Caribbean night sky whose original she had sworn never to lay eyes on again, she cuddled. We were floating under the fire of dueling cannons, my arm over her shoulder, my hand suspended over her Minnie Mouse T-shirt, when I stealthily palmed her braless breast under Minnie's ear, and she shuddered. In pleasured reaction, I thought, to my index finger's stroking her nipple. But she pulled my hand from her breast, and for the rest of the dark ride mentally sailed inward, smiling to herself. At the attraction's end, she jumped out of the boat, one hand rummaging her handbag as she rushed ahead out of the landing's dim light to the blinding sun of Adventureland. I saw her reach the restrooms behind a souvenir shop, her white shorts and T-shirt glaring in sunlight as she turned and, finding me, raised a triumphant fist whose content I knew: a tampon. Smiling after five anxious days, she waltzed into the Womens' Room...

The phone rang. The machine answered: "The lawyer Eduardo

1

Loperena isn't taking any more cases..." The caller hung up.

Why had my mind drifted to that horrible day at Disneyland? Fingers still on the keyboard, I realized that to the left of the type-writer I had been peripherally staring at a grinning Mickey Mouse holding out a receiver, the upright phone that Winston left on his otherwise empty desk. I hid the little prick behind the file cabinet.

That morning Judge Weinstein signed the final decree. Our mar-riage lasted seven years, lived in an area of the North Bronx where My People had yet to migrate. Last night I dreamed that because I had complied with Graziela's every wish—I left My People to their problems, closed my low-income office, joined a high-powered Manhattan firm—she called off the divorce.

I awoke, of course, to the first day of the new life of the bearded face in my bathroom mirror. Leaning to trim my now salt-and-pepper beard, my nose became a prow steaming through breath-fog toward the Big 4-0. I wiped away the fog. The beard had become a bad disguise of my youth.

I grew it after receiving Harvard Law School's acceptance letter. A liberal Political Science professor at Smith Wesson College was impressed that I, a minority student, was keeping a 4.0 average and advised that I could do more social good as a lawyer than writing the radical poetry for which I was famous on campus. An outfit called the Wheatley Foundation was offering fellowships to minority students who applied to law schools. He knew people at the foundation and suggested Harvard, where he also had some pull.

Before that moment being a lawyer had never crossed my mind. I was born to write and had moved beyond radical poems to writing stories. But if I saw a serious choice between writing and becoming a Harvard lawyer, it was not just false but indescribably stupid in the eyes of Mami Lalia, who characteristically sledge-hammered her common sense: the son of a woman who sewed bras in a factory had a moral obligation to embrace that opportunity. But working dressed every day in a pinstripe suit and wing-tipped shoes! The beard served as my private symbol of solidarity with Fidel's *barbudos*. Now its gray just aged me.

White foam entirely covered it. In a few strokes the razor removed it. In seconds I was a wondrous spectacle of bare-skin from my neck to the twin bays of my receding hairline. I combed back my thinning, limp hair, once a ball of revolutionary, Afro-style curls.

I finished one letter and aligned another sheet in the roller. Before Winston left, we agreed that he would take over my last two *pro bonos* and I would handle remaining office chores. So here I am, in a practically bare office, dressed in a lawyer's suit either from habit or because I am not quite sure myself if I am really ending this career, typing letters to clients.

I couldn't have typed one on our old fat I.B.M electric without running out of correction tape. Thankfully, our secretary Karla made us get this electronic upgrade because, as she put it, we were two progressive lawyers working as if oil lamps still lit up the streets. You type into a small, word-processing window that allows you to make corrections before printing. Then overnight our cool technology became obsolete beside the personal computer. Winston purchased one when the original high price came down. Neither of us learned how to use it before he took it with him. A technological revolution was taking place just as Winston and I were retiring as revolutionaries.

I was first shown the Shining Path toward social justice by Brother Albert, my teacher at St. Peter's School. He taught us of our Christian obligation to make a better world. That lesson traveled with me to high school at the exclusive boarding Excalibur Academy in a suburb of Boston, which I attended thanks to Brother Al, who recommended me as a minority student worthy of one of the full scholarships they were offering "to exceptional students of color."

At Excalibur I met "progressive" and "artsy" friends who introduced me to a more radical vocabulary— "Yankee imperialism," "colonial exploitation," "racist capitalism" —words that later inspired my revolutionary poems at Smith Wesson College. But Brother Al continued to be my conscience, even after I graduated from Harvard and later as I defended the rights of My People, what I've done since passing the Bar, earning the honorific "The Community's Lawyer" from a columnist at *The Daily News*. I boarded the train to Excalibur determined to keep my promise to Al to remain committed to justice, not knowing that Boston would be the first stop of a train of Current Events scheduled to carry my life to my opening this office partnered with Winston—and now to close it.

Winston and I met at the law firm Kukla, Franklin and Oliver. He had just passed the Bar and I was studying to take it. Under his guise of another blond white-guy, he was a "radical" that the firm didn't know it had hired. In a secret ceremony he had recently married the Puerto Rican community leader Isela García. (I only knew her from the news because, after Excalibur and Smith Wesson College, I really didn't know The Community.) About to leave the firm anyway, he saw no point to disturbing the mostly conservative partners with the news of his nuptials. His letter of resignation was already written when he heard that I had been hired.

We were instant seventies brothers, a match made in leftist heaven. I had just broken up with Louise Hobson, and to prop up my fallen spirit Winston would stop by my office. One afternoon he laid out his plans for us. Isela was recently named director of a huge community service program, his first major client in an activist practice to represent such organizations as well as to defend victims of racist, exploitative capitalism—what society considered simply criminals. I welcomed this avenue back to The Community, so when I passed the Bar, we opened this office.

Of course, we came to revolution from different directions. Winston was drawn to struggle by intellectual empathy, not by marginalization in the flesh. Case in point: he was genuinely pissed when he heard about my rookie run-in with Clarence Ferguson, a senior partner who conveyed to my face his personal objection to the firm's "fashionably hiring a concession to Affirmative Action, even one from Harvard." I reflected then asked: "Well, does telling me this make you feel 'better,' or should I say 'intestinally relieved?'" Ferguson kept his smirk walking away. After that, word spread that Loperena suffered from a 'tude problem, and that if I was still at Kukla, Franklin after sassing a partner like Ferguson, that was proof that my ass had been saved by white guilt.

Inviting Fergie to a drink to discuss the latest movies—I had recently seen Elia Kazan's *The Last Tycoon*—or, knowing that he too was a Yankees fan, to talk baseball, was out of the question since the creation of Time. For him my body was composed of civil-rights-issues flesh and Counterculture bones. I breathed not oxygen but leftist cliché.

But for the very reasons that others saw me as an enema abrasively introduced as good social medicine into a job opening for which their friends were more soothingly better qualified Winston saw in me a comrade. He related everything rumored about me in his white presence because, denied the exhilaration of actual victimization, his engine of social commitment ran at full throttle on the narrative fumes of such experiences. Once those stories stopped working their enchantment and Reagan smiled away the Great Society, Winston possessed the privilege to walk away from the ruins of the seventies.

Marrying Isela in the seventies to divorce her in the eighties was a testament to his good eye for political fashion. Now, attired for the Reagan Era, he could quit our low-profit activist practice to make good money with his Republican cousin's consulting firm in Seattle, "the most livable city in America," also the perfect place to replace the plump brown Isela with a leaner, pink All-American Gal. Because for Winston, the WASP former socialist no one could pick out from a line-up of Republicans or Russian spies, home is any quiet corner of this country, his social commitment a canned generational vogue with a shelf life.

On the other hand, my home, home on the range was MINORI-TYLAND in AMERICA, THE THEME PARK OF SOCIAL STRUGGLE. If Winston was free to advance into the eighties, my genes kept me in the seventies, fighting for people of color, whether rhetorical color or real, my revolution not just ideological but biologically hardwired.

Winston left looking sheepish, taking my words of understanding his departure as just classy rhetoric. He couldn't imagine that I, being the "minority," understood his desire to leave behind the seventies to surf into the sunset on a crapped-out Marxism's long ideological fart. He couldn't imagine that if I possessed that freedom, I would have used it in a heartbeat.

I mean that white *americano* freedom to walk not weighed down by bullet-proofing against the Oh-God-I-gotta-be-tolerant-now stare at the exoticism of my Mediterranean swarthiness, my hair curled by a renegade African gene, and the anger in my black, Otherness eyes. And that other freedom from the predictability of this discussion, My People's incessant Conversation on our minority condition, repeated out of the need to justify ourselves before a culture at whose pallid imagination we should simply marvel.

All my life my unpolitical dream was to return to my childhood island Paradise, a boy's aspiration that the seventies turned into a baroque political idealization, a liberation from Yankee clutches following the lesson of Cuba. In that vision My People were still homogeneous, not either islanders, "real Puerto Ricans," and alienated *newyoricans*, and we were all paradoxically simple and sophisticated, rural and post-industrial, innocent and militant, forever singing on the country road as in Rafael Hernández's song, "Y alegre el jibarito va,/ cantando así..."

Well before Winston talked of leaving, that inhaled seventies smoke had worn off, and I began to see things as brutally as they struck me. My People had changed and I was never going to be replanted in the tropical flower pot of my "roots" now that we of the mainland had been disowned, no matter that throughout our lives we drag behind a bleeding umbilical connection torn from that placenta. Even if one was not born there and even if one has never been there, one preserves *la isla* on a mental map, our essential X that marks a place to be from. For if anybody needs a place to be from, it's we Ricans in the U.S., that land that is my land, that land that is your land although not exactly right here nor exactly over there either. Having no place to be from, we continually remodel that plasticine place from which we progressively lose touch even as, whether to bury a relative or settle an inheritance, we still have to return, not with the advantage of the indifferent tourist to a resort

6

unreality but to a reality Bedlam whose patients all wear the same threadbare Americanization.

No greater collective illusion than boarding a jet plane to return, three hours and fifteen minutes to a memory that Time swallowed up. Approaching the Luis Muñoz Marín International Airport, the plane descends, bumping down cloud stairs until its wheels thump onto the runway, delivering a lifetime of accrued social angers. We pick up our luggage in air conditioning that, even though one may know better, deceives in reassuring that we've arrived at the place where everything that we've always felt out of sync will be set right. But what awaits are kin who forgot you are related, by family or by culture, who stare at a misguided pilgrim, face disfigured by decades of self-doubt and anger en los Estados Unidos. They demand to know what the hell you are who can't speak fluent Spanish and bring a gift of defensive brusqueness, saying this as they get more bilingual, more Americanized, berating you to convince themselves that they know what the hell they are, blowing that fart out of asses on which is tattooed, as we all have, the American flag.

arrival at US

This tattooing takes place in every island maternity ward, the doctor also an ambassador from Washington, coaxing out babies who can later serve in the U.S. armed forces or give birth to more babies who will. My Bayamón Hospital birth certificate certifies my American citizenship to the country that claimed me at the outer edge of my mother's womb, the country whose mechanism for attaining our equal participation, when successfully used, stigmatizes for having resorted to claiming that equality.

I gave up my practice when I realized that nothing I achieved in a courtroom would liberate us from that scam, nothing legal would redeem our three-dimensional complexity from being two-dimensional props in The American Story. To achieve that freedom I had to start fresh in another country, the one I invented and proclaimed to myself, Nowhere.

Winston's leaving only spared me my having to explain my new liberation even more unrealistic than our now defunct Worker's Paradise: the unlitigated, un-talk-show-worthy, untalked-to-death equality on Main Street, U.S.A. that he enjoyed since birth. That place where I would never have to repeat any of this rant.

I phoned for a Chinese lunch then rolled another sheet into the typewriter. The phone rang. The caller let the outgoing message play completely. "Socrates, you there?" I picked up. "Carlos?"

"Hey, my maaaan!"

After more than twenty years Carlos sounded as he did when we both lived on the second floors of adjoining buildings and from his fire escape he called me to come out to my fire escape so we could hang out, two stories over our block...*the street's asphalt our turf for stickball, with manhole covers for home and second base; the tar plant across the street, its wall perfect for King, Queen and Jack played with a pink Spalding ball; the bodega that never once closed beside the empty lot that remained a rat-infested dump until a public housing project bulldozed it, our buildings, and the entire street off the municipal map...*

"Hey, Soc, you there?"

"I'm here. It's really great to hear from you, Carlos."

"Well, that makes me feel real good, 'cause I been meanin' to get in touch with you. I see you're a big deal in the community. Seen you in *The Daily News*. I brag to my friends, that's my man Socrates, my little brother, the big lawyer. Many times I thought of calling but I know you're busy and my situation is crowded too with all kinds of shit..."

...Muscular Carlos, who started pumping the weights he got for Christmas after seeing Charles Atlas's physique so many times on the back covers of comic books, who bounced the pink Spalding ball off the stoop faster than any other player, who held the King's square longer than any pretender, whose stickball bat could only hit home runs, the same Carlos who would also sit out on the fire escape alone for hours and sketch the rows of build-ings, the domino players in front of the bodega, the tar factory trucks being filled with big black cans, sketching because he was born with the ability and wanted to be a commercial artist, what his mother told him his father was...

"...so I didn't want to just crash in on your life, you know."

...and my protective big brother, always watching out for his skinny best friend, once sending that bucktoothed crybaby Georgie Adamici home bawling

8

with a broken nose because Georgie had lost his mind and tried to push me around after he heard I had been alone with his sister in their apartment.

"Well, Carlos, I'm glad you called because I've been thinking about you too."

"Oh yeah?"

A door I meant to open only a crack suddenly flew wide open. Now Carlos waited for me to walk in, say what I had been thinking about my forgotten, closest, discarded friend.

"So, Carlos, what are you up to these days?" I gritted my teeth, knowing what Carlos had been up to for a long time.

"Oh, you know, independent businessman, and I was doing very good, but it looks like hard times are coming, and that's why I'm calling you, little brother."

I almost repeated my answering machine message about not taking any more cases.

"As I said, I'm hitting some hard times now. Not just in my business. I been working solo since my wife split last year."

"I'm sorry, I know how..."

"No kids. I mean we did have one, but he died...anyway that's the past."

"How's your family?"

"Before I met my wife, my whole family started dying, man. First my abuela..."

Hooked-nosed Doña Perla, whom Mami Lalia paid to take care of me after school, ever cooking beside her Spanish radio soap operas. She must have been over ninety.

"I'm sorry, Carlos..."

"...Then right after my abuela died, my moms found out she had a tumor in her breast. She didn't last a year, man. My aunt was already gone a long time before. So things are like that, okay."

...Carlos' mom Vivian wore tight skirts and on my entering puberty, always got me horny. Her older sister Nicolasa came home from the shirt factory and walked around the apartment in wired brassieres, her big tits bulging out. Carlos' family, crammed into that one-bedroom apartment identical to ours, adjacent to our bedroom wall...

9

"But I didn't call to talk about that." He cleared his throat. "I got this problem I need some help on."

"You need a lawyer?"

"No, man, I need somebody I can trust. I need to move around, have to travel light. I need to leave a couple of suitcases with you." After my silence: "Not what you're thinking, man, just paper. A lot of valuable papers. I need to leave them somewhere for a while. Are you catching what I'm pitching, Eddie?"

"I think so, but Carlos..." He was calling from a street phone and a recorded voice was asking for another deposit. His coin jingled down.

"Listen to me, man. I gotta hurry. Nobody in my business knows nothing about me and you. Everybody thinks I'm talkin' out my ass when I talk about you anyway. Just in case, that's why I'm calling and not going to your office. Unless your phone is tapped, nobody knows nothin' about this call."

"Who's after you?"

"My competitors, Soc. You can't step into this. This is street shit not for you. Just write down my will."

"Your will?"

"Now, understand, I'd like to get the suitcases back, but life is life. So let me just leave you my will."

"But is this illegal money, Carlos. I won't be able to execute your will."

"Soc, Soc, just listen to me, okay? I never said nothing about money. But this is my will: If something happens to me, those important papers are yours, little brother."

"Carlos, I can't—"

"Don't, don't, don't, Socrates, I ain't got time. I got things to take care of real fast, so I'll be in touch with more details. Later, bro." He hung up.

I stared out at nothing, wondering how without moving I had stepped into a forgotten room in the blueprint of my life. Now that I planned to resign as professional minority citizen from this culture as packaged for My People, to leave The Community behind, Carlos calls for me, croaking from the middle of our sociological swamp.

Chapter 2

No picture in my memory archive fit the description of the person named Big Carlos, connected to Colombian sources, greaser of the palms of crooked cops to muscle out competitors, overseer of a network of neighborhood distributors. The voice on the phone didn't belong to Big Carlos but to the face I last saw.

I was home for my first Christmas break from Excalibur. Mami Lalia sent me to deliver a girl's party dress she had finished, her side business. On the way back I bumped into Gerry Duffy, who was in Carlos' class at St. Peter's. He was pulling a loaded grocery cart for his mother. He introduced me to her as the kid who had gotten that scholarship to a boarding school. She looked sadly at Gerry.

When I got to our block, Carlos was sitting on my building's stoop. Something wasn't okay with him. Mami Lalia told me his aunt was receiving chemotherapy for intestinal cancer and that his mother had recently lost her job. Carlos and his mom weren't getting along over a man she was seeing.

It was great to see him. He missed me too. I asked about kids we knew from St. Pete's. "Don't know much, don't hang around here. I stay with a girlfriend by Morrisania." He heard that Richard Bell won a city-wide track medal at St. Dominic's High, and that one of the Hungarian kids who arrived at St. Pete's after the Budapest uprising got an Irish girl pregnant.

"Those Hungarians were really two and three years older than us. They stuck them in our seventh grade class because they couldn't speak English."

I told him about seeing Duffy and that his mom didn't seem happy for me that I was attending Excalibur.

"Everybody's jealous, man. You're lucky to go to that school, get the fuck out of this shit neighborhood. Just don't forget your people down here. How is it up there?"

I described the country scene, the dorms, the brand-new gym. I told him the girls were pretty but not sexy like ours, most of the guys snobs. He listened transported, the way he traveled every time I returned after a summer in P.R. and told him stories. He took a few seconds to come back. "Man, I don't know if I could make it there. If one of those snobs looked at me the wrong way, I'd pop him one."

I sometimes felt that way too but didn't tell him. "I miss hanging out with you."

I really did miss him and felt very lonely but would rather be up there than on our block. I asked him if he was going to be around but he said that his girl was waiting for him. I thought about maybe asking him if we could meet in Morrisania but I always heard it was a tough neighborhood. The next day and the day after that I tried to find Carlos at his abuela's, but he was out.

On Christmas Day I went by his house to leave him some socks that Mami Lalia had gotten for him, but Doña Perla explained that he got into a bad argument with his mom and spent Christmas Eve with his girlfriend. Doña Perla sent Mami Lalia a fancily-packaged *turrón,* a Spanish nougat. I figured that when he got back, he'd call me, but a week passed and nothing.

On the afternoon of New Year's Eve, I saw him crossing the street, his Navy pea jacket open as always even though the day was cold. I opened my window and hollered out to him. I put on my Army fatigue jacket and ran downstairs. He looked bad, his eyes red, his muscular shoulders slumped. He had come to wish his family a Happy New Year and his mom's guy was already there. They almost

fought, so he stormed out. He didn't know when he'd be back. "If
I don't see you before you go, remember, you do your thing, little
brother, do everything to be all right for the both of us."

Mami Lalia was removing rollers that straightened out her curly
hair. New Year's Eve night we always spent at the apartment of
Matilda Cintrón in Brooklyn, where many from Bayamón yearly
gathered, and where we had to arrive early so she could help cook
the food. She had already put on her make-up and her light cinnamon cheeks were soothing to look at. Because I slept on the sofa
bed and didn't have a room, I got dressed in her bedroom while she
finished getting ready in the bathroom.

When I came out she looked me over, not looking at my suit. She
knew how I was feeling about Carlos. "*La mamá de...*Carlos' mother
dates the kind of men I wouldn't look at. It breaks my heart to see the
direction he's destined to take, but you can't do anything, so don't
lose yourself in trying to save him." Then she lowered her voice
as if somebody could hear her tell me that Carlos' family and ours
came from different stock. They're more like the people coming to
New York now from the island, *jíbaros*, not like our family. "Most
Puerto Ricans like us really stayed back on the island. Even in that
Carlos didn't have your luck in life."

The day after I returned to Excalibur I wondered if Carlos even
heard me describe my school through his pain of not having a home
anymore. I thought that he might be having a hard time remaining
my friend because some inherent difference had determined that
I would be the one plucked from our neighborhood to attend this
nicer school.

That summer, thanks to a lifeguard course I took, I got a job at
St. Mary's Park pool. When I got home, I was too tired to go down
to the street. I set a lamp by the window to read on the fire escape.
One night, instead of reading, I noticed how the neighborhood had
changed—or noticed more impatiently how pathetic it had always
been. People dropped wrappers and dirtied the street. Men on the
sidewalk drank from beer cans in little brown bags. Music blared
out of every window and neither husbands nor wives cared that

the whole block heard them fighting. I gave up on seeing Carlos.

In the last week of August Mami Lalia left work early to meet me in front of Alexander's Department Store on Mahdorf Avenue. I needed new clothes to begin the fall semester at school. I was looking at winter jackets when I saw Carlos over by men's suits. I went over to him, and we hugged. Mami Lalia stayed by the coats. Carlos waved at her. She waved back tepidly.

He looked pretty sharp in a three-quarter length black leather coat, a black turtleneck sweater, and a gold chain with a girl's name in gold hanging from it, Alicia. I asked if we could hang out later. He said he was meeting his new girl, and held up the gold name. That summer he worked at Central Park selling ice cream until he met Alicia at a party. "Alicia is older, runs her own business. I'm making real money working with her." He was attending a public high school now because Vivian said she couldn't afford to pay St. Dominic's tuition.

Mami Lalia called me back to the coats. I asked him to write, told him that my mother can give him my address. He said he'd get it from her. After that, for weeks I'd call home and ask if Carlos came around to get my address. Mami Lalia always said no but I'm sure even if he had, she wouldn't have given it to him. That fall his family moved away from our block. Mami Lalia claimed not to know where they had moved even though at the bodega she picked up every *chisme* on anybody. I kept pestering her, and she finally spoke frankly. "*Carlos sólo*...Carlos would only show you street ways. I prefer that you stay away from him, make new friends. Your getting that scholarship was a blessing from San Judas Tadeo, his sign that you should start fresh."…

Did Carlos actually call me today and propose something impossible?

The phone rang. Gustavo Sánchez O'Neil, Mayor Koch's Deputy Mayor for Hispanic Affairs, left a message to call him back. He was running for Congress and wanted me to manage his campaign. Ever since I made a name for myself, he had been grooming my political potential: "You can affect millions of lives in the most direct way, not through some plodding legal system." His only logic understood that I was closing my practice to cash out on my renown as "The Community's Lawyer" for a more lucrative political career. For him closing my practice to write would be the equivalent of aspiring to become a subway violinist.

Yesterday while packing files I found the first chapter of a manuscript that I had started, who knows, almost five years before. Louise Hobson had planted the idea that I write a minority testimonial because they "were hot nowadays." When I decided to start, I was already married to Graziela, who threatened to leave me if I didn't stop. "You've already wasted your valuable law career on My People, so at some point you invest your time on making money and looking ahead and not back. Besides, since when do you consider yourself a 'victim' of this society to write a sad 'minority story' about it."

I had no intentions of writing as a social victim although I didn't know where it was going. The first chapter talked about my first seven years in Bayamón's hills, where my parents lived in basically a large shack, well before my father decided to bring us to New York, not realizing that he was still carrying a dengue flu bug that brought on his death that first winter. But Graziela really wasn't why I stopped: I was capable of getting hooked and winding up broke and alone in some roach-infested apartment.

My problem was that I didn't just want to write; I *had to*. Stories would materialize before me superimposed on my real experiences, then I would archive them, the characters still haunting me. But I had to contain the impulse. One day a mother called because her son was being held at Riker's Island on a heroin-possession charge. I recalled the afternoon that Carlos took me to a party in the apartment of an older girl everybody called Dotty the Slut, where I first saw somebody shooting up. That mother's voice made me think of how Mami Lalia would have reacted if she saw me among that kind of people. A story occurred to me about an impressionable young man at that party whose mother comes looking for him. Karla, who could decipher my face, fanned before my eyes papers that required my attention. In a blink, abandoning a lawyer's career to write seemed as ludicrous to me as it did to Graziela.

Hated losing Karla, the proudest little fat lady in the world, an assertive Ecuadorian choo-choo transporting her freight of efficiency. Her chubby-cheeked, slant-eyed, mestizo face patiently smiled at my laxness as she moved from desk to copy machine to desk and file cabinet and back to copy machine. She provided structure and organization. She reminded me that the pager only worked if it was turned on. Under her eye, this letter that I just stopped writing for the third time would have been written. Máximo Modesto and I arranged to have her report the following day to his law office.

I returned to my letters that were getting harder to grind out. Winston and I partnered to free the Third World from the tentacles of capitalism, treating every courtroom battle as a world-informing theater. And we confronted police brutality and discrimination in housing and employment. We won class-action lawsuits to improve the bilingual education of newly arrived children. And of course, I won the case of William Guzmán. But just as often we saved the asses of pathetic clients like the misery piled on my desk.

"Dear Mr. Camacho: According to the judge's order you were supposed to..." At sixteen Nicky Camacho discovered a talent for stealing and stripping cars. He was given probation and ordered to visit a therapist weekly. My letter sent him to Modesto and reminded him of the consequences if he attended therapy only once.

Lourdes Castro was accused of leaving three sleeping children alone while she trotted off to dance in a neighborhood club. The building caught fire, and her children were saved but traumatized. Lourdes swore she just went to the club to get milk money from Sis, who corroborated the story. A hung jury. Her new attorney was going to be Francisco Suárez.

Then came Piri Amador, accused of rape in a hallway. According to him, the panty-less victim sat on the stairwell with her legs wide open, her big-lipped *chocha* throwing him kisses. How was a real man supposed to react? He simply zipped down his fly, moved in and then out, zipped up his fly and walked off whistling Zippideeduda. His aunt testified that she'd heard the two laughing in the hall. She asked, why didn't that girl wear panties? Piri walked.

The rape victim is filing a civil suit. Modesto now has his file. Only the tip of the pile.

Nicky's letter done, I got up and stretched, walked to the window. In the weekday activity on Westchester Avenue under the elevated Pelham Bay subway My People went about their lives cleansed of Original Sin by my revolutionary consciousness. Along both sidewalks they walked in and out of stores, climbed the stairs to the elevated subway station, waited for a bus. How many belonged to the sorry kind, not "like us" as Mami Lalia warned, lost-cause *jíbaros* like those on my desk or like, her assertion was painful, Carlos. Or was Mami Lalia just exporting her island prejudices? Did Brother Al seek out that scholarship for me because he saw that difference? I didn't feel that different. Carlos had been like my brother.

Along Westchester Avenue a mother pulled a shopping cart loaded with groceries as her little boy, about ten, steered a stroller with a toddler in pink. The tilted shopping cart was the same as Mami Lalia's. I was pushing Rosy's stroller. The three reached the corner and turned out of sight, to my starting point before Harvard Law School, before Smith Wesson College, before Excalibur, before Rosy was sent back to P.R. so she wouldn't get raped by a lowlife Bronx *jíbaro* or grow up a morally loose *americana*. Before...

I returned to the typewriter.

Lourde's and Piri's letters were done before the Chinese lunch arrived. Munching on pork lo mein, I tore out the previous day's page on my desk calendar, crushed it into a ball, lobbed it toward Winston's empty basket, scored. Karla's eyes reprimanded my puerile behavior. I flipped calendar pages. Tomorrow I expect Dr. Maritza Islas, accusing Mahdrof University of bigotry in denying her tenure.

I only agreed to see her because she'd been referred to me by Isela and I liked the sound of her voice. Ironically that night Mahdrof's noted sociologist Father Thomas Stevens was being feted for his contributions to My People both as *padre* and sociologist scholar. Sánchez O'Neil, a university trustee, sent me tickets. I had stopped attending such leadership powwows to please Graziela, who wanted to keep our contacts with The Community to a minimum. Now I was free to attend but given Sánchez O'Neil's sowing rumors that I was about to make my political move, his way of pressuring me into managing his congressional campaign, I had a better reason not to attend.

Since my separation from Graziela, free to be me, I lost any doubt that despite my pinned-stripped ectoderm inside beat the heart not of a politician but of an artist and not the kind of artist of which Sánchez O'Neil was a bona fide genius. But my future still a blur, I had to make a living, so I couldn't just discard everything Sánchez O'Neil proposed, which of late was offering me as a Hispanic vote magnet to Governor Mario Cuomo's re-election effort.

I agreed to attend a Sunday Brunch, look into what Cuomo had in mind, Sánchez O'Neil's job referral that came at the price of having to make a guest appearance at his Barrio luncheon for Harlem leaders. After that, blank calendar pages, my only commitment a flight to P.R. for Rosy's Fourth of July wedding. I had just swallowed my last bite of egg roll when the phone rang.

"*No te...*I didn't want to bother you, but I didn't know who else—" I picked up with a greasy hand.

Yvette was calling about her boyfriend, arrested for stabbing a cop. I heaved a sigh—*what jíbaro fool stabs a cop?*

"*A la verdad*...Actually, it was an accident, and the policeman is still alive."

"*¿Cuándo*...When did this happen?"

"Last night."

"Was he resisting arrest?"

"It was an accident, believe me."

"Where is he?"

"They took him to the 40th precinct. His name's Esteban...Esteban...Cabrera"

Cabrera. Cabrera?

I threw on my suit jacket, and went downstairs to my Camry, which I kept parked behind the Greek-Cuban Deli. At the first red light I asked myself what I was doing. I wasn't supposed to be taking any more cases. But this was for Yvette.

Detectives Dalton and Murray and a new uniformed officer seemed disturbed that I was there to represent this...Esteban Cabrera.

He was brought out handcuffed, looking out of slits of eyes puffed into black and blue golf balls. We sat in a small room with a desk. Dalton and Murray lingered and my look inquired why they didn't leave. "Eddie, this guy confessed." Paunchy Dalton, in a gray suit over a white knit shirt, was red-faced Irish. His big red nose breathed heavily owing to a sinus problem.

I peeked into Esteban's slits. "Is Bell around?"

"No, he's out. Don't get mixed up with this one, Eddie," Murray chimed in. Wiry, gaunt, ghostly pale and calm, in a black suit he could pass for a priest but wore blue jeans with a well-worn, brown leather jacket. "With three cops on top of him, he kept kicking and shouting 'I kill you friend. Me.' and some other stuff in Spanish. Don't waste your time."

"You have a list of the witnesses' names?"

"Cops who were there and Callahan himself."

"That's his name?"

"Yeah, and he's got a wife and two kids."

"So Callahan was well enough to make out a report?"

"The cops who were witnesses made out the report. Callahan was still conscious when the ambulance came."

"Let me talk to this guy."

"Eddie," Dalton said, "you don't need this kind of case. It's a piece of...well, you know." They stepped outside, became shadows behind the door's frosted window.

Esteban said that he had recently arrived from Puerto Rico. He had no family in New York except for a sister he didn't know. Her name was Graziela. His sister's phone and address were in his wallet. I opened the door and requested the wallet. Graziela never mentioned a brother, neither did my mother-in-law. This guy didn't resemble Graziela in any way. He was dark, with a little bulbous nose not like hers. Hers was aquiline. His black hair was tightly wavy, not straight like Graziela's.

When an officer returned with the wallet, Esteban removed a

slip of paper with the name "Graziela Cabrera" at my old address. "*Nunca nos hemos*...We've never even seen each other. I thought I'd meet her at our father's burial but she never showed up. Her mother hated my existence. I was the son produced by her husband's cheating on her, so she taught Graziela to hate her father and me. My aunt found out her address. She thought it wrong that I didn't know my own sister."

Dalton opened the door, said something. He spoke again, "I said, can he sign the confession now?"

"No way."

"Come on, shit. We drag this guy in here bragging at the top of his lungs that he did it. What? Puerto Rican lawyers can't get cases?" For the officers I was a "Portorican" pain in their *cojones* with a Harvard degree up my ass. "Maybe I just get my rocks off breaking your green Irish balls."

"Okay, just do what you're gonna do. This asshole's as good as gone," he shouted at my back on my way out the precinct, Esteban's predicament no longer front-page in my mind.

Public schools were now on summer vacation. If Graziela and her new man hadn't taken off, I could call—but one syllable from me would be the duration of the call. When I reached the precinct door, Richard Bell entered. "Eddie, what's up? New client?"

"Maybe, good to see you again. Gotta run." A couple of years before I bumped into Bell in the Bronx Court House. He was one of St. Peter's School's few black kids, and the fastest track runner in our school. Now an NYPD detective, he'd been recently transferred to the 40th. "Remember Gerry Duffy? He was transferred too. He's my partner." Still muscle-toned, his hair was nearly all gray, the hairline receding. He asked if I kept in touch with my buddy Carlos, if I knew what he was doing now. I did. The court part door opened and Bell was summoned inside. We shook hands. When I tried to release my hand, he gripped it harder and tugged me closer. If I wanted to get in touch with Carlos just let him know.

Foggy connections between cops and suspect neighborhood old friends I had witnessed before. What stayed with me was the possibility of contacting Carlos. I told Graziela about bumping into Bell, mainly to share with her how strange that a cop should so casually offer to put me in contact with a known drug dealer, but she didn't believe my story. I was the one who had inquired about Carlos. Her index finger shot up to warn me that if I planned to stay married to her I shouldn't even think of that meeting, that I should come to terms with the person I became since the day I took that train to Excalibur. "You may make a living by preaching that everybody is equal and nobody is better than anybody else, but if I married you, it was because you are not a community 'brother.'"

Isela could have passed on Esteban's message to Graziela. But I wanted to confront my ex-wife for not telling me about this brother although I also knew that bringing up her father's adultery was to set a match to her most flammable theme: the evil of Latin men, really why we got divorced.

"You're just like all of them, no different." One hand went to her forehead, and her head fell as she heaved a sigh of exhaustion, from living with me, from living. I was sitting on the bed watching her get ready to go out because, after finding out about Yvette, she had declared us over. In vengeance she had fixed herself to pure *latina*: lips red, eyes lined larger and vibrant, body potently perfumed, dress accenting every curve, killer high heels, a woman I had never seen. I did supply her with a righteous reason for the breakup. But I was also taking hits for every Latin man in her life.

Elsa Sapato, a client, first made me aware of that *latina* anti-Latin man syndrome. She was the organizer of a rent strike in her South Bronx building of mainly single moms. Winston and I fought off the landlord *pro bono*. In gratitude, Elsa and her sister strikers invited us to their celebration dinner at her apartment. At the last minute Winston backed out to attend some political caucus and, not to slight those grateful women, I went. As the other women worked in the kitchen, Elsa, who was designated to entertain the *abogados*, served me a beer and sat beside me on the sofa.

Her pale sagging cheeks were heavily rouged, and she had gathered her frizzy black hair to one side behind her left ear. In a red

21

dress and heels, she looked like a big-hipped real woman, not the maintenance man she passed for in daily, big-butt jeans. Her lament of Winston's absence explained why she had spruced herself up. "*Sé que*...I know he's married, but I like his kind, not like these men around here, useless, liars, traitors."

"*¿Crees*...Do you think he's a saint?"

"No, but he's not Latin. I prefer men who aren't. Ask any of these women and they'll say the same thing. If they could, they'd avoid Latin men."

Mami Lalia once expressed the same. While searching for a job around the time I was born, my father took up with a woman. When I was nine and we were living in New York, Mami Lalia belched out that old pain to a neighbor. "*Nuestros hombres*...Our Men will always hurt you," she added, then gestured with a deep sigh, "our men are like that and there's nothing anybody can do."

Graziela once quoted to me the same words from the mouth of her mother Mercedes, a short frail woman who compensated unhappiness with God's recompense in His own way. Graziela loved her mother but hated her example of forgiving her husband's sexual betrayal to preserve social respectability while silent anger ate away her insides. Her resentment of her father was the real reason why she asked to be sent to live with her aunt to attend high school in New York, where she had planned to attend college. For Graziela, in other words, "Puerto Rican" didn't mean coming from a place with beautiful beaches and lush tropical vegetation and a warm Hispanic culture but the damnation of coming from three hundred square miles of men like her betraying father.

I once asked her if I was the first Latin guy she dated. That, she answered, was none of my business. But patently some post-traumatic stress had been carried over into our marriage because treachery was not just expected but almost wished for. I once accused her of doing everything to have her anger reaffirmed, and she got really furious, unforgivable my presuming to know her better than she knew herself. Losing her temper was her way of avoiding an honest exchange especially when she might have to backtrack. Such tantrum smokescreens dissolved as soon as she achieved her objective.

Real retribution she prepared calmly, with deliberation, the way she monitored my affair with Yvette. Discovering it was her proof that despite my "disguise of the enlightened college-educated new man" I was "the typical macho." My cheating I saw as a bit more nuanced.

Long before I met Yvette, Graziela had distanced herself and I could pinpoint the exact moment: on the day that, having recently passed the Bar Exam, I mentioned that we could now start a family. She reeled. After my postponing so long, she interpreted that I had given up on having children, and she had been willing to forego motherhood to support my commitment to my career. My sudden, supposed flip-flopping was a breach of a tacit contract.

I had always said I wanted children and actually passed the Bar exam sooner than the national average, a fact that made no impression on her. Since that conversation, the "pressure" I put on her to have a child epitomized my oppressive male package. Somehow, it was also symptomatic of my disease of being a Latin male.

We had both married under false pretenses, two veterans of the Civil-Rights era dreaming that we could rescue a lost ethnic essence. For my part, I was seeking my roots on the rebound after my having to stop seeing Louise Hobson, a relationship that had left me in an identity crisis. In a seventies *Roots* phase, Graziela may have genuinely believed she was over her phobia of Hispanic men in finding me acceptable when she was really attracted to my estrangement from The Community.

One day I confessed that I had idealized her according to the *Roots*-consciousness that we had all then been high on, adding that I soberly came to love her true person, hoping that my heart speaking from its open vault would inspire her to dial the combination to hers. But it didn't. She didn't need all that information, she said. By then I was committed to my practice with Winston and identifying with The Community, inadvertently proving that I was like "all of them." In the end, it was easier for her to wait for me to provide the ineluctable provocation of Latin men for breaking up a marriage.

My defense, I admit, is as old as Time: in Yvette I groped for feelings I couldn't get at home. Not just sexual feelings. Graziela herself didn't realize how she had reduced me to a symbol of her culture's treacherous men. I became a two-dimensional symbol again as I had been in Louise's social world, in the country I was offered. Yvette was my oasis of warm feelings in three dimensions.

Chapter 3

I walked two blocks from a parking spot on Riverside Drive to Graziela's West 87th Street brownstone only to realize that I had overlooked the intercom. Refusing to buzz me in was power too irresistible. But all I could do now was press the button. No buzz. Steps descended behind the door's translucent window. A short, bespectacled chubby woman in a flowery summer dress and monk's sandals opened the door and immediately blocked my entry, inquiring what business I had in the building.

"I'm expected at 3A, but the buzzer's not working." She gave me a body-length scan, my lawyer's suit and tie possibly better qualifying me for entry. She pressed the button. Empirical proof gave me the privilege to pass.

A dog's barking from a higher floor got louder as I climbed the stairs. The barking was coming from a third floor apartment that faced the street, from Graziela's 3A. I walked around the stairwell railing to her door, paused to gather courage, remind myself that, after all, I was a lawyer there on business. The dog barked behind the door, and a man's voice ordered, "Sylvester, calm down."

David Marlboro's presence muddied matters. He was a theater lighting technician who had been after Graziela even when she was married. His heavy footsteps went into another room then returned, "I'm going to walk Sly." A chain rattled over the floor. Sylvester sniffed at the bottom of the door, his paws scratching.

Their door had a button under a peephole, and I was about to press it when behind me I heard thumps climb the carpeted stairwell. An elderly black man, keys in hand, nodded. He had a full head of snowy Afro-hair. He used two keys to open 3B, then turned and smiled before entering and shut the door. My pressing 3A's button produced a chime. Sylvester barked and sniffed even more feverishly.

Graziela's eyeball appeared in the peephole. Sylvester barked. "Quiet Sly," she hollered, then inquired, "Who is it?"

"It's Eddie. I need to speak to you."

She didn't open. "What do *you* want?"

"I'm here as your brother's lawyer."

"My brother?" The security chain scraped against the door, one lock clicked.

"Grace, why are you opening? And what the fuck is he doing here?"

"Let me handle this, please. Just take Sylvester out."

Another lock clicked and the door opened to a family tableau: the six-foot, brown-haired Marlboro in straight-leg jeans, a sleek Doberman barking and panting at the end of a chain, and the barefoot Graziela in shorts and T-shirt, her hair now pixy cut and dirty blond. A flicker in her stare betrayed her taking note of my clean-shaven face. Marlboro held back the panting Sylvester.

"So what's this about?" asked Graziela.

"Your brother. He's in big trouble."

"What are you talking about? I don't have a brother. Is this a stupid excuse to harass me?"

"You're half-brother, the one you never told me about."

"He told you to call *me*? I don't even know this guy. How did he have this address?"

"He had our old address. Somebody had given it to his aunt."

"Who contacted you?"

I started to say Yvette but caught myself. "This is pretty serious, Grace. Attempted murder—of a cop."

Sylvester lunged, and Marlboro pulled him back. "I gotta walk the beast." Marlboro was pulled by Sylvester out the door, not acknowledging me. He added out loud, "I want your guest outta here by the time I get back."

"Why didn't you just call? Why did you come here?" She was containing anger.

"I figured you'd throw down the phone before I got a word out."

"Well, that's true. But why are you coming to me with this?"

"You're the only blood he has in this city. Can we talk inside?"

"No."

"It's common courtesy. I think it extends to lawyers and exes."

Graziela sighed. "Look, I really don't know what we have to talk about."

"So I just tell this *jíbaro* that this woman he thinks is his sister is too sophisticated to..."

"Stop!" Her look telegraphed a desire to throw the door in my face but she stepped back.

The high-ceilinged studio apartment had a well-lustered Parquet floor. A small kitchen to the left of the door. A sleeping loft framed two windows that afforded little daylight. Out of one jutted an air conditioner that kept the room pleasant. Graziela sank into a leather chair under a lit floor lamp. I sat by the air conditioner. In the lamplight she looked younger and nubile. A healing bruise haunted between her right cheek and ear.

"So what's the name of this person who's supposed to be my brother?"

"Esteb—"

"I don't get it, Eddie. Of all the lawyers in the world, why do *you* have this case?"

"It was Yvette."

"Ah, your big-assed barmaid."

"I'm not seeing her. She didn't know who else..."

"I don't care. How did she know he was related to me."

"She didn't. It was this Esteban..."

"Esteban?" Her eyes climbed the wall above my left shoulder and up to the sleeping loft.

"Yes, like your father, coming to think of it. Anyway, the cops beat him up pretty bad. They don't like to see their brother cops stabbed."

She stared at the Parquet floor, exhaled hard. "I don't know. It's that world. A million miles away from me. I don't even know this guy."

"Grace..."

"Don't lecture me, Eddie!"

"I wasn't going to lecture. I was only going to tell you that I can't take his case because..."

Sylvester was panting up the stairs.

"That was fast. You better go."

Sylvester pawed at the door. Marlboro's keys jingled. The door opened and Sylvester ran in, straight to Graziela, who stood up to rub his shiny ebony head. "Hi, baby. High'ya. High'ya." I passed Marlboro, who threw the door behind me.

Before I got to the top of the stairs the neighbor in 3B turned two locks and opened the door. The elderly man pressed an index finger against his lips, a finger cut off at the first joint, and waved me in. After closing the door, he whispered. "You a lawyer, right, and somethin' to that girl, too? I was listening, sorry."

"Hi, I'm Eddie Loperena."

"Sam, Samson Magnus, pleasure."

"Yes, I'm a lawyer and her ex."

"Well, that's good. I mean for what I'm gonna tell you. She's a beautiful girl, so I don't think it's right that white boy beat up on her like he does."

"He hits her?"

"That's right, hear the screams all over the hall."

My stomach turned into a fist.

"Makes me angry, nice girl like that let herself get beat up. I never see no family. That's why I'm jumpin' in like this, if you don't mind."

"No. I appreciate it."

"Well, I hope you can do something for her because, like I say, that ain't right, and she don't seem to have nobody."

"Her mother is old and not well, lives in Puerto Rico. She's got people there but...I don't know what I can do. It's her life."

"Well, I'm a retired taxi driver, and now don't really go anywhere except walk to the deli and the supermarket. I can still drive, still got my license up to date, but I can't afford a car, insurance, gas. This building is rent controlled and I been here a long time. So I'm here all day and can hear everything and get to live their lives without meaning too."

"That can get tough."

I took out a calling card, pointed out my pager number. Samson let me out as furtively as he had invited me in. I stood at the top of the stairs listening. For what? A reason to bang on the door, act like a jerk-off rescuing knight?

Sunset bled over the West Side. Maybe Graziela was right. We should both just walk away from Esteban. No point dropping his problem on her lap when she hardly knew him and had problems of her own. She no longer belonged to that "world." Neither did I. Disagreeing on where we did belong tore us apart even though we were never actually together.

After graduating from Hunter, she and a girlfriend toured Europe. Her father left her two plots of valuable land, and with no plans of returning to the island, she convinced her mother to sell them. With the money she visited England, France, Brussels, and Germany. I asked her why she skipped Spain. She just shrugged.

I, on the other hand, had saved my summer job pay to take a student charter flight to Spain. My Venezuelan friend Luz Vitali at Smith Wesson convinced me that while my poet's radicalism worked for showing off among Americans, I should start to rescue who I culturally was from my true roots. I took her advice that summer. The average *madrileño* was stiffly different from us, especially in those rigid Franco days. But traveling south I discovered the Andalucía of Lorca and Picasso, close to Arabic Africa, the origins of the version of Spanish that My People spoke, where the people sounded more like us.

Maybe if Graziela had had my experience in Spain, a sense of belonging to a wider world, she would have seen herself and us and all of us differently. Once in Spain I decided to take a ferry to Tangier. Not to smoke hashish like my black Bronx buddy Blane was waiting to do. On vacation from a tour in Vietnam (where he crossed paths with Carlos, who got shot in the ass and lucked out when they sent him back home), he was the only black guy at a disco full of Germans in Málaga.

I took in Málaga and the next day, I grabbed a bus headed further south to Algeciras with plans to hop a ferry that crossed the Mediterranean to Africa. I sat in the back row beside a window. A mother sat beside me on my left, facing the aisle, serving as bulwark between me and her two restless young boys also contained by the two-seat row in front of them. The father sat sidesaddle with feet in the aisle in front of his wife, watching over his family. They looked *gitano*, clothes ragged and poor.

The parents were dramatically mismatched. She was much younger, fair and wan, a Renaissance madonna, hair covered with a kerchief except for tiny hair rings crowning her temples and forehead. That delicacy clashed with her dirty red calico dress under a man's brown suit jacket with the cuffs rolled up. Beside me she was a wax statue staring at the floor of the aisle in the direction of but really past her husband.

He was short, very dark, his black hair combed back, and frightening was a diagonal scar that cut deep from his left eyebrow, caving the bridge of his nose, to the right side of his lips.

He disciplined the rowdy children in a language I didn't understand. I guess because I was observing, he spoke to me in his language, and I said in Spanish that I didn't comprehend, looking to see if his wife understood me at the very moment that a cockroach crawling out of her jacket's breast scampered up to her shoulder and up to her neck, continuing into her hair. At that instant, like one of those Disney robotic figures, the woman suddenly lifted her head, turned to me and asked in a slow voice, as if narcotized, "*¿Ere' moro?* Are you a moor?" I shook my head. She said, "*Parece moro.* You look like a moor." Her eyes returned to staring at the aisle.

At Algeciras a storm farther out kept me from taking the ferry to Morocco. At the pier a young Arab asked me in Spanish something I couldn't answer about the schedule. Perhaps my different Spanish accent prompted him to ask where I was from. To simplify things

I said "Puerto Rico." He pat his heart with his fist, "*Español! Somos hermanos!*" The backlog of passengers meant I could never get to Tangier with enough time to make it worth the trip and return to catch my charter flight. From the pier I looked out toward Africa that I could not reach but now seeing myself there too, not as just Eddie from the Bronx but as Eddie from the wider world.

When I spoke to Graziela of my trip, I shared the pleasure of the novelty of being surrounded by people who *expected* me to speak Spanish, of being thought a *moro* and embraced by that Arabic guy as brothers in a lineage, of discovering a wider world in which to belong, where Lorca's *gitanos*, like us, struggled with their country's disdain, especially under Franco. She just made a face.

That was a turning point because until then we had enjoyed the same things and appeared to share the same world with Isela and Winston. Excited that I had met her, the courtship was short. Neither of us had family in the city, so we appreciated the importance of having each other and decided to marry, which we did in City Hall. Winston and Isela witnessed.

In love, I was in denial that our differences ran that deep. A trip we had to take to the island so we could introduce our mates to our parents was tense but I also blamed both our families. Then a year into our marriage, after I had committed myself to defending My People with Winston, she began to express what she had been covering, that she felt a million miles away from "that world."

Given her close friendship with Isela, I had always assumed that most of her friends were Ricans. But Isela and I were exceptions. Her friends mainly came from the theater and she kept "that world" and her private one apart. What she really saw in me, a Rican not in the theater, I started to contemplate too late. Ironically now I was driving across Central Park to the East Side on my way to the Bronx to see the woman who fulfilled the sense of place that Graziela had taken from me, Yvette.

Chapter 4

The Danubio Azul Restaurant, named after the favorite waltz of its proprietor, Rodrigo Cuevalonga, was an oasis where public school teachers and local small businessmen met for lunch and later after-work drinks. This Danube, however, ran through not an imagined Austria but through the Puerto Rico romanticized in the restaurant's murals of sugar cane fields and cobbled streets of colonial San Juan.

In anticipation of the late daily crowd, the air conditioner was on high. On a barstool closest to the door, Armando Casanueva worked on his daily drunk. He was the younger of two brothers who owned Casanueva's Super Furniture. Their ads played on Spanish TV, "Casanueva para su casa nueva" (Newhouse for your new house). Marcelino, "Mark," mostly ran the business and closed the store, leaving Armando to get his drink. Mark wouldn't be caught dead socializing in the Bronx. He married an *americana* and lived in New Rochelle. I never saw Armando sober. Every night he left the bar soused and miraculously drove to Northport. He struggled through an alcoholic haze to recognize my beardless face.

Yvette behind the bar had no problem recognizing my bare face. A smile was her reaction. She pointed to our corner table. Bearing a scotch on the rocks, she also delivered her silky cinnamon complexion, her green eyes, her extravagant hips, her waist like a wasp's, but couldn't join me just then. She went over to Rodrigo, spoke something to which he nodded. She returned and sat.

I got to the point. "*Vine*...I came to tell you that I went to the precinct as a personal favor to you, and I'll represent him at the courthouse in an hour, but I can't take his case."

She assumed the silence of a student listening to a teacher.

"I got him a good lawyer. And there's another reason why I shouldn't take this case. Esteban, if you can believe this, is Graziela's half-brother."

No reaction, then she burst out in laughter. "*Cuando*...When he told me of a half-sister named Graziela Cabrera, I wondered. He showed me the address and phone number but I never knew your exact old address and you never gave me your home number. I didn't call you right away because I was afraid his sister was your Graziela. Then I heard those court-appointed lawyers just throw you to the wolves."

"Graziela isn't the only reason. I'm closing my practice."

"Why?"

"Many reasons."

She seemed to gather that it would take more time to explain and said that she had a real break due and could take it now if I wanted. I almost told her no. My mission was done. But this unfinished scotch and my eyes full of Yvette. I agreed. Thanks to the scotch, Eduardo had also emerged and couldn't take his eyes off Yvette's curvaceous form as she leaned over to whisper into Rodrigo's ear. She returned.

"Well, how did it happen? Was Esteban drunk?"

She gasped for oxygen to gather the energy to tell the story yet again. She met Esteban at a friend's party. He started coming to the Danubio occasionally on his nights off from work, the night shift at a company that produces boxes. His visits somehow hadn't coincided with the off-duty cops who had made the place their hangout. Sometimes they tried to hit on her, nothing she couldn't handle. That fatal night Esteban stopped by when three cops were present. None was in uniform, and she had been too busy to explain that those guys were cops.

"He usually sat close to the register at the other end of the bar, the cops always closest to the door. Rodrigo had asked me to get a couple of quarts of milk from the deli next door and when I came out from behind the bar I passed one of them sitting on a barstool and he stuck out his arm and wrapped it around my waist. I asked him to remove it and he said out loud, 'Who do you think you are?' Esteban came over, shouting at the guy to get his hands off me. The cop told him stay out of it and his two friends came up to Esteban, who whipped out a switchblade and pointed it about a foot away from the cop's stomach. The cop had released me and I shouted out to Esteban that they were cops and to put the knife away because the whole thing was over. But he felt understandably threatened and was too angry to listen. The cop didn't believe Esteban was going to do anything and went to take the knife but his foot got caught in the bar stool so he appeared to be lunging at Esteban, who just stood his ground. In a way, it was really the cop's fault."

Her head fell. Narrating the event exhausted her. "Let's talk about something else. This has me sick. You look younger without the beard." Her face—red lips, perfect white teeth, eyes two glazed smiles—entranced her lover and servant Eduardo, who observed her delicate fingers pick up my empty scotch glass. He followed her gait to pour another drink.

We met on the night that Isela Chase's South Bronx Community Services Association held their annual dinner-meeting at the Danubio. By then Grace had stopped accompanying me to Community functions, always with a good reason. This time she was directing her school's production of Brecht's *Mother Courage* and was too tired. After that night, before heading to the North Bronx from my office, I began to stop by the Danubio to escape our quarrels at home and find refuge in her world—the one from which Grace was never convinced she had already escaped as a college graduate and high school teacher.

No matter how far she had gone in her life an inner voice convinced her that she was still not yet free from her kind. Our Civil Rights generation's determination to debunk that self-loathing bounced off her for whom Anglo Saxon people had always been superior, and whose escape from our meager horrific world would not be complete until she escaped from its men.

Yvette too had been betrayed by a Latin man. Her little girl Rosita's father one day simply disappeared. But Yvette didn't ascribe her husband's irresponsibility to her culture or as evidence of a damned genealogy. Yvette acknowledged that for a woman the *americano* world promised more stability, and of course, material security. But she hadn't met an *americano* that wasn't slumming with her, expecting her to be cheap. And she couldn't abandon herself to its sexless premeditation. To her *americanos* seemed terrified of the primary business of life, feelings, their human side drowned in being legalistic about everything. And, "frankly, I could never find the sexual side to their men."

Yvette laughed at Graziela's declaring herself a feminist, which to Yvette meant those women who railed against high heels, burned bras and walked around in men's work clothes. "I don't have to look like a man to stand up to one." She wanted her man to be sensitive but he had to be physically masculine and feel inside like a real man. To Yvette, Graziela's aversion to becoming a mother seemed grotesque and pathetic. Yvette felt privileged, not oppressed by the ability to bear children. Yvette's contrasting comfort with me as a man seduced me away from Graziela's constant indictment.

In other words, Yvette's nurturing an old-fashion male consciousness allowed me to be Eduardo, who wanted to experience being simply a male attracted to a warm woman, not caught between clashing worlds ever sociological. In the Danubio I was on the moon receiving the reflections of Yvette's earthy feelings, never upscale nor downscale, neither "white or black or Puerto Rican." Well, anyway, that was how I romanticized our affair until Graziela found out.

I knew better than my rationalizations, aware that Yvette was a figment of my hypocrisy. She was a beautiful oasis but also a simple woman who at the end of my odyssey could not be my home. Eventually I had to be honest with myself, and break off with her because she deserved to find someone who wasn't just using her. That pact with myself explained why, despite the second scotch that usually made Eduardo incorrigible, I resisted answering yes to her inquiry if, after the court, I would return to the Danubio.

On my way up the Bronx courthouse stairs my pager buzzed. Samson, I thought, was calling to report a crisis, but it was Graziela's home number. I called back from a public phone. Busy. After the arraignment, I called again. Busy.

The next morning she called my office. She confessed that she had regretted not flying to P.R. to attend her father's funeral, and now felt that she owed him at least helping out her brother. She had decided to visit him at Riker's. I warned her that Riker's Island was a real horror show and not a TV movie she could surf away from with a remote control. A long barge of silence sailed the length of the phone line. "I'll deal with it."

For the rest of the day I typed more letters. It was almost three o'clock when Graziela called again. "The bus to Riker's was full of those messed-up people I had wanted to avoid all my life. I was on the verge of getting off the bus and forgetting about Esteban. When I got to the prison, I was numb. Esteban sat in a cubicle, and we talked through a telephone. His face is my father's but darker and beaten so badly. Is that legal?"

"Máximo Modesto will address that."

"But why can't you take this one case? Are you just getting back at me? What happened to the defender of the community?"

"I can't go into that now. If that cop Callahan dies, with photos of his family all over the news, who's going to let a spick like that off? If Max can't help him, nobody can."

She said something that the pay phone operator spoke over. There was a silence. I had never felt her so sincere, so present. She repeated: "I said that I could pay you."

"Grace, we can just have dinner."

"No, Eddie, don't. We can't. If you want to go back, go back to before you met me. I have to go." She hung up.

She was right about going back to before we met. Reflecting on how she was incapable of seeing me as anything but a two-dimensional emblem, I became nostalgic for the person for whom I thought I truly existed in three dimensions, Louise.

Chapter 5
Louise Hobson

There I was, floundering in the white and gray of the Old Regime at a penthouse cocktail party of partner Troy Oliver, feeling every bit the pre-Bar exam, progressive Mr. Nobody—until I saw her. Black radar eyes, trim body, divine legs wrapped in the primo textile of a woman's gray business suit, expensive high-heeled shoes, and an artistic coif, exhaling from head to toe that beauty of confidence that I admired in an older woman. After a day of complaining about kissing the ass of the world of wealth, I was drawn to her elegant materialism. Her ocular invitation empowered me to walk over.

"Do you think," I asked, "that we should interrupt our conversation with introductions?"

"Of course not. So what's that you were saying about *me*."

A butler exchanged our empty wine goblets with full ones, then Troy Oliver, martini in hand, presented himself to welcome me to his house. "I see you've met Louise, looking exceptional as ever." He quickly excused himself to circulate.

"So Eddie it is. Fast Eddie?"

"I come in on cue."

Somewhere playing, a musical sound track wafted us out to a

late Thai dinner, during which I learned that Louise sold hot new artwork as investments to corporations and executives. Todd Oliver was a client. She sold him most of the considerable art in his duplex penthouse. She invited me for a nightcap at her West Greenwich Village townhouse furnished with exquisite antiques and adorned with fabulous modern art. As I knew we would from the second we laid eyes on each other, we crowned the night on her King-size bed. Like everything else she did, she indulged in her lovemaking unabated.

She looked older in the morning, but the pleasure of being with her, body and house, was not lessened. Over breakfast our conversation continued uninterrupted from the night before without indicators of exhausting. Our relationship took off. On weekends I accompanied her on tours of Soho galleries, or to visit studios of artists she represented. At galleries she lectured in my ear—about art and anecdotes about artists—as she squeezed my arm.

Her whispered art lessons aroused a dormant music I hadn't heard since my days at Excalibur when my roommate Teddy Katsavos discussed his abstract paintings always piled leaning against the wall of his side of the dorm. Teddy had been my only other close encounter with art. Being with Louise even evoked my teenage love for Dixie Culpeper, my first muse, for whom I wrote my first poems. In my delirium, one day I mentioned that I used to write poems.

"I told you that my late husband was a lawyer. I didn't tell you he was also a novelist. He didn't have a best-seller but one novel was purchased by a movie studio. They did nothing with it. When I first saw you, something in your eyes reminded me of him. My gut told me that you naturally gravitated to art and not the law. You're a smart bastard who's going to be one great lawyer, but it's that hidden side I'm attracted to. So you wrote poems. When am I going to read them?"

I couldn't imagine her reading those political protest poems and ethnic identity poems, in retrospect thin, always read before sympathetic crowds opposed to the Vietnam War and cheering on the Third World. "They're in a folder in a drawer of my old papers, which my mother keeps in Puerto Rico. Most weren't very good."

"But surely you must have gotten the urge to write at some point after college."

"The urge did come up. But I had to fight it."

"How about writing your story as a minority person. Those memoirs are hot nowadays and you have a story to tell. Few minorities go from the South Bronx to where you are. I can get you in touch with agents who are clients of mine."

Yes, but who would be interested in a life that seemed so lucky? I hadn't run with a street gang. I'd never been to jail or gotten hooked on heroin. Far more titillating would be the life of Carlos and the things Mami Lalia had heard about him at the bodega.

Her suggestion had catapulted me very far away.

"You really do need to write. Why don't you move in with me. You can write that book we both know you need to write."

"First I pass the Bar."

"You can study for it living here, then write."

Her wanting me to live with her took me by surprise. Once expressed, she couldn't hold in expressing the hollow feeling after I left every Monday morning and having to wait a week to be with me. What sane lonely bachelor in a modest West Side studio would decline living with her in that marvelous house?

But there was more to contemplate as a permanent resident of her world, whose initial liberal embrace was beginning to wear off, her friends' reservoir of cordial empty exchange having been depleted.

Where I expected innocuous chat or winks of solidarity with the social and racial righteousness that I embodied, still foremost in their minds into the eighties, I was receiving more genuine mono-syllables and that dumb look whites give when caught unprepared to perform mannered pluralism. That our idyll had run its course with her friends was signaled at a recent birthday party for Jeffrey Todd-Jones, one of her best clients.

Jeffrey, a young investment banker, had invited Louise, I guess expecting her to come alone because when he came over to welcome her and saw me he gave a look of surprise, not of pleasant surprise, rather of unexpected resentment, and not just for my being in his house but, I sensed, because I had crashed into the private party that was his life. Louise either didn't notice or chose to say nothing. I believed that I had let that look roll off my back, but that night in my sleep I saw Jeffrey's face morphing into Juan Acosta's at Smith Wesson and returning to Jeffrey's.

The face changed but not the look in the eyes—even though Juan's eyes were brown and Jeffrey's blue. Their look penetrated my Harvard lawyer armor so they only saw a New York Rican guy who didn't belong in their party of a better social class. They kept asking what I had come there to deliver, a pizza, and why was I still hanging around with a drink in my hand. A single outstretched, shared hand tried to give me some bills for a tip so I would leave. Instead of taking it, I mined my seventies revolutionary self-confidence of knowing that I was the planet of the oppressed rising up against supremacist bigotry. In my dream I heard my mantra in the voice of Eduardo, who didn't shut up after I woke up.

In my waking life Eduardo had already been undermining my original excuse for attending the party where I met Louise. Sure, I had a professional obligation to network among colleagues, but maybe deep down I took Nicholas Gainsay's advice at Harvard that I get better experience first at Kukla, Franklin before jumping into the political fray with the Puerto Rican Legal Task Force really only to put off returning to the Community. Sure, I still talked about defending The Community but now Louise was inviting me to become someone even farther from that alienated person I had started out being—ironically to write a book about that confusion.

Louise's deference to the dreaming writer had transiently seduced even Eduardo, and so I had convinced myself that with her I could simply be the generic person stripped of sociological evocations. But being with her also meant living in her world, and Jeffrey's look roused the dormant Eduardo, setting off a Roman candle of identical eye messages that I had been archiving in denial. Sidelong glances from her friends not fooled like their dear Louise, who although esteemed for being sharp, self-assured, and aristocratic, was perhaps feeling devalued by age or why else allow herself to be used by this much younger, "obviously climbing Puerto Rican," as I overheard a couple describe me.

In sum, by then her proposal that we live together was imperiled by that social bacteria, which I was trying to laugh off as American folk charm but that Eduardo wouldn't forgive for a second. In the end, of course, however grand my relationship with Louise, I couldn't allow myself to be trapped in a social world whose calculus of preconceptions precluded imagining that this Puerto Rican could climb on his wits and that if I lived with Louise it was because she made my prick stand like a ballistic missile.

Our relationship had to progress but it was advancing to no place where I could continue to be the person I had a glimpse of when being alone with her. My flying to Puerto Rico for a weekend to negotiate with some contractors for work to be done on Mami Lalia's house provided a seam. On our last Sunday, I rose early, got dressed. I was serving us coffee when she came out of the bedroom. Her silence evinced the perspicacity that never failed to excite me: she had known for a long time. Nevertheless, I said what had to be voiced, that the following weekend I would be flying to the island and after that our relationship could not continue. Her sad nod expressed understanding. She wished me a good trip and returned to the bedroom.

I didn't call her for three days after that. I almost called her on Thursday before flying. In Puerto Rico I caved in and called on a Saturday night, fortunately got her answering machine and hung up. That night, when I called New York to get my messages, her voice was on my machine. She extended an offer to give me time "to think over what you really want. I don't have to live in New York if that pleases you. But please keep in mind that I adore you."

When I returned to New York, for over a month she called once a week during work hours, intentionally, it would seem, to find me not at home so she could leave a message, "just wondering how you are, how everything is going," making it harder for me to survive missing her. Finally she left a longer message that ended with "I decided not to bother you anymore. I'm sorry you need to think about so many things when life should be simpler." After hearing that message I had a hard time resisting her and especially missed our long and rich and sexually stimulating conversations, about art, about anything—in other words, I just missed her. With her I truly felt a sense of place and without her I was lost. I had cast myself from her to sail off to what Eduardo kept calling "home," having no idea where that was. I listened to her final message several times, experiencing flashes of fantasy that argued that I chose wrong and that maybe Louise could actually be home. Eduardo pressed the erase button.

Chapter 6

By this time Eduardo was not the only counter force. Winston and Isela, monitoring my emotional decline, had plans for me. "Louise was really the wrong woman for you at this time of your life," Isela advised. "She's much older than you. What about children?"

That far ahead I hadn't thought.

"Your better nature told you to end it," Winston contributed. "You need somebody closer to your normal life. I apologize for coming down so hard but I think it a shame you're losing time by creating these emotional confusions. That's what you get for chumming up with the other side. I didn't go to that party. You shouldn't have gone either. No point. You had a mission."

"I was new to the firm. Single. Just trying to get a feel." I winked at Isela. Winston missed the humor. For him the broken-down world was going to be fixed without a laugh, and the firm misread his seriousness. By then too the three of us were convinced of the kismet of a future partnership. Isela had already concocted a remedy to put on a fast track the overcoming–love convalescence of her husband's future partner. The first step was to convince me to join them at the annual fundraiser of the Boricua Footloose Theater, on whose governing board Isela sat.

I completed the trio promptly in front of the theater but we didn't just enter. Isela and Winston exchanged smiles, then waved at somebody behind me, an approaching young woman. Isela's good friend Graziela Cabrera was just shy of my height, with black shoulder-length hair, light brown eyes, emitting a pleasant perfume. Isela informed that Graziela was a high school drama teacher who occasionally works with the Boricua Footloose Theater. They graduated in the same class at Hunter College.

The Theater's top floor of five, a large rehearsal loft, was crowded with a tossed salad of business people, politicians, and theatrical patrons that either Isela or Winston or Graziela knew. Greetings dispersed us, I unfamiliar with anyone. Finally, wine goblets in hand and munching on canapés, we reunited just as an imposing man in a gray suit walked out to the center of the large room and introduced himself as the City Councilman Gustavo Sánchez O'Neil.

Tall, handsome, blue-eyed, Sánchez O'Neil flaunted a full head of mostly black hair with silver streaks. Speaking into a microphone, he toasted the theater's founder, Miss Danira Román, who once worked opposite Gregory Peck as the beautiful Indian princess in the movie *Spotted Pony*, and who never succeeded in movies but who now earned Sánchez O'Neil's praise for founding the Footloose that "constantly reminds us of the cultural wealth of a community misrepresented by its material poverty." Miss Román stepped out into the adulation and welcomed all with a histrionic graciousness. Middle-aged and plump but ever pretty, she seemed directly descended from Arawak Taínos. Her bright orange summer dress accented her smooth brown skin.

Sánchez O'Neil stepped forward again and introduced the evening's guest of honor, "the man who over the years has supported the Hispanic community's theater and made this fundraiser possible, the theatrical producer and founder of the New York Shakespeare Machine, Mr. Josef Pepp." The smiling Pepp stepped out, waving. A short man with parted hair and a boyish smile, he looked spiffy in a pink shirt, white tie, white suit and white shoes. In the microphone he thanked Sánchez O'Neil for the introduction and Danira Román for her bringing theater to poor communities by means of transportable stages because, "as everyone here knows, my first love is theater and I believe that *latinos* will make up a key part of the future of New York theater, which means American theater."

He waited out the hall's applause to introduce the famed actors from Puerto Rico, Natalia Guerra and Rufino Pacino. Rufino wore a black Nehru jacket with a bone-white scarf wrapped around the collar. His blond hair was shoulder-length and he sported a goatee. His average height was humbled beside the statuesque Natalia, a brunette who filled out a red minidress with full hips and long milky legs balanced on red high heels. Pepp held out the mic as Natalia read their prepared statement: "Our island is here today in spirit to acknowledge the contributions of this theater to Puerto Rican theater. As representatives of the Institute of Puerto Rican Culture, we bring a jumbo jet of *orgullo*, pride, to snow upon this gathering." A round of applause.

The actors melted back into the crowd and Pepp introduced the "Poet of the People," Usmail Rufo, a brown chubby man with a bulky salt and pepper pony tail of wavy hair that had receded to the crown. One hand carried a tube of rolled paper and the other held a stuffed, black LP record sleeve. He wore jeans and over an army fatigue shirt, a half-white and half-black vest spotted with circular seventies "cause" buttons: "Free the Chicago Seven," "Stop the Cuban Embargo," "Jíbaro Sí, Yanqui No," "Give Peace a Chance." Pepp announced that the Shakespeare Machine would soon produce on Broadway "A Toilet for the Turtle," a play based on Rufo's poetry. "Robert De Niro will play the Turtle, a Puerto Rican janitor who falls in love with a woman in his building and discovers that she's his lost sister."

Pepp passed the microphone to Rufo, who held up the black record sleeve over his head and pulled out of it a bit of white latex. He claimed to have invented a special condom that "Of course, doesn't fit me." The crowd laughed. He unpeeled a black sheet over the LP sleeve to reveal, in white letters, "Nixon Condom." "You just slip your whole body into it and you're protected when you screw the whole country." I had heard him tell that joke, a recycling from the glory days during the war.

"I wrote a poem for Danira on the bus on the way here and made copies." He unrolled the paper tube and distributed the poem. "I didn't know how many to make, so you can share." He paused for the poem to go around. "So here's the bit. 'Poem to Danira:'"

It's like this bus
I'm rolling in
down some fancy neighborhood
to your house, our house,
where we wouldn't be
if you wasn't on stage.
It's like this bus
over the bumps,
stopping so many times
for passengers
and footloose
like your theater,
picking us up,
picking us up,
picking us up
to take us through
these fancy neighborhoods
where our people ain't
to your house
where we live,
where we come to give
a standing ovation
to ourselves.

The room sighed and ooooed then broke out in applause.

Pepp stepped forward and hugged Rufo and so did Danira Román, who planted a smooch on his forehead as the crowd regaled them with more applause. When the applause leveled off, Danira made the closing remarks, a history of her struggle to bring the island's theater tradition to this community. As she spoke, my thoughts drifted to

Rufo, who when as a young poet he read at Smith Wesson in my freshman year. I emulated him for the next three years.

Danira Román was finishing her expression of gratitude to her patrons when I caught Graziela eyeing me. She looked away. Sánchez O'Neil leaned over to tell her something that made her giggle when I heard Isela whisper behind my left ear. "When we were students, I told her to try out for acting, but she said she came from a working-class family and needed security. That's why she teaches theater and doesn't act. She often taps Gus for money to bring theater groups to her school. But nothing else connects them. I would know."

From Hunter College Isela went straight into Johnson's Great Society, soon directing a huge anti-poverty program in Spanish Harlem. Her endearing smile, bouncy demeanor, and posturing at being the mothering Puerto Rican woman camouflaged a surgical third eye that could cut through a skull of steel to scan an opponent's brain. That gift allowed her to withstand many a male leaders' testosterone efforts to get their hands on her program's voluptuous budgetary chest. Never forgetting a face or detail, she knew everybody in city government and whoever was important at the State and Federal levels. So when she assured me that Graziela had nothing to do with the City Councilman, I could take that to the bank. Isela applauded Ms. Román's closing words, then finished her report, "Graziela is a person with very high standards, sometimes maybe unrealistic, and Gus is...well, to start with, he's married again and that's something that Graziela would never fool around with."

Winston returned from the wine table after "touching base" with every local Democrat en route. Politics energized Winston. A gene drove him to ejaculate the seeds of his egalitarian vision. Stories of discrimination in the work place aroused him as another might be by a scene from *Lady Chatterly's Lover*. Every touching of base minutely advanced social progress, and he was born to hasten the future. I left Isela and Winston for a refill of wine and they walked over to Graziela as Pepp was giving her a peck on the cheek before leaving her to chat with Danira Román.

I had nobody to touch base with and so was returning directly with my refilled wine glass when I paused before the sight of Isela beside Graziela, a study in contrast. Darker, shorter Isela wore her hair in a short Afro, medium-high heels, and an above-the-knee turquoise dress of loud, abstract, African designs. Lighter complexioned and taller, Graziela's straight black hair cascaded, and she wore a subdued Navy blue dress hemmed at the knee. In flats, she was taller than Isela in heels. Isela's body language was vivacious, electric, arms dynamic. Graziela's body language was reserved; both hands held on to her wine. When we were first introduced, I couldn't tell if that reserve just expressed her nature or her really not being interested in meeting anybody, having been cajoled to meet me by Isela, who was waving me over.

"I was just telling Graziela that you're a poet too. You should show her your work because as a school teacher she could use good material that her students could identify with."

If she reads them great poetry, they'll identify with it.

Usmail Rufo happened by and gave Isela a big hug. She celebrated him as "a genius, this man is simply a genius." She introduced me. Rufo remembered that I had published poems in *Palante*, the weekly published in El Barrio by the former gang turned into a political party, The Young Lords. "I remember. I used to like your stuff, good revolutionary stuff, bro. What you up to now?"

"I'm a lawyer now."

"Hey, here..." He searched through the pockets of his vest. "Here's my card. Give me a call and we can hang out, man." He turned to Isela. "I used to read him back when I was starting out, all ri-i-i-ght," he said, his head nodding rhythmically, his two thumbs up, as he stepped backwards to take his leave. To Graziela he added, "So long, *preciosa*."

I read his card: "No Fool In Productions. Usmail Rufo, Poet, Writer, Actor, Performance Artist." The busyness of Rufo's life reminded me that I had abandoned my original ambition.

Isela and Winston had drifted over toward Sánchez O'Neil.

"So when do I get to read your poems?" Graziela combed back

a handful of hair behind one ear. Her eyes courted me.

"They're old poems..." I was having the same conversation I had with Louise but now I felt free to show my poems to someone who surely shared their viewpoint—even if I didn't think much of them. "...but I'm open to negotiation."

I looked around at the surroundings of eyes neither surreptitious, ambiguous, or encoded. I was in The Community. Basking in Graziela's flirtation, I belonged to My People.

PART TWO

ADVENTURELAND

Chapter 7

Professor Maritza Islas's strictly business glad-to-meet-you hand nearly speared my gut. Seduced by her voice, I agreed to take her case as my last client. I apologized for the starkness of my office, explained that she was my last client. She glanced around and gave a look of wondering why I mentioned anything. A short, pretty brunette, she wore a blue blazer over gray pants and black pumps and carried a fine-looking dark purple leather briefcase. Her black hair was stretched tightly back in a bun. I offered her a chair and coffee. She nixed the coffee, sat, swung one leg over the other, and got straight to her case.

She was a tenure-track, Assistant Professor of Spanish who had published substantial papers, given talks at conferences, and worked on departmental committees, but Mahdrof University denied her tenure. "*No puedo*...I can see no other reason for their denying me tenure except that I am a woman and a *latina* and not a very religious Catholic and Mahdrof University is a Jesuit school." She removed a stack of file folders from the briefcase. "These contain data I've compiled on the college's practices in the hiring of women and minorities."

I glossed their content. "*Creo*...I think some of these memos build a case. How well do you know Father Stevens?"

"Stevens is chairman of Sociology. Puerto Ricans are his academic specialty."

"I gather you don't get along with him."

"He has something to do with this, I'm certain."

"Being the eminent sociologist specializing in Puerto Ricans, he also became the community's Great White Father. He means well but he's very much the missionary, and unfortunately feels threatened by types like you and me who make him feel unneeded. Also, ironically, the college counts on him to keep at bay the South Bronx that threatens to devalue the campus. His projects involve people from the community, spreading diversity in the employment rolls, and leaves the college free to concentrate on recruiting students from the Midwest. Stevens may be a big friend of the community, but he's a Company of Jesus man first. Have you given him a friendly call?"

"We say hello. He addresses me expecting the little girl role that stupid *latinas* play before priests. Also I disagree with his patronizing interpretation of Latin American culture in general and Puerto Rico's in particular as I articulated in my review of his *From the Oxcart to the Subway: The Puerto Rican-Americans*."

"Hmmm. Please don't misconstrue what I'm about to recommend."

"Well, I'll tell you after I hear it."

"Stevens will be receiving a community service award tonight at a benefit dinner-dance at the Sheraton. I don't normally attend these things but I would this time if you decided to accompany me—to help your case, of course. Today's Thursday, shouldn't interrupt anything important."

She pondered the ambiguity. "What would I gain from being there?"

"It's sponsored by NICHE, the National Initiative of Committed Hispanics for Equality, which invites community leaders and politicians and corporate community relations reps who donate to its scholarship programs. Some of the politicos oversee agencies that fund Steven's programs. He wouldn't expect you there, might give him reason to think twice about who you are and who you know. Also I want to introduce you to a good friend, who'll probably be a Congressman in a couple of years, but even more important right now, he's a Trustee of Mahdrof."

As if looking out at a Macy's fireworks display over the Hudson, her eyes filled with tiny sparkles. We agreed to meet in the lobby of the West Side Sheraton. Before leaving, she asked about my fee.

"Well, I really am closing my practice. Your message on my machine touched a nerve, an issue I had raised with my trustee friend about Hispanics and tenure at the college, and this is a service to the community that he could perform in his own interest. I don't see your case going beyond a few phone calls, no expense that should deter you from proceeding, I assure you."

"I would prefer a clear financial statement at the end."

The idea of attending the Sheraton shindig came at a great sacrifice. Showing up at those functions after years of not showing would send an unintended signal among political animals who couldn't imagine any other future for the beardless me than investing the equity of my community renown in anything else but politics. I called to RSVP.

On the way to my car behind the deli, I heard Louise's warning that politics would ruin every chance of my ever writing anything of merit. Steeped in that thought as I passed the elevated subway's newsstand, I delayed in reacting to the evening's *The New York Post* headline. I went back to the newsstand: "PRECINCT DRUG SCANDAL, DA" and in smaller print "Link Bronx Stabbing of Cop." I read the report on the way to the car.

The Danubio Azul restaurant on 149th Street was identified "as the corrupt precinct's watering hole, where an off-duty officer was recently stabbed...The Bronx DA said that his office is investigating a possible connection between the cop's stabbing and allegations of drug corruption." Normally, I would have jumped on this muckraking case. Now I wanted no part of it.

I had just enough time to get to my apartment, wash up and dress. By the time I got to Manhattan, I was regretting having led with my littler head in inviting *la profesora* and sentencing myself to an evening of political *abrazos*, hypocritical schmoozing, and narcotizing blather. I also arrived just after the last allowable post-7pm street parking filled up nearest to the Sheraton, and could only find a spot on 47th Street, just off the Avenue of the Americas, along whose length west to 7th Avenue lowlifes loitered in front of grungy hotels and hookers intercepted every male passing through.

Up ahead a pair of prostitutes chatted. One was a busty, frizzy-blond black woman with bare shoulders and wearing the most mini of skirts. By her side a long-ponytailed, platinum-blond white colleague in hot pants reported something that required her demonstrating it with dancing gyrating hips. As I passed them, black Busty turned to me: "You like titties, do you, honey? Wanna go out?" Steps ahead, a black guy and a white guy sat on a condemned building's stoop as they drank from bottles in brown paper bags. They were talking loud about something but stopped to watch me parade by.

Just off the corner of 7th Avenue, three more hookers milled about, separately modeling an array of professional attire: miniskirt, hot pants, tight pants. A Buick that rolled by at that moment pulled over by the group. Four young white heads were visible from the rear window. The black hooker in a miniskirt conducted the negotiation, speaking into the driver's open window as her two colleagues milled behind her. I was passing their meeting when the *latina* of the waiting two, seeing me approach, stepped up to me. Her toothpick legs paced in skintight, silver-fabric pants. Atop her pretty face rose a swirling, black merengue of hair. She made her pitch in a hickey island Spanish, "*Nene, ¿quiereh salil?*"

Her girlish *jíbara* voice evoked a remote collective innocence— *back before My People made the first non-European, transoceanic passage from Hispano to Anglo America, back to when My People still possessed a human, non-politically-charged identity, back to before our becoming walking totems of gringo notions of supremacy*—a fleeting sympathetic rumination that must have doodled itself over my face and encouraged her, despite my walking off, to call me back, but this time in an almost baritone English, "Hey, macho, come back. Let's talk about it, baby."

At the Sheraton, heartland-looking blond flight attendants in uniforms waited as a hotel doorman hailed them a taxi. An Asian group lined up to board a chartered bus. African men and women in colorful dress, just arriving, accompanied their luggage being carted from an airport service bus. In the balmy summer night, intuiting that any relationship with the *profesora* was going to end as strictly business, I suddenly didn't want to walk into the hotel.

Maritza waited in a lobby sofa chair. Seeing me, she stood, a soldier at attention, although her black hair was now let down, cascading in curls, and the knee length of her black dress revealed— pedestaled on three-inch heels—a pair of legs that made me bite my tongue about second thoughts. She was wearing a silky scarf that wrapped around her neck and hung behind her back, and instead of that afternoon's briefcase, she carried a dainty black purse that hung from one shoulder. Her made-up eyes sexily showcased an otherwise business-only dead-fish look, taming any impulse I might have had to compliment her. I was also immediately kept in check by her bayonet hand, extended to just shy of stabbing the middle button of my blue suit. I shook the bayonet and we proceeded to the ballroom.

A bald pianist with a Genghis Khan mustache played background piano notes at the edge of an island of instruments set up for a full band. The piano's soothing notes wafted throughout the ballroom, whose tables around the empty dance floor were filling with the creme de la creme of the New York Rican Dominion: community organization presidents, mayoral appointees, corporate community representatives, political aspirants, and young, successful profession-als of the I-no-longer-really-look-Hispanic variety. There were also non-Ricans whose candidacies or businesses counted on The Community. In front of the band arrangement was a dais. The wall behind the band displayed a banner: "National Initiative of Committed Hispanics for Equality."

At our assigned table sat mainly people I knew, all the men in suits and ties and the women in evening dresses. The dapperly bow-tied Anselmo Principio first recognized me after first staring briefly to make sure that, though beardless, I was the person he knew. He shot up to shake my hand vigorously. The completely gray-haired Anselmo was president of the Gaudi Soft Ice Cream Franchise. His wife Sally was a principal at a Manhattan middle-school. Her large red-framed glasses matched her dress. The quite senior Jaime Sefardí, owner of Sefardí Fancy Bagels expressed the table's pleasure at having me at the table. His wife was the more corpulent fifty-ish Alma. And a firm handshake came from the elegantly graying Jackson Merit III, a Corporate Vice-President of Community Relations at Con Edison Electric Company, who introduced his classy-looking date, an educational psychologist, Dr. Corita Gamble-Parker, who wore a modest Afro and from whose neck hung a pair of reading glasses. Next to her sat Maritza, whom I introduced to all as a professor of Latin American literature at Mahdorf University, and I sat between her and Anselmo.

At such moments of The Community's recognition, I was reminded that I had indeed made a name since Winston and I joined forces with the Puerto Rican Legal Task Force to sue N.Y.C. to provide bilingual teachers and translators to assure clear communication with parents. That victory made us Community players. After that both *The Daily News* and *The New York Post* reported on our role in the Egyptian Paper Bag Co.'s settlement with the union over the company's sneaky way of discriminating in job advancement. Both papers then described as heroic my blocking a Korean speculator's attempt to harass his Latin tenants in four square blocks of the North Bronx that he wanted to vacate for a new wave of Irish immigrants who would upgrade the property value.

The real media attention, of course, came with my successful defense of William Guzmán against the feds, charged with being an accessory to the bomb-planting of his brother Timoteo Guzmán, "Timmy the Terrorist" as *The Daily News* called him. The English-language press didn't celebrate that I got William off but, following the lead of the Spanish-language *El Diario*, began to acknowledge me as the Community's paladin. That celebrity made me a honey for political bears. The fact that I was making this rare social appearance generated more than the usual display of stroking that to the naked eye made me appear to wield considerable political clout, and after the first exaggerated handshake, I caught Maritza glancing at me with naked eyes.

After our first drink Maritza the soldier seemed at ease, and after a second drink, I felt licensed to get personal, inquire what island town she was from. She grew up in Guaynabo, a well-off suburb, and came to New York never planning to stay longer than it took to get her Ph.D. at N.Y.U. Her goal had always been a job at the University of Puerto Rico's Río Piedras campus. But the competition was tough, so she stayed in the city waiting for an opening. Mahdrof was not where she expected to stay, but still, given her meritorious academic C.V., she couldn't believe what was happening to her bid for tenure.

"*A proposito*...By the way, I told you that Isela Chase recommended you. I met her at a Latina Professional Woman's Conference in Chicago." She lowered her voice, "Truthfully, I attended that conference mainly to build up my case for my tenure. I really feel that the problems of Hispanic women in this country don't have much to do with me. I even have a hard time identifying with my Hispanic students, who are mainly English-speakers, and, to be frank, English is too foreign to my soul. Puerto Ricans from here—" Luckily as she began her review of "Puerto Ricans from here," the waiter arrived with a tray of dinners stacked under steel-covers.

Alma Sefardí looked at her entree and celebrated the ethnic symbolism of the roast pork steaming beside a serving of red beans and white rice. As if Alma's observation also proved another point about "Puerto Ricans from here," Maritza rolled her eyes toward me. She leaned to whisper in my ear, "...As I was saying, Puerto Ricans from here have settled permanently, which was not my ambition, and I'm sorry but I simply don't identify with them. Our people at our best are not represented by mainland people who only project being poor, having no culture, which is the basis of Father Steven's career and Mahdrof University's—" I brushed my index finger against my lips as my eyes panned the table.

She changed the subject, keeping to a low volume. "I hope nothing I've said offends you, Eddie. Can I call you that? Everybody else has been doing it."

Of course she could. *But if you want to leave so badly, why bother with tenure?* I addressed the simplicity of roast pork.

Maritza was apparently not hungry. "I really forgot that you're from here yourself. It's just that your style and manner didn't give the impression you were raised in New York. Neither does your Spanish, I guess—" I looked away at a table consisting of English monolinguals and English-lopsided bilinguals and, not counting her, two predominantly Spanish speakers. Felicitously Jaime Sefardí and Jackson Merit III and Anselmo had been carrying on a conversation on the Mets and Yankees. Dr. Corita knew Sally Prinicipio, a sister in education, and the two were discussing one of Mayor's Koch's public school initiatives. No one really had much to share with Alma Sefardí directly across the large table, a simpler woman whose husband happened to make a lot of money from selling bagels. Lacking a conversation to distract her, Alma kept looking our way but fortunately from her distance couldn't hear Maritza. She smiled, casting us, I imagined, in a *telenovela*.

Jackson Merit addressed Jaime to comment extra loudly, "Gus seems to have chosen his campaign manager."

Jaime chimed in, "I think maybe Eddie's too busy for politics." He raised his wine goblet to Maritza, "and I wouldn't blame him."

Anselmo and Sally looked at each other amazed at Jaime's remark in front of Alma. Dr. Corita rose from her chair, picked up her small handbag, and excused herself. Jackson got up to accompany her out the hall. Anselmo excused himself to go greet someone who had just come in. Sally, an older woman with her hair dyed blond and a political calm about her, tried to soothe things by commenting in Spanish on Alma's dress. Alma was plump and dull, making any dress, however fashionable, look plain. Sally did succeed in making Alma feel flattered, and with that confidence she began chatting away in English on where she purchased the dress and how it had been marked down, and where Sally would find treasures herself.

But that conversation didn't let Jaime off the hook. Once Alma finished reporting on that dress store and Sally returned to chatting with her husband who had returned, Alma—too emotional to realize that Maritza and I were watching—whispered to Jaime an earful.

As Anselmo reminded Sally in English about the guy that he had just left to greet, Maritza whispered, "*Con toda franqueza*...Quite frankly I would have a hard time befriending a Puerto Rican who spoke only English or a fractured Spanglish, that sort of thing. Your Spanish, in fact, made me feel better about your taking my case."

I chewed the last of my food.

"Members of our Community," resounded the amplified voice of a tall, swarthy man in a tuxedo on the dais, "guests from other Hispanic communities, leaders and captains of industry, *Buenas Noches*. I am Raymond Clark Classen, President of NICHE." Applause. Clark Classen thanked all for attending and for their support over the years. The first order of business was the dinner he hoped we all enjoyed and now the highlight for him, the honor of introducing "...that great man who for four decades has worked to improve the lives of our people, who was there for us at the state level, who was there for us at the federal level, the one we simply call *Padre*, Father Thomas B. Stevens." The short, white-haired priest in a black suit and white collar walked up to the dais, crossing the crowd's standing accolade, which to make the seated Maritza join I had to tug at her hand.

His milk-pale head lowered in boyish modesty, from his jacket's inner pocket Stevens took out folded papers, and reading from them started narrating a chronology of Puerto Rican migration to the U.S. mainland: "...They were an agricultural people pushed out by an industrialization initiative. They encountered resistance, bigotry, rejection, and I as the son of Irish immigrants know well that history as a very American pattern..." The entire hall adored Stevens's uplifting futuristic vision of inevitable Puerto Rican rise in pursuit of the American Dream. "That's right," shouted Alma Sefardí across the table, "The Italians are Latin like us and they made it," forgetting that she was present only because she already had.

As he spoke, the silver haired Gustavo Sánchez O'Neil arrived accompanied by his towering, stunning colleague, the African-American former model and socialite turned civil servant, Star Anita Crommet, City Commissioner for Consumer Affairs. They waited at the fringe of the ballroom's dance floor as Stevens concluded by praising "...this gathering of community leaders who symbolize the triumph of a resourceful people, their wealth of humanity and generosity, the richness of their culture."

The crowd's resounding applause served as cue for the six-foot-three Deputy Mayor to begin crossing the dance floor, waving to all sides, usurping the hall's cheers for himself. Theatrically extending his arms, he walked up to the dais and gave the padre a huge *abrazo* and turned to wave to the crowd, hugging Steven's shoulders, locked like a political ticket, basking in even louder applause that finally subsided from exhaustion.

Meanwhile, behind them, the musicians reunited with their instruments were ready and Clark Classen returned to invite the guests to "put on your dancing shoes." At that moment, from another microphone, in Spanish the bandleader Wilfrido Lamm introduced himself and his Dominican merengue group Los Genuinos and suggested that "*Todos*...Everybody loosen up, forget the serious affairs you important people carry around in your head all day." At the stroke of his hand, nine tall, skinny black musicians in green jumpsuits multiplied themselves by constant movement, playing a hyperkinetic merengue.

For what living flesh doesn't respond to the rhythmic electrostatic of a striated gourd stroked by a long-toothed fork? And whose torso resists writhing to the primal African thunder of taut leather? And whose feet can refrain from shuffling to the hip-lubricating, rhythmically stuttering Dominican merengue brass? Few turned a deaf ear to that libidinous call, among them Jaime and the still pissed-off Alma with her arms crossed, and, of course, Maritza and me. Our dramatic isolation gave me the moral support to inquire if she cared to dance. To my surprise, she said yes.

My philosophy about dancing: a couple's ability to harmonize in dance is a trusty indicator of the potential for spiritual and any other kind of intercourse. Case in point: Maritza held me at bay with a rigid right arm. Halfway into the number, her limbs relaxed, her resolve perhaps softened by the lyrics of Wilfrido's big hit about a woman so alluring that the singer begs to know what spell she had cast, accusing her of inhuman cruelty. When the air space between us shrank to little more than an inch, her black hair tickled my nose and I inhaled a blend of perfume and hair spray.

The moment seemed right for addressing her as a woman and not as a client, but conversation would have undone the progress made. When the dance ended, Sánchez O'Neil, who had been dancing with Star Anita Crommet, excused himself with her and walked up to me. He shook my hand vigorously, histrionically. "I swear"—quick look at Maritza—"I hardly recognized you without the beard. Looks great, very mainstream, Eddie"—smile at Maritza, whom I finally introduced. Sánchez O'Neil was now thrice-married and recently thrice-divorced, a track record fatal to another, less popular and charismatic politician.

Her "*Buenas Noches*" prompted him to respond in his *jíbaro* Spanish, "*Peldóname, pero no noh ehmoh conocido*," which he also felt the need to translate. "I don't believe we've met." My having brought her to speak with him about a problem she was having at Mahdrof made him glow 100 watts. He signaled to Star Anita and followed us to our table. On the way my beeper went off. Not Graziela's home number but the same three-number exchange, which caused me to worry. I excused myself with Maritza to call from a lobby phone.

Samson answered. "Mr. Loperena, I'm sorry to bother you, but you said to let you know. That guy's going crazy, must be twisting her into a pretzel from how she's screaming. I wish I could give that motherfucker the ass-kicking he deserves."

I struggled to calm myself down. "Call the police, tell them that a woman's life is in danger. I'll call her number, then call you back."

Graziela's phone rang several times before somebody picked up and immediately hung up. Another try, a busy signal. Dialed again. Marlboro answered calmy. I listened for background sounds, Graziela cursing uncontrollably, the dog barking. Marlboro became impatient, "Hello, hello."

"Is Graziela there, please. It's Eddie Loperena."

"Yes, well, she's sleeping right now."

Marlboro covered the receiver, and a muffled shouting exchange could be heard. "Look, don't call back. Leave her alone. You're harassing her." A background banging on the door. He threw down the phone.

Out of coins, I went to the front desk, told them it was an emergency and a local call. Samson reported that the police were at the door, talking to Marlboro. "Shh. She's talking now. Man, she's saying they were both yelling at each other, that's all. Damn, damn. What's wrong with that woman?"

Unable to do any more than the police, I realized that my confronting Marlboro would require a persuasive illegal weapon. I thanked Samson for calling me.

"Okay, you the lawyer. You know what you're doing. I'm going to have me a shot before I go to sleep."

"Yeah, I know it's tough. Have that drink."

I stood at the entrance to the ballroom in no mood to return to the table. Maritza was dancing with Sánchez O Neil, a *bolero*. No stiff arm, just warm accompaniment, following his every step although at that moment she created a foot of space between them and talked as he nodded, trying to keep in rhythm. I stepped aside to allow a woman to exit the ballroom.

"Eddie, is that you?"

I recognized the voice.

"I wasn't sure if it was you without the beard."

Louise looked much older than the face I pictured when I heard her voice. In a black evening gown with a lace cape hanging from one shoulder, she emitted the same charming elegance.

"You still look gorgeous, Eddie. And don't bother to lie about me. I've read about you and the troublemaker you made of yourself."

"What are you doing here?"

"My husband is a Vice-President of Citibank, a patron of NICHE."

"How's your art business?"

"The art market went through some roller coaster phases. My husband convinced me to take it easy for a while. We don't need it. I just like to work with artists, you know. Hamilton Kukla tells me that now you've really made a name for yourself. I think they want to approach you again."

"I don't know where I'm going right now."

"Did you ever get back to writing?"

What if I had taken up her offer? Surely I would have written but not this story. And would I have stayed with her as she aged? Or would she have run from me out of fear that I would leave her because she was getting old and didn't want to be the one left behind...?

A tall gray man in a dinner jacket came up behind, put his arms around her shoulder. She introduced Anton Polander. "Meet my friend Eddie. He started at Kukla, Franklin. Now he has his own practice."

Anton greeted cordially, then suggested to Louise that they had better leave.

"We have another one of these functions to attend on the East Side. Eddie, it was wonderful seeing you again." She stepped up and gave me a kiss almost on the lips. They walked away, she looking back and waving one last time. Seeing Louise and seeing how much she had aged transported me, reminding me that Graziela had been the cure I had hoped for finding myself at last. *...screaming, twisted like a pretzel.*

Wilfrido and the Genuinos took a break. The Deputy Mayor for Hispanic Affairs was still being lectured to by Maritza, the two now standing by our table.

"So I hope that Maritza was able to explain her situation."

"Yes, she did quite clearly. And I promised her I would look into it."

Maritza grabbed her purse and plucked out a business card that he took, grabbing her hand as if it belonged to Blanche in *A Streetcar Named Desire*, assuring her that he'd be making calls on her behalf. As if billing me for that favor, before returning to his table, he reminded me of the luncheon with Harlem community leaders the day after the brunch with the Governor he had arranged for me. Maritza, excused herself, left the hall, purse in hand. Alma Sefardí rose to accompany her.

With everybody else schmoozing elsewhere, at our table

remained Jaime and Anselmo and Sally Principio and me. Sally commented that her granddaughter attended Mahdorf and might have taken a course with someone that fit Maritza's description. Her granddaughter spoke highly of her as a teacher although she complained of her being too demanding. Jaime, taking the opportunity of Alma's absence, whispered to me that Maritza sure was a looker. I hadn't recuperated from bumping into Louise, from seeing how old she had gotten. Father Stevens materialized at my side.

He thanked me for attending, taking a quick glance at the empty chair beside me with a woman's scarf over the back. He extended his hand to depart just as Maritza returned refreshed, makeup, fragrance, animus. Stevens shook her hand too, greeting with overacted pleasant surprise, prompting her to feign being equally pleased. He proceeded to greet Jaime and Alma.

Maybe he had seen Maritza dancing with Sánchez O'Neil and had come to poke into the quality of her connection to me and the possibly future congressman. I could bring the University bad press, and Sánchez O'Neil always looked to secure more federal funding for his endless sociological study of Puerto Ricans. A hand squeezed my shoulder.

"So how's the community's hero lawyer?" It was Celestino Hunter (formerly "Cazador"), publisher of the second-largest Spanish-language daily, *Nuestras Noticias*, and the African-American-oriented tabloid *The Brooklyn Community Post*. I got up to greet him.

Beside him was his wife, Minerva, a big-boned brunette who directed a community outreach program for Mathias College in Nassau County. The paunchy, balding Celestino was wearing a dinner jacket, Minerva a blue evening gown. They were on their way out, when he caught who I was without the beard. Minerva stood with arms akimbo, her countenance letting the world know that this having to wait for Celestino was how she spent her life. He asked me to step away from the table and I guessed also from Minerva. "Has the Governor's office gotten in touch with you yet?"

"I'll be at that brunch."

"Well, really give it serious thought. I mean, let's be honest, you're on everybody's wish list. You've proven yourself to the community. You're legendary, man. You are the Hispanic vote. What everybody asks is, why isn't this guy running for office himself? Oh, who's the beauty?"

"She teaches Latin American lit at Mahdrof."

"A *profesora*. That's perfect for your public image, and of literature, that's sexual therapy for the Poet Man. Don't tell me different, Eddie, you must be looking for *some* elected office." I gestured to Maritza to come over, mainly to change the subject. The pleasure of Celestino's meeting her was so obvious that he didn't get to say more than "Eddie tells me you teach literature" before Minerva stepped forward. I was introducing Maritza to Minerva when Father Stevens materialized again, this time between Celestino and Maritza.

Stevens greeted Celestino warmly, then caught Maritza off-guard by pointing out to the publisher that she was another example of Mahdrof's commitment to the Puerto Rican community. The *Noticias's* photographer took a picture of his boss and Stevens flanking Maritza. Visibly zonked by the cleric's hypocrisy, Maritza looked for instructions from her ring-corner lawyer, but Stevens waved me forward to appear in the photographs, *"Bueno, Bueno,* the community's El Cid."

Pictures taken, Minerva Hunter's strained face finally worked its voodoo on Celestino, who throughout the photo session had been darting sidelong, adulterous glances at Maritza. Publisher and wife departed and the smiling Stevens wandered off, leaving Maritza and me to return to our table, Maritiza having no more reason for staying except to recuperate from the jolt of Stevens' hypocrisy.

Wilfrido Lamm announced that his next musical piece would be his popular merengue hit "That Baby Girl Is Crying for Her Milk." Energized by its tempo, I took Maritza's hand to lead her out on the dance floor, but she pulled back. My spontaneity overstepped some boundary. She was tired and was going home. She didn't decline my offer to drive her.

On the drive uptown I reassured her that Sánchez O'Neil would act on her behalf. "...He can give Stevens a call but that might not be necessary. Stevens got the message tonight. That's what he was telling us at the end."

She was still zonked by Stevens' chumming up to her in front of the photographer.

"Well, in a community newspaper a photo with the publisher and a Puerto Rican woman professor from his university implicitly endorsing him can go a long way with local politicians who financially support his projects."

"It's a world so different from mine. For him I represent 'The Community.'"

"Are you saying that New York isn't Puerto Rico?"

"No, I mean I don't identify with a world in which everything is reduced to social politics. I can't imagine any of those people talking about literature or culture."

"Politics is where every group new to this country first invests its genius. It's only now that some are finding time for art and literature."

"Yes, on this side of the Atlantic, and most of it is not very good, everything so naive, but on the other side we are conscious of having a literature, and a good one, which is what I teach."

"Unfortunately, the community here still thinks that politicians, social scientists and journalists say it all."

"And where are you?"

"In my car, driving you home."

"You know what I mean."

"I'm somewhere between those people back at the hotel and you, if that's a place."

"Sánchez O'Neil told me you have a great political future."

"I'm a product of the seventies, liberation, Third World, etc. I was committed to justice for My People. I didn't know that I was building a political career. If anything, for me, politics was just an excuse to write."

"What made you decide to become a lawyer?"

"A professor recommended me for a minority fellowship to attend law school. The opportunity just fell on my lap, really. I thought I was going to be a writer but I couldn't turn down an offer to attend Harvard Law School, so here I am, being your lawyer, doing my poor best to impress you."

She changed the subject, "But I heard you with Stevens. In English you're an American, so why don't you just be one thing?"

"Legally, you're an American too."

"But you know what I mean. I'm just American on paper. You talk to him like his equal, you share the same underlying semantics."

"You mean the same 'lying semantics.' That's true, but outside of official business, post offices, voting booths, selective service, and jury duty, things start to get foreign and unless I keep to a set script that makes me American, I start to look exotic. For example, for me to be *really* American, I have to see myself as a Latin intrusion on Anglo Saxon innocence and express sincere contrition and demonstrate how far I'm willing to cure myself of that defect of being a sinful Latin."

The West Side Highway traffic became a river of red brake lights. To diverge from The Conversation, I asked her about her roommate whose voice announces her answering machine message. "Oh, Wanda. She's a feminist radio producer, very active in Third World and women's causes. She's really a terrific person. She—"Emergency flashers ahead. Two lanes were being funneled to a one left lane, past the scene of an accident better viewed from Maritza's side. Two police cars, a tow truck and an ambulance surrounded an overturned minivan, the punched-in driver's side face-up. Medics attended to a black woman on a white sheet, a red stain by her head. Someone still inside the van was being helped. Thump, thump. An officer in a Dayglo vest tapped his nightstick on my Toyota's hood, waving me on.

We had pulled away from the scene but Maritza kept her gaze out the window. "I don't know. I just know I can't stay here all my life."

"Because here cars have accidents?"

"No. That lady was about fifty something, and I thought of myself here for another twenty years and dying here."

"But that's what tenure means. And you want it."

"I just want to be secure, besides I've earned it. I want the recognition."

"By the way, I was curious about your chat with Alma in the ladies' room?"

"Oh, God. We were both looking in the mirror, fixing ourselves up, and she told me that I was lucky to catch you at this perfect moment, now that you're divorced. I was putting on lipstick, so I just nodded."

I almost asked what were the odds that Alma's comment wasn't so ridiculous. But she changed the subject silently, staring out again. "I understand that you write poetry."

"Who told you that?"

"Isela said you would sympathize with my case because I taught literature and you were a poet."

"I don't anymore, and they're in English."

Maritza lived near the Mahdorf campus, on Webster Avenue, in an Irish pocket still resistant to being consumed by the South Bronx. I pulled up in front of her building, and she thanked me for the ride. She requested that I send her my bill.

"This matter isn't resolved until you have a letter in hand. Besides, I didn't do much except enjoy the company of an attractive woman."

"When that letter arrives, I would feel better if you billed me properly."

She opened the car door then paused before stepping out. "If all night you spoke Spanish like a literate native speaker, why don't you write in it."

"I live here so what's the point? And speaking isn't the same as writing, and I'm not even writing in English."

She turned and disappeared into her building. *And if I did write in Spanish, what would I gain? Would you and "our" entire island be more welcoming, less distanced than now when I sound, as you say, like a native speaker?*

I turned the ignition key but just stared down the length of deserted Webster Avenue, determined not to get pissed off, not to give anybody that pleasure. I turned on the radio. Playing was the overture to Rubén Blades' "Buscando América." Heavy South American Andean drums, the epic of a hemisphere marching ascendant to a triumph where the meek finally inherit the earth. Eduardo still loved that song but I now hated its idealism. The Bronx was now

Latin America, but no signs of any victorious marching. As for unity, go ask Juan Acosta, for whom I was ghetto riffraff at Smith Wesson, and Pilar Meléndez, who rolled her eyes when at Harvard Dean Nicolas Gainsay addressed us together as Puerto Ricans. And now Maritza.

The hour was a little past nine, but a Wilfrido Lam merengue still undulated under my skin. Yvette would still be working at the Danubio. After a day of Graziela and Maritza, I craved a woman who simply saw me as a man.

Chapter 8

Eduardo took over the wheel and drove me to Third Avenue. Down its length from the Bronx's northern city limits to its piano-shaped southern hump along the Harlem River used to run the elevated Third Avenue Subway line. Mami Lalia and I took it when she wanted to shop uptown. While I was at Excalibur, it was dismantled, tons of steel pillars uprooted and rickety wooden stations demolished. But even on the brightest day my memory of those elevated tracks still darkens Third Avenue.

Southbound to 149th Street I toured its landscape of guys dealing, hawking with hand signals. I stopped at a red light, and a car pulled up next to me. The driver rolled down his window and honked but at that hour on that avenue I wasn't going to engage in conversation. I didn't wait for the green light to hit the accelerator and neither did the other car, blocked from catching up by so many double-parked cars, but managing to follow me past three green lights. Up ahead at a wide commercial intersection the traffic light changed to yellow, and from around the next corner to my left flared a flashing red light that I hoped was a squad car's.

I ran the red light, turned left in the direction of the flashing light, just swerving around a car about to make a right north onto Third. The flashing red light belonged to an Emergency Services Ambulance. I sped on. In the rearview mirror, the car pursuing me had to brake to avoid crashing into the turning car I had swerved around. At the next corner I turned right onto a dark, residential street, where I pulled into the space by a fire hydrant, shut off the motor and lights. After several minutes with no sign of the other car, I pulled out, peering constantly into the rearview mirror.

The Danubio's regular crowd filled the bar. I passed Armando on his stool nearest the door and sat at mid-bar. To my left two standing men with briefcases at their feet discussed something that Mayor Koch was doing that pissed one of them off. Next to their left a trio of two women and a man laughed about something. To my right just a guy drinking and then Armando and, at the bar's curved end by the wall, two new Irish drinkers who had to be cops, one tall, in a black T-Shirt with khakis, the other in a plaid shirt and faded jeans. Tall looked at his watch, then both took their beers to the window by the neon Budweiser sign and looked out. Yvette, wearing a black miniskirt and bare-shoulder blouse, was at the cash register down at the bar's end to my left and hadn't yet noticed me. The jukebox was playing the Celia Cruz hit, "*Toro Mata.*"

A short new barmaid with blond frizzy curls introduced herself as Nani. She reminded me of somebody. She got as far as asking me what I wanted when Yvette showed up behind her to instruct that someone by the cash register wanted a beer. Would I prefer my scotch at our usual table? She was due for a break in ten minutes. I had just looked up from our table when Richard Bell and another Irish guy walked in and immediately huddled with Tall and Short Irish.

Short Irish, wiry, with red curly hair was vigorously shaking his head at Bell, who tried to get closer to him as Tall black Irish held him back until Bell backed down. The guy who came in with Bell then stepped in, apparently having final say because he ordered the three to have their discussion out on the sidewalk. The two with beers put them down on the window ledge and followed Bell. After a long exchange outside, the first two didn't return. Bell did and followed them with his gaze out the window. The remaining Irish guy ordered two beers. *Duffy, Gerry Duffy*. Bell had said they were now partners.

Duffy was my sixth and seventh-grade classmate at St. Peter's School. He and Carlos were put in the smarter "A" eighth grade. I last talked to Duffy that day when he returned from shopping with his mom. Practically bald now, he vaguely resembled the dirty-blond, pug-nosed kid.

"*Bueno*...So, are you here because of Esteban?" Yvette sat beside me at the square table.

"*Sólo*...Just here to see how you were."

"Oh, I thought it was because you heard. Callahan died. Mr. Modesto called to tell us."

Now Esteban was really up shit's creek. Instead of taking her break, she had arranged with Rodrigo to get off work early, but she needed to close out.

The jukebox started playing "*Solamente Una Vez*." A middle-aged couple went out on the small dance floor. I watched them dance, slowly swaying to the rhythm. They swirled around until they stood in my line of sight of the off-duty cops. I looked away, at Nani, who smiled.

"What's up, Eddie?" Duffy in a windbreaker and Bell in gym clothes. "You almost got us killed back there on Third Avenue."

"What did you guys want?"

"We wanted to know if you're defending that Esteban guy. We don't think it's a good idea. Everything you touch ends up stirring up politicians and Puerto Ricans. We don't need the publicity."

"What are you now, detective? Not bad."

"Yeah, but I didn't luck out like you."

"What do you mean?"

"Big shot lawyer. Harvard. My dad and uncle were cops, but this country treated you a little better."

"What does that mean?"

"You didn't have the best grades, but you went to that fancy boarding school."

"That was Brother Al. Remember, all the Irish parents didn't want him to be our teacher because they said he was a commie. How're you doin', Bell?

"Can't complain, Eddie."

They had something else to say, looked at each other. Duffy started to speak when Yvette returned, purse in hand. The two just split back to the bar.

"¿What did they want?"

"They're old schoolmates. Do they come around?"

"No, first time. The other two were here the night with Esteban."

"I don't know what they really want."

"I'm free, so we can leave."

"I don't think I can just walk out. They had something else to say. Let's do this." I palmed my car keys, put them in her hand. "I'm going to the Men's Room. Go out and start my Camry parked up the block, across from the Chinese take-out."

She got up and headed for the door. I went to the john and had just finished a piss when Gerry came in. He didn't enter for the facilities, just waited as I washed my hands.

"Eddie, there's a piece missing in a puzzle, and me and Bell got this hunch that you have it."

I had just finished drying my hands and we were face to face at the door.

"Me and Bell want to sit down with you and talk about your buddy Carlos."

"I haven't heard from him in more than twenty years."

"Yeah. Look, we're not patient guys." He opened his wind breaker, allowing me to see his gun. "Can't just be coincidence that Carlos disappears, your guy Esteban stabs one of my guys, and then of all people you pop up."

"Well, if you shoot me here, I can't help you, can I?"

"We want to hear from you real soon." He stepped aside.

Yvette was waiting for me, engine running, beside their unmarked car, which was double parked and blocking me in. She got out, told me to drive, and ran into the Chinese take-out. In a few seconds she came out with a Chinese teenager, who got into the car parked in front of mine and drove it out.

Yvette jumped in, shut the passenger door. In the rearview mirror

Duffy and Bell were leaving the Danubio. I pulled out with head-lights off, paused at the corner to watch their car light up, then turned at the corner and pulled over. When their mirror reflection crossed the intersection, I turned on my lights and continued as Yvette's hand lightly stroked my knee. "Papi...Papi, you're really nervous. Let's go to my place. My little girl's on the island with my mother for the summer, and these guys don't know where I live."

Yvette's stroking made me forget about Duffy and Bell and think of Graziela. Mami Lalia never celebrated my marriage, and I constantly had to give her the excuse that children would come after I was secure in my practice. For a while she faked accepting our parenthood timeline but knew better. "*Tu carerra...*Your career is a good excuse for you but a better one for her. She might actually get pregnant, which would not make her happy because the poor girl doesn't know how to be happy. I would feel sorry for that child and for you. She doesn't want to be a mother. A woman can see that."

Mami Lalia understood that I fooled around with Yvette in search of the warmth my marriage lacked but just as a dalliance, not prog-ress. Yet on this night she was my fearless Venus in this "street" world. She was probably the finest person I knew, but I had to chuckle internally at Mami Lalia's reaction if after all my searching for identity, all that fancy schooling, I had brought home Yvette, proof that I was continuously in need of San Judas Tadeo's intervention.

Chapter 9

I got to my office the following afternoon to find among the day's mail a manila envelope with the Brooklyn return address of a Charles Atlas. Inside was a wooden matchbox that contained one car key and two tiny keys. Handwriting on yellow post-it slip on the box read, "Wait for my call, Carlos." I listened to my phone messages

Luis had to make an emergency trip to New York for a client, and wanted to know if I would be free on Monday night. Sánchez O'Neil was making sure I'd be at Governor Cuomo's Sunday brunch. Maritza let me know that our night at the Sheraton had already produced some action on her appeal for tenure. That morning she received a memo from the head of the appeals committee and her chair said he suspected a turnaround in her favor. She was inviting me to a dinner with her roommate Wanda on Monday night. Yvette let me know that she had a beautiful night. The novelist Upton Wane requested an appointment to meet with me for a book project, on the highest recommendation of Sánchez O'Neil. Numerous other calls were hangups. The phone rang. Anxious, instead of screening, I picked up.

"Eddie, I received a review that's going to come out this weekend in the *Times*." It was the novelist Bonino Feliz, who sometimes published under the nom de plume Felix Goode. "Can I sue the *Times*? They're going to misrepresent my book completely."

"How?"

"Look, the title of my novel is *Drumbeats from a Small Planet*. You hear me out and see if I have a case."

"Bonino, I've got loads to take care of, send me a copy of the book and the review..."

"No, listen, just listen. I'll be brief. You're a writer, so you can understand my feelings. My novel is about these Caribbean island people who are invaded by a fleet of aliens with skin like wet rice paper and no body hair. The authorities call them Mogools. They are 'transformers' that can change anything they want to whatever they imagine. The Mogool's ability to transform palm trees into brick buildings and dirt roads into superhighways overwhelmed the island people, who came to accept the Mogools's indoctrination that they are superior beings and that the island would be better off under Mogool rule."

"Bonino..."

"That was just the background. I'm coming to the conflict. Life became hard in the countryside because the Mogools took away the islanders' appetite for tropical foods. Islanders abandoned their farms to work in the factories and the luxury hotels the Mogools had materialized. In time enough islanders were convinced that the Mogools had proven they were superior beings and civil war broke out, with half the islanders convinced that life would be better lived as Mogools and urging them to relocate the island in the Mogools' galaxy. That's where my hero comes in, Bori Quoi, who saves the island from Mogool illusions.

"Bonino, get to the point, what did the reviewer misrepresent?"

"They labeled it an *ethnic novel*, man. Can you believe that shit? I just happen to publish this novel under my real name, so this bitch comes up with this interpretation that's just a bunch of stereotypes. She recommends the book for schools, especially and I quote, 'for the positive image it portrays of his people.'"

"But if the review is good, how are you going to prove damages?"

"I'm a science fiction writer! I put some amazing stuff in that book! I want to talk to movie producers, not teachers. And what really pisses me off is that they reviewed it alongside this memoir

Memory from Hunger by this Chicano guy Raymond Reyes, whose family used to pick fruit. Apparently got so assimilated that he couldn't talk to his humble parents anymore. You'd think becoming an English speaker was like traveling to another fucking solar system. Let's get back to my case, Eddie."

"Bonino, I'm not taking any more cases. Maybe the reviewer is right, maybe you were born to write ethnic science fiction. Why don't you write a novel about an ethnic computer programmer who programs only in ethnic computer languages?"

He didn't find that funny, but I promised we'd get together soon. I was about to call Maritza and ask if I could bring Luis when the phone rang. This time I screened the call. Carlos started to leave a message. I picked up.

"Socrates, did you get what I sent?"

"Got it."

"So you can pick up the suitcases right away?"

"I don't know if I can do this, Carlos."

"Soc, what's the problem, man? You just pick up a couple of suitcases and put them away for a while, that's all."

"I don't even have them yet, and they're already getting dangerous for me. Last night Gerry Duffy...you remember him?"

"Yeah, I know that Irish fuckface."

"He showed me his gun and said you had something he wanted."

"Yeah, he may want it...Look, I'm talking a couple of weeks at most, then I'll be out of your life. Don't start thinking too much, man, don't let me down."

I heard the word *again*. "Let me help you some other way. I know people."

"You don't know this kind of people. This is street shit and you gotta stay out of this. Just hold the suitcases for me. And you gotta get them today."

"And I'm leaving for P.R. in a couple of days..."

"That's okay. I don't need them right now. If *you* got'em, *I* got'em. I can't stay on the phone, so don't make this harder for me. Just do me this favor."

"Suppose I don't get back. I was going on a long vacation. And I'm going to close this office soon, so you won't be able to call here."

"I'll find you, man. I haven't got much time to stand out here talking. Listen to me. You know the Cross County mall in Yonkers. The larger key in the matchbox is for the trunk of a white '76 Sunbird with North Carolina license plates parked in front of Sears. The other two smaller keys are for the two suitcases in the trunk."

I took notes from habit while trying to build up the determination to disappoint him, debilitated by my still hearing him say I would let him down *again*.

"So that's it, Soc. Just pick up that stuff today. Oh, the suitcases are tagged, one and two. Just in case you have to open them, open number one first. Now I gotta go. He hung up.

Carlos used the word "stuff." Was it really just paper in the suitcases?

I agonized over the word, mindful also of the time. If I was going to get those suitcases, I should do it before sunset and in plain view, hoping that whoever might be tailing Carlos might be deterred by witnesses. In short time I was driving north on the Bronx River Parkway, still mulling over the possible dangers. But no matter how possible those dangers, I kept seeing Carlos at a pay phone, hearing him ask me not to let him down *again*.

The white Sunbird with the North Carolina license plate was in the Cross Country Mall lot as described. I drove past it, pulling into an empty stall three cars away. I got out of my car and walked toward Sears, surveying as I walked. In Sears' entrance foyer, looking out at the lot, I feigned using a public phone. Being close to dinner hour, the lot was beginning to thin out and within a reasonable radius I didn't see any waiting drivers or passengers. No reason to stall as whoever was out there would see me approach the Sunbird whatever strategy I used. I was either going to go through with this or I wasn't. The car next to the Sunbird had pulled out so I moved my Camry into that slot.

I stepped out and opened my trunk first, then the Sunbird's. Two medium-sized, old brown suitcases. A dirty rag beside a toolbox reminded me I would need it. My passing the suitcases from one car to another and closing both trunks took seconds. I used the rag to wipe what fingerprints I had left on the Sunbird. On the way home I drove checking constantly in the rearview mirror. I pulled straight into my building's garage.

My building was a safe haven because the address wasn't in my name. After Graziela threw me out, I sublet my apartment from Bonino, and not expecting to stay so long, I never formalized it as my address. My postal address was my office. I carried the suitcases to the elevator. When the door opened, out stepped my neighbor Mrs. Daly and her ten-year-old Andrew. Mrs. Daly was an obese middle-aged woman who gave special attention to her flowing, youthful blond hair, which called attention to her pretty face. "Oh, are you just coming in from a trip?"

"My sister's getting married in Puerto Rico. I borrowed suitcases." Sensing a conversation coming on, little Andrew, whose blond hair spiked out every which way, complained that the library was closing soon. Mrs. Daly wished my sister well. In my apartment I put down the suitcases and sat on my sofa, staring at them as if they were about to speak to me, give me some advice. Each had a tag as Carlos said, marked with a large 1 and 2 in black. Again I heard the word "stuff" and couldn't leave matters there.

The suitcases were locked, two old-style latches clamped down so I opened the matchbox for the keys. I lay the case tagged "1" on its side. Fitting the key into the first lock hole with my shaking hand wasn't easy. One latch popped up. I needed to jiggle the key in the second lock before the second latch popped up. I paused before lifting the suitcase lid, dreading that out of some deep-seeded resentment Carlos had used me as mule. I lifted.

Rows of piled, neatly arranged "valuable papers," whose imagined value made me shut that suitcase immediately. Hoping that the first wasn't just bait, payment for my keeping the second that might contain "stuff," I aimed the key at the locks of the suitcase tagged "2." Under its raised lid, a duplicate of the first, rows of piled "valuable papers." I closed that lid, locked both suitcases and stored them upright in my bedroom closet in the shadow of my suits. *Why did I have to open "1" first?* The ringing telephone nearly emptied out my intestines.

My calls to this apartment were redirected from my office, so I normally let the machine answer. *Beep...* "Eddie, it's Gus. Just on the phone with Nicholas Gainsay, the Governor's campaign manager. I knew he was your dean at Harvard, but you didn't tell me how close you were to his family. Well, this is so great for your new career. A slight change for Cuomo's brunch, more like a late breakfast. Be there at 10. Cuomo knows all you've done, just wants to meet you personally, protect himself from whatever skeletons you might have in your closet. "...*beep.*

I tried to calm my nerves, but the phone rang again. Graziela wanted to express her gratitude. I picked up.

"Hi. I just wanted to thank you. That lawyer Modesto is doing his job."

"I told you he would. I'm glad. Are you okay?"

"Yes. I...don't know. I'm torn about this. Esteban reminds me so much of my father who I never forgave. I have to go. Thank you, again."

"Wait—"

She had already hung up.

I sat on my bed, feeling up to my neck in "street shit," stranded in the world that terrified Graziela: *Don't you even think of calling Carlos. You don't come from the same worlds anymore. You yourself told me how you felt after playing the Barrio brother with that guy Silvio when you were in college...*

Chapter 10
Silvio

A freshman at Smith Wesson, he looked city-rough. His almost blue curly hair and vulnerable, angry black eyes reminded me of Carlos. Grown up in El Barrio, Silvio felt strange on that upstate rural campus. I was a junior, famous on campus as radical poet when he sought something of home, approaching me in the cafeteria to share how much he liked my poem "Honk If You Live in the Bronx," which he'd recently heard me read. He said he didn't believe that "so-called real-PR from the island," Juan Acosta, who was going around discrediting my revolutionary commitment to My People.

Days later he was in my dorm with a copy of Piri Thomas' *Down These Mean Streets*. Said he had some questions to discuss with me. "I'm not black, so my island family didn't reject me that way, and I'm no drug addict and I never went to prison." Thomas' book mostly reminded him of Claude Brown's *Manchild in the Promised Land*, a book about being black, "not about all of us in El Barrio." I agreed, pointing out another indication of its imitating that earlier book. Thomas wrote of being a merchant marine. At some point he mentions that he traveled the world, even stopping at Puerto Rico. But that experience is not included in his finally-edited story. The entire book is about his imprisonment from 96th to 125th Street.

Silvio hadn't caught that detail. Another time he brought me recent issues of *Palante*.

Silvio seemed really unsure of why he was at Smith Wesson. His gifts of conversation about books and poetry were just to win my friendship because he wasn't artsy and didn't demonstrate an interest in reading if not assigned for a class. But I felt bad about leaving a fellow Rican alone on campus, especially one who reminded me of Carlos. In late October, days before a weekend when coincidently we both planned to be home (or he decided to go home after I told him my plans), he told me that his mother had invited me to dinner.

His family lived on 117th Street, just off the part of Park Avenue where commuter trains come up from Manhattan's underground after passing the swank part and look down at the grungy Barrio. When I arrived, a Ray Barreto LP was playing a little loud. Silvio introduced his mother Ruth Cachola, a short fair woman with cropped brown hair, light brown eyes and a curled-in, paralyzed left hand. She was wearing a Betty Crocker apron that she used to clean her good right hand to properly greet me.

The house was very neat, the sofa and sofa chair covered in clear vinyl. Silvio and I sat on the sofa as out of another room appeared a great-looking young woman with long hair black like Silvio's. His sister Felina had mild island manners and, although a high school senior, spoke in a Latin womanly way, not in an American teeny-girl style. A pink sweater emphasized her frontal development and her bell-bottom jeans modeled her full, smooth limbs. She didn't sit with us because she had to help her mother. She lowered the music volume.

Silvio suggested that after dinner we see a movie. We were deciding on the film when Silvio's dad Ray Cachola arrived, a tawny hefty man with calloused hands. In accented English, he apologized that he couldn't shake my hand because they were dirty from his working on the boiler. He welcomed me to their "modest home," sounding very respectful, making me feel a little embarrassed. He excused himself to wash his hands. The building's superintendent, he kept its entrance and halls clean.

His wife called us to the table that Felina had set up with side dishes, rice, beans, an avocado salad. Ray approached the table reporting to Ruth in Spanish that the day's *bolita* numbers came out sixes back to back. She asked him to come to the kitchen. He came out carrying the main course, a roast leg of pork, a *pernil*. Ruth finally joined us at the table. Ray did most of the talking, staying in Spanish.

What did Silvio and I have planned for that evening? Silvio told him about our possibly seeing a movie. Ray suggested that afterwards he should bring me around to be surprised. They both smiled cryptically. Ray suddenly remembered to tell Ruth that someone named Charlie Lugo was back in prison, the *bolita* numbers guy told him that afternoon. Ruth shook her head, her face a pained expression.

Charlie was her nephew, she explained, from a part of her family with which she'd lost touch because "*ellos viven*...they live, let's just say we don't live that way." Charlie attended high school with Silvio but never graduated and began hanging around with the wrong people. Ray interjected, "*Sabes*...You know, life is funny. Charlie had been in prison for one year for possessing a gun and that probably saved his life because he didn't get drafted. My older son Hiram was not in prison, and he was drafted. He's in an infantry unit in Vietnam and I worry every day. Now Charlie's up for dealing, twenty years. At least Silvio can't get drafted."

Ruth asked me how I liked Smith Wesson. I answered that it was a pretty nice, with many cultural and political activities, but that college was a lot of work. Ruth seemed surprised to hear there was so much to do because Silvio complained of being bored. She expressed her surprise to Silvio, who shrugged his shoulders and said in English, "Eddie's a big shot over there, a poet, you know, I told you that." Nevertheless, she expressed pride that Silvio was attending college. "*Obtuvo*...he earned high grades in high school and Smith Wesson gave him a full scholarship. At first I was worried because he had never lived away from home."

Ray Cachola interjected that he liked that Smith Wesson was near the Catskills, a stone's throw from Plattekill and *Las Villas*. They all expressed shock that I hadn't heard of *Las Villas*. "*Son como...*They're like being on hilltop in Utuado, with Puerto Rican places that play our music, serve our food," Ray said. "When we go, you can meet us with Silvio. It's so close."

Ruth asked me what I planned to study. I was majoring in English, thinking of teaching, and my certainty seemed to cause her to turn her face to Silvio, who looked away. "Silvio expresses no interest in anything."

"Freshman year is that way," I interjected.

Silvio was a totally different person at home. To anything either Ray or Ruth asked him, his usual fast, rhythmic street English deferred to his halting, poor Spanish. Felina was more fluent in Spanish even though she was the one born in New York. Ruth seemed to be reading my thoughts when she asked if I took classes in Spanish because Silvio needs them. Glaring at Silivio, she flattered me for speaking it well because "it was important that we all continued to speak our language."

I didn't want to answer, but she was waiting. "*Estoy tomando...*I'm in an advanced Spanish class, a literature course." Ruth said that Silvio took them but they didn't do any good. As rationale Silvio reminded his parents, that as he had told them, I attended a very exclusive boarding school. That biographical detail possibly had something to do with Ruth's redundant effort to make me aware of Felina, who I was told had seasoned and practically cooked the roast pork. And while Ruth had served Ray and Silvio their meals, Felina was asked to serve me.

As she did, her hips were at my eye level, that curvature lingering in memory during the dinner when I struggled to keep my eyes off Felina's olive skin, her large black eyes, her cranberry-colored lips, and my imaginings of the extensive, smooth topography below her neck. At the end of the meal Ruth suggested that if we boys had plans to go out that we should take along Felina, who protested her mother's boldness but in jest.

Silvio wanted to see *Shaft*, but the next showing was too late. *Dirty Harry* with Clint Eastwood was playing on 86th Street at an hour that we could make. As Felina got ready in her room, Ray reminded Silvio to bring me around after the movie. Felina finally emerged in a tan spring coat, her face touched up. I put on my Army fatigue jacket and Silvio threw on a bomber jacket.

Out on the sidewalk Silvio became his extroverted self in English. Felina too suddenly became a New York girl. On the subway ride to 86th Street we guys entertained her with stories of life up the Hudson. Silvio described the students mockingly. "Those white kids all think themselves hot shit, walking around us as if we're some kind of smelly trash. I'm just glad that Eddie's there. And, sis, you've got to see these jokers dance."

On the moderately occupied subway Silvio gave his rendition of their dancing, an exhibition that prompted Felina to laugh and laugh in the same wild way she had laughed at every other dumb thing Silvio said. I wanted to overlook her silly laughter because I enjoyed her smile, her black hair falling back with every burst of laughter, and especially because every time she leaned forward in laughter, her left hand gripped my thigh.

Silvio's demeanor changed the second we exited the subway at 86th Street. As we walked along the Upper East Side on the way to the theater line to purchase tickets, he looked around as if someone were ready to pounce on him. He was more himself while the movie was playing, reacting to the coolness of Clint Eastwood's aiming his Magnum into the punk's face and saying "Go ahead, make my day." It was a nice night for October, so after the movie I suggested we get a beer. In those days during the Vietnam war, with so many young guys getting killed doing a man's job, in New York State the drinking age was lowered to eighteen and we could socialize in bars. Silvio reminded me that Felina was underage.

I changed the suggestion to coffee. But Silvio seemed restless to get back uptown. He had promised Ray to deliver me in time for something but wouldn't say what. Felina rolled her eyes and Silvio warned her. She assured me it was nothing to fear. Once inside the subway station Silvio became his old self and reviewed the film's highlights in a way that kept Felina in stitches. As he joked, I kept seeing that stiff person on the East Side sidewalk.

Carlos used to behave the same way when we went ice skating in Central Park. We always just walked straight back to the subway from the rink. One time I slowed down to look around at a world presumably forbidden to us. I stopped to look into a Florsheim Shoe store window, at shoes that cost $100 bucks, a high price back then, wondering if one day I could have shoes like that or even live on the Upper East Side. Carlos waited on the sidewalk outside the airspace of the store's windows, rigid, his shoulders raised as if he were suffering from the cold, which it wasn't. He never even closed his coat when it was really cold. I asked him what his rush was because we weren't late to get back home. "I just don't like being in this neighborhood, man, that's all."

We exited at the 116th Street station, and Silvio entertained us the entire way to his building. Once inside, I started toward their first-floor apartment door but Felina grabbed my hand and led me behind the stairwell, three steps down, to the building's sheet-metal rear door, which was unlocked. Silvio opened and switched on a bare bulb outside, lighting up a concrete backyard closed in by a chain-link fence that separated their building's clean backyard from an abandoned building's backyard cluttered with mounds of junk. A padlock to a gate in the fence was already unlocked, and through a path cleared through the junk-heap, we crossed to the other building. The sheet-metal rear door to the other building was unlocked, and Silvio pushed it so we could enter the basement dimly lit with a yellowish bulb. As Silvio shut the door behind us, I heard voices. They got louder as we walked along a narrow corridor when I also heard a rooster crowing. I asked Felina if she heard it, and she pursed her lips, bursting to laugh.

Another crowing amid louder voices behind another sheet-metal door in front of us. Silvio pushed it open and I gazed in disbelief. The large basement was well-lit, its walls lined with shelves holding cages that contained roosters. A crowd of shouting men, four deep, bandied fisted cash and frantically cheered on something in a circular space enclosed by what looked like an empty, two-foot-high wading pool. We marched around the crowd of men to reach Ray Cachola, who stood on an elevated platform to our left, from where one could look without obstructions inside the circular ring where a pair of bloodied gamecocks clawed at each other. Ray had to shout to ask if I had ever seen a cockfight. I shook my head. Felina kept her back turned to the arena, her pretty eyes taking side glances at me.

A sudden outburst from the crowd drew my attention back to the ring. A bloody, radiant, brown rooster lay finished, a thin geyser of blood gushing from one eye. Felina, without turning to see, grabbed the sleeve of my Army fatigue jacket and yelled into my ear that she was going upstairs. Ray Cachola handed me a cold can of beer, grabbed hold of a mop and two buckets, and went down to the arena. The whisking mop painted the floor with light strokes of red, which he then covered over with sprinkled sand from a blue plastic bucket.

Silvio asked me what I thought of the operation. Just then I could honestly say that I thought it was cool. It was underground and radical. It was *jíbaro*-dom and fuck *los yanquis* wherever they roam. I didn't see then what would become clear years later in Puerto Rico, when William Guzmán would show me his fighting roosters.

Two rooster owners began priming their contenders for the next contest, each pressing down the wings and legs as he jabbed his bird's beak into its challenger's face, friction to spark fury. Set loose, the birds began slashing, cutting, stabbing as they squawked. Bets crossed hands, men cursed, cheered, and then booed at one rooster that, after receiving a few bloodletting cuts, was peddling around, defending more than attacking. For being a coward, he was cut so deeply that his insides popped out.

Silvio tapped my arm and signaled with thumb up that we should go. Over the crowd noise I yelled out my thanks to Ray, left him my half-empty beer can, and followed Silvio back across the contiguous backyards. It being past eleven, I told Silvio I would go to thank his mother for dinner and say goodnight to Felina, then be off.

Ruth Cachola was watching a movie on a Spanish television station. She reminded me that I had family on 112th Street. Felina saw me to the door, where to my surprise she gave me a long, sweet kiss. Not knowing how to turn down a surprise like that, I kissed her back, and I supposed I would follow up with a phone call. But once back at Smith Wesson, the thought of calling her or seeing her again made no sense.

That year I had become good friends with Juan Acosta's ex, Luz Vitali, who although not coming close to looking like Felina and to whom unfortunately I was not sexually attracted, had aroused a new level of pleasure: sharing intellectual things with a woman. Luz helped me recover my Spanish, which now I practiced by reading out loud to her from my assigned works of Spanish literature. Aside from her looks, Felina and I had nothing more to share.

I managed to avoid Silvio on campus until one night he showed up in my dormitory room to tell me that a friend of his father's who bought a farm near Plattekill was going to drive into the city for the weekend and had offered to give him a ride on Friday to return on Sunday. Silvio was inviting me to come along. The idea of going home for the weekend on a free ride clouded my remembering that Silvio and I were not destined to have a long friendship. With whatever motive—to make me jealous or get me off the hook—he also let me know that I shouldn't feel obligated to call Felina because she'd met a guy at a dance.

That Saturday night we met at a Latin singles bar he'd heard about, The Daiquiri, just a few blocks south of 96th Street, in the Upper East Side he didn't like. It was full of Rican business-types, a world unfamiliar to me, and I looked forward to mingling with the interesting-looking women. But the minute we got there Silvio expressed discomfort. These women, he whispered, probably won't dance with the likes of us. "Look at those guys and the cars parked outside. We're just a couple of students." He insisted that we go to a place called Manny's #1, farther north into the Barrio.

Manny's was full of a rougher-looking crowd not necessarily any younger. But Silvio seemed relaxed there, getting in several dances while I danced only one time then stayed by the bar and observed Silvio do his thing. When he stopped to check on his wallflower friend, he spotted a new pair of women at the far end of the bar and went directly to introduce himself. He waved me over. I was introduced to Sylvia and her cousin Lucy.

Sylvia's large, golden, half-moon earrings glittered as she moved her head, giggling it up with lucky Silvio, who, because her tight short skirt receded almost to her crotch, also got an orchestra view of her thighs. I was left with her plain-Jane cousin Lucy, whose longer dress revealed nothing and who waited for me to say something. When I was finally about to say that awaited thing a big guy standing behind Silvio shoved him forward, causing his drink to spill over Sylvia's legs and brief lap.

Silvio swiveled in macho rage to face his hefty, six-foot-plus opponent who waited to see what the squirt Silvio was going to attempt, which on second thought was nothing. Silvio sheepishly apologized but had already lost his stride with Sylvia, who joined by Lucy had walked off to the Ladies' Room, wiping herself and her skirt with a napkin,.

The incident had been brewing. In his excitement to rap with Sylvia, Silvio cut in front of that tall guy, obstructing his view of her legs and the chance to hit on her. The guy gave me his pissed-off look. Taller and bigger than either Silvio or me, he wore an Afro and over his black wool sweater a gold chain with the large gold figure of an assault rifle. He at least kept his cool until Silvio, showing off before Sylvia, gestured widely with his arms and almost poked the guy's face with an elbow that the guy pushed way, causing the drink to spill.

Before the girls returned, Silvio told me to follow him to another cool place he knew a few blocks uptown, but I passed on that. He then invited me to a beer at his father's cockfight arena but I didn't want to go there again or with Silvio anywhere else, except that I had to ride back to the campus with him. That Sunday, for the duration of the trip upstate I needed to study for a test but had to listen to Silvio and Benjy, the driver, dispute over the best salsa bands. I felt bad about not being able to hang out with Silvio but I couldn't be myself squeezed into Silvio's narrow world north of 96th Street.

Term papers and catching up for final exams kept us from getting together, and I didn't call him over Christmas Break. When we came back for the spring semester, I didn't see him on campus. I asked around and a student who worked in the administration office told me that Ray Cachola had an accident, went on disability, and his family had moved to Puerto Rico. Silvio opted to go with them. The news hit me hard. I thought about Silvio, about Carlos. Couldn't separate them for weeks. Now Silvio could also get drafted. Did I let him down by leaving him alone at Smith Wesson?

I had been introduced to this *americano* world much younger while Silvio underwent culture shock. After crossing that invisible border between worlds, maybe he needed me to make that transition possible, which also required that I spend more time where he was still more comfortable, north of 96th Street. If he didn't see a place for himself outside of El Barrio and a good reason such as Ray's condition came along, his making the sacrifice to stay in college was unlikely.

Or was it his responsibility to confront the challenges of our situation with or without me? Was his father just an excuse? Did he simply quit, like the cowardly rooster that pedaled around till that slash emptied his guts. I imagined Silvio drifting far behind me, morphing into the figure of Carlos who stayed in the world he knew, afraid of manhood in a world in which he intuited he would not fit. Or did they both intuit what I didn't, their ending up nowhere, what happened to me?

PART THREE

FRONTIERLAND

Chapter 11

That Sunday I had to attend Governor Mario Cuomo's brunch. Originally I was going not just to get Sánchez O'Neil off my back. I was exploring new career possibilities. Now with Carlos' suitcases in my possession and the possibility of a disastrous conclusion, my job hunting seemed purely hypothetical. But the last thing I could do was to demonstrate a loss of interest. Being sought after by the Governor of New York and being wooed to manage the campaign of an almost shoe-in Congressman weren't opportunities one backed out of without drawing curiosity, especially the curiosity of enemies. And I wasn't without those who coveted my advantages, who would make a career of finding out why I would mysteriously turn down those very advantages.

To make the possibly useless long drive out on the island at least pleasurable and as well repay him for looking out for Graziela, I called Samson to hire him as my driver. He agreed enthusiastically, and the following morning he was promptly on the sidewalk in sunlight, dressed in a tight-fitting plaid suit, distinguished-looking with his snowy hair. He opened the door for his passenger in khaki pants and a blue knit shirt. After a quick inventory of where everything was on the Camry dash and an adjustment of mirrors, he was ready.

"Now, where did you say this Shag Harbor was?"

"Sag Harbor."

"Sag, like tits?" From the inside pocket of his suit jacket he produced a map. "Sit back and relax, Mr. Loperena."

I asked him to tell me about himself.

He was born in Florida. He was a teen when his parents moved to New York in the thirties. Got married only once. "My children come around now. They didn't use to when I acted like a motherfucker. I smoked weed and snorted the good stuff, but the bottle, you understand, liked that way too much. One night I dropped in late at night and slept off a drunk for a whole day. Next morning, my wife and the kids had moved out to live with her sister. I tried to call but my sister-in-law is practically a minister, so, well, forget that. A month later I woke up one morning and said, 'Goddamn.' I picked up the phone and called my wife. Now, she's passed on, you understand. I told her something had changed in me. She said, 'yeah, so what? Again? Man, how many times you going to change.' I tried to explain but she just cut me off, 'The day I see you in a church, praying with decent folk, I'll think about it.' She hung up. But she gave me the idea. I stayed sober on the weekend to show up to church on Sunday, sober as a motherfucking judge and singing like James Brown. My wife be coming in with her sister and looking at me like a wild bear the preacher had dragged in on a chain. She didn't come over to talk to me and I didn't go over to talk to her.

"Which was okay because in this churchgoing solo I started to meet some decent-looking ladies. Man, those ladies know how to make friends fast. Got invited to dinner, to the movies. All that time that I'm drinking like a fool and looking for pussy, the church was where it at. They knew I was married but when that midnight hour came, man. And they was very understanding in church, walked past you with a simple, 'Good morning, Mr. Magnus.' So my wife was seeing me too too happy. She told the preacher she could see I was a changed man but didn't know how to get close. That's how he explained it to me. I called her up. Sure, she'd have dinner with me. So that was it. The preacher got his piece of me, I got a piece of his pussy, and now my wife wanted in on the action. She came back and we lived good in that apartment until she died two years ago. Cancer."

The yacht, the pride of some Democrat donor and ironically named Dalilah's Man, was easy to spot among the more modest surrounding flotilla. Overcast of a storm forecast for later had already moved in. Nicolas Gainsay met me on the deck, drink in hand. His bushy seventy sideburns were gone. His thinned out frizzy dark-brown hair showed blotches of baldness. It took him a few seconds to recognize me. "Eddie, my boy, how good it is see you?" he said hugging me. "You look great, and Candida and I really couldn't feel prouder of your work."

I introduced Samson as my friend.

Gainsay guided us to the rear of the wide deck, where a young tall blond guy in a white linen coat poured Bloody Marys and screwdrivers to a crowd that also schmoozed around a spread of breads and cold cuts. The men, like me, mostly wore summer khakis and knit shirts, the women knee-length shorts.

Candida Gainsay had aged considerably, no longer resembling Jackie Kennedy as she used to, not even an aged Jackie Kennedy. In a white blouse and beige shorts, her hair was now all gray, closely cut and covered by a N.Y. Mets baseball cap, her legs cellulite-plump. She extended her hand to someone Gainsay said he wanted her to meet, surprising her, "It's our Eddie!"

Her face beamed, her eyes becoming tearful as she hugged me maternally. "Oh, my God, it's so great to see you."

I asked about their daughter Flora. Smiling somewhat cryptically, she answered that Flora and her daughter were just fine. Gainsay excused himself for interrupting, noting that we could catch up later, pointing toward the food table where, he said, a couple of people had expressed interest in meeting me. Candida joined us.

Gainsay introduced me to State Comptroller Edward Regan, a bald muscular man in a running suit, and I had already met State Attorney General Robert Abrams, attired as if for a tennis match. Gainsay spoke in a tone of introducing a protégé of whom he was most proud.

"Politics next?" asked Abrams. Before I could answer, a woman apologized for interrupting. Gainsay introduced Constancia Vaselini, the early fortyish Governor's personal secretary. Dressed unlike the other women on the yacht, she wore a coral-colored blouse and a calve-length skirt as gray as her all-business demeanor, punctuated by black-framed glasses. "Mr. Loperena, I'm glad we can finally meet." Constancia spoke with a mild English accent. "I didn't mean to interrupt but the Governor has asked me to speak to you before he does. If you can come with me."

I let Regan and Abrams know it was a pleasure to meet them and hoped we could chat later. Attorney General Abrams raised his glass, "Look forward to it!" *Which gave me a chill.*

Constancia and I went just out of earshot. "Before you speak to the Governor, I need to meet with you, but I just realized that I have one matter to take care of first. I'll look for you on the deck." I nodded, returned to Gainsay, who was piling cold cuts on a roll. I prepared myself a sandwich and as I poured myself a cup of coffee, I caught sight of Samson in a chair against the railing and biting into a bagel. He smiled, raising his coffee cup. I raised mine.

Gainsay led me away from the crowd. "You don't know how proud it makes me feel to be here with you, on the verge of working with the Governor. You know how our family has always felt about you. Greeting cards aren't the place to tell things. I left Harvard for N.Y.U., you know that already. I wanted to get back to my New York roots. But my family went through some strong times coming out of the seventies. The sickness of our era."

"Flora?"

"No, Flora straightened out, no more pot. You know that she gave birth to Aisha Margarita, my gorgeous grandchild, my pride and joy, and she's now working with the gay and lesbian homeless. That Cuban revolutionary who knocked her up when she went there to cut sugarcane suddenly reappeared, wants her to help him get to the U.S. And, of course, you remember little Abigail. Well, figure, she's a stockbroker. Doing pretty well for herself. No, Candida was the one who had it pretty rough. She went through a severe cocaine phase. But everyone's still here, thank God, and loves you to pieces."

For a second Gainsay was the same progressive Dean at Harvard, my hair hadn't thinned out and lost its curl, our seventies still gleamed in his gaze, and I once again was fueled by the revolutionary commitment that inspired poems and later my activist legal causes. Gainsay saw Ms. Vaselini heading our way. He looked forward to our getting together afterwards.

Ms. Vaselini escorted me to a cabin furnished like a studio apartment, where she asked me to sit across from her at a vinyl island counter. She glossed over notes on her clipboard. Her eyes were a light brown, her black hair in a bun except for strands that fell along both cheeks. "My report on you says your problem is you don't show off enough. And that you don't have the look, I mean that you don't seem very representative of most people's idea of—index and middle fingers of both hands twitching in aerial quotation marks around—"Puerto Rican." To begin with, "You have a very privileged education. Hmm..." She continued to gloss her sheets. "Would you categorize yourself as representative, to the extent, of course, that anything *is*? Would you say you still feel the pulse, if pulse, of course, is the appropriate figurative expression? Would you say you still have a feel for the community from which you came but which you also left?"

Her Continentally-accented English that thoroughly enjoyed its own sarcasm, self-conscious that her every sentence sizzled with a wit that the listener, if he could ever be her peer, would also appreciate, were hallmarks of an insufferable kind of Argentine.

I didn't answer.

"Mr. Loperena, could you please answer my question?"

"Oh, I understood it to be rhetorical."

Not pleased, she exhibited another *porteño* hallmark: a bluntness with which she herself was eminently impressed. With an in-your-face without actually lifting her head from the clipboard, she expressed being glad to see Hispanic leaders with my educational background because "tragically so many got ahead in ethnic politics with only street smarts—at great expense to the Hispanic community." And to test my ethnic pride even more she appended, now lifting her head and looking directly at me: "To be specific and frank: you are quite different from any Puerto Rican I ever met."

"Well, I usually find I'm different from *everybody* I meet."

"Of course," she returned the sarcasm. Her head floated over the clipboard.

"Ms. Vaselini, is your interview supposed to get as anthropological as you're making this?"

"Well, the Governor consults me on Hispanic opinion, and I am trying to get a sense of who you are. To be honest, I expected somebody quite different. To begin with, I was told you wore a beard."

"I shaved it off a couple of days ago."

"You were married and are now divorced. No children. What do you think went wrong?"

"According to her I did every possible thing to bring it about."

"What I'm trying to get at is whether she can get back at your character, did she find you in bed with another woman or something ugly like that."

"I was never in bed with anything ugly, no. I did her a legal favor, in fact, something to do with her half-brother."

She lifted one, two, three sheets on her clipboard. "We know. We've got to talk about that. We don't think it's a good idea that you defend that man who stabbed the cop, especially now that he's died." She paused as if to get my reaction. "Well, what's your comment?"

"Someone else is representing him."

She let fall two sheets on the clipboard. "Oh, are you still an advocate of Puerto Rican independence or was that a sixties thing?"

Outside the storm had started, and the yacht was rocking.

"Well, Mr. Loperena, I need a response to that question to give the Governor."

"Ms. Vaselini, how long have you been in this country?"

She pressed back her glasses against her nose, sat up, took a deep breath and looked me squarely in the eyes. "The Governor asked me to clear up a few things with you."

"Well, because you are a public consultant on Hispanic Affairs, your qualifications should be public knowledge. Isn't that so?"

"I came fifteen years ago from Argentina."

"Now try to follow this argument that I will attempt to develop as clearly as my unrepresentative skills permit. Your boss wants to give the impression that he cares about the largest sector of Hispanic votes, mainly from Caribbean people, and he makes his assistant and Hispanic advisor somebody from a country where people see themselves as the Aryan race among other, impure Latins. Let's just concede right away that your country is indeed whiter, closer to Europe, and steeped in Western Civilization. Explain where that pedigree warrants that you, except for being Italian and Southern Italian at that, should be the one whispering into the Governor's ear insights on those whom you plainly consider inferior Latins, what you refer to as *tropicales*. Or another way of looking at this is to wonder if the Governor is simply blind to your obvious superiority and that explains why he has you performing this minority duty."

Ms. Vaselini capped her silver ballpoint pen and stood up. "I'll see if the Governor is ready to see you. Please wait here."

Amid the rocking, Ms. Vaselini struggled to keep her balance and exit decorously. The boat's engine growled and lamps lit up the dimmed cabin. Listening to wind and rain, and feeling a bit nauseous from the rocking, I suddenly had my fill of New York State political prospects. I shut my eyes and took a deep breath, envisioned myself walking out, driving back to New York and... what? Returning to Carlos' suitcases in my closet.

Ms. Vaselini opened the cabin door, stepped in with the Governor, introduced me and departed.

Mario Cuomo was taller than I imagined him in person. He had a full head of tinted dark hair and smiled exuberantly, placing his hand on my left shoulder as we shook hands. He smelled of onions and lox. His Italian genes rewarded him with a suave, genteel manner; his height gave him a commanding presence.

"Eddie, let's sit down and talk. We might have to make this very brief." The boat's swaying caused his butt to almost miss the stool.

"Before we begin, what did you say to Connie? She came out... peeved, shall we say?"

"I asked her a few things she might have misinterpreted."

Mario Cuomo, son of Italian immigrants, was the poet of immigrant imagery in speeches that ignited the patriotic fervor of the "marvelous rainbow that makes ours the greatest country on this planet." According to Sánchez O'Neil, his multicultural vision was not just rhetoric. "He's Italian, *latino* like us!" And genuine, I was assured too, was his respect for my work in defending My People. That's why Cuomo wanted to hang me like a mojo rabbit's foot on the Democratic Party's key chain. My pissing off Ms. Vaselini, however, seemed of a great concern.

"Okay, let's get on track. When you hear my projects to improve housing, education, drug rehabilitation, you will agree with me that this clash of personalities is minor and incidental. Can you join me without being a problem to getting there is what Connie wanted to find out? And what about this guy who killed that cop?"

"I'm not involved with that case."

"That's terr—"We both listened to the noisy rain and sounds of brunchers scampering beyond the cabin door. "How closely tied are you to the accused's sister, your ex-wife? I frankly wish you were married, had a couple of kids."

"So do I. Maybe you can line up some candidates. Is Ms. Vaselini free?"

He chuckled. "I need you clean as a hound's tooth, Eddie. We'll be sending out rumors that you're going to become a judge or the Commissioner of Human Rights. But conservatives dislike you intensely. They'll disinter skeletons, believe me. Your closet has to be clean."

Ms. Vaselini opened the door, her hair no longer in a bun, but dripping wet over her face, her glasses fogged up. She was holding a large golf umbrella that she closed to step inside. "Governor, we've moved everything inside—" The boat pitched, and Ms. Vaselini was thrown in pirouettes landing with her face on my lap. My stomach felt queasy but the governor stood up and ran to the not-so-far farthest corner and unloaded. After retching several times, he composed himself, stood straight, wiped his mouth with his handkerchief, pushed back his hair, and excused himself. He exited with great decorum, slamming the cabin door that didn't shut but swung open.

Meanwhile, Ms. Vaselini lost her glasses and was struggling to keep her balance on the thrashing boat as she looked over the general area, although obviously she couldn't see much without them. I stood up to help her, and her glasses slid off my lap. I picked them up and handed them. She thanked me, giving a forced smile although a changed humbler look. Furious rain entered through the open cabin door, and she offered me half the ample golf umbrella. Together we walked out of the cabin's rising stink, Ms. Vaselini steering us to the main cabin's door, where I had no desire to be in closer quarters with more questions on my future plans. But Samson could be in there. I was about to ask Ms. Vaselini if she had noticed him when I heard yelling out on the dock. She generously kept me dry by the railing as I watched the governor's chauffeur shouting into the driver's window of my Camry. Samson had apparently outwitted the chauffeur when the storm started and coolly positioned my car in front of the gangplank before the chauffeur could pull in the Governor's chariot. I was about to walk out in the rain when Ms. Vaselini offered to keep me dry up to the gangplank. When we got there I thanked her. Her messy hair made her look younger and more lightened up. "The Governor will get back to you."

I regretted not getting the chance to say goodbye to the Gain-says, appreciating in retrospect how deeply ran my relationship with them. Gainsay had opened his arms to me as the son he never had. He would have been pleased if I had stayed with Flora, whose fixation with pot constantly made me think of my broken promise to Carlos that I wouldn't use it. Instead she went to Cuba in support of the Revolution only to be knocked up by a "New Man," who was just another shit man. Another road not taken, another story to archive.

Chapter 12

The next day when I got to the Ponce de Leon Restaurant on 116th Street Sánchez O'Neil was standing in a parking spot by a broken meter directly in front, keeping it available for me. On a sweltering day he was characteristically in a suit. I came dressed as community leaders do, in a short-sleeved shirt.

I stepped out of my car, expecting to proceed to the restaurant door, but Sánchez O'Neil wrapped an arm around my shoulder and remained immobile. "I know that the governor's secretary was a tough appetizer but she's not the main course, so you shouldn't have wasted your smartass words on her. Anyway, for some reason she approved of you as his Hispanic vote charm. So let's see what he comes up with."

He lifted his arm and I thought our intimate session was over, but he stepped in front of me and held up both hands, "Eddie, I just need a few seconds to compose my words here. I need you to be nice to these people. They're not so sophisticated, but these are the real People you always talk about. They're also my votes and I invited you as my guest." That said, he patted down his suit jacket, and he ushered me toward the restaurant door. We weaved around tables of people having lunch on our way to a reserved back room.

His guests sat around one large rectangular table. Three center seats that faced the open door to the restaurant's main room were empty, presumably for him and me and perhaps another tardy leader. Seated to Sánchez O'Neil's left I had a clear view all the way to restaurant's window facing 116th Street where a police car had just double parked in front of the restaurant giving me an unpleasant rush. A cop came in and talked to a waiter as Sánchez O'Neil performed the introductions.

Except for the wiry, bald Jake Goldstein, a Democratic party campaign adviser, I knew everybody else at the table, so after shaking Jake's hand, I only needed to nod and send a collective wave. Present were the dagger-bearded Jamal Kinshasa, president of the Council for Leadership and Afro-American Dignity (CLAD), dapper in a dashiki and African skull cap, and his wife Sheshona MacNamara Kinshasa, a plump, dark-chocolate woman lavishly wrapped up in a turquoise and brown African tunic dress, who lit up the room with a smile as radiant as Yvette's. (The cop had ordered a take-out lunch that he was carrying out.) Then came the New York Rican lawyers, Evaristo "Call me Teddy" Miravé and Roberto "Buzz" Tencuidao and last the flamboyantly blond State Senator Patria Gómez Mitchell, famous for her Spanish-only campaigns in her Barrio district—forcing news reporters to accept translated transcripts—and, ever at her side, Sarah Juanita Cabot, her bilingual translator-secretary. The irony about Patria and her campaign was that she was married to Kipper Mitchell, an *americano* millionaire, who like her two previous *americano* husbands, didn't speak a word of Spanish.

Sánchez O'Neil started the ceremonies by underscoring not having to list to all present the challenges that minority communities all faced. Heads bobbed in agreement. Unemployment was rampant. Hunger was especially serious among our schoolchildren. So much work was needed to improve our pitiful education statistics. Heads continued to bob. Our kids are not even flunking out, just disappearing, swallowed up by the streets.

"—And too often found dead!" interjected the translator Sarah, pausing to get another message from her boss, Patria Gómez Mitchell: "The crack epidemic and the educational system are conspiring to kill our children."

"Yes," added Sánchez O'Neil, "drugs continue to plague our communities and corrupt our police and destroy the lives of our children..."

Cocktails arrived as Sánchez O'Neil reiterated the importance of his effort to get to Congress and help both the Hispanic and Black communities. He paused only to pop into his mouth a slice of warm Spanish *chorizo* sausage appetizer that everybody else was chomping down.

The introductory remarks over, he signaled to the waiters, who in minutes served from two deep pots of paella. Official discussion deferred to gastronomy until Sarah who, as Patria poked her fork into a clam, read her translation of a pre-written statement about the rights of brutalized Hispanic women. When Sarah finished, the table applauded, then after more recess for eating, Sánchez O'Neil got up.

"I know, as you all do, that the grievances and afflictions in the Hispanic community are shared with our African-American brothers and sisters. That's why I've invited the Kinshasas to join us. As I said earlier, I want this campaign to be a coalition of communities and not be seen as just an effort to install a Hispanic in Congress." As he spoke, a pair of black women, dressed in what looked like white nurse uniforms, entered the restaurant. One held up to her bosom a picture of the Sacred Heart of Jesus. The other passed around a tall white collection cup. They almost reached the back room before the manager cut them off. They politely departed.

"That's why I have invited to this meeting Mr. Eduardo Loperena, whose legal battles for the good of both our communities you know well. Few men in this city have his reputation of commitment to our struggles. The black community knows how he has cooperated with their causes, which after all, are our causes too. The liberal sector knows and has recognized Mr. Loperena's accomplishments over the years. But what few know and you are about to be among the first to know is that he is taking another career step by beginning a new phase of his important work as a political leader."

I couldn't believe that Sánchez O'Neil authorized himself to make that public declaration about my career change.

"Eduardo Loperena has come to be with us here in solidarity with my campaign and its commitment to our entire Harlem community. I don't want to impose on him the obligation to give us a speech because I know that he spent yesterday at a special meeting with the Governor and hasn't had the time to prepare a statement. But I will ask for a few improvised words. For he is a proven champion of all our causes, and that's why I am proud to introduce him to my campaign team." Teddy Miravé and Buzz Tencuidao shot up and applauded and the rest of the table also stood and applauded.

I stood as everybody sat. Took a deep breath. "I am really here as an observer, but I do want to thank you for coming and supporting Gus's campaign. He too is a proven leader and mentor of our broader minority community and will devote the same respect and concern for the well-being and progress not just of this East Harlem district because his goals as Congressman..." As I spoke a commotion started up in the main dining room. I also felt the buzzing of my pager, but I continued with more boilerplate as the waiters in the main dining room tried to remove a gruffy young man hugging an almost life-size statue of the Virgin Mary. Sánchez O'Neil took note of what was happening and broke into a smile.

As I finished my praise of "his record of commitment at the local government level and for his campaign to become our voices and ears in Washington," he gestured to one of the waiters to come over, whispered in his ear. I was thanking Sanchez O'Neil for the honor of inviting me to this lunch with such distinguished community leaders when out in the main room the waiter to whom Sánchez O'Neil gave instructions rescued the young man about to be removed from the premises.

Sanchez O'Neil thanked me again for my presence, prompting more applause. "Yes, applause well deserved for his words here and for his record with our minority communities. And now, my other special guest has just arrived, one of the examples of the cultural contributions we are making to this the city of art and culture, the celebrated street poet and prison playwright, Noel Angel, whose play *Shortsighted* was nominated for a Tony."

The waiter had to forcibly drag in Noel, bearing his Virgin Mary and looking around with glassy, floating, frightened eyes. Not much taller than the plastic or fiberglass statue, Noel had unkempt curly hair and a pimply face downy with soft blotches of black whiskers. He wore faded, torn blue jeans and a dirty sky blue T-shirt with an embossed Puerto Rico flag surrounded by a ring of words that read "Kiss Me I'm Puerto Rican."

Sánchez O'Neil led him to the empty seat to his right, trying to peel Noel's fingers from the Virgin. But just as the lady was about to leave his hand, Noel yanked her back, embracing her obsessively. Instead of sitting in his chair, Noel shuffled up to Patria, stroked her blond hair, and made a whining, pleading sound, holding out his open hand, "Five bucks, just five bucks."

Sánchez O'Neil behind him pulled out his wallet and took out a twenty. "Here, you are, poet and actor. That was genius." Sánchez O'Neil pointed out that "this artistic genius has been performing the reality of so many of our people whose lives are mired in drug addiction and despair. The ability of Noel's performance art to bring out the poignancy of this condition is exemplary of his great contribution to our cultural life."

As Sánchez O'Neil spoke, Noel took a deep, clammy, loud sniff, wiped his nose with the back of his hand, and sat in the Deputy Mayor's chair. The Virgin fallen by his side, he began to wolf down what was left of the paella in front of him, munching and sniffing, lost in his own world.

Sánchez O'Neil, caught off-guard, was still able to continue his performance, "And now you can tell by his exaggeration that he wants us to become sensitive to the hunger of our communities. Excellent, truly excellent." Then, as Noel Angel sucked noisily on an empty lobster leg shell, Sánchez O'Neil, apparently having exhausted superlatives, concluded: "and in summary, with Mr. Loperena here and the arrival of our street genius Angel, all present can be proud that our table is blessed with two fine poets."

"Three," Sarah the translator interrupted, making the table wait as Patria Gómez Mitchell fed her more Spanish. "Do not forget that my book of poems was published by my family in Puerto Rico when

I was sixteen." While Sarah translated, Patria struggled to dislodge something caught in her back teeth. "Five," Sheshona and Jamal said in unison, staring at each other rather proudly, and out of Sheshona's large African-design leather bag emerged two chapbooks of poems. Sánchez O'Neil's eyes moved around the table with the glee of a kindergarten teacher about to praise the entire class.

"Four." Everybody looked at me. "I don't consider myself a poet anymore."

I heard myself as if some other person had spoken. My pager buzzed again. I pushed back my chair from the table. "I'm sorry but I have to leave." Sánchez O'Neil apologized for not telling them that I had informed him earlier that my schedule left me little time to be with them that afternoon. Excusing himself, he accompanied me, and once out of earshot, grabbed my arm. "Eddie, what are you doing? You've got to get down off that high high horse. This is our reality."

"Yeah, I know. I'm sorry. I just got beeped for something urgent."

"Maybe if you want to live with the *blanquitos* in P.R. But this is us here. We live in the Third World."

"Don't forget to take care of Maritza."

"I'll be taking care of you too, so don't let me down."

"Gus, I've got something on my mind. We'll talk later."

I truly admired Sánchez O'Neil's capacity to harmonize anything: Noel Angel drugged and pathetic repackaged into performance art. Gus was the genius performance artist and Noel his prop. *Get off your high, high horse.*

Samson was paging me. I called from a street phone. He was fearing for Graziela's life after what he heard that morning. *What can I do? Bang on Graziela's door, then what?* I hadn't planned on going to the West Side. Luis Villanueva was arriving from PR that afternoon, and then we were attending Maritza's dinner.

I drove as fast as I could, but it took me almost as long to find parking three blocks away. By then there was no apparent motive for knocking on her door. "Man, things are quiet now, but that girl had a bad time of it this morning. She was crying. Dog barking like crazy. I heard her man slam the door and didn't hear him come back." That Grace used to be my wife made him take her suffering personally. He looked shaken up. "Can I get you a something? Gin on the rocks?"

"Fine."

From the kitchen he thanked me for the day on the yacht. "Boy, I had fun. Eyes moving everywhere, clean sea air. That's a big deal for an old man like me who doesn't get around. I enjoyed it, and I thank you. And that serious-looking girl who took you away. Nice body under that formality. I'll be right there."

Samson's apartment kept all the touches of his deceased wife, maybe exactly as she must have taught him to arrange it. Large doilies spread over the arms of an old green sofa. Lace-bordered curtains. He returned from the kitchen, handed me the drink.

I took one sip and we heard footsteps climb to the third floor. The door of 3A opened and then shut. Marlboro's voice could be heard demanding to know why Graziela was on the phone because he couldn't get through. She said something inaudible that didn't satisfy Marlboro, who called her a backstabbing slut, a cunt. As he said these words things were crashing. He wanted her "to explain why the fuck she disappears for hours so he didn't know where she could be reached." *Crash.* "Who are you fucking, who is it? Your cocksucking ex, isn't it. He's still around, isn't he." *Crash.* In the background, weeping, mumbling, Grace's voice begged him to stop. "No, you're wrong, please stop, please." I ran out to the hall and banged on the door.

"Fuck off, whoever it is."

"It's Eddie Loperena, open up."

"Oh, yes, yes." Marlboro opened the door, and as he was about to throw a punch, Graziela jumped on his back and embraced his right punching arm.

"David, no, David, he's a lawyer."

"I don't give a fuck what he is."

"Eddie, go, get out of here." She was bouncing up and down, choking Marlboro, who tried to shrug her off.

"Eddie, just go. This doesn't have to do with you."

Marlboro was either drunk or on something. He's eyes didn't look anywhere. I looked into her eyes. I wanted some kind of explanation. "Why are you doing this to yourself?"

"Because I love him, see." She kissed his ears and neck. "See. He's my man." Her eyes brimmed with tears. I turned around. Marlboro threw the door.

I went back to Samson and apologized because I couldn't continue our visit. He understood. Downstairs I sat in my car with the engine running and the air conditioner on, staring through the windshield as the sun began to descend over Riverside Drive and the Hudson River. I tried to think of anything that would erase the mental picture of Graziela hugging her most important symbol.

The equation had never been more concrete and clear: Marlboro embodied everything she wanted in life and I symbolized everything from which she wanted to flee. To all the women I had ever known I was never a person but a symbol of something. I exaggerated. I didn't feel like just a symbol to Louise and certainly not the person who produced the man Graziela married, Luz Vitali...

When I introduced Luz at our graduation, Mami Lalia's great pleasure seeped out of her eyes and smile and welcoming arms, and Luz expressed her great pleasure at their finally meeting, "habiendo oído de...having heard the great mother you are." Luz handed me a business-size envelope and apologized for having to leave us immediately but her parents were waiting. She kissed Mami Lalia on the cheek, adding that she should be proud of her son, who someday will be an important leader. When she said this, she paused to look into my eyes, half-smiling, which made me feel like shit. "La barba, ...The beard, I have to tell you, makes you look even more handsome, intellectual." She gave me a last hug and light kiss on the lips then was gone.

Her departure left Mami Lalia unhappy, angry in fact. My reminding her that Luz had sent that postcard last summer from Venezuela was redundant. She hadn't forgotten who signed the postcard and, when introduced, knew right away whom she was meeting. "A la verdad...We were really just good friends," I said in pathetic self-defense.

Mami Lalia sighed hard. I took her arm to lead her to the graduation reception, but she pulled away. "Cualquier mujer...Any woman with a pair of eyes can see Luz cares for you very much." She spun toward the reception. I introduced her to professors and friends. She was cordial but distracted, looking around. Luz and her family did not stay for the reception. At Mami Lalia's request we left early. On the train ride home, she spoke practically nothing and shut her eyes, whether to sleep or just to avoid talking to me. I took out Luz's letter:

Querido Eddie,

Ya sabes cómo...*You already know how I feel about you, but I respect the fact that love doesn't always come with a guarantee that the other person will love you back. I understand but can't help feeling that one obstacle to your seeing my true feelings and your feeling the same way toward me was that you were so conscious of yourself not as a person but as a symbol. In your poems, you write about being this thing "Puerto Rican" and you want your people to be free. But however "revolutionary" that might sound to your supporters, you are really giving in to all the garbage that American culture put into your head. You want to be special even in a way that is humiliating because it makes "the Man" feel guilty. Well, he doesn't and if you just accepted that you are a really bright, good person who happens to be studying to improve his station in life maybe you could have seen me as just a chubby girl who really wanted to be with you and not the Venezuelan from a rich family beside the Puerto Rican from the Bronx. In practical terms, of course, we would be separating anyway toward different lives, I headed for medical school and you off to Harvard, so maybe you were wiser as this day would have been even more difficult at least for me. I wish, of course, the best for you and leave the door to our friendship always open.*

Love,
Luz

Mami Lali waited several days to bring up Luz. Then, out of the blue over dinner, she asked why I didn't respond to that young lady Luz's genuine feelings. I looked down at my plate. I realized then that she wasn't just standing up for Luz. The genuineness of love was her cause, maybe because of her own lost love she once spoke about to a visiting woman friend when I was younger and presumably distracted and uninterested in adult conversation, lost in my imagining the combat of toy soldiers. I figured it was the genuine lost love that she preserved archived in letters wrapped in a red ribbon, which I once found while rummaging among her things in a closet.

"Sus padres...*Her parents are traveling with her across Europe for the summer," I said, thinking that information spoke for itself. I imagined the campaign Mami Lalia would have mounted much earlier in the year if she had seen the pictures of Luz's father's unending ranch in the Amazon. I wouldn't have heard the end of it if she knew that we had briefly been lovers even though I really wasn't attracted to her chubby body, her walk a kind of waddle. She was Juan Acosta's girlfriend, from which I concluded that class to class loyalty overrides physical attraction.*

I resorted to my old excuse. "I won't feel right about establishing a serious relationship until I move out of our stinking neighborhood." I said this containing the memory of what I felt when Luz walked away, grateful that she taught me Spanish, made me literate, sent me to Spain thinking I would take her so I could see myself in the wider world but unable to feel for her what she deserved, the love that wouldn't come naturally.

But Mami Lalia believed in the power of love. "Una mujer...*A woman truly in love would overlook your temporary condition. She knew your worth. She could see into your soul and saw you in the future, not now. And her eyes, her entire body can't lie because she's a real woman. In love a woman like that would walk with you to wherever and as far as you must go, down this block if it were engulfed in flames."*

I laughed off her traditional Hispanic-woman romanticism, "Claro... *Sure, for you love may be that old fashioned sacrifice but nobody loves like that anymore. Besides, where would things have ended with me in Massachusetts and her in San Juan in medical school for the next four years, and then her residency who knows where."*

"Maybe she chose to be a doctor because there was nothing else worth doing without the one man she cared about in the world."

I had never given that possibility a thought but stood my ground, answering that modern women don't think that way, that Luz was committed to having a career.

But Mami Lalia just smirked off my modernity. "If I had known about her in time, I wouldn't have let you run away like that afraid."

Outwardly we reached a stalemate but inside I knew she had won, hands down. She had touched the very reason why I held out from telling her the full story about Luz: because I felt ashamed of my reason for not letting myself feel for Luz what she deserved, my feeling socially less, an excuse Mami Lalia would have heard as cowardly talk. Next to Mami Lalia's wisdom, so often my college education seemed worthless, and this time she was right about Luz, who I truly believed would have strolled with me down 136th Street if the buildings were engulfed in flames.

Chapter 13

Witnessing Graziela's defense of Marlboro to put me in my place left me with no fortitude to confront Maritza's island pretensions that night. But I had invited Luis, the son of one of my aunt's neighbors, with whom I serially grew up through my summers on the island. Luis wasn't the typical islander because his dad was Jewish and from Georgia even though he came out more Puerto Rican than American although somewhere in between like me.

He too became a lawyer and was also nosediving into middle age, so when I opened the door to greet him, his once thick black hair had thinned out even more than mine and what remained was totally gray. His cynical smile was still there but if before he pitied the stupid planet, now he smiled falsely defiant not to let the planet know it had won. He said he was in New York for some fun before leaving for Delaware to get some depositions to settle some islander's inheritance dispute. I'd quickly learn that he was actually escaping the miserable state of his marriage with his wife Yolanda.

Of late a tour guide through the island's haute circles, Yoli fell in love with a woman Brazilian systems analyst she met on one of her tours. They flew off to Rio de Janeiro, originally for a two-week vacation that stretched out to two months. For Luis, her absence became an all-consuming torture unrelieved by intensive psycho-therapy. This sojourn to the mainland provided a distraction. "*No*

*Tuvimos suerte...*We're not lucky to have grown up when we did. Sexually, today is a horrible time to be a man," he lamented. "And now I can't even be a boring husband. Maybe, I thought, it's just *our* women, on our looney island. So I've come here, far away, to relax my mind. So, help me, tell me *your* problems."

I thought of Grace's kissing the hand that beats her.

"Oh-oh. Maybe you shouldn't."

"*Un día difícil...*A hard day. Let's just have a good time."

On the way I double parked by a liquor store to pick up a couple bottles of wine. When I returned to the car Luis asked me to describe the friends we were visiting. I told him that my client's name was Maritza, a graduate of University of Puerto Rico, and he asked "Maritza Islas? I know her. She comes from an uppity family and wouldn't have anything to do with me, and I'm sure she wouldn't with you either, you Newyorican. If she was a woman who came from where we came from, your being a Newyorican is a manageable misdemeanor. For her kind it's a capital offense."

"Well, she's made that clear."

"If this is the same person, in the seventies she was a radical-chic socialist, if you can believe it. She used to date guys who had traveled to Cuba and cut sugarcane in support of the workers of the world, and thinking about it now really makes me laugh. All she ever wanted in life was to be a princess."

"You should hear her argue for her tenure. She was complaining about being turned down because she's a woman and a Latina and a feminist."

"She's a *blanquita* who wants tenure. She wants equality first, then she wants to be treated like a princess. What's her roommate like?"

"According to Maritza, Wanda is a very active gringa in Third World and woman's liberation. She's the founder of the Feminist Womancasting Radio Project, which womancasts programs on Third World women."

"Ah, she's more for you. An *americana* who gets off on Latin American revolutionaries. And for her, just being Latin American makes you a revolutionary. Is she a feminist who looks like a woman or one that looks like a man?"

"Maritza didn't describe her physically. She did say that Wanda was attractive, that I would definitely like her, and that she was tall."

Wanda Freed looked down at the pair of average-height men at the door. She wore no makeup, leaving her fair skin looking washed out. Her long auburn hair had strands of gray. She wore a black T-shirt with the large red words "Brigada" above the face of Nicaragua's hero Sandino. Underneath that icon breathed her huge braless breasts hard to avoid staring at, being practically at our eye level.

In excellent Spanish, she welcomed us both and thanked us for the bottles of wine, pressing them tightly against lucky Sandino. She invited us to proceed into the living room past the dining area, where the dining table was set, an uncorked wine bottle breathing in the center. Her long legs in tight jeans silkily transported her into the kitchen. "*Martitza*...Maritza's getting ready in her room. She'll be out in a minute."

In the background played the voice of the Argentine singer Atahualpa Yupanqui, one of the Latin American "New Song" artists. *Luz Vitali had introduced me to his music as she had introduced me to almost everything good since I met her.* Wanda was back from the kitchen. "Would anyone care for a Cuba Libre with real Cuban rum?" She explained that she had just come back from taping a radio program at the Fourth Third World Woman's conference in Camaguey and smuggled back some Havana Club. Wanda took a few minutes to bring out the drinks on a tray.

"Eddie, Maritza says you're a poet. I'm familiar with some Nuyorican poets. I taped a couple of them for some programs. Mike Elgarito, Citu Labiera and María Santa Estavez, have you heard of them?"

I had but didn't know them personally.

"Have you done any legal work with the Independence movement? A few years ago I produced a fundraising concert with Roy Brown and other singers from the New Song Movement. Mercedes

Sosa, Silvio Rodriguez. I'm also good friends with Rubén Berríos, the leader of the Puerto Rican Independence Party. We met in a Non-Allied Countries Conference in Nigeria. Do you know him?"

"No, not personally."

"Maritza said she's related to him on her mother's side."

Luis came into the conversation. "Then we definitely know each other!"

Maritza happened to step out of her room at that moment, her raven hair loosely falling to her shoulders, wearing black slacks and a long-sleeved white silk blouse with a wide collar. She and Luis looked at each other as if they couldn't believe their eyes. They hugged in joyful reunion. An inner glow in Maritza's face emitted the rays of a person I had not met, this one giddy and free, among her own people.

"*No lo...*I can't believe it. Luis and I studied together," she celebrated with Wanda. "We worked in the student independence movement together. Wow, I don't believe it. What have you been doing?"

"*Bueno...*Well, I'm a lawyer. I have a little boy. And you, Eddie tells me you're teaching and fighting to get tenure."

"*Ay*, yes. I finished my degree and thanks to Eddie, my tenure case is being reviewed. I invited him to dinner to thank him. Excuse me. Eddie, how are you?" She gave me a peck on the cheek.

Maritza asked him a barrage of questions. What did he know about the guy they used to call Quasimodo Belpré? And remember the afternoons in the Cafe La Torre, the student hangout. Luis broke the news that the cafe was turned into a loud-rock Lum's. What happened to Little Machito Reyes and his cousin Couscous? And that crazy old Professor Paloseco, who used to come in drunk to class and proposition the girls? And how could they forget that anti-independence gringa professor of English who gave everybody who advocated statehood a B or better and made everybody else go through hell. "Her name was Sarah Mumphrey but Luis just reminded me that the students called her 'Sarah Mambeech.'" Maritza cracked up, "I had forgotten that." As she laughed, she looked at me once, an insignificant look.

On the stereo, the Cuban Silvio Rodríguez was now singing, *"To build this wall, bring me all your hands."*

Wanda didn't get the joke about the professor's name. Maritza explained the way that Puerto Ricans intentionally misuse English phonetics, which Wanda knew but didn't get the joke this time. "Said in a thick Spanish accent 'son of a bitch' is popularly mispronounced 'saramambeech,' and because her first name was Sarah and she was a madame bitch, that's how she got that name."

Luis broke in: Did Maritza remember the mass demonstration to protest that pro-statehood act of blowing up the statue of Eugenio María de Hostos. Maritza started to explain to Wanda who Hostos was in Latin American letters and his importance to Latin American and Puerto Rican history but Wanda already knew, mentioning that she had also read Hostos's famous essay on the education of women.

Luis described the march. "It was like a big party, with music and singing. Overhead, in open-bottomed helicopters, federal agents photographed everybody and everybody waved upward as they sang and danced and gave them the finger. You know, Roy Brown started his career singing at marches like that one and his American father is a colonel or something in the Army. Roy's mother's last name is Ramírez. I recently found that out."

Wanda excused herself because the food was just about ready to serve. Maritza started to get up to help, but Wanda insisted that she stay and entertain their guests. Wanda's huge breasts rose to the occasion as her long limbs sauntered into the kitchen from where savory aromas were wafting. She went in and out of the kitchen several times, each time bearing a bowl or dish that she placed on the table.

"*Todos*...Everybody, come to the table," Wanda called out, but she herself went to play a background cassette by Willie Colón, starting with the cut "*¿Cuándo llegará?*"

Maritza and Luis moved toward the table without interrupting their reminiscing. By now they had retrogressed to their childhood, their infancy. The Palmolive soap commercials, the Klim chocolate commercials, the fifties Diplo Comedy show that only the first TV sets

118

got to see. I remembered them from my boyhood summers, but those memories didn't authorize my joining in their special communication. Between them, there was not the layer of redundant American culture; they settled into those unadulterated, shared memories.

Wanda pointed to the large bowl, switching the conversation to English. "...This Ropa Vieja is made from a recipe given to me by a Cuban *santera* I once lived with in Queens. Maritza prepared the red beans from scratch, soaking them all day, something she confessed she hadn't done since she was married."

Maritza had never said anything about being married. "My ex-husband hated having to eat canned beans. Imagine the thought of being enslaved by a man who couldn't bear to eat anything but freshly-soaked beans while I tried to finish my dissertation. As if I didn't have a career of my own, like a stupid fifties hausfrau."

The food was delicious and the conversation deferred to everyone's savoring it thoroughly, also deferring to Wanda's switch to English until Maritza asked Luis in Spanish to fill her in on the island's gubernatorial campaigns. Luis started to detail the chances of the three parties in individual townships. Then he remembered a juicy scandal involving a strip-club dancer and their former independence-supporting but now Commonwealth-supporting classmate, a candidate for re-election to the local Senate, Juan Acosta, "who everybody suspects has shady connections—"

Maritza corrected this slanderous information because her family was good friends with the Acostas, and "nobody I know gives any credence to those rumors."

Luis diplomatically changed the subject, "Well, the stripper has a paternity suit against him, and you know how everybody's eating that up. Oh, wait till you here this one about the Governor's son..."

"So, Eddie," Wanda addressed me in English, "do you think New York Ricans should have a say on the island's political future." Wanda chewed on a forkful of *ropa vieja* as she waited for my reply.

"As lawyer, I see arguments on both sides. Personally, even though I grew up here, I'd like to have a say but I can understand why islanders would object."

"Well, *do* you support independence?"

"I always have although I think we don't have a clear idea of who we are."

"Oh, I know many people who would dispute that. They would just say that you're projecting your own lack of definition as an assimilated *newyorican*."

"Well, that only reflects the preconceived level of thought your 'many people' have mapped out for us. What I meant was that our collective underlying psyche hasn't reconciled the past with the present. Our traditional culture has been retrograde, machista, classist and racist, so independence can become a perpetuation of oligarchy, traditional gender values, racism, making it difficult for modern women and working-class people and black people among us to cuddle up to nationalism without thinking of going back to the worst in the past..." As I spoke, Wanda stared at me either left speechlessly impressed or bored on the verge of falling into a wide-eyed coma.

I put my monologue into overdrive: "What I mean is before American culture swallows us whole, we must throw off U.S. colonialism and liberate ourselves, with bombs and guns, if we have to. Do you know what I mean?" Wanda's milky cheeks flushed once again as she nodded enthusiastically. Her bosom progressively inflated as well. Even Luis and Maritza had stopped talking to listen to my performance. "It's no different than what our oppressed people here in New York must do, liberate ourselves from racist and capitalist oppression. We have to put our lives on the line if need be. That's what I, a Puerto Rican, am about."

Wanda picked up the wine bottle, refilled everybody's glass and offered a toast to those words. And as part of the toast, she waved her goblet between Maritza and me, "and to the prospect of tenure thanks to our revolutionary lawyer."

The wine bottle in Wanda's hand, I had read from the label, was a mixed metaphor from Chile, from the sun-ripened vineyards of the murderous Pinochet regime that Henry Kissinger helped install after he put out a hit on the democratically-elected socialist

Salvador Allende. When she put the bottle down, I pointed to the label, "Politically problematic."

"I'm sorry. My father, who doesn't always understand my politics but knows I'm a fan of Latin America, bought me a case of that wine, which regrettably was bottled under Pinochet's regime."

After the *café con leche*, we all settled into the living room, where Maritza served Felipe II brandy. Luis and Maritza got into a discussion about Latin hit tunes of the forties and fifties, and Wanda interrupted their banter with her encyclopedic authority: Maritza was confusing Mon Rivera, the 78 rpm wax record master of the *plena*, with Ismael Rivera, originally lead singer of Rafael Cortijo's band and the 33 rpm LP *plena* king, who happened to be her favorite. She brought out a batch of cassettes from her room and played one of my all-time favorites, "*Mataron Al Negro Bembón*," Cortijo's classic version of Bobby Capó's brilliant fifties satire on island racism. Wanda started to dance to it alone, her moves so uncannily un-Nordic, fluidly Latin, that Eduardo couldn't take his eyes off her enormous body. He got up to join her.

Dancing with Wanda was pure joy. Our every move synchronized as if we'd been partners for years. What turns or variations I improvised she responded to instantly, escalating the pleasure up to a peak from which I began to reflect on my ineptitude with Graziela, who never liked to dance with me, our missteps emblematic of everything else in which we as a couple never harmonized. *But why had we danced so well together when we dated? Why did she soak the beans the first times she cooked for me? Why the folky ethnic touches in her performance of just a Puerto Rican woman looking for a compatible partner and then gradually that shield of feminism that she used to justify her hesitancy at our carrying on a true marriage? Her then-best-friend Isela seemed to have been coaching her at being a real Puerto Rican woman, which was what she said she wanted to be when we met. But it wasn't just feminism that stood between us; it was my expecting that we have a child, her fundamental disdain of Latin men, and ultimately her head being screwed up by self-hatred, by this culture, and her seeing that portrait of herself in my Rican face.*

121

Thanks to Fidel's rum, Pinochet's wine, and King Felipe II's brandy, my mind had drifted off but my body had not lost a step and, coming back to the present, I suddenly had spectacular Wanda dancing before me, her smile of total abandon. Spinning around in my wine-and-rum-and-brandy state, I also noticed that Luis was dancing with the equally unleashed Maritza. I tapped Luis's shoulder and he good-naturedly took rhythmic steps toward Wanda.

But Maritza hadn't been dancing with Luis as much as with herself and hardly noticed the exchange. Cortijo's band was coming to the part of the song when Ismael again parodies the judge who tucks in his own fat lower lip to answer the accused that his victim's having big lips wasn't a just cause for deserving to be killed. I made the mistake of adding that "That song should be Puerto Rico's national anthem."

Maritza gave me a haughty look. I apparently lacked the authority to make such pronouncements. But Wanda thought it perceptive. She crouched before the cassette player, changed cassettes, hit the play button, and grabbed my hand. "This is a great *merengue* by Johnny Ventura." My arm around Wanda's waist, I held on for the Magic Mountain and the white water ride of a Dominican *merengue* with her. Just then my pager sounded. I resisted its summon. The music began and I started dancing but too mentally split to enjoy it and apologized to Wanda. I looked to see who it was. It was Samson.

Wanda confessed that her room was a mess and asked Maritza if I could call in her room. Maritza led me to her bedroom door and pointed to the phone. I gazed at her, haughty, shielded. Was that forbidden quality what made her attractive to me? Or was I attracted to the hidden woman inside, the one who came out for Luis, the savage dancer, maybe an indescribable fuck? Whoever she really was, the sheen of her black hair and the proximity of her body molded in black pants momentarily diverted me from my reason for making the call.

"What?" She was annoyed at my look.

"Why do you make yourself so difficult to charm?"

She pointed to the telephone again and walked away. Before

dialing, I sat on her bed and took a deep breath. Samson at that late hour. I didn't know if I should even care anymore. In the dresser mirror I stared at the public ethnic symbol staring at me. Tired, I felt myself drifting to the threshold of sleep until stirred by the sensation of a hand wrapped around one side of my neck while lips lightly kissed the other side.

In the mirror I saw Wanda's fallen hair and her hand descending from my neck into the open collar of my shirt, the sensation thrown from the mirror, like a ventriloquist's voice, into my body. We were engaged in a kiss when Maritza called her out to help find the songs of Sylvia Rexach in her collection. When Wanda didn't respond, Maritza called again. Wanda sighed with good-humored resignation. She touched my lips with her finger and left me to make my call.

Luis drove because I couldn't. I had closed my eyes not to think and slid instantly into a dream of the summer in Puerto Rico when I was fourteen and fell in love with Tina, a thirteen-year-old dark gypsy of a girl. Her father, the brother of my Aunt Dina's husband, was a blue-eyed Spaniard and her mother an island Indian-looking mulatta. Their seven children came to this world in almost every possible hair, skin and eye color combinations, red hair to blond, fair skin to brown, black eyes to blue. Both parents were spiritualists, the mother a medium.

Two nights a week her parents' spirit-chasing friends gathered at another house on their block as their seven kids and their friends stood in the shadowy carport, peering in through the Miami shutter windows hoping to see weird activity and listening for strange sounds. The shadows of the carport afforded me the privacy to embrace Tina and kiss her in the humid summer night. I was crazy about this baby-fat girl, this frolicking pony with her midnight eyes and wild, wavy black hair and smooth, beautiful, milk chocolate face.

Later that year, Mami Lalia received a letter and told me that she had very sad news about that pretty girl at whose house I had spent much of the summer, and in my dream, Mami Lalia told me again that she had just received word that Tina suddenly came

down with meningitis and the next day was dead. But in my dream
I also realized that when Mami Lalia told me the first time I was too
young to understand loss, and now being told again in this dream
Tina's death hurt deeply. A loud moaning awoke me. It was the
wind lamenting through the car's slightly open window.

The cop at the police barricade listened to Luis' explanation that
I was the lawyer Eduardo Loperena and the ex-husband. He spoke
into the walkie-talkie and given instructions to escort us. We left
the car by the barricade. In front of Graziela's brownstone investigators moved about marking and measuring. The cop presented
me to a detective who came out of the building. He asked me about
her mental state, how long she had been living with Marlboro,
how well I knew him. I answered with my eyes on the bloodstains
splattered over the brownstone steps and over the entrance to the
garden apartment. I was told she didn't die on impact. She died
at the hospital. The detective thanked me and went back into the
brownstone.

The whole block it seemed was either at a window or out on the
street. On the curb in front of the investigation scene protected by
two cops a crowd had formed around a sudden bright light before
video cameras. A news reporter held up a microphone to a face I
couldn't see through the crowd but whose voice I recognized. "The
whole building knew of this travesty. This racist man held this
woman captive. The neighbors say that they could hear him beat
her..." I moved closer, peered through the crowd. Sánchez O'Neil
in a dressy, embroidered *guayabera* was talking before the cameras
of Channel 9 and Channel 11 and Channel 5.

Hearing him go on was affecting me, and I felt the need to go
upstairs to speak to Samson, but at the top of the steps, the cop
guarding the door wasn't impressed that I was the victim's ex-husband. He passed along my request to enter the building into his
walkie-talkie. A voice answered something incomprehensible that
the officer interpreted as instructions to tell me to wait.

Milling with Luis in front of the brownstone stairs, I had to listen
to Sánchez O'Neil's voice picking up steam. "Her neighbors had

complained to the police of his verbal and racist abuse and the law enforcers did nothing to save the life of this poor woman. I can only assure you that as Deputy Mayor for Hispanic Affairs I will push for a thorough investigation of the Police Department's handling of this case and that justice be done if a crime was committed..."

His politically feeding on Graziela's corpse provoked me to stomp toward the video camera lights, not heeding Luis's plea that I keep my head as he followed me. I got as far as the outer edge of the crowd, which wouldn't let me through. My shoving finally got me behind the taping cameras, Luis beside me. At that moment I began feeling as if a sperm whale rolled over and over in my stomach. Dizzy, about to faint, I reached out to grab Luis and grabbed instead the back of the shirt of the Channel 9 cameraman. Luis caught me in time, the commotion prompting the three cameras to record me because Sánchez O'Neil, on recognizing me, came forward to prop me up and make me part of that night's breaking local news.

"Here we have the victim's ex-husband and my good friend, one of the city's most respected lawyers, who has devoted his life to fighting for social justice." Putting his arms around my waist, with me woozy before the glaring camera lights, he continued, "Doesn't life hold such ironies that this man, defender of so many victims of this racist society, should have to experience the pain and heartache of seeing someone he cared for perish in this way."

The Channel 9 reporter actually tried to interview me. Did I still love her? Why did I show up? Did I think that her boyfriend pushed her? Sánchez O'Neil intervened, "Isn't it obvious that he is sickened by this tragedy? I am certain I speak for him when I ask you to leave him alone at this moment." Saying this, he straightened me up, and I stood on my own.

But somewhere near the middle of his last sentence I felt the first acidic belch, seeming to others like a dramatic effort to speak despite my pain, drawing the attention of the three cameras and the three reporters's microphones and all the spectators. In other words, that complete array of eyes and media witnessed my volcanic upchuck of puke. The half-digested *ropa vieja*, the avocado salad, the Havana

Club *Cuba libre*, the Chilean wine, and the Spanish Brandy erupted over the microphones aimed at my face and all over Sánchez O'Neil's fancily embroidered *guayabera*.

Before someone rescued Sánchez O'Neil by the arm, a second retch, coming while the Deputy Mayor was still in shock, showered over his well-polished shoes. By this time the camera crews had scrammed to directly in front of Graziela's brownstone. On the bright side, my discharge was so well-behaved toward its host that all Luis had to do was offer a napkin that some onlooker handed him. He left me seated on the curb while he ran to the corner deli to get a bottle of water. I caught a glimpse of the Deputy Mayor for Hispanic Affairs as his assistant delicately fit the soiled *guayabera* into a plastic bag and he jumped shirtless and barefoot into his car.

Picking myself up from the curb, I watched the investigators still busily at work around the area where Graziela fell. At that point, apparently what the camera crews were waiting for, a pair of officers came out of her building followed by Marlboro followed by another three cops, one the detective who had earlier interviewed me. Marlboro was booed by onlookers as he was hustled into a patrol car. He wasn't in handcuffs. His eyes were red and he looked boozed up.

I looked again at the bloodstains over the brownstone's entrance. Graziela was gone. My mission to make her see me and herself as persons and not symbols was suddenly aborted. I would miss loving her even if she never managed to love me. A large plastic bottle of club soda materialized in front of me. I thanked Luis and washed out my mouth, spitting out the foulness between two parked cars. Graziela's death was an unwanted purging—as after a severe operation, the malignancy absent, the cause of the pain was the extraction. I cleansed my foul soul over and over with half the quart bottle of seltzer.

The cop now let me enter the brownstone. Luis chose to wait downstairs as I went up to Samson, who was really shaken. "That white boy kill that beautiful girl, I know he did. I heard her screaming. He was drunk and throwing things around. Cop tells me he says he was too drunk to do it and too drunk to stop her from doing

126

it, but I don't believe it." He looked at me, across the abyss of my silence. "It's all bad and it hurts, man. You know why."

I hugged him. "You're a good man, Samson."

A yellow plastic strip pasted across Graziela's door announced a police investigation. On the ride to the Bronx Luis and I didn't speak. In my mind I traced Graziela's life's walk over the burning coals of self-disdain. She adored the cobra and it finally bit her. Her allowing Marlboro to drive her to this. Her inviting Marlboro to push her. Her instigating Marlboro to encourage her. Her pampering Marlboro to be paralyzed to help her. She probably didn't tell him about Esteban, not to publicize her umbilical cord to "that world," and her secrecy angered him. Marlboro thought she was calling me.

Chapter 14

Luis left me a note held down by a refrigerator magnet, thanking me for the evening with Maritiza and Wendy and giving his condolences. Last night lingered as a bad dream and Luis' note imposed its reality. I called Mami Lalia. She was saddened by the news, said she will pray for her. "Who notified her mother?" she asked. I hadn't thought of those details. I called Isela but got her beeper. She called back in minutes, said that she hadn't been at the scene of the tragedy because Sánchez O'Neil had called her immediately and so she went straight to the hospital. Graziela had already died.

Isela made the funeral arrangements and called her mother Mercedes. She also reserved two airfares, for Mercedes and her nephew, to come to New York. Her aunt too was coming. Graziela never wanted to be returned to her place of birth. She had always said she wanted to be buried in Woodlawn Cemetery in the Bronx, where as a student she would go to read because it was peaceful. Mami Lalia also asked me if I was going to attend the funeral. I saw no point to it. Marlboro would be there and I might cause a disruption. Also, I had to put Graziela behind me.

Driving to my office seemed to take twice as long, the traffic flowing in slow motion. I only had a few more letters to write and then sort through old files to store or destroy, and even that felt as if I was about to do heavy lifting. But I didn't want to stay at home entertaining memories. I had just rolled the first sheet into the typewriter when someone knocked on my office door, which as a rule was kept locked, requiring that Karla buzz open.

My first thought was that Gerry Duffy dropped by to catch up, but Sánchez O'Neil identified himself, knocking impatiently. I buzzed and he breezed in, ever armored for battle in his blue suit, red tie, some mild cologne, and now carrying a small paper bag. "I was in the neighborhood. I'm glad you were smart enough to come to work. I thought you might want some coffee and Cuban-Greek baklava." Out of the bag he served me a cardboard coffee cup, a wax-paper-wrapped piece of baklava, and a napkin, then sat at Winston's desk across from mine.

"Sorry about your clothes last night, Gus. I was at a dinner and had too much to drink." *But I know you are here for another reason.*

"I had plastic bags in my trunk. So let's skip that." He bit into the baklava, chewed for a while, sipped coffee. "I know you still cared very much. But please forgive me for being rash in what I am about to say." He spoke cleaning his hands with a napkin. "Don't abuse yourself over Grace. I knew her before you did. She'd been looking for Marlboro or somebody like him. And her relationships were always abusive. So were his. Just before you came along..."

I insisted.

"Okay, I'm sorry and you're right. We should be looking forward."

He picked up his baklava again, took another bite. "Mmmm, good Cuban baklava."

"Thanks for coming all this way to deliver it."

"Well, as I said, I was in the neighborhood." He chewed while preserving a wide, mouth-shut grin. He took a long chug of coffee and wiped his mouth. "Okay. This is important. We have to iron out a couple of things. First, the Governor thinks you're a brilliant guy, maybe too brilliant for your own political good. I'm also very seriously concerned about that incident at the restaurant. The group understands you're important to the election team. But there's a serious, grievous 'tude problem that has to be worked out. These people respect you, Eddie. You're the community's champion. You don't take shit from the Man. You whip his ass in his talk. But they also need a man of the people, and I've been noticing that you've gotten impatient, distant and maybe you think yourself better. Now, are you with us or are you going to run off and become some downtown law firm's token minority? Because I hear things, everything that goes on, and I see through walls, Eddie, that's how I survive. I was having a conversation with Isela about you and we both agreed that deep inside you're down on the community, that it's too small-time for you and you want to get out of it and its politics, the way that Winston did, leaving her for his new eighties life in Seattle. Because you know that's Winston's America, not ours."

"Look, I know better than to think I'm going to work out as a clone of Winston. And I know that you can use me, but frankly I don't know if the community needs me. It needs somebody like you. You have the stomach I don't."

"Eddie, I need you, and they need you. But after that luncheon the Democratic party rep recommended that somebody else manage my campaign. I still want you, but I sense that you're disappearing, forgetting the work we have to do..."

"Gus, I really do appreciate the importance you're giving me and you're looking out for me, but right now I need to take a little time off, get some perspective. Tomorrow I fly to P.R. to my sister's wedding. When I get back we can talk fresh. I just need to look up at the sky, eat roast pork, and clear my mind. By the way, I am really very sorry about throwing up on your clothes, but that show you put on before the TV cameras at Grace's death scene, turning her death into a political drama over racism, pissed me off."

"I thought you didn't want to talk about her?"

"I'm talking about you."

"She dumped you, Eddie, and you know why. I knew her and her circumstance. If I didn't show up, the police and the press would've whitewashed the thing as a lover's quarrel. It was more than that and you know it. That's why you showed up there, not just because you thought you still loved her. I was there so that New York knew that this Marlboro was a racist pig. Admit it, you really do care about us and what touched you about the tragedy is what touches me and our people, so get off my back about that, okay?"

The irony of Graziela's becoming a symbol of "our people."

Sánchez O'Neil climbed up grass roots that grew in asphalt, helped along by good looks and the height that he carried like a sign from the gods. He graduated from high school in 1956, three years after Fidel launched his attack on the Moncada Barracks to start the Cuban Revolution, and nine years before Martin Luther King, Jr. marched his movement to its climactic moment at Selma. While the world created the setting for his future success, Sánchez O'Neil worked in construction, getting involved in union work. By the early seventies, after Tejerina had galvanized Chicanos to confront the Anglos and the American Indian Movement had made its stand by taking hostages at Wounded Knee, and Washington was already shelling out money so that Blacks wouldn't burn down their own neighborhoods, Sánchez O'Neil was married and father of two kids.

All those years he saw the vaporous skywriting and keenly observed the drama unfolding. He trained himself in mainstream diction, imitated the proliferating black activists and soon was organizing rallies to intimidate the city. Over time, he was awarded the management of a string of community service programs, each new one with a larger budget than the last. With the opportunities those positions afforded for him to use his looks, performance skills, and political acumen, those turbulent decades served him better than three law degrees.

"Gus, so you think Marlboro killed her?"

"I'm sure of it, and I'm putting pressure on the D.A. Your friend Samson says he heard it all. Marlboro likes the kind of women he can dump on, so he can feel like a big shot. White sickness. He used to live with a black girl. When she heard about what happened, she called the *Post*." He paused, a silent apology for having gone there.

"Let me get to the other reason why I'm here. I have a proposal, but before I lay it out I just need to give a little speech because I'm trying to figure you out. You're too honest, Eddie. Politics is theater, only on a big, unruly stage. And the only way to talk to so many people is to become something larger than life, a stereo sound system, so things must get exaggerated. You must become a well-meaning liar. That's what less gifted people like us must do, but I get the sense that inside you laugh at that, at people less gifted than you trying to accomplish big things for great numbers of people. I'm trying. But I know I need you, Eddie. You sharpen my own thinking. You cut through legal walls I can't even scratch. But you have to learn to control when to use your gifts and when to let things ride. That's why I want you to consider very seriously what I am about to offer."

He actually sounded earnest.

"Look, I can understand if you lose patience with our puny little world down here, so I thought you might see things differently on a bigger stage, that we're really part of a bigger story. Across the country, we're trying to organize Hispanics into a single voice, using the English Only backlash as a unifying issue. There's an important regional meeting of Southwest Democratic organizations scheduled in L.A. in less than two weeks. The Chicanos invited me to be one of the principal speakers, but I can't make it. I have a campaign fundraiser scheduled the following day. Instead of canceling, I figure that you could serve as the perfect stand-in. You fought for bilingual education, so many of them out West have heard of you. Your speaking in LA will get your feet wet, show you the wider picture of what the larger Hispanic community is trying to accomplish. Maybe after seeing that bigger picture you'll appreciate my work and feel better about managing my campaign. There's an honorarium that'll pay for your trip to PR with something left over. Treat this gig as an extension of your vacation, take in L.A., take in Disneyland. I can call some Chicanas who could make sure you have a social life out there. Now, I've taken the liberty of faxing the organizers a professional bio and news clippings of you. The talk will be provided by my office. Are you game? Oh, before that there's a stopover at Miami, a dinner meeting with the lonely Cuban caucus of the few Democrats there to boost their commitment to

Hispanic unity, just touching base, a dinner and the next day a few words I'll provide for you as guest speaker. I added this on so that the Cubans could get to know you."

The phone rang. Afraid it might be Carlos, I picked up before the machine answered. Yvette was calling to give her condolences. She also expressed how hard it was to break the news to Esteban that his newly discovered sister was dead. I apologized that I couldn't speak because I had someone in the office. She understood but couldn't contain the other reason why she called: the murder charge against Esteban had been dropped. The police witnesses were now testifying that it was an accident. She apologized for keeping me on the phone. I promised to pass by the Danubio.

Sánchez O'Neil grinned. "So now you know. I was saving that news as icing on the cake. Ah, Yvette. I can read her all over your face. Modesto is bragging about what he did, which of course everybody believes you really did, but I brokered that deal. Esteban's not going to be charged with involuntary manslaughter. Reckless endangerment in the second degree, a misdemeanor in this state. Cuomo asked me to get on it because he doesn't want you to be connected. The next election year is going to be a Democratic year, and nobody wants to fuck this up." He paused. Sánchez O'Neil can detect the pulse of a spider. I was fearing a call from Carlos.

"Looking forward to your trip to P.R.?"

"Just to get away."

"Have you picked out a wedding gift for your sister?"

"I mail-ordered a pasta machine a couple of weeks ago, and I'll give them some money."

"Oh, that's nice." Sensing that I had relaxed a bit, he returned to his sermon: "Eddie, those meetings with the Hispanic national reps will bring you back to the battlefield. Harvard, political ideals, legal briefs are important but those people at the restaurant, they're your bread and butter—and mine. We're all not as deep-thinking as you, okay. We do the best we can with what we have. But we have people being fucked over and they need us to help them. The seventies gave you the breaks, but the next step is to get dirty, down and dirty again in the same way that you made your reputation in the courts. Unless you want to work with clean hands. Is that what you want? Okay, end of sermon. My people will be in touch."

I didn't remember having agreed to make his political speeches. I also didn't disagree in favor of Sánchez O'Neil's leaving right away. The last thing I wanted was having him curious and even using his resources to investigate what could be preventing me from embracing the future he was serving me on a silver platter. Once he was out the door I sighed in relief but wanted so much for Carlos to finally call, reclaim his suitcases. I would be lucky if I just survived without finding myself in prison or the target of Gerry Duffy's gun. *And if they kill Carlos, what do I do with myself and the suitcases?*

Chapter 15

Sanchez O'Neil wasn't gone long before I heard the mail being deposited into the box attached to the door. I was about to get my mail when there was another knock. This time I went over to Karla's receptionist desk, picked up the phone receiver and held it to my ear as I buzzed in whoever it was. Into the office marched Figaro the deli's fastidious delivery guy, with two other people. He was rail thin and always wore skin-tight pants, his heavily greased black hair combed straight back. His father was a Cuban musician, touring when he met his Yugoslavian mother. It was never clear how he got to the Bronx, the murkiness surely something to do with his sexual orientation. I told my imaginary interlocutor that I'd call back.

Figaro introduced me to a very dapper blond guy in a white suit, powder blue shirt with a white collar and a pink tie, accompanied by a familiar-looking beauty. "Dis is da novelist Upton Wane and dis, of course, ees Leesa Carr Caro. De boys cookin' in the deli was goin' cr-a-a-a-sy gwen I tell dem." He arranged chairs for my two guests.

Leesa Carr Caro was truly a sight in a dark green suede leather miniskirt and matching emerald high heels, as striking as when I first saw her in a production of The New York Shakespeare Machine's Teatro Latino Fest, *Chimichurri on Steak* written and directed by the Uruguayan Agostino Hammerstein, the male pseudonym of the feminist playwright, Angela Plotnik. The illness of the Uruguayan actress Josefina Lluvias gave the leading part of Nancy to her understudy, the continently loved Puerto Rican actress, Lisa Carr Caro. As Nancy, her voice was deep, her Uruguayan lilt surprisingly convincing, but her real allure was those big, sensitive, wounded black eyes. Graziela had known Leesa since she was an aspiring actress studying at Hunter. Now, a decade later, there she was in my office, hips slightly larger, pouting red-red lips, flashing shoulder-length black hair, and strongly aromatic with perfume. A silent-film exuberance in her eyes expressed the pleasure of meeting me, having forgotten that Graziela had introduced us.

"Mr. Wane, I apologize for not getting back to you..." I had completely forgotten his call requesting to meet me. Compensating, I told him that I had recently read the *Times* book review of his most recent novel, *Slow Wheels on the Asphalt*, set in East L.A., about a car executive kidnapped for ransom by a gang of Chicano low riders. I told him how much I enjoyed his previous novel, the megahit *The Hollywood Rider*, about a Hollywood born-again Christian motorcycle gang member by day and by night the stalker of the movie star Betsy Harjo, who tormented her with poetic, mesmerizing, pornographic letters whose power over her was such that in the final gripping courtroom chapter prosecutors and lawyers battled over the definition of free will. "...Too many things have been happening and I must leave tomorrow for my sister's wedding in Puerto Rico."

"Call me Upton, please. Sánchez O'Neil told me what just happened, about your ex-wife, and I'm sorry to barge in like this but he recommended you so highly and warned that I had to catch you before you left. So I took the chance. Have you had lunch? Can we go somewhere and talk?

"I really haven't got that much time. We can talk here." I asked Figaro to bring me a Cuban sandwich and a glazed donut. My guests didn't want anything. Wane beat me at pulling out his wallet, plucked out a twenty, and told Figaro to keep the change. Figaro opened the door, and seeing the mailbox, I asked him to bring me the mail. I rifled quickly through the small batch, pausing at a thick business envelope from a Charles Atlas. I put it on top of the pile, and excused myself for getting distracted.

"Eddie, I'm here to see if you can help me with my new novel. It's set in the Bronx, but a little further south. I was interested in the Bronx precinct corruption being reported because my novel has something to do with a situation like that. I heard you were involved in that case."

"Somebody got facts wrong."

"It's really your savvy I'm looking for, not about that particular case, a technical consultant who can read my drafts and let me know if the setting feels authentic. I'm from the West Coast, and I know that Latin scene. Sánchez O'Neil talked of you as someone with a reputation as a writer—"

"I was a poet in college and that stuck."

"That's okay. I know your community has working writers out there but your reputation as lawyer also appealed to me especially after Sánchez O'Neil said you were the brightest guy he knows and best of all that you know this Bronx inside and out, its 'pulse' was how he put it."

"What's the title of the novel?"

"*The Bronx Brains*, about a character named Tito, a college graduate who returns to the community and turns two once-warring street gangs into his organized crime family that takes over the local drug and gambling business. The organization grows into an underground local government that gives loans and invests in local businesses, even funds community projects and doles out scholarships as good public relations for their organized crime. The cops and the regular mob join forces to cut Tito down."

"Sounds great. Where does the great white hero come in?"

Wane tossed a smile over his shoulder at Leesa. "Well, there is a central white character, of course, someone with whom the mainstream audience can identify. Clint Dare has been stationed in the South Bronx to start a task force that will end Tito's career and nail some cops who have been on his pay. I should quickly add that my agent has already sold an option to a movie producer, so that your role can also extend to becoming the film's consultant."

"So you need a native guide in and out of Fort Hitachi."

Wane smiled again and nodded. "You can put it like that."

The chance of being involved in a writing project comes now? I glimpsed at the return name on the top envelope. Charles Atlas.

Figaro, I hoped, was the one knocking. I buzzed and he walked in his runway-model way, to place a bag on my desk. I thanked him, and he walked back to the door, pausing behind Leesa to pinch his nose.

"This project sounds really interesting, but I'll be on vacation for a week and then I have some commitments."

"We can do this long distance. You read the manuscript, give me your impressions."

And what happens if this book takes off and then the movie and then all hell breaks loose if Carlos hasn't picked up his "papers" and is connected to the scandal that has inspired Upton Wane.

"It's really very tempting. In fact, I would do it on the condition that you comment on my manuscript, connect me with an agent..."

"That would be a done deal."

"But I simply can't at this time."

"Well, I'm really sorry because I have a hunch you would be good for this project. Can you recommend anybody else?"

"Have you heard of Bonino Feliz? You might know him by the name Felix Goode. His novel was reviewed last Sunday in the *Times. Drumbeats from a Small Planet?*"

"Yes, I saw it. I mean I didn't read the review because it was science fiction. Well, I'll look into this Felix."

Leesa Carr Caro gave me a farewell peck and a great smile as they left. How much it hurt having to give up this opportunity to work with Wane, coming closer to doing what I had always wanted because I had to babysit Carlos' suitcases.

I ate my Cuban sandwich, staring at Carlos' bulging business envelope. He used his old address on 136th Street, our street that no longer existed. Done with the sandwich, I wiped my hands and picked up the envelope, wedged my finger under the glued flap, and the phone rang. I let the machine answer. Maritza started to leave the message that Wanda found out about Graziela while watching the morning news. I picked up.

"*Gracias*...Thank you for calling. And thank you for the dinner last night."

"*Bueno*...Well, you earned it. How hard has this been on you? Did you two stay friends?"

"No, not really. We didn't communicate very well. We were in touch because I recently introduced her to a half-brother who's in legal trouble and wanted to reach her. She'd never met him. We could communicate about that but nothing more."

"Wanda also sends her condolences. I should say that you made another fan." A long silence changed the subject. "So what are your plans now? You said were closing your practice." The remark came from a different woman than last night's sterner-face. I felt freer to address her, be more up-front as I had determined to be with her before last night's sad event.

"I'm being offered things. But I'm taking a week off. Tomorrow I'm leaving for the island. My sister's getting married on the Fourth of July."

"Fourth of July, what's that about?"

"Her fiancé's apparently a piece of work."

"Well, I myself am leaving for the island tonight, which is another reason why I am calling, to let you know in case you need to reach me. I'll be with my family for the summer."

"That's great. Maybe you can be my date to my sister's reception." That just came out, instantly assuming a gravitas that prompted a molasses-thick silence.

"As I said, I'm going there to be with my family and don't know their plans, so I can't give you an answer right now." She left me her mother's number and I gave her Mami Lalia's. I didn't know what to make of the conversation.

I finally opened Carlos' envelope. Inside were folded handwritten pages of yellow pad paper:

> *Socrates, my man. I can't say too much on the phone. Read this letter then maybe burn it. As I told you I been following your things. In the papers. The community scuttlebutt. I always knew you'll do all right for yourself. We were just split down the middle, different lucks. Remember that I was the one in the 8-A class! I wasn't a dummy. But when the coin went up, it came down heads and that was you. I always thought about that coin, man, alot. That's life, that's it and there's nothing to do about it. But I know you. You weren't making money to keep for yourself. Friends of mine say look at these political dudes grabbing here and there and everywhere, fuck, then they come fuck with us. But I know you, man. Then I seen your office address. What you doing up in the Bronx defending people who pay you piss compared to what other bastards out there making?*
>
> *I don't want you to feel bad about staying away from me. A good thing happened to you, man, and the first time you came down to our shit block from that school I could see we were going in different directions. That's okay, man. Don't feel bad because it wasn't your fault. I kept away too. I didn't want you to hang with people I knew, bitches that would get pregnant to get a piece of your white boy luck. I didn't want you to start wanting to be cool and snorting shit just to hang. I knew how your moms felt about me. She told somebody who told somebody, you know the shit, but she was doing right, little brother."*
>
> *Its crazy. The world, man, is crazy. You got to go to all those schools and I know your not making what you should, and I stayed on the street and now I got more than I need. Than anybody needs. I know it wasn't right. Almost got killed a couple of times, and I had to do some mean things to survive. I admit it. I'm not fucking innocent, bro. But I tried to quit, get out. I never forgot that we attended St. Pete's. I guess that I had chances to do something else. I know guys who were getting scholarships and chances, like you, but I couldn't stay in school after I got out of my house. My mom*

lived with this guy that I wanted to kill. Fucker I knew beat her. Then he left her and then she kept hitting me for money. When those chances came for minorities, I was already in this shit and making money so I couldn't stop. It was hard starting over, min- imum wage, school. Couldn't do it.

When my moms died and I almost got killed from something that went down wrong, I had enough. Then I met this girl. She was waiting for somebody on the stoop of a building where I was doing some business. She didn't belong there, different. She was a college student and a girl friend of hers was coming down. I talked to her. I really liked her. I know I could never get anywhere with a girl like that, not with what I do. I don't know, I was just tired. I look back and don't know how I got here. I wanted to quit but what do I do? Work for a fucking minimum wage? And where do I go with this brown spick face and this ME after all this time in the Bronx. I tried everything. I drove with my old lady of that time in a brand new car, carrying mucho cash, in every direction but into the Atlantic Ocean. Its frightening out there. As my nigger brother Opine says, we the shit and they the fan, so anytime we try to get together, that's it.

And my stash couldn't buy me a decent place. People ask what my profession is. Dig it. Just look at my shit face and they know, they know what this is good for. And anyplace I went I couldn't find no decent place to live that didn't ask for my credit. Credit rating, dig it. And everywhere we <u>could</u> go had the BUSINESS, man. I even went to PR, stayed with my girlfriend's family in a public housing project. I looked for that beautiful place you talked about when you went down to your family. I could see other people lived there, but my kind of people live in a fucking cage and I could never get to that place. I could afford those places, where everybody was different from me, but they looked at me like some trash. When I looked for an apartment nobody would rent me what I could afford. Everybody just assumed that I was going to bring trouble, more trash like me. We lived in public housing where motherfuckers argued with machine guns. And blabbing tongues *from all the way here, from the Bronx, reached over there because they know you, they know who you are.*

I almost got killed again over the BUSINESS, man. I had to do bad shit again. I don't know if I killed a guy to defend myself. I shot and split, then flew back to New York. My girl wanted to stay so I said goodbye. Fuck it. Then I needed money again and things got fucked up here too right away. Some guys have been doing a number on me, some cops. I can't go into it, not your business. So I fucked them back. So things are really hot for me now and the Sheriff and his maricones are after me too.

Looks bad, little bro. But I got this plan, to skip. I don't know what's going to happen. I can't be in touch a lot because that will only bring you problems. I'm thinking of being like that guy we once saw in that TV show, The Man without a Country. I got that idea thinking about you. We saw that show together. I figure I can ride around from motel to motel forever across the whole country. If I do and I mail you a letter from different places, you'll know it's me because of my name. I'll be Charles Atlas with my Dynamic Tension, building muscles.

My problem right now is what to do with all my valuable papers. As you probably know by now, it's a lot. As I told you on the phone there's nobody left for me. You're it. If something goes wrong and some dumb reporter tries to dirty you up, just say I once hired you as my lawyer. Say something that makes it look that way. I left you some pictures that will make police brass shit in their pants. Use them to fuck them back. But I wrote this letter because I know you. Don't start with this idealist crap, man. Because it's shit out there. They're all full of shit out there, the police, the priests, the government. And I know you, you've been working your ass off to save all these people and you probably still live in some shit apartment in the Bronx.

So I just don't want to die somewheres knowing you made some fucking white cops go around smiling. You take this candy. You take it and eat it and say it's oh so good. Take yourself home to the Puerto Rico you always talked to me about when you came *back every summer, the place I never seen because I only got to see our people from the shit side. You got good credit, so use it for me. So you do that, you go home for me, for me, your big brother. Then go kick ass. Tell'em all to go fuck themselves because they can't touch us. <u>Do it for you and for me</u>. So take good care of yourself. Charles Atlas.*

P.S. Don't forget to burn this fucking letter. And when you empty the suitcases, start with the one marked '1', and at the bottom find the pictures.

Chapter 16

The Danubio Azul's air conditioning was doing a poor job of venting the strong smell of garlic. The jukebox was playing "*Rosa, Rosa*" by the Argentine Sandro de America. I had called Yvette to let her know I was coming but she wasn't behind the bar. I stood beside drunk Armando at his usual stool, and Nani came over. Yvette had taken a late lunch break and left word that I should be patient. I didn't realize that I was staring at Nani's blond frizz until she asked if there was something wrong. I just smiled, shaking my head.

I asked Nani about the new waiter in a black vest, white shirt and black bow tie, standing among the dining tables. He had a full head of wavy gray hair. Nani introduced me to Domingo from the bar. He tipped his head, smiling broadly. She said he used to have his own *cuchifrito* in New Jersey, retired, and now just wants something to do part-time. Rodrigo himself always waited. Nani whispered, "*Creo que...*I think Roddy is just getting too old."

Nani confirmed if I wanted my usual scotch, and Armando beside me said in a voice as if I were at the other end of the bar, "Hey, Loperena, how come you don't drink rum and coke, like everybody else in this place. I mean, you, a big deal Puerto Rican, are supposed to drink rum and coke. That's the law of nature." He paused, drifted staring at his drink, then suddenly came back, "Hey, why don't you answer me when I talk to you?"

"*Basta*...That's enough, Armando," Nani intervened as she served me. Armando meekly retreated to his mental cave.

More customers trickled in for dinner. The bar filled out. Suddenly everybody was looking toward the door. I turned to see. Yvette had entered wearing a curves-revealing light blue dress, showcasing her cinnamon beauty, her auburn hair freshly coifed in lustrous swirls. The men at the bar whistled. Rodrigo tossed out verbal long-stemmed roses with the voice of a singer of *cante jondo*. Domingo applauded. Enrique Lin, the Honduran-Chinese cook, taking a breather from the hot kitchen, also applauded.

She looked radiant. Behind her in the window under the Budweiser sign a car rolled slowly by, paused, and two male passengers looked inside.

Yvette turned, "*¿Qué?* What?"

"*Nada*...Nothing, I'm just a little jumpy."

She led me to our table. I took my scotch and Yvette asked Nani to serve her a Brandy Alexander. I invited her to dinner. She apologized for making me wait.

That morning she had visited Esteban. "*Acababa de*...He just started to know Graziela, so the news hurt. He hardly reacted to the news that he won't be charged with murder. Mr. Modesto said the he could be bailed out tomorrow. I want to thank you for helping us."

"I didn't do very much..."

"You did and you always do so much for me. You went to see Esteban when I called. You got Modesto to represent him. You look at me in a way that makes me proud of myself."

Her fixing herself to look so great made it difficult to tell her why I came. I changed the subject. Had Duffy and Bell come by again?

"The news reports of a cop's being killed here had given their little off-duty gathering attention they didn't want, so they must have moved on to another place. I was really happy when you said that you were coming."

She knew that I was leaving for my sister's wedding. She didn't know that the trip would be longer, that I would be traveling after that, and I wasn't ready to tell her that I didn't think it was good for either of us if I came back to her again. I told her about seeing Leesa Carr Caro.

"Leesa Carr Caro! She acted in the novela *Like a Rag.*" Yvette remembered that Leesa played the abandoned, bastard daughter of a bottled-soda company CEO. "She was left to grow up in poverty and raised by a black granny vendor of codfish fritters, but she grew up to be a gorgeous blond who does literally anything to climb to her father's society." Then she expanded on Leesa's bio, filling in details on her failed marriage to "the Mexican singer Antonio Volvo, who everybody knew was having an affair with the Spanish actress Petra Celestial, who physically assaulted Leesa in a Madrid café. She grabbed her..."

As Yvette gave me every detail she knew of that scandal, I happened to glance at Nani, who had been reminding me of...*Georgie Adamici's little sister Josephine, a frizzy blond. Their fatherless family was famous on our block because their fat widowed mother, her Georgie, and Jo herself fought constantly. The whole block heard their voices from their open window. Georgie and Josephine would even say "fuck you" to their mother, something inconceivable to Carlos and me. That Josephine talked dirty also bolstered her being known as a* puta, *a reputation enhanced by her physical development way beyond her fourteen years. Comforted by that reputation, Carlos offered to pay her five dollars if she would let him see her* chocha. *She accepted and Carlos got to see it, even put his finger in it, as he boasted to me, describing the experience in detail. "You do it too, Eddie, man. Pay her, it's smooth and pink."*

But I was too shy to make Josephine that kind of offer. Knowing that about me, the next time we were on the stoop the next Saturday afternoon, Carlos called her over as she came out of the bodega. She was wearing jeans and a T-shirt, what she always wore, and carrying a Macy's shopping bag. Her tits were pretty-good sized and she had been wearing a bra for a while. Then Carlos shocked me when he came right out and said it, "Jo, listen, my buddy here Eddie wants to see your cunt, so he'll pay you five bucks, okay."

Jo didn't respond how she was supposed to, happy go lucky. She looked down the block, her blond frizz and Roman nose profiled against the black empty space of the tar factory's open garage across the street. Carlos nudged me with an elbow, making a facial gesture that told me to pick up from there, which I found myself doing to my amazement. "Come on, Jo, I really want to see it." She said, "Okay, when Georgie takes my mom to the doctor's. I'll wave from my window to signal it's okay." Only now, in recollection, did I realize that she never stopped staring up the block and then left without looking at either of us in the face...

"Eddie, are you all right? You don't look good." Yvette's palm was on my cheek.

"I'm okay."

"Before I took my break, I made a deal with Rodrigo. I gave up a day off that he owes me if he covers at the bar for me later tonight."

"What about Esteban?"

It was Yvette's turn to tread silence. "He's really a sweet person, but when I saw you again..."

I called Domingo over and ordered food.

The jukebox played "*¿Qué Sabes de Linda.*" That old song sung in Daniel Santos' fifties macho-amorous voice turned the Danubio into a bar in some small mountain hamlet in P.R. Distracted, I listened far from Yvette and without a compass. *Where was Eduardo now to tell her, honestly, not words of love like Daniel Santos' but words to hammer at her heart, to tell her that I must stop coming to see her, called away to a life unknown because...?*

Yvette tugged at my chin, turned my face toward her. "You don't relax for one second."

At that moment Armando Casanueva fell from the barstool. Commotion erupted as a gang of men ran to help him: Adelberto López and Frank Sánchez, followed by Luis Rivera, Joe Rivera, Justino Rivera, Tomasito Rivera, Moises, and Tony Rivera—none related. Armando fought off the attention, insisted he was fine.

In shame, he tried to leave but Rodrigo held him down on the stool, ordered Domingo to bring a black coffee. Armando balked and Rodrigo threatened to call his brother Mark to come and get him. The possibility of enduring that shame, of being drunk in the South Bronx and picked up by his brother, shut down Armando's resistance. He sat tamed. Poor Armando, unhappy because he only found refuge in this Bronx while residing in Northport and detesting Northport unable to live in this Bronx.

My scotch glass empty, Yvette gently plucked it from my hand and walked her mellifluous walk to the bar. Nani said something to her, and Yvette gave her the glass to refill and went behind the bar to the cash register. Under the bar's overhead lights, Nani's frizzy curls glittered...*even before Josephine's fat Mama waddled out of sight around the corner beside Georgie, Jo was leaning out the window, waving at me to come upstairs just as Mami Lalia called me up for dinner from our window. I ran upstairs and asked for permission to eat a little later, so I could go with Carlos to see Georgie's train set.*

Mami Lalia was adjusting a hem on the sewing machine while dinner cooked. I reminded her that I never got to do anything with my friends because during weekdays I had to come straight home from school and by the time she arrived from work it was evening. This argument touched a tender spot but her permission was for no more than a half hour or I'd be grounded the following weekend. I had to get five bucks but didn't dare ask. Carlos called up and I shouted down that I'd be right there. Carlos was excited as I was supposed to be. I hoped to work something out with Jo about the five, maybe just have her keep our secret that nothing happened.

Carlos waited for me on Jo's stoop. Her building consisted of "railroad apartments," right and left of the hall, the rooms in a row with front and rear entrances. I was about to knock on the rear kitchen door when the living room door opened. Sunlight from the street window behind her turned her into a silhouette, so I couldn't see until I approached that the zipper to Jo's jeans was open, revealing her panties. I asked if for sure her mother would not be back soon. She shrugged off my worry, took my hand, led me to the sofa, where she pulled the jeans down to her knees. Her legs were creamy white and chubbier than they looked in jeans. This was my moment of truth: "Jo, uh, I couldn't get the..."

But before the words came out, she placed my hand on her belly, whose warmth and smoothness made me stroke her stomach in circles that edged downward until my fingertips grazed over her muff. My hand dove further down, into the wetness in her crack where my middle finger just sank in. Jo pulled down the panties and leaned back. "Don't you want to see it?"

Of course, of course I wanted to see it, and I got on my knees as she spread out on the edge of the sofa. Oh god it was so pink and incredible. I wanted to smell it, but she pulled back my head, sat up, and rolled up her T-shirt to pull down her bra. I couldn't believe the sight of her tits. I touched them softly, I cupped them in my palms, I wanted to suck on them and leaned over to do it but again she pulled me off. I pleaded with her. I offered to get ten dollars and pay her later. She pulled up her bra and rolled down her T-shirt, pulled up her panties, and whispered in my ear, "I only want to do those things with someone who is my steady boyfriend." I positioned her flat on the sofa and crawled over and on top of her, kissing her neck, about to kiss her on the mouth, about to volunteer to become that chosen person, her steady boyfriend, when we heard heavy footsteps on the landing.

I leaped to my feet, and she ran to her bedroom, pulling up and buttoning her jeans. I sat in the living room trying to look nonchalant to greet Mrs. Adamici, who luckily for me, had no Mr. Adamici to beat the crap out of me. The person at the door, however, didn't have a key and knocked. Jo looked in the peephole, whispered to me, "It's your mother." She stretched her T-shirt over her jeans, turned the two locks and opened. She greeted Mami Lalia with the calmest voice, "Oh, Mrs. Loperena, hello." My mother walked in, surveying the scene, sniffing the circumstances. She informed me that I'd been gone almost an hour, that Carlos was already home.

"Well, Georgie had to leave to take my mother to the doctor's, so, um, Eddie just hung around for a while." *Mami Lalia looked at both of us and ordered me home. I was too tired to eat. My balls ached with the pain of being full with desire for Jo's body, which kept flashing in my mind in countless naked positions. At one point during dinner Mami Lalia started to say, "Si tu padre...If your father were alive..." but she must have thought over what she was going to say and her eyes got wet. All that night, she surprised me by treating the matter with silence. Instead of furious, she was sad.*

"I'm sorry I took so long. Nani forgot how to enter a traveler's check in the register and didn't want to ask Rodrigo, so I had to help her."

Dinner arrived and we ate. She was still too impressed that I had actually met Leesa Carr Caro. After the entrees, Domingo brought us two coffees and a flan to share. Nani called her again. Yvette apologized. My eyes imbibed her silky walk. How easy, after a couple of drinks, to fantasize being hers as she would want. Nani waited, apparently useless if cute as a button.

"Jo must have the hots for you, man. Oh, man, you're going to go steady with that slut? That's the word she's telling her girlfriends. Well, at least it won't cost you five bucks every time." I really never understood what was wrong if Jo became my steady girlfriend. I avoided her after that, not because I didn't want to see her but because Carlos and "everybody" on the block thought the idea ridiculous that anybody should like Jo.

Yvette returned with two snifters. "I'm sorry. This time she ran out of brandy at the bar and she doesn't have access to the stock. I knew you would like a little brandy, so here." She sat and there was a pause. "I can tell that you're already in Puerto Rico. Is there somebody waiting for you there? Would you tell me?"

"No, nobody's waiting. What's waiting for me is my sister's wedding and then a commitment to travel, give some political talks."

"Maybe you'll meet a woman at the wedding, somebody that you deserve to have."

Olga Guillot's classic ballad *Teatro, Lo Tuyo Es Todo Teatro* ("Acting, Everything You Do Is an Act") started playing on the juke, and Yvette tugged at my hand, leading me to the middle of the Danubio's small dance floor, where she wrapped my arm around her waist, just at the rise of her hips. Resting her head on my shoulder, she hummed the tune as the length of her body felt like a warm mold of my own, totally surrendered to our dance, our perfect physical harmony. *Of course, according to Graziela, I always held her wrong and danced all wrong. Looking back, I could have spent a lifetime trying every possible way to hold her and always manage to hold her wrong. I had to remind myself that Graziela no longer mattered. "You want to be with your People, then stay with your barmaid."*

Yvette stopped dancing and refused to budge. She clutched the back of my neck and pressed firmly, whispered in my ear: "I don't care if you are flying away tomorrow. And I don't care what happens after that. Tonight you are going to be with me. So get whatever it is or whoever she is out of your mind."

PART FOUR

FANTASYLAND

Chapter 17

A coldly air-conditioned cab delivered me from the San Juan airport to an unusual welcome at Mami Lalia's house: the carport was empty, the porch gate was locked, and my key didn't work. I remembered being told about the changed house door and security gate locks and listening distracted. Doña Teresita, who lived across the street, called out "Licenciado," waving me over to her front porch. I left my suitcase by our porch gate and crossed.

A thin, Indian-looking woman with silver hair in a bun, Doña Teresita lived on her porch, ever peeling potatoes or removing beans from their pods, a living security camera of the block's goings on. First she welcomed me home. Mami Lalia and Rosy were so busy with wedding arrangements they had to grocery shop at the last minute, she duly informed. Out of her apron pocket she pulled a set of keys for the new locks. for the house door and the porch security gate. Lunch was prepared on the range.

Mami Lalia's house belonged to one of the earliest cramped, affordable "urbanizations"—this one near Bayamón called Lomas del Paraíso—popular at the time of the island's industrialization and rising middle class. Each house started as concrete square unit quartered into rooms, a flattened dirt ramp for a carport and a patch of front lawn. Over decades increased income made possible each unit's expansion and particular design, propelling both the property and social value, inviting more upscale condominiums to burgeon in its environs, adding additional value, giving some cache to our regional address even as our particular house kept its original, increasingly conspicuous and embarrassing modest configuration for years as a rental.

My father Baltazar purchased it with a small inheritance as down payment but, being a man from the hills, with only agricultural skills, with no place in the industrializing and rapidly concrete-pouring island, he couldn't get an island job to keep paying the mortgage. This was why he heeded the government's propaganda to consider the new jobs available in the garment industry left vacant by upwardly-mobile Jews on the neighboring isle of Manhattan. Mami Lalia agreed to the move only if my father rented out the house and promised that we would return to live in it.

We came to New York, and he died with in the year. Mami Lalia's sister's collected the rent, deposited the mortgage payments, and looked to necessary repairs. Over the years Rosy and I added the concrete fence wall, two additional bedrooms, a cement carport, improving on the pink paint job Mami Lalia gave it, making it look it look like a doll's house. Rosy chose a mellow green with a lower facade of stylish, brown masonry. Rosy made sure that inside the furnishings reflected the house's escalating appearance. Most recently we added the crime-preventing ivy-leaf-decorated iron work that secured the windows and caged in the carport and porch—the same iron work that imprisoned every house on the island. Only the backyard mango tree rose free in the sun to drop its ripe fruit on the roofs of three different houses similarly imprisoned.

After I graduated from Harvard, Mami Lalia felt free to leave New York and live in her own home. Still relatively young, she got a job dispensing food in the dining hall of Sagrado Corazón University and lived with Rosy, who had recently graduated from Puerto Rico Junior College and landed a job in Jetstream Mortgages and Finance. Second only to the satisfaction of seeing me become Somebody as a lawyer, this *casita* that she now enjoyed in retirement was the crowning material dividend of her almost thirty years invested in New York, her bedrock on Earth through whose front door I walked into the aromatic embrace of whatever she left warming in the pots on the electric range. Under the cover of the larger pot, my favorite: pig's feet and *garbanzos* in a red sauce.

I disposed of my suitcase in my bedroom and returned to serve myself and gleefully savor the rind fat, sauce, white rice, garbanzos, disregarding my conscience's reminders of the lethal doses of cholesterol that I wanted to eat, did eat, and thoroughly enjoyed eating, down to the succulent, articulate toe bones. I promised myself to repent for the joyful poison by henceforth moderating the urge to satisfy my cravings for every one of the island's deadly culinary recipes.

This promise I knew would be difficult to keep what with the morning white buttered bread and overdrive espresso coffee, the high noon feast of the equivalent of or actual pork chops, larded white rice smothered under red kidney beans in a tomato sauce thickened with the starch of potatoes or yams, all modulated by the coolness of a half avocado, a vinaigrette lettuce-and-tomato salad and helped down the gullet with more fresh white bread and a *cerveza* and finally, even if lunch was not yet thoroughly digested, a serving of leftovers for dinner. Yes, during my days on the island, my battle was to be uphill to fend off the predestination of every islander to become a Caribbean beach ball.

For the moment, however, I was pleased that the day was typically hot, that a breeze was slapping a low palm tree frond against the Miami windows, through which wafted the voice of the originally New York Rican Nydia Caro singing her Spanish version of the Swedish group Abba's "Fernando." At that very moment the wheels of my Boeing-jet-soul thumped on landing, and I heard the fully booked cabin applause.

The wall phone by the kitchen door started ringing. I wasn't yet ready to be back in New York but Rosy or Mami Lalia might be calling. Just then Rosy's Mazda pulled into the carport. She burst in through the kitchen door and, not seeing me in the dining room, picked up. "*Hola.*" The call was for me. "*Se le digo*...I'll tell him as soon as he gets here."

Rosy had lost weight. Her hair tips were tinted blond. She was wearing white shorts and a yellow blouse with a gold sparkler tiger, whose tail and hind legs curled around her rib cage. She didn't notice me step up behind her until she hung up and turned around. "Shit, you scared the hell out of me."

"I didn't want you to tell Sánchez O'Neil I was here."

"He wants you to call him. His Spanish is terrible. Oh, since when have you become so important that you can't even give your little sister a kiss?" Standing there, smiling with her arms open, her head slightly cocked, for a second she resembled our father in the photograph hanging in Mami Lalia's bedroom. Her given name was Miriam Rosalinda. Rosy inherited our father's physical appearance of Canary Islander, where her complexion type was common. Her skin was always pink. After playing in the sun, Rosy never tanned, always looked pink.

Those years of our growing up apart took their toll. I never knew her well and she wasn't prone to displays of self-analysis. She simply smiled and showed her love, covering any darker emotions that may be tearing her apart. Only once did she open up briefly and that was to tell me where I could stuff my older-brother advice. So when I learned that she was marrying a guy who advocated statehood for Puerto Rico, I knew enough to keep my opinions to myself—although I couldn't help wondering if she was unconsciously getting back at me for all the years that Mami Lalia played favorites by sending her to school down here, even if for her own good, to grow up to be a decent Puerto Rican woman. And so what if her betrothed advocated something ridiculous? Rosy was deserving of overdue happiness.

She almost married in her late twenties. He was an evening student about to graduate from Inter American University in Business Administration. Two months before the wedding, as part of a corporate trainee program he was flown to Miami, where a Colombian woman seduced him. Latin American women on the prowl for Puerto Rican men as conduits to acquiring a "green card" are the bane of Puerto Rican mothers. He married the Colombian who, after gaining her legal residency, divorced him. He came around again only to be sent to hell. Since then suitors rained on her defensive umbrella but quickly beaded up and rolled off.

Her fiancé George, a devout Yankee fan with no interest in baseball, made it past the growling dogs guarding Rosy's heart to the relief of Mami Lalia, who after meeting him extended her unique sort of encouragement. She advised Rosy not to forget "that, considering your age, even though George had been married before and looks a bit boring, he comes from a very good family, is a lawyer, and men looking to build a family are becoming scarcer since so many are liking men these days."

Mami Lalia opened the kitchen screen door, put down grocery packages, and let out a loud Ay!!!! of felicity as she ran up to hug me. Did I serve myself the lunch she prepared? Do I need help unpacking? And before she forgot, Luis left word to call him. After storing groceries, they had to look in on the woman working on the bridesmaid's dresses, and I was ordered to get settled and rest. I called Luis at his office. He was unable to chat, and we set up a meeting for that evening.

Mami Lalia had turned my small bedroom into a museum of my memorabilia. A shelf on the wall above my bed displayed track medals, three of them won as part of a relay team in which I ran first leg and Carlos ran the last leg. Another shelf on the opposite wall was a gallery of graduation pictures from St. Peter's School, Excalibur Academy, Smith Wesson College and Harvard. On the wall over the head of the bed hung certificates of honor and merit. The diplomas that I had taken down from my Bronx office would find their way into this museum.

I emptied my suitcase, hung up or folded clothes, stripped to my underwear and stretched out on the near-antique mahogany bed with high posts at each corner, of the days when we still needed to sleep protected by mosquito nets. Mami Lalia was sentimentally attached to this bed, in our family since she and my father lived in on a Bayamón hilltop, and I wanted it in my room. I turned on the tall fan and dozed off until Rosy awoke me so I could shower and dress in time to meet with Luis.

We met in the last light of sunset at a new bar called The Sensual Sea, a large canvas-covered terrace facing the southern Atlantic in the hotel district Isla Verde. Its oblong polished wood bar dominated the center of the terrace. Given the nice ocean view, the place was probably busier on weekend nights, but at this weekday dusk only two couples sat at tables and a trio of female tourists at the bar. A waitress was lighting candles for the evening's more romantic mood. Luis waited at a table by the ocean, with a view of the waves crashing at the terrace's rocky base, a table perhaps better used to stoke a first date.

He rose to greet me with an *abrazo*, and once I sat realized that he chose that table because of its topographical view of the barmaids. It was also apparent he had arrived earlier enough to get in more than one drink. Night falls early in summer in this part of the Caribbean, and I looked out at the darkening Atlantic under a brightening full moon. Distant across the darkening horizon sailed a cruise ship's triangular constellation of lights.

One of the barmaids—the four wore hot pants—came to take our order, a long black pony tail falling down to her admirable butt. Her enormous almond-shaped brown eyes inspired one's desiring from her more than just a drink. Luis ordered "*Otro*...Another double Dewar's." I ordered a single. Our eyes followed her shapely hips and legs. "*Buenísima, no*...Really hot isn't she? This is my favorite place, worth coming just for these women and this cool breeze, the crashing waves." He looked out to the Atlantic and fell into a rabbit hole.

The waitress returned, served our drinks. He chuckled.

"What's funny?"

"Nothing"

She asked if we wanted anything else.

"Yvette?" I asked.

She smiled, nodding.

We took in every step of her gait back to the bar. Then, out of nowhere, he asked, "So what happened with Maritza?"

"I invited her to Rosy's wedding but didn't get an answer. She's down here, left me a phone number."

A grimace of skepticism. He glowered at his drink, heaved a sigh. "I promised Yoli that I would cut down on this. I promised lots of shit. She came back home the day I returned from Delaware, and I didn't know how to react. She had left looking like Jane Fonda at the height of the Vietnam War, and when I opened the door, I saw a fifties Puerto Rican woman incarnate in one of those monk-brown dresses women wear who make promises to a saint, with matching white belt, white handbag and shoes with fat white high heels. She was plumper than she was when she left and her normally pale face was powdered geisha-white, with her lips maraschino-cherry red."

Yvette returned with a little bowl of peanuts. Luis paused to render homage to her return to the bar. He took another swig of his drink. "Okay, where was I?"

"Lips, maraschino red."

"Oh, yeah. So I didn't know how to react. She regretted how she had treated the greatest man she had ever known." He took another swig. "She promised never to refuse *any* of my sexual requests, including acquiring a taste for semen. Can you believe that?"

"Well, did you immediately apply the scientific method?"

"I mean, can you believe that she would suddenly return a reformed woman, that woman *in toto* some woman writer praised in a book as The Total Woman—Oh! And no more pills or condoms. If she gets pregnant, she said we'll just have another child."

A moment of silence rendered a salute to the extent of Yoli's commitment, braving the perils of another kid like little Otto José, who from the age of four knew that he wanted to be a real estate agent. Other kids played video games. Otto assessed the value of any property.

"What happened to her in Caracas?"

"She begs that I forgive her running off but swears it was the best thing that could have happened to our marriage. Now she supposedly has no sexual doubts about herself. Apparently while in Brazil her friend—now that dike bitch is only her *best friend*—was religiously reborn, and in their weeks together, Yoli too caught that religious bug. Christ, she now says, told her to come home and be a good wife. Christ supposedly also turned around her best friend, who now claims that she's looking for a macho mate—while still writing supposedly Platonic letters to Yoli. So all those goodies I'm getting come at a price. I have to thank Christ every minute of my life for marital bliss although, I have to admit, she was never so hot."

Luis ordered another round. He thanked me for being a good listener because he felt better. For a while we both looked out at the dark night and ocean, listening to the waves. The next round arrived and Luis stared at the scotch for a long time before he dared to grab the glass and gulp down half the drink. Then, with the fury of the Atlantic's crashing waves, his cresting rage confessed that Yoli's string of postures, fads, poses, transformations had taken their toll. In sympathy with the poor guy, her evolution flashed before my eyes: the once pot-smoking hippy in braless tie-dyed tanktops, the blue-jeaned student nationalist chanting for Puerto Rican independence, the boy-cropped feminist, the over-the-hill punk rocker, the suburban wife and mother, and now the former middle-aged Lesbian and born-again Christian *mujer puertorriqueña*.

"If it weren't for Otto José, my love on this planet more than anything save my deceased mother, I would have run out a long, long time ago. I think you have it better up North in that way. I don't think you would ever be happy here with these crazy women. Can you believe this, tomorrow we're headed for a Charismatic Christian gathering in Sao Paolo."

My attention had turned inward to Graziela. I saw her standing on the window ledge, screaming into Marlboro's face to let her go but not specifying whether inside the room or outside the window. I suddenly wanted Luis to shut the fuck up or change the subject. Luckily he was talked out, and their flying to Brazil in the morning rescued me from getting up and leaving him there.

On the drive back I tried to recover but the imagery would not let up: the barmaid named Yvette and Luis' ranting on about Yoli, who like Graziela didn't know who to be. Couldn't sleep when I got home, so I sat on the porch, listened to the two-syllable whistling fugue of the *coquí* tree frogs, trying to get farther from my New

York life. But the *coquis* failed and the Atlantic wasn't wide enough. I needed to give back Carlos his suitcases, get my life back.

On the kitchen phone I called my answering machine: *Beep... Beep...beep...*"Eddie, Gus, your message with my secretary didn't say your flight time. If I don't hear from you by noon, I'll call you down there."*...Beep...Beep...Beep...*"Hello, Mr. Loperena, this is Gigi Ropanueva calling from the Planning Committee of United Spanish-Speakers of America in Miami. This is just to touch base with you and confirm your meeting with Miami USA in preparation for next year's National Conference of Hispanic-American Unity in Denver. Please call 305-I-M-A-YANK."*...Beep...Beep...Beep.* Maybe Carlos was the one calling and hanging up.

In my room I turned on the bed lamp. When I sat on the bed to remove my socks, on the wall directly across I noticed an addition to the museum of my accomplishments that wasn't there when I last looked. Encased in plastic hung the Smith Wesson literary journal *All the Above* opened to the page on which appears my poem "Don't Let Me Die in Disneyland." I laughed to myself recalling the night that I naively announced at dinner that I wanted to be a poet.

I had come home from Smith Wesson, a sophomore, two days before Christmas Eve. I knew I was going to shock Mami Lalia by arriving with my hair no longer combed out straight but boasting of my natural curls in an Afro. But she contained her obvious initial reaction and embraced me with seasonal and maternal joy. Rosy, brought from PR to be with us by Mami Lalia's older sister, my Aunt Guillermina, commented on how funny my hair looked but nobody picked up on that just yet. I thought I had survived but the storm was brewing.

On Christmas Eve the table was bounteous with tropical succulence thanks to Aunt Guillermina. Short and thin, her hair cut manageably short, and wearing silver frame glasses, for any family reunion she could be counted on to prepare a banquet. For this visit, she prepared a feast of roast pork loin, *pasteles* she had frozen rock solid and wrapped in towels for the flight, coconut eggnog and even a sweet guava paste that she made from fresh island guavas that survived the Department of Agriculture's poking smuggled a. boxed Heavy Duty Maxipads.

By dinner time snowfall had repainted our street into a white postcard scene as we enjoyed my aunt's culinary delights and, except for Mami Lalia's occasional glances at my hair, the mood was absolutely spiritual right up to the moment, over the white-cheese and guava dessert, when she asked me, "*Bueno*...Well, what's going to be your major, what do you plan to be?"

In my junior year at Excalibur I had dabbled at writing poems like those I read for English classes, by Shakespeare or Shelly or, better yet, John Keats. Later, inspired by the "underground" readings among Excalibur's artsy group, especially my black friend Skeeter McTeer, I had also secretly attempted to write like Allen Ginsberg and Leroi Jones, never showing my efforts to anybody. The first ones I revealed were those that gushed out my love for Dixie Culpeper, which disappeared with Dixie. At Smith Wesson, where my writing radical poems was making me a campus star, I believed that my destiny was to be a poet but intuited that was not an answer Mami Lalia wanted to hear. "*Creo que*...I'm leaning toward a major in English, and be an English teacher."

I may as well have answered that I was studying to be a corpse.

Rosy, then thirteen and speaking better Spanish now that she was studying on the island, interjected that being a teacher sounded great.

Mami Lalia turned to Guillermina, who shook her head over her food. I knew by heart the roll call of my cousins who were making or had made themselves Somebody. In Mami Lalia's Somebody firmament, only three professions glittered: lawyer, doctor, engineer. Maybe because of the holiday spirit, she neither exploded nor broke down. My appending that an English major also qualified me for law school perked her up, putting on hold an honorable burial in a dignified casket. Then, believing that the specific career that I had not yet revealed might make her proud, I blurted out that I had also started to write poetry and that the students have reacted very favorably.

The non-response was deafening. That was when I lost control of e revolutionary poet persona, "*Pero*...But," I started out trip over my limited Spanish, so I switched to English, as to speak up against the poverty and exploitation r community, against our colonial status, the slaughter of the innocents in Vietnam, the racism in this country."

Mami Lalia looked back dumbstruck. Her life had come to an end. "*Lo veo*...I see it in your eyes," she reacted, "that same anger of those young black men in the news. I should have realized it when you came home with that hair." She got up from the table, walked to the bedroom, and shut the door. Guillermina sat stunned in her chair.

I myself was at a loss for words. For not just the poet emerged out of nowhere when I started writing at Smith Wesson. I discovered that my soul was seething with an anger that had been hiding somewhere in me and that in poems gushed out as volcanic memories and unsettled scores with American culture. My memory of an Excalibur English teacher who had made plain his disapproval of the administration's liberal gesture of infesting that distinguished school with ghetto vermin and who shaved points from my real grade because he didn't believe that I could have written my submitted essay became the marrow of a poem on the killing of Che Guevara. The snide remark I overheard a townie baker make about a black customer became the leavening of my poem "Mrs. Tetona," about the nasty behavior toward me by the first teacher I had in my Bronx grade school before I was put into St. Pete's, when I was still learning English, which included these lines:

> ...but I wasn't bad or stupid,
> even if not an English muffin
> made from white dough,
> just whole grain me.

That poem went over big with my sociology professor, an advocate of bilingual education.

Guillermina sat chewing on guava paste. Rosy made matters worse by yapping about how she liked poetry and offered to recite a poem that her class had recently memorized. Guillermina asked her to recite it later. Mami Lalia returned to the table mysteriously calm.

She commented, "*No hemos*...We haven't had coffee." Guillermina had already brewed the coffee and began to heat the milk. Mami Lalia, her hands clasped as in prayer, seemed to marshal every molecule of will: "I spoke to San Judas Tadeo. I know he will win you back from the dark forces of anger." Confident that her prayers had set in motion the necessary intervention, she focused on the happiness of having her family together, "Christmas is about Christ and family and these worldly things should not interfere."

Coffees served, Guillermina joined us and Mami Lalia asked her, "Guillermina, how are your children? We haven't spoken about them."

My aunt delivered on cue. "Margarita, Guillermo, and Hugo are all fine. Margarita, you know, graduates from medical school this spring. Guillermo completes his law studies next year. But little Hugo really has me overwhelmed. He's been awarded a special NASA scholarship in the sciences, so he might be studying engineering at M.I.T, where he has always wanted to go." In other words, my cousins were becoming Somebody.

Mami Lalia had come a long way to display my poem. Reading it again for the first time in years, I wanted to read more of the plans I had put aside. From the top chest drawer I took out my old manuscripts of the stories that as lawyer I had started but never finished. I read through those pages until my eyelids fell and I either heard or dreamed I heard a rooster crow.

Chapter 18

Rosy's knock on the bedroom door roused me out of a deep sleep. She didn't wait for a response to stick her head into the room, "Eddie, some woman reporter is on the phone. She called yesterday and I didn't get a chance to tell you." In pajama shorts I groped to the kitchen phone. The caller was Anita Blanco Mann, the arts and culture reporter of *El Nuevo Día*. "*Oh, bien, Licenciado...*Oh, good, Counselor, I would like to interview you about the planned national Hispanic conference and, as you can understand, the mainland position regarding the coming island plebiscite on our political status."

Sánchez-O'Neil at work. "*A la verdad...*I'm really down here for my sister's wedding."

"Oh, I know. It will be announced in the paper, and I plan to cover that wedding on the society page..." We weren't "society" but my future brother-in-law was. Our whole family chipped in for this wedding just not to be shown up although considering the social concession George was making in this second marriage, the arrangements were no more than his family assessed that this union merited.

"...because I know the groom's Skywalker family and that they have long supported statehood. That George is marrying your sister on the Fourth of July seems like a marvelous metaphor of a permanent union on the day of the union of the United States, such an inspiring idea."

"Look, I really didn't come down to make time for interviews..."

"Well, maybe we can find a few minutes at the wedding."

"I can't promise that."

After I hung up, Mami Lalia came to tell me that Doña Milagros, who sewed Rosy's gown from a design by George's cousin with a fashion studio in the Condado, was going to Rosy in her bedroom for final adjustments while she had to rush off to pick up the bridesmaids' dresses with my cousin Ana Liza waiting in her car. I could greet Ana when they returned. None of that information seemed to warrant her look of distress. "*Mira...*Look, George is on his way to meet you and to bring your tuxedo, so you will have to play host. That means that you two men will be alone without the watchful eye of a woman."

Because men are handicapped by nature to behave foolishly if left unattended by womankind, she was especially concerned that her smart-aleck son might jest about the politics sacred to George, an ROTC graduate who was disappointed that the Vietnam War ended the year he graduated from college. So I had to promise to discuss nothing of substance.

Rosy waited to announce her engagement with George after I was back in New York the last time I was down here, her way of protecting her fiancé from her big brother's political sarcasm. Since then, between my marital problems and my practice, I was too busy to come down, so my first view of George was when he showed up at the open door, holding up a wooden hanger with my tux, smiling amiably. "*Buenos días, cuñado,*" he said with a smile, adding a firm *abrazo*. We both expressed the pleasure of finally meeting.

Mami Lalia explained to George about Rosy and her gown, inviting him to sit in the front porch, where it was cooler and suggested to me that I serve him whatever refreshment he wanted. She excused herself again for having to leave. I thanked George for bringing the tux and excused myself to hang it up in my bedroom.

George Skywalker Carrión was like the proverbial little teapot, short and stout, at least an inch shorter than Rosy. He had a soft golden face, his dirty-blond crew cut giving his head the shape of a fish bowl. Being a lawyer, on paper he was Somebody, but according to Luis, among his brothers in jurisprudence he was famous for holding an informally-tallied island record of lost cases. He quit litigation to specialize in negotiated settlements. He was also known as Sausage Fingers in honor of his short fat digits. Family influence allowed him to excel at his only apparent God-given talent, bandying about his maternal surname Carrión, in the genealogical line of two island Supreme Court justices. Typical of fifty-caret surnamed islanders who come into this world as low wattage bulbs, he bore the smugness of somebody much more accomplished.

That George proposed to Rosy, not of his social standing and whose brother was the notorious radical *newyorican* lawyer was understood by Mami Lalia to be San Judas' handiwork and interpreted by the Skywalkers to be God's consolation prize. In an increasingly perilous world now rampant with AIDS, this was his *second* opportunity to have domestic stability, the first having been annulled because the girl from a truly fine lineage shortly after the wedding proposed that they both take a vow of chastity and devote their lives to prayer and good works. Five years after the annulment George was still wasting his best years with Army reserve buddies who if not drinking and picking up tourist women at the hotel bars spent their weekends running around topless in fatigue pants and shooting paint balls at each other in El Yunque rain forest.

Seeing the joy of grandparenting fade and increasingly anxious to cuddle any creature born of any minimally suitable human candidate, his folks considered Rosy just above a bar that they lowered. She was a junior-college graduate and her brother was—to put it in the curative wording in which her future mother-in-law described me to Mami Lalia—"a celebrated lawyer abroad." Rosy's growing up here most of her life paid off as buffer against the Skywalkers' having to socially reconcile, in addition to her descent from a nothing-lineage family, its having left the island with the diasporic riffraff to New York. Less talk was given to the fact that Georges' class credentials was a lineage with poor material dividends or to his having proven himself to be a low-grade catch among his privileged kind.

George, to his credit, boasted of prizing Rosy more proudly, she being Americanized from having been partly raised "up there" but without the truculent, en garde hard edge of a *newyorican* girl. Marrying Rosy was untraditional for his class, but as he enhanced it, wholly consistent with his determination to erode the island's inferior Hispanic culture from which he envisioned a complete English-speaking upgrade even though after that salvation he and his ilk expected to continue to enjoy its traditional undemocratic class deference.

But that reality was for the future. For now, in his white shirt and gray slacks, his welcoming words sounded far more *jíbaro* than one might have expected, with every terminal "r" turned into an "l," a phonetic trait unique to Puerto Ricans, and his initial "rs" pronounced gutturally, like the French and Rio *Cariocas*. Also, like every Spanish-speaking Caribbean, he aspirated every terminal "s" and, like an Andalusian, he shortened intervocalic d's of *ado, edo* (and only in extreme rural cases, *ido*), respectively resulting in *ao* and *eo* (and *ío*): *condenao, peo, metío*. In short, his politics aside, in Spanish he lost the look and feel of a Yankee Doodle Dandy.

He sat on the Swedish wood patio sofa that Rosy had recently ordered, his back to the dining room window, and I positioned one of two accompanying Swedish chairs to face him, with my back to the door. Before sitting, I offered coffee, what I still needed that morning, in Spanish and he asked for a glass of cold water in English. I served the coffee and water on the glass top of the patio table between us. Continuing in English, he expressed his sincere pleasure because we finally met. I shared the sentiment. He said he missed New York, where he had some great times.

He was the kind of islander Army veteran who had adopted the Southern-drawl English he picked up in the military, taking pride in speaking more genuinely by completing sentences with a long "ma-a-a-an" and sometimes with an elastic "shi-i-i-i-t" for even more authenticity. He asked me how I liked being single again. "Ma-a-a-an, from what I hear you don't stay lonely long, Eddie." Then, lowering his voice and turning around to peek through the window shutters behind him, he asked: "Is being single, you know, paying off?"

"Shi-i-i-i-t, ma-a-a-an, it's great."

Taking my answer as a macho challenge, he came back with a mature, worldly tone to explain his willingness to "give up" his own sexual freedom, "because I've really satisfied myself, shi-i-i-i-t, you know what I mean." Then in silent hiatus we sat sipping our respective beverage, at least one lawyer under a gag order. I made the first significant effort at nonvolatile conversation. "How did you get the name Skywalker?"

"My great-grandfather was one of the colonels who landed at Guánica during the Spanish-American War. He was later stationed here."

I was about to turn the corner to avoid minefields, but George stepped in.

"How bad is it up there in New York. Shi-i-i-i-t, people tell me stories. My neighbor is a retired professor of Economics. A few years ago he was invited to a Puerto Rican Studies Program they were opening in some university in New Jersey. The university couldn't find any local Puerto Rican with an advanced degree, so my neighbor got offered the job. Sh-i-i-i-t, he tells me he lasted six months. The students were a bunch of pro-Castro radicals who wouldn't let him teach his classes and..."

The phone rang. I excused myself to pick up in the kitchen. It was Luis. He was at the airport and couldn't call sooner but that morning he had received a call from Harmony Slaughter, a columnist for *The San Juan Star*. "Her paper had received a press release from New York about your coming down here. She's a pushy bitch, and I owe her favors, so I couldn't get out of giving her your address on the condition that she call first. Did she call?"

"No."

"Well, she said she planned to interview you after investigating a story near your mother's house. I'm sorry, Eddie. Oh, one more. I got a call from an Arturo Avellanet. He needed to talk to you. He sounded old, sick, said it was urgent. He called your Bronx office several times and the machine answered, but he didn't want to leave a message. He said you gave him my number as a last resort."

"He's the father of a former client. I have his number." *Maybe it wasn't Carlos but Arturo who kept hanging up on the machine.* I called Arturo. William Guzmán answered. He needed to meet with me, was willing to go anywhere. After the wedding I only had one free day. Visiting him would at least give me the opportunity to spend a day in the country.

When I got back to George, standing at the porch gate was a heavy-set woman wearing round metal-framed sunglasses, a straw fedora, and a loose, below-the-knee-length denim skirt. She carried a dirty beige canvas tote bag. Her big, sunny smile showed lots of gum. "Good mornin'" Another Southerner. "Licenciado Eduardo Loperena. I recognize you from the press photo. I'm Harmony Slaughter from the *San Juan Star.* I meant to call but I was so close by." She looked around at the gate grillwork restraining her. "Can I come in?"

I nodded and she opened the gate.

"Gus Sánchez O'Neil and I go way back. He always lets me know when he's coming down or something important is happenin'."

I introduced George as my future brother-in-law and offered her a seat on the other patio chair, facing George and me. Harmony removed her sunglasses, lay her hat on the low table, smoothed down her graying blond hair with puffy, petite, dainty hands, then removed from the tote bag a small cassette recorder. She placed it on the table close to me, pressed the record button. Her thick gams were hairy.

"I've been covering the controversy of the forthcoming plebiscite on the island's political status. Gus' office called to let me know that you were visiting our Isle of Enchantment, and it occurred to me that you could provide yet another—and I should add—important perspective on the subject, the view from the mainland." She took a sidelong glance at George and asked if maybe we could move to the living room. I explained that the living room was poorly ventilated and besides I would have to leave George alone out on the porch. I explained that "I only came down for the wedding, so I really didn't come prepared..."

"Oh, I'll just be writing a short vignette, a profile of a prominent visitor sort of thing. I don't need formally prepared statements. Besides, I think you would agree with me that you represent a very positive and improved image of how many see Puerto Ricans in New York. So you would be helping the cause of communication, don't you think? So how do you feel about mainland Puerto Ricans participating in any plebiscite on the island's status?"

"Well, that's for politicians to decide..."

"Well, what political status do *you* favor?"

"I'm nobody to come here to tell anybody how to vote." *I favored independence when I thought I belonged, now that hot potato is on some-body else's lap.*

"But isn't it true that you've publically spoken on the subject often and said," quoting from notes, "The only viable choice for the majority of Puerto Ricans is independence." I gauged the intervals between George's gulps of water.

"Excuse me, *Licenciado*, do you remember saying this in a *Daily News* interview?"

"That was during the trial of William Guzmán. I was speaking in a cultural context."

"Can you elaborate?"

"I was responding to a question of what would motivate two young men born and bred in New York to become nationalists of an island they hardly knew because they wanted to see their culture survive, making the only viable choice independence. Being a colonial 'Associated Free State' erodes our identity and builds up an appetite for a statehood that will never come..." I caught myself too late.

George stomped his foot as he uncrossed one leg to cross the other. His squinting eyes were fixed on the sun-white, steaming street.

A squeaky voice interrupted the interview. "*Buenos Días...*" The bird-thin, eldery next-door neighbor, Doña Juanita, was standing at the porch gate. "Can Doña Lalia spare some Spanish parsley. I need it for my beans."

I invited her to look in the refrigerator. She climbed the porch steps, greeted all present, and entered the house.

"You were saying, *Licenciado*."

George shot up and marched into the house.

"I just said," lowering my voice a notch, "that statehood is not likely to happen."

In the background, I heard George ask Rosy through the bedroom door how much longer the fitting would take. I didn't hear her answer as Harmony asked me "to elaborate on the bleak prospects for statehood, considering that so many here remain hopeful," finishing her statement just as George returned quietly behind me when I thought he was out of earshot.

"Statehood isn't ours to simply proclaim, and it will also mean that the Slaughter family will feel safe to come down and decide to buy out this lady next door and the house after that and the one after that and realtors won't sell homes to any native islander who won't be able to afford the going rates and might even devalue the property, so inevitably the natives will all be clamoring for a Civil Rights Bill. For true *americanos* like yourself, equality is something that doesn't have to be legislated. That's not the case with minorities, which is what islanders would instantly become even in their own cultural setting. We know that history already, in the Southwest, in Hawaii, in Alaska. All we'll get is a future of civil rights litigation. Statehood would just be like a marriage for money with a man who is rich but stingy and who outlives you."

"Oh, but, using your own analogy, wouldn't you definitely be assured of a better life?"

"True enough. The well-off white ones. Not as easy for the darker half. From the vantage point of living hand to mouth, the servant's quarters and a secure job sounds just fine. The dog of a rich man does live better than a poor man—but as a dog."

George jumped out from behind me, darting his sausage finger at Harmony Slaughter. "Are you going to actually quote this guy who grew up in New York on what we should be doing with Puerto Rico."

"Hey, buddy, keep out of this, will ya," Harmony snapped.

Rosy came out to the porch just in time to see George's sausage finger still in the air. "*Jorge, por favor, ¡tranquilízate!*"

"You two against statehood are working together. What *you* want to do is to use *him* to sink statehood so you can preserve this phony Commonwealth. I've read your pieces, Ms. Slaughter, and I know you're married to that left-leaning painter hired by the government to go around painting folkloric Taíno Indian designs over the walls of public housing projects, a capitalist who exploits the poor and calls himself a progressive. That party hack, like all those stupid Popular Democrats, still go around believing their party is the party of the *jíbaro*, a sad symbol of the hillbilly that doesn't represent anybody anymore."

Rosy gently tugged at George's arm, "Baby, *Papi, por favor*. This is so shameful." But George didn't budge and neither did Harmony.

"Ramón is an apolitical soul, Mr. Loperena, a pure artist." Harmony's voice was low and sounded hurt. "His Nativity scenes in a miniature wooden-shack slum are yearly commissioned by the San Juan Mayor for public display, movingly representing the real slum dwellings at the foot of the El Morro fortress wall." Addressing George: "My husband is a fine Puerto Rican artist struggling to create his art and you should have the decency to refrain from belittling him for his beliefs. He feels proud of being Puerto Rican. It's his right to defend the Commonwealth formula."

George, now in Rosy's bear hug, and though receding, couldn't be restrained from shouting. "Oh, so your husband defends the Commonwealth, and he feels proud of being a what? Your husband is an American! There is no such thing as a Puerto Rican citizenship."

"Oh, *you* know what I mean."

"No I don't. Shi-i-i-t, I only know that he wants to keep this bullshit Commonwealth. What I wish is that he had stayed back where he was born, in the slums of New York because as you yourself know, your dear Ramón is just another *newyorican*."

"He was born and raised here, mister, and he only worked in the Barrio for ten years teaching kids art. So that's how much you know. If the likes of you is supposed to represent America, I would give back my citizenship!"

That answer shut George up while Rosy managed to finally tow him into the house. Harmony sat again, daintily tucking her denim skirt, revealing part of her mutton, unshaven legs. She patted down her hair with her gentle hand and took a deep breath.

The neighbor Doña Juanita had stood frozen by the doorway during this exchange, afraid to come out. When Rosy managed to rein in George, she thanked me for her fistful of parsley and asked in a whisper what the fuss was about.

"*Nada, Doña, diferencias políticas..*"

"*Oh no...*I don't get involved with that." She left to cook her beans.

The seamstress Doña Milagros followed, an almost skeletal black lady with thick square glasses and her hair wrapped in a turban. She came out bearing the empty box that had contained Rosy's gown. She bid all a good day.

"You speak Spanish quite well. People here, as you know, find that those from..."

With that question, I had come to the limit of my patience and tuned her out.

Harmony was waiting for my answer to a question. "I've asked the question twice, if you can just give me a brief summary about how you see Puerto Ricans in New York today, half a century after the great migration, just some statement."

"About the life of every Puerto Rican in New York?"

"Well, I think you know what I mean, Mr. Loperena. Your impression of your community's condition there." A car slowed to a roll and parked in front of the house. Mami Lalia stepped out.

"Ms. Slaughter, have you seen Spielberg's movie *E.T.?* Well, Puerto Ricans in New York phone home but nobody answers. I think the appropriate metaphors are there."

She winced, shut off the recorder, and thanked me for my time, crossing paths with Mami Lalia, who immediately inquired about George.

"*Está...*He's in the room with Rosy."

She shook her head, "*Nunca*...Never fails."

A young man carrying three piled boxes that covered his face followed her into the house. Once he placed them on the kitchen counter I realized that the man was actually my cousin Ana Liza. I last knew her as a dolled-up, flowing-haired feminine coed in short skirts and high heels. This incarnation wore a boys' haircut, a black T-shirt, baggy fatigue pants, and a sweat band around each wrist. Her welcoming "*Bienvenido*" growled from the depths of the earth. We embraced, her hug a vise. Ana Liza, forearms and biceps rippling, then carried the three boxes into Rosy's room.

Mami Lalia started preparing lunch. "Are you taking anybody to the wedding?"

Ana Liza came out of Rosy's room. From a distance her downy mustache appeared more pronounced. She went out to the car. I answered Mami Lalia, "No." *Should I try Maritza, again?*

Ana Liza entered the house carrying two more boxes that she took to Rosy's room.

"Well, my concern is that you not be alone because if a woman isn't around to bring out your better instincts, you'll only behave stupidly. That's why I thought that maybe, if you didn't have anybody..."

Ana Liza walked out of Rosy's room again. Her sweatbands swung to the rhythm of her walk as she crossed the kitchen to the dining table, where she pulled up a chair, turned it around and mounted it as if it were a saddle.

"*Bueno, Eduardo*...So, Eduardo, it's been a long time." Up close, her mustache hairs were holographic, becoming lighter or darker according to the angle of light. Her forearms were thicker than mine. Her biceps burst out of the T-shirt. Under naturally long black eyelashes, her black eyes twinkled. I asked how her work was going.

She had completed a masters degree in Social Work and worked as a psychotherapist. "*Soy terapeuta de mujeres*...I'm a woman's therapist. I also run a barter cooperative of professional women. I give therapy to a woman dentist and she fixes my teeth, like that. I know all about *you*. Aunt Lalia keeps us well informed."

Mami Lalia asked Ana Liza to try on her bridesmaid dress so adjustments can be made. Ana made obvious her dread. She entered Rosy's room and George came out. Before he said anything, his future mother-in-law invited him to have lunch. He declined. His army buddies were throwing him a bachelor party. The phone rang once and Rosy apparently picked up in her room. Showing his breeding, George expressed his pleasure at our meeting, extended his hand and, as we shook, Rosy stuck her head out to shout that I should pick up the phone. A woman named Maritza was calling.

Chapter 19

Maritza's agreeing to a dinner date goosed me with the optimism that maybe she might grace my sister's wedding with her company after all. I picked her up at her mother's large, Spanish-tiled white house in Guaynabo, its design compromised by two solar panels and a black dish antenna. The driveway curved around a well-tended, circular garden that led to a three-car carport with a Mercedes convertible in the middle beside a Ferrari coupe.

I parked Rosy's Mazda behind the Mercedes and walked to the porch, where separated by an empty wicker patio love seat before a low center table, to the left Martitza sat in a rocking chair and to the right a svelte woman sat back in a cushiony white wicker patio chair. Her meaty white legs were crossed, her black hair thickly lacquered, and her pale face lightly rouged, smooth of wrinkles. Her bright yellow dress decorated with daisies matched her white leather sandals with a row of little white leather daisies over the toes. Stretching out her hand that sparkled with a sizeable-carats diamond engagement ring and a diamond-studded wedding band, Doña Ayxa Vergara de Islas smiled a sunrise to say that she was "*encantada*" to finally meet me. Words could not express how much she appreciated my helping Martiza get tenure.

My response that Maritza deserved it, given her academic work, prompted Doña Ayxa to comment on how cultured I spoke Spanish, and as if to reward me she offered something to drink. But I was hoping to take in the sunset where we were going. Already on her feet to serve me, Maritza excused herself to get her handbag. In her absence, the sun in her mother's smile set instantly. She pointed to the love seat, and I sat. She looked away, toward her garden.

"*Ah...Ah*, New York. My husband Alfredo, may he rest in peace, used to take me often." She paused. Before her eyes the evening air was screening an old reel, of her husband in a double-breasted suit at the Palladium, leading her in dance to "*Mambo, Qué Rico el Mambo*," holding her close then spinning her. Suddenly the music stopped and she looked up, at nothing. *Loperena...Loperena*, I don't know any Loperenas." She looked at me and smiled.

A red Porshe convertible came up the driveway. A young couple stepped out of the car. I was introduced to Martiza's brother "Billy," pronounced "Beely," in khaki shorts and white shirt, and his wife, Ana Mulet, in fashionable red hot pants and a yellow blouse, the matching colors of her sunglasses. Beely gave his hand and Ana just smiled hello. Doña Ayxa volunteered that "*Ana es...*Ana is from the Mulets, the Cuban public relations family. Her father admired the United States so much that they only spoke English at home and sent her to English-speaking day care and English-language schools. Now the poor dear sounds like a Newyorican, her Spanish is so bad, but she's so beautiful that we forgive her. She represents Elizabeth Arden."

Maritza returned with her purse, and Beely asked to borrow her VCR for the weekend because theirs was on the fritz. They were going to see videos taken by their friends Arturo Cohen and Juan Acosta on their trip to Colombia and a two-week-long Amazon expedition. Doña Ayxa expressed disbelief that anybody could stay in a jungle that long. *Natural habitat for that snake Juan Acosta.*

Beely didn't look like anybody in the family. His skin was albino pale and his nose was flat, his cheekbones high and his blond hair tight, naturally kinky but combed out and moussed wavily over his head. He sniffed a lot, constantly stroking his nose with the back of his hand, and he seemed to have a 1-event/1-day programmable

VCR for brains. Everything he said was hyperbole, *crazy*, *wild* or *great*, and maybe from living with the Spanish-deficient Ana, he habitually translated himself, saying everything twice. "*Oye, Mari, préstame tu VCR.* Can you lend it to me?"

Maritza returned with a peach leather pouch hanging from her shoulder and had changed from sandals to heels with peach leather webbing. We were set to leave when Beely remembered: "*O, y te hice la llave.* I made a copy of the key you wanted." He searched through his pocket and pulled out a car key dangling on a ring with a leather Porsche-logo tab. In the process of removing it, out of his pocket popped a dollar bill folded into a miniature square cushion, the kind for which I had to defend clients. Ana swiped it up, complaining that Beely was such a little kid sometimes. She tugged him by the elbow into the house.

I delivered the de rigor *enchanté* to Doña Ayxa, who reciprocated smiling confidently, having elegantly informed me that Martiza wouldn't consider someone with my nothing Loperena pedigree. To distract from the added ignominy of escorting her to Rosy's Mazda, as I opened the passenger door, I described the great view of the place where we were going, a ploy that backfired. "I may have already been there," she said, "a place owned by a family friend."

Seconds out of her driveway Maritza inquired about my plans now that I was closing my practice. "*Creo que..*I think I'm starting a political career. I've been interviewed by Governor Mario Cuomo, and Sánchez O'Neil wants me to manage his Congressional campaign..."

"*Y después...*And after that?"

"I have to wait for the results of this political experiment." *And my being a Harvard lawyer, "The Community's Lawyer," and now sought after by the governor quite obviously is not enough to elevate me above a* newyorican, *so what difference does it make what I do after that?*

El Restaurante Mirador del Valle wasn't her family friend's place, but wasn't far from it, also on a Cayey hilltop, offering the same panorama of the Atlantic to the north and, distantly south, the Caribbean, the romantic view the reason to eat out on the terrace. With tropical rain looming, we picked a table safely against the lounge's display window and next to its glass door.

Martiza had a *chisme* to share about her tenure case. "Apparently my back-stabbing chairman had reserved my tenure-track line for a Cuban nun who had been formally convicted of plagiarism in another department."

"Well, a Catholic university favors a super devout Catholic, a company woman even if she's a plagiarist."

Maritza ordered a glass of Chardonnay and a shrimp salad. I ordered the same. In the sparsely-populated lounge a one-man synthesizer band was setting up, a chubby guy with an obvious black toupee, wearing a white, short-sleeved *guayabera*. Into the lounge walked three women. I excused myself, stepped around to the sliding door and entered the lounge.

Consuelo López, a Somalian-looking, strikingly beautiful M.D., opened her arms. Connie grew up in pre-gentrified Park Slope, Brooklyn, and like me received seventies minority scholarships that, in her case, made possible her becoming a pediatrician. I provided legal counsel to community health programs that she either administered or advised.

Her hair was longer than when I last saw her, no longer a then-stylish Afro, and her red cotton dress was tight at her now wider hips. It had been years. She got married, divorced. Her daughter was entering N. Y. U. Her teenage son was with his Cuban father in Miami for the summer. Her companions, Gabriela and Mayte, were also New York Rican doctors on vacation, all practicing in Hartford now, completing an attractive trio in heels no one would guess were three MDs. They had planned to have a drink in the lounge but seeing a storm coming, immediately decided to leave before it started.

"You won't believe this, Eddie. Last week I was at a conference on public health in Caracas. I was about to quote you, and said 'My friend Eduardo Loperena' when a Venezuelan doctora was all over me, asking about you."

"Luz Vitali."...*who Mami Lalia could see truly loved me even if her father did own ranches in the Amazon, for whom I could never feel more*

*than friendship, hard as I tried, because she deserved more, capable of pass-
ing every test that for Mami Lali proved that a woman truly loved a man...*

"How is she?"

"She's a doll. She's married to a Venezuelan doctor. Every summer
they volunteer to work for Doctors without Borders. You obviously
performed your usual magic. I was so jealous, but I loved her. I told
her you were married and lived in the Bronx."

"I'm not married anymore."

"Oh, well, then you can enjoy the evening with us."

I pointed to Maritza looking in.

Maritza had pushed her chair back and crossed her legs to be
presented, smiling, as a professor of Spanish at Mahdrof University.
I introduced Connie as a public health doctor for whom I did legal
work. Connie switched to Spanish to address Maritza, "*Mira...*
Look, in this ungrateful world, I'm Loperena's biggest fan because
nobody stands up for Puerto Ricans in New York more than this
man. So take really good care of him for me." She gave me another
major hug before departing.

Maritza's smile was gone the second that Connie turned.

The waitress came with our shrimp salads. She asked if we were
having dinner. Maritza sharply answered no. As I bit into a shrimp,
she commented on how nice 'Connie' seemed, an exercise in good
breeding more than sincerity. Maritza bit into a shrimp, looking
out, perhaps at the lightning or at a farther, inner distance. Across
a gulf of silence over the small table, I apologized for interrupting
her on the conspiracy to replace her with that Cuban nun.

"*Dije...*I said everything I had to say. And 'Connie' also expressed
my gratitude for your helping 'us Puerto Ricans in New York.'" A
huge lightning bolt lit up the tropic zone, this time eliciting a gasp
from the entire, now full, terrace. "So, did you date?"

"No, I did legal work for her programs. We were both married."

"Well, she sincerely meant it about being your fan. Women can
see certain things."

"What do they see?"

"Body gestures. The way she looked at you—and at me."

"What kind of look did she give me?"

Burdened, she heaved a sigh, sipped on her wine.

"I'm just curious to know what you women see so clearly that men don't see."

"Are you trying to convince me that you didn't notice it too?"

"What?"

"Her eyes, the way they lit up when she looked at you."

"Show me."

She grabbed her purse, marched into the lounge now in candle-light, and wove around three couples dancing to the lounge singer's Spanish version of the Brazilian Roberto Carlos' "Amada Amante."

A continuous crackle of lightning lit up the sky. Rain pelted the terrace's Plexiglass cover. Totally dark was the eastern horizon and still sunlit the edge of the farthest west. When Maritza returned, radiant, her make-up refreshed, the singer switched speeds to "*Compadre Pedro Juan baila merengue.*" I grabbed her hand. She slung her purse belt over her shoulder and acquiesced to a dance.

The *merengue* is seductive, not aggressive like a *bolero*, which is really intended to be danced body to body and cheek to cheek. A Platonic *bolero*, bodies apart, is a big nothing. But the *merengue* allows you to get erotic starting out as *agape*, natural movement toward steamy perdition seeking its darkest extreme, a tight, fast, hot "*apambichao*," bastardized from Palm Beach.

The singer slid into a wacky medley of standards that he *merengue*-ized—a "What I Did for Love" *merengue*, followed by a "To All the Girls I Loved Before" *merengue*, followed by a "Hava Nagila" *merengue*—one door joyously opening to another transporting me closer to Maritza's *alma* as she allowed me to hold her longer, closer, brushing my cheek against hers, until our pressed bodies, rhythmic and harmonious at last, could fit as one in the shadow of the leanest palm tree on the sands of Palm Beach.

The medley ended the singer's set, and back at our table, catching her breath, Maritza removed a Spanish fan from her pocket book, splayed it, and fluttered it over her face. Her sweating forehead looked baroque with little wet curls as she arched her head back fanning furiously. But more than cooling down, I realized, she was trying to come to her senses.

The rain had let up. Startling her, I stopped her fanning hand and invited her to the cooler edge of the terrace. She picked up her hand bag, stored the fan. Standing beside me in the breeze-busy dark with distant lights, she inhaled deeply. Both her hands gripped the railing, fingers massaging the steel. "*No puedo*...I can't accompany you to your sister's wedding tomorrow. I'm sorry."

A monstrous flash shocked the entire region. Rain again drummed loudly.

Settled back at our table, I asked about the topic of her dissertation. "Gabriela Mistral. Why?"

"I like her poem 'Pan,' about bread and love."

"You're confusing me."

"How?"

"Why don't you ask me why I can't go with you to the wedding."

"Because you wouldn't tell me even if you knew."

"What does that mean?"

"Do you know?"

"Because I don't want to lead you on."

"Okay, that sounds good."

"Don't be arrogant."

"I think your explanation was a good try."

"Take me home."

The rain worsened as I paid the check, and we got soaked rushing to the car. At her mother's home, her good breeding thanked me for a pleasant evening.

Her pulling back after briefly giving in to her feelings didn't hurt as much as the root of her reversal. On the drive to her house, where Maritza heard silence, I was stirring my molten center so it didn't cool and set in the humble cast in which she had presumed to pour it. I had traveled too far in the face of white, gringo, Yankee, *americano* ethno-diversity babble to be flattened again into a two-dimensional prop of her identity confusion or to give a flying fuck about her puny island oligarchy.

Chapter 20

The following note was taped on my bedroom door: "Having not heard of any other woman you are taking to my wedding, I recommend that you call Susana Santo Coto. The number:...." In the morning I needed to get a clarification on being stuck with a blind date, but Rosy, steaming milk in the kitchen, preempted my question, "Just in time. Here." She poured the hot milk into a cup half full of black coffee. "There's fresh bread on the table." She opened the fridge and extended the butter holder. "Mami's in her bedroom getting ready and left you the *El Nuevo Día* opened to the page with the picture of your friend." I asked her again to explain this blind date.

"Susana's my Maid of Honor, and her car's in the shop. Mami and I will be going to the wedding in the rented limo, and you'll be driving my car anyway. Besides, you didn't show up in time to rehearse, and she can help you with what to do. She's my good friend who needs a ride to the wedding. If you care to know, she's a natural blond, divorced, and is an officer where I work, Jetstream Mortgages and Finance. But I warn you. She's very attractive and a darling person."

Rosy was an apostle of Mami Lalia's doctrine that a womanless man lives in peril of driving his libido off the high peak of his ego. Law school hadn't trained me for Rosy's tactics, so I took my coffee to the dining table, where *El Nuevo Día* was open to the page with

Sánchez O'Neil's's photo: In the foreground of a group, he grinned under the arm of the also grinning Jessie Jackson. The caption, in Spanish, identified the civil rights leader and the Deputy Mayor, "the Manhattan-born son of parents from Arecibo, who was running for Congress." If I had been in New York, most likely I would have been in that photo with Jesse, whom I had met at several conferences and confrontations.

Rosy returned to the table to remind me not to forget to let Susana know when I would be picking her up. I thought I answered okay but my attention was arrested by the male face behind Jesse, an Excalibur classmate I had lost track of, Skeeter McTeer. After he had stopped writing to me at Smith Wesson, I found out that he had dropped out of Temple University to find himself in the hippie life on the West Coast. Skeet apparently found his path just as I lost mine.

Rosy stuck her head out of her room, half her hair in curlers. "Pick up the phone. I called Susana so you two can introduce yourselves."

We were both pleased to meet even if over the phone. Apparently counting on my fortuitous availability as a driver, Rosy had shown her some news clippings of me, allegedly just so Susana could recognize the person who came to her door. We agreed on a time for me to pick her up. I was about to enter my room to get dressed and the phone rang. Rosy picked up in her room. I had just shut the door to my room when I heard Rosy scream. In her bedroom that two lamps lit up because the Miami shutter windows were shut so air conditioning could protect Rosy's coif against tropical humidity, Coqui was propping up Rosy's faint head as Mami Lalia in curlers was plumping a pillow behind her neck to rescue from the headboard the hairwork that Coqui had already done.

"Whoever called said something that caused Rosy to faint," Coqui explained. Pillow and Rosy's head in place, Mami Lalia ran to the bathroom and returned with a folded towel wet with herbal-laced alcohol. Placed across Rosy's forehead, the towel's pungent aroma worked, and Rosy came to. "*George, algo...*George, something happened to him."

Sounds squeaked from the phone receiver still on the floor. I picked up the phone and receiver, "*Diga.*"

"Yes, well, my friend, who might I be talking to."

"Eddie Loperena, Rosy's brother."

"Oh, good. Look, I didn't mean to upset your sister."

"What happened?"

"Well, it's a long story. Let me just talk *macho a macho*, so can you step away if the womenfolk are around."

I took a few steps away, lowered my voice. "Sure, let's hear it."

"Oh, yes, you're from New York too. I've been up there. I know how frustrating we out-of-towners can be on you, with your timing I mean. So, Eduardo, you're name's Eduardo, right.

"Right."

"So me and a bunch of George's Army buddies gave him a little going-away party at my place at Isla Verde. Now, you see, we know what George likes, so we had a Fourth of July special for him, a gorgeous Swede."

"Who am I talking to?"

"Oh, yeah, I forgot my manners. I'm Gilbert."

"Okay, Gilbert, can you tell me what you told my sister that made her faint?"

"Ah, yes, New York. Well, now as I was saying, this is *macho a macho*, remember. Okay, so Georgie took off with Dina, that was her name, and we hadn't heard from him all night."

"So you told her this?"

"No, I'm trying to explain but you keep interrupting me. Now this is *macho a macho*."

"So where is he now?"

"I'm getting to that. There you go again, New York. Well, he gets back here this morning a nervous basket case, with his middle finger set in a cast. He thought he couldn't explain the cast to your sister without giving away that he wasn't telling the whole story, you see. This happened to his hand with the car door when he dropped Dina off this morning. He called me and I had to take him to the hospital to fix it up. So I made the mistake of not warning her first that he was all right. I started by saying we had to take George to the hospital. She screamed. Next thing I was talking to space. But George is home now and, hell, he'll be at his wedding all right. Only thing is his middle finger looks like a big fat dick."

When I hung up everybody was waiting to hear. *George sólo...* "George only hurt his hand. He had been drinking with Army friends."

"Aghh, those Army friends," Rosy growled as Coqui helped her get up. I was about to shower and get ready when Rosy asked me to stay while Coqui worked on her hair. This being her day I pampered her, sat on the bed, totally receptive. She asked me if I wasn't a little curious about Susana. It was a rhetorical question because she started telling me Susana's story anyway. She was practically done when the phone rang again, and Rosy had Coqui answer it quickly. The caller was Sánchez O'Neil. I took it in the kitchen.

"What the hell are you trying to do down there. Did you read Harmony Slaughter's interview of you? You sound like a radical. You're supposed to speak neutrally, not divisively."

"I don't remember saying anything divisive, so I don't know what she's quoting."

"Write a letter to the editor and accuse Harmony of misquoting you."

"Gus, today is Rosy's wedding."

Resigned that I wasn't going to write to the editor, in a slippery about-face, he said that he'd take care of it. "I understand that I have permission to answer in your name."

"Fine, do that. What about the speech I was supposed to receive for L.A.?"

"Jesus, Eddie. I've been so pressed with my campaign and the issues here that I completely forgot. How about The Effects of 'English Only' on Bilingual Education? That was going to be my topic."

He urged me not to forget that it was a political talk, so I didn't have the freedom to ejaculate freestyle. And about the stint in Miami: "It's simply a dinner with those lonely Democrats down there and then a meeting the following day. You can read them an outline of what you'll prepare for L.A. Again, bi-lingual education and language are the keynote issues. The plane tickets will be at the airport: L.A., by way of Miami. In Miami, you'll be met by Gigi Ropanueva. She'll host and introduce you to the head of the Cuban delegation, a guy named Antonio with the ironic surname, Heras de Castro, who once was a *barbudo* revolutionary and is now a banker and mango juice magnate. But he likes to be called Wally. Okay, gotta go. No more interviews or statements that don't simply say, this is the best place to sun and surf, okay? Oh, did you catch my picture with Jesse yesterday?"

"You looked like a Congressional candidate. Did you get a chance to talk to the guy standing behind Jesse?"

"No, is he important?"

"He was a classmate of mine at Excalibur."

I had to find a copy of the *Star*. Rosy told me that a couple down the block recently moved from New York and got the *Star* delivered.

Harmony Slaughter's column was called, somewhat threateningly, "In Harmony's Way":

"The celebrated New York lawyer Eduardo Loperena is in Puerto Rico for the Fourth of July weekend. I caught up with him the other morning on the *balcón* of his mother's house."

Asked about the upcoming plebiscite, Mr. Loperena, a man of average height incommensurate with his stature, told us that he saw independence as the only viable solution. Frankly, it's difficult to imagine why a man so obviously formed up North should hold that position but Mr. Loperena feels that the island's culture is at risk. He is, after all, famous among the ghettos of New York for supporting the underdog.

"He demonstrated a certain touchiness about his Spanish, which is surprisingly better than we hear from *riqueños* from New York but I did not belabor the point. When asked how he saw the state of the mainland Puerto Rican community, he seemed to want to dodge the subject. He suggested we all see the movie *ET*, which according to him sums up the story of the immigrant. That, I confess, went over my head. For those of us who take an interest in the development of *boricuas* abroad, Mr. Loperena was somewhat disappointing as its spokesperson, especially given his reputation as the poet of the courtroom. But we know he's here to enjoy our beaches and palm trees and wish that he returns to New York with fond memories of this Isle of Enchantment."

Chapter 21

This was everything Rosy told me about Susana.

A recovering victim of Everywoman's struggle for self-determination, she was now thirty two. At twenty-two she married Abdul Roberto Nazar del Valle, an officer of the Royal Nova Scotia Bank and half owner of the restaurant Alps Blanque Challet. A sudden change in personality caused her to plummet from the social heights as Señora de Nazar del Valle, and now she was a working woman who lived in an upscale but less than ostentatious condominium.

Her life changed the day she had to wait for her dentist who, the assistant explained, was treating a patient only in need of a minor filling but who being pregnant was unlikely to return on schedule and so was also getting a cleaning. The word pregnant struck Susana, who hadn't been able to get pregnant. Equally as fateful, someone had left in the waiting room Betty Frieden's *El Mystique Femenino*, which Susana browsed, Friedan's words affecting her instantly. In the time the dentist removed his patient's plaque, the half chapter that Susana read of Friedan started removing that plastic outer layer that Susana called a life.

On the drive home, she stopped at the bookstore. As Abdul met late into the night with his partner at their restaurant, she read every page of *El Mystique*, painfully acknowledging that she wasn't a person but an appendage to her husband, whose money kept her thinking about nothing but the latest fashion, manicured nails, and perfectly coifed hair. She woke up determined to change her life. That morning she threw away her cosmetics. That afternoon she shocked her hair stylist by insisting on having her pampered mane cut short and from that day on only wore blouses and pants. The transformation provoked a violent response from Abdul Roberto.

The Middle-Eastern-descended Nazars, of a complexion a touch more sautéed than stir-fried Mediterranean—a swarthiness that in his monetary case island upper crust saw as a currency green—had married Susana mainly for her blondness and sense of fashion. Understandably, then, he cursed that stupid androgynous hairdo and that face without makeup, so yogurt-pale she could play Swedish Death in Ingmar Bergman movies. Hoping that jealousy might rescue his wife from this phase, he went public with one of the dolled-up women he'd secretly been seeing, only confirming Susana's suspicions why she hadn't gotten pregnant, deprived of the optimal statistical probability of the most active sperm.

Susana packed her things and left the marriage, and, despite her lawyer's pleas, took the feminist high stand of demanding nothing material from him at the divorce. Her parents helped finance the purchase of the Caribbean Towers condo in Hato Rey, actually with a mortgage from her father's friend's company Jetstream Mortgages and Finance, which also gave her a job.

Her B.A. was in *Estudios Hispánicos*, a major she chose thinking that her material security was expected to come from a man, but she learned the ropes of mortgages fast and advanced to the level of officer. She also befriended Rosy, who from the vantage of her post-traditional new identity, was Everywoman, a victimized sister. Under Rosy's influence and with a reborn desire to attract a man, Susana's feminism evolved from its fundamentalism to a compromise with nails, hair, cheeks and lips that allowed her once again to exhibit the charms of the original Señora de Nazar del Valle. If she hadn't found somebody in the last six divorced years, Rosy reassured me, "it's because really good men are scarce and she deserves a prince."

Punctually I arrived in my white tuxedo at her Caribbean Towers pad on the eleventh floor. A perfumed breeze escaped out the open door into the hall. *"Hola, Eddie."* Her eyes were green. Her blond hair was in a bun. Her marble-smooth neck was highlighted by a velvet choker. Her cheeks were rouged, her modest-length nails were lacquered pink. Her eyes made nanosecond inquiries. It was a sort of clumsy, less than romantic situation: she was wearing a full-length, Asian-themed bathrobe because I was also there to deliver her bridesmaid's gown. She welcomed me in.

Her apartment had white walls, the furniture made of rattan. A racket of chirping birds came from the balcony. An oblique, northwestern exposure brightened the living room with early afternoon light. On clear glass bookshelves in a breakfront propped for exhibit were the classic art covers of three oversize tabletop books, *Michelangelo, Rafael, Leonardo.* Her cassette stereo played a piano concerto softly in the background. Prominently on one wall hung a framed print of the islander Impressionist Francisco Oller's "The Student," whose original, I remembered reading at the Smith Wesson library, hangs in the Louvre. She asked if I minded sitting on the balcony, where an even taller condo provided a nice shade and the temperature was pleasant.

Along the balcony's wall were arranged four bird cages on stands: two cockatiels chattered beside a pair of finches next to two king-fisher birds next to two lovebirds. On a small green marble-top coffee table, Susana had set two cloth napkins and two wine goblets. She invited me to sit in one of two rattan chairs with a view of San Juan harbor, then excused herself to return with a bottle of chilled white wine, already uncorked, and a dish of Gruyere, green grapes and wheat crackers, which she positioned on the coffee table. She poured me some wine, and excused herself again to put on her gown.

So far this assignment to pick up Rosy's friend was painless. Enjoying the wine and the view of distant San Juan Harbor, I lost track of time so she seemed to simply materialize looking radiant in her bare-shouldered, sky-blue bridesmaid gown. She poured herself wine and sat in the other chair. Rosy had given her such wonderful advanced publicity of me that she had been looking forward to the pleasure of just meeting me. "*A la verdad*...Actually, you sounded like the more interesting driver of *any* driver she offered. Chin-chin."

"*Cuántos*...How many did she offer?"

Susan served me some pieces of cheese with a cluster of grapes. "You were the only one." The birds chirped loudly. "Sometimes they squabble when they think I'm in danger."

Actually, Yvette had flashed across my mind. The contrast was so extreme. In my mind vI was walking up the four flights of dingy stairs to Yvette's modest, clean apartment. Her dresses always engraved her sensual form in my brain. Dance music constantly played on the stereo. Yvette was everything Mami Lalia had turned me away from, the woman always receding behind my train of Current Events. Susana, on the other hand, seemed like the perfect match for a political rising star, she being the one combination beyond the science of American doll makers blond *and* Latin. I had always hated the predictability of my being expected to look for blond. My first instinct was to louse up this match-up before it got anywhere.

Susana apologized for Rosy's effort at matchmaking. "Her nature seems to abhor a vacuum. I honestly just needed a ride. What I got was a full dossier on your work in New York."

"In my short career as driver, I've never been treated so well."

"I don't have much experience as a passenger. I should be more careful."

"Do those books mean that you studied art?"

"I first thought I wanted to study art history but settled on literature. Studying our language was the patriotic thing to do at the time. Latin American literature was emerging even though we were still into Spaniards of the Generation of '98. Some exiled writers of the Spanish Civil War were our professors. Pedro Salinas. Juan Ramón Jiménez."

The loud braying intercom sounded. The birds went crazy. Susana looked away as if she heard nothing. Another buzz. She told me to disregard it and poured more wine into my glass. Two more buzzes but nobody heard them. "Now, Counselor, tell me about your interest in literature. Rosy said you were a poet in college."

I explained that the law was not my first choice, that I had majored in English, and thought I wanted to be a writer, but...I was interrupted by a different buzzing, this time at the apartment door. The birds acted up again, fluttering up and down their cages. Susana wore a frozen look, expressing nothing in particular, just smiling.

"Maybe you should answer."

Whoever was at the door knocked, almost a pounding. Susana, face still frozen in smile, went to answer. I remained seated, content to just hear. Susana greeted. An inaudible conversation ensued. Then metal-tap-heeled footsteps clomped on the ceramic tile floor.

"Eddie, excuse me, I want you to meet someone."

In the living room beside Susana a thinly mustached, tawny police officer in a light blue uniform, his closely cropped hair wet with sweat and pressed against his forehead from wearing the cap he bore in the crook of his arm. He tapped a riding whip against one palm, explaining his blown-out pants and high black boots. On one collar lapel of his short-sleeved shirt a Puerto Rican flag pin and on the other lapel a U.S. flag pin. About six inches taller, he confronted the less-empowered me in a foppy white tux, his stare a criminal investigation.

Susana introduced the *Licenciado* Eduardo Loperena "*el hermano...* my friend Rosy's brother from New York, who has volunteered to drive me to his sister's wedding. My car, you know, is being repaired." Before me stood Wáshington Matamoros.

Wáshington's grip on my hand was firm, prolonged. His black eyes challenged me to a duel. "*Cuáles...*What are your intentions with Susana?"

After freeing my hand, I asked Susana in English "What did he say?"

Wáshington looked to Susana, "*Qué...*What, is this, one of those stupid *newyoricans* who can't speak Spanish?"

Susana, smile intact, shrugged her shoulders.

Wáshington paced, tapping the horse whip against his thigh, Il Duce at the Ethiopian campaigns. The cockatiel let loose a whistle a hardhat might aim at a woman passing a construction site, but not for one second did Wáshington's eyes veer from mine.

The ugly downstairs intercom buzzer sounded and Susana backed up, not taking her eyes off my standoff with Wáshington, pressing the intercom button with her thumb. "*Diga.*"

"*Disculpe...*Excuse me, it's Ramón. I'm sorry to bother you but the officer, I tried to explain, it's about the horse."

Wáshington went over to the intercom. "*Ramón...*Ramón, I already made it perfectly clear to you that I have that horse trained, and tied to that tree he won't disturb anybody. He will not cross the yellow lines into the other parking spots. I guarantee you that."

"I know, officer Matamoros. I don't doubt that, but I'm only the porter, you see, and, well, the people have come to me to complain that your horse is trained to stay within the yellow lines but he's not trained to keep the space clean."

"Thank you, Ramón. I'm very sorry," Susana broke in, glaring at Wáshington, "The horse has dirtied the parking lot again. So please take care of that right now because I will not be embarrassed before my neighbors." Susana opened the door.

The humbled King in check, before departing Wáshington gave me a silent-movie look of disdain. I smiled stupidly and said in English, "My pleasure."

Susana leaned against the closed door and sighed heavily. Slowly her smile came back. "*Bueno...*Well, where were we?" She covered her mouth to mute an urge to burst out in laughter, then whispered, "That was brilliant."

I looked at my watch. Wáshington had consumed what extra time we had.

Chapter 22

On the drive to the church Susana confirmed the accuracy of her biography according to Rosy only in more circumspect language, a marriage and divorce, getting used to being a working woman, and "*una fase…*a crazy phase in which I had to find myself, when I made some choices that I now regret." I gathered she referred to Wáshington. She inhaled deeply, "My divorce left me confused. I didn't want to be a haughty class-conscious porcelain doll anymore, so now I have this uncouth man around my neck. I'm sorry you had to go through that scene."

We were on Rt. 2, passing now abandoned, dilapidated old-money homes waiting to be sold so the profit from the land could be split up by descendants and then sold to a condo developer. "Secretly I've envied the life of our people in the United States. For a woman…" She paused as we passed a mall with neon signs announcing Sears and a fast-food pantheon—Pizza Hut, Kentucky Fried Chicken, Burger King. "You see, we have these things, and life is modern here too, but our island men don't change that much. That's why I notice that Puerto Rican men who have lived outside, they're different. But we're not supposed to like that." She seemed unburdened of something she had been wanting to say. What Maritza saw half empty Susana saw half full.

She changed the subject, or only appeared to. "I've been to Los

Angeles and New Orleans and Atlanta. I did spend a couple of weekends in New York with my husband and after my divorce two weeks with a girlfriend, a teacher in Manhattan. She gave me a tour of where some of her students lived. The neighborhoods were horrible, what many of us here think about when we think of Puerto Ricans in New York. That wouldn't be my New York. And I'm sure it's not yours. In our New York I wanted to stay and live in for a few years. Broadway plays, museums, art galleries."

When we got to our parish church, Our Lady of Guadalupe, Rosy looked lovely in her wedding gown in the afternoon sun at the church entrance but she was crying on the shoulder of Aunt Providencia, who stroked her back. Six other aunts stood around her lending support. Mami Lalia contributed the shade of a parasol. Seeing Susana and me arrive together made her face glow. I asked her why Rosy was in tears.

"*No es...*It's not the end of the world, but it's important to her. The priest had promised that construction on one wall would be finished by today. There's part of a wall, then a huge sheet of plastic. Rosy was going to wait in the church but she came right out because she couldn't stand the sight of it."

Spain's lingering weapon against the Protestant Americanization of Puerto Rico is keeping it stocked in Iberian clerics. The island may be an American territory but its soul was still a Spanish colony. Father Gerónimo, a Spanish priest wearing bifocal sunglasses, introduced himself to me. He has apologized to both families because he did assure both bride and groom that the construction work would be completed. That was what the workers had promised him. Water damage from the last hurricane required repair, then they discovered a foundation problem. Gerónimo himself just got back from New York yesterday only to be as disappointed as Rosy. He left a message on the bridegroom's answering machine.

Everyone was reassuring Rosy that the photographer could avoid the wall, that the ceremony would be beautiful and she would have a great reception. The sight of Susana lifted her spirit and while hugging her friend she smiled smugly at me. I greeted six aunts with a kiss each when we were all approached by a trim short woman with red-dyed hair way longer than one would expect of a woman past fifty, at least on this island, wearing very stylish purple-rimmed glasses. Mami Lalia introduced Doña Lola Beauchamp de Skywalker, George's widowed mother, who asked me to just call her Lola "because she didn't feel like a Doña yet."

I whispered to Susana that, for a reason I couldn't explain just then, to keep Rosy in the church before George arrived. Maybe once inside and emotionally caught up in her ceremony, with Susana holding her hand, Rosy wouldn't get to ask George why he never got the Father's message nor clinically inquire about the morning he hurt his middle finger. Susana convinced Rosy that she should first see George in the church and the circle of women agreed and accompanied her.

The truly contrite priest shared with me his own disappointment. "*Como*...As I left recorded on the groom's answering machine last night, the contractors had sworn the work would be done by yesterday, but you know how things work in this country."

"*Territorio*...Territory, Father," George interjected in his light blue tux with tails, provoking a glare from above the rim of the priest's sunglasses. "I just got your message. So our wedding has to take place in a plastic tent?"

"No, not a tent. One wall, only the rear half is covered with clear plastic. I'm very sorry, son, but I don't believe you'll want to cancel your wedding now, so let us please proceed. We have another wedding scheduled after yours."

The huge plastic curtain covering the rear half of the church's wall to the right as one entered did look shabby but didn't spoil the joyful spirit of the small church packed with friends and family, the Loperenas and Cabezas and Montalvos beside the full wall with stained-glass windows and the Skywalkers, Adornos and Vegas by the half wall with the ugly plastic curtain. All sweltered in the three o'clock heat scarcely relieved by regularly-spaced, noisy, upright fans and breezes from the flutter of women's Spanish fans.

At the rear of the church Rosy came out of a side vestibule, accompanied by Susana and Mami Lalia, who were joined by the ushers and bridesmaids. Bride in white, groom in sky blue, ushers in white and bridesmaids in sky blue. I was slow to catch on: the colors of George's statehood-aspiring New Progressive Party. Anita Blanco Mann will have a field day. Susana being the maid of honor, she took her position at the head of the parade, turning once to smile at me. A pair of children, a boy from one family and a girl from the other, were poised to lead the procession, the girl to strewn rose petals.

Mami Lalia pulled me aside by the arm. "*Esa mujer…*That woman Maritza called just after you left to pick up Susana. She asked you to call her when you can. I didn't want to forget to tell you."

A bald guy in tails behind Mami Lalia introduced himself as George's brother, Samuel Skywalker, also the best man. "*Me llaman…* They call me Sammy. I've seen you in the newspaper. I'm a lawyer myself and a great admirer of your work up North." We shook hands. Taller than George and fairer-complexioned, his baldness was billiard-quality and there was something arresting about his dark eyes. "I should correct myself, I *used* to be a lawyer. I stopped practicing some years ago. I'll enjoy speaking with you later, for now I must ask you to line up with the ushers."

Sammy stood between lined-up bridesmaids and ushers and thanked everyone for attending the rehearsals, requesting that we keep to the tempo of the organ march. He guided Rosy by the hand to the front of the procession and gave a hand signal to the organist above us. To "Here Comes the Bride" we proceeded to the altar where George nervously wiped a handkerchief over his brow, his wrapped middle finger giving the bird to the entire church. Awaiting at the altar, wearing those sunglasses, the Spanish priest—perhaps the greatest obstacle to George's wish for statehood—awaited to consecrate this union.

Chapter 23

For this Fourth of July wedding reception the Bayamón Lion's Club had been turned into a huge patriotic tent, with red, white, and blue ribbons radiating from the central chandelier and covering the walls and a pair of miniature flags—Puerto Rico's and Old Glory—waving atop every flower arrangement on every table. A slightly larger pair of crossed flags also waved behind the five-inch porcelain couple on the three tiered-wedding cake, and as backdrop to the wedding party table elevated on the stage, alone and proud hung a theater-curtain-size Stars and Bars.

The tables filled up as the five musicians of "Nero's Hot Band," as imprinted on the large base drum, played a cha-cha arrangement of "As Time Goes By." George editorialized in his wedding party assignments on the hall stage, putting Sammy at his extreme right, followed by his mother Lola, by himself and Rosy directly in front of the pedestal-elevated cake, with Mami Lalia off-center, Susana and then me farthest to his left at the end of the table.

The newly waxed dance floor was defined by a semicircle of tables that extended back toward the hall's rear, where drinks were served at a bar by Lion men on the left and dinner was served by Lion wives from a table of food on the right. The busy hall transported me to the ceremony honoring Father Stevens at the Sheraton in New York and to wondering why, after our disastrous date, Martiza called me on the day of the wedding.

Lost in thought, I didn't realize that I was being rude to Susana, who on finishing her meal excused herself to greet someone she knew from Jetstream Mortgage. I resented Rosy's assuming that I was going to bring the date she wanted me to bring but I shouldn't have been unpleasant to Susana. Once the tables were cleared for dessert, up to a microphone in front of Nero's band stepped the Head Lion, Ito Flores. Susana returned bearing a tray with our servings of coffee and flan. I got up and pulled back her chair. "*Pasaba...*I was passing the dessert table."

Flores proceeded. "*Para este...*On this so special day, as a tribute to George, his fellow Lions have prepared a program that will make this celebration unforgettable in the hearts of his family, friends and, of course, his lovely new bride Rosy." Lights dimmed to total dark as Flores's amplified voice announced: "Here, direct from the Club Amapola in the Raquet Club Hotel, Afrodita, Poetess of the Caribbean."

Conga drums beat loudly as on the center of the dance floor a spotlight shone on a bleached-blond and shapely dark woman in a skin-tight, sequined, emerald-green body glove, arms dramatically outstretched, her head dramatically back. To the congas' toning down to steady, faint beats, her hand gripping a microphone with a snaking long cord slowly approached her mouth as she lowered her head, shut her eyes. Suddenly the congas erupted again and Afrodita opened her eyes, pointing to a Klieg light to dramatize the first lines of Lorca's "Romance of the Moon Moon."

She recited with a passion that turned her glittery, sequined body into a surreal, green moon that Lorca himself would have probably loved. Her concluding, sweeping hand representing the little boy intensely *mirando* Lorca's moon was rewarded with abundant applause and whistles. She took bows, breathing heavily, then paused, took a breath, composing herself for the next delivery, one of the Cuban José Angel Buesa's puffed-up love rhymers. In her rendition Buesa's dominant, confident male persona became a woman powerful enough to rip in two a man's telephone-directory-thick heart. This poem too elicited the same great wave of applause as her treatment of Lorca.

The lights came up again, and Afrodita apologized that she could only offer an abbreviated version of her nightclub act but wanted to conclude with her own poem, written for George and Rosy. A copy of "*Con Alas*...On the Feathers of Unmeltable Wings" was provided in the folded program at each setting. She turned to face the wedding table and, as if the soul of the poem were pooled in her palm, she extended one upturned hand toward the new Señor and Señora Skywalker, prompting applause. When it subsided, she read: *¡No teman el vuelo juntos/ altos sobre un mundo sin amor!...*

> ON THE FEATHERS OF UNMELTABLE WINGS
> Fear not your flight together
> above a loveless world!
> Fly, fly on magical wings,
> Strong with the feathers
> Of white turtledoves,
> Inseparably bound
> By your unending love.
>
> Fear not the sun of love!
> Nor does your bond betray
> Like the wax on the wings
> Of fallen ancient Greeks.
> The sun of love is mild,
> And eternal holds the glue
> Of true passionate love.

Lorca should have been so fortunate as to receive the standing ovation that Afrodita's poem received. She threw a kiss at Rosy and George standing with the audience that applauded until Afrodita disappeared into a room off somewhere past a door behind the bar.

The hall went dark again. Head Lion Flores announced, "*directo de*...straight from a tour of the flamenco clubs in Spain, Sant-i-ago!"

A taped, loud Spanish guitar was joined by other taped guitars and the recorded voice of a *cante jondo* singer. In sudden spotlight, the rail-thin Santiago cut a profile before the wedding table: in a black flamenco jumpsuit, a white shirt, with one shoe on its toe, the thumb and index finger of a hand that also palmed a castanet clutching the bottom of a gold lamé bolero vest and the hand holding the other castanet tipping a flat flamenco hat. He stood immobile throughout the guitar prologue whose pause was his cue to spiral the elevated hand downward from his hat, clattering castanets as he began to tap his heels, stepping in rhythm, whirling, his stare at the audience radiant—an Italian actor before a *mangia* pair of tits—concluding in the same opening pose, but with one castanet in the air, "Olé." The audience applauded wildly.

Santiago then posed again, assuming another fatal look. This time both hands held out as if to be handcuffed, castanets lightly tapping in the quiet of the hall's anticipation. To more recorded strumming of guitars and singing, he began an explosion of tapping heels, turning and crisscrossing arms, an explosion of dance whose finale was to fall on one knee and from inside his vest pull out a fresh rose extended to Rosy. The audience shouted "Olé" and gave him a standing ovation as he remained in that pose, heaving to catch his breath.

The applause got louder when he got up and walked to the stage, where George reached down to take the rose and give it to his bride. Santiago's proximity allowed me to confirm what I had suspected ever since he first turned to face the wedding party. The spotlights went black again and in the dark he hurried around the applauding tables to the back.

I excused myself with Susana and stepped down from the stage, crossed the dark dance floor as Flores announced the show's grand finale: "The duo Tony and María, to sing a repertory of songs from *West Side Story*." They started their rendition of "Somewhere" as I followed Santiago's path past a door behind the bar to a corridor, down which after the restrooms, light framed a shut door behind which I heard Santiago's voice. I knocked. Sammy opened and only then did I notice that he wore eyeliner. "Ay, Santiago, you have a special guest."

He was in his socks, pants and vest removed, still wearing the white shirt. He didn't immediately recognize me.

"Eduardo Loperena. Without the beard."

"Wow!" He embraced me firmly, giving me a kiss on the cheek. "How are you? Sammy, this guy saved my ass."

"Oh, well, that was important."

"I mean it. I mean it. This guy saved my life."

Santiago was originally Jimmy Crespo, a skinny Bronx kid who began to hang around with some older boys, seasoned car thieves. Jimmy got caught when he broke into his first car and became one of my *pro bonos*. In court I presented his unfortunate biography as melodramatically as I could. His mother was an alcoholic. His father was a junkie who fortuitously overdosed on heroin during the trial. The story moved the woman judge to give him a second chance. He got two years on probation in part because Isela Chase, by-then a reputable leader, agreed to hire him in one of her community service programs, and through her, Jimmy met new friends, learned new ways.

Sammy's pink bald head and outstanding eyes stood behind me in the mirror.

"When did you become Santiago?"

"Sit, here," pulling up a chair "I'll tell you while I take this makeup off." He spread cold cream over his face. "One day I went to Central Park with some friends and there was this free flamenco show. My mother constantly played flamenco records but I had only seen her dancing it. My friends weren't interested, so I told them I'd catch up later and sat in the first row. One of the men dancers kept looking at me. I didn't know I was gay at the time, you know, so I felt funny. Anyway, afterwards I hung around the dressing trailer, I didn't know for what. One second." His face clean, he picked up a pair of jeans folded over the back of a chair and put them on.

Outside, Tony and María were showered with applause for their "Somewhere" and started to sing "María...The most beautiful sound I ever heard..." Sammy said "María" was one of his favorite songs and stepped out. Jimmy removed the white shirt, folded it and placed it in a canvas overnighter. Out of it he took a T-shirt that he pulled over his head, a souvenir of Walt Disney World, an embossed castle with the words "The Magic Kingdom." He rushed into the bathroom and came out with his hair wet. He combed it back.

"Sorry. I gotta run to a show at the Hilton tonight. So when this dancer came out of the green room with the group, he recognized me from up front. He asked me if I liked flamenco. I told him I did, which I realized just then that I really did. Well, one thing led to another, and he gave me lessons. My moms loved the idea. She had always told me that as a teenager in Puerto Rico she studied flamenco with a teacher who studied under the great Carmen Amaya. She said that maybe I caught the flamenco bug because when she was pregnant with me she went to the New York World's Fair about ten times to see Antonio Gades dancing in the Spanish Pavilion. I think it was because she'd get drunk and play Manitas de Plata records every day. She died two years ago, by the way.

"She didn't care if this guy was gay neither. But this guy was my ticket, man. I worked with him and his group about five years. He had many friends with bars that gave us gigs. Then I went to Spain, worked and studied with some gypsies. Then I hooked up with the hot group I'm with right now. I just worked this gig here freelance, but the troupe I work with is appearing at the Hilton all this week. Why don't you come by?"

I explained that I only had one free day before taking off. I had to see a former client.

Jimmy put on his flamenco hat and assumed a flamenco pose, clutching an imaginary vest. "So, what do you think? All I need now are my shoes." He pulled out a pair of sneakers, put them on, tied the laces.

" I'm really happy that everything is going great for you, Jimmy."

He lost his smile as he carefully stored the hat in the overnighter. He told me that Francisco, the dancer at the Central Park show, was dying of AIDS, and that he himself was HIV positive. He didn't feel anything yet but was scared. "I'm taking some medicine but nobody seems to know nothing about it. I don't know what's going to happen. All I know is..." switching to Spanish, "*Jimmy ya no existe, Eddie.*" Assuming a flamenco pose again, snapping fingers over his head, "*¡Soy Santiago, Olé!*" He had to run. He picked up the overnighter, gave me a quick *abrazo* with a kiss on the cheek, and grabbed the door handle just as Sammy opened the door. Santiago gave him a kiss on the cheek, then left. I was about to follow when Sammy extended his arm across the doorframe.

"*¿Cuál es...?* What's the rush?"

"My true love is waiting. Sorry, Sammy."

Tony and María passed me on their way to the green room. Also the Spanish priest still in sunglasses and now obviously drunk. He passed raising a glass in salutation on his way toward the Men's Room. Sammy followed him. I entered the ballroom as Nero's band played Hector Lavoe's salsa hit "*Ohé Oh Oh.*"

On the way to the wedding table I brushed past Susana dancing with some guy. I had just sat in my chair when Rosy came by, holding up the hem of her gown. She had warned me not to leave Susana alone because there were single men around. "I know you just gave my friend a ride and you're not really her date, but Susana is a very attractive woman, so don't take her for granted."

I explained about Santiago. She wasn't impressed.

Susana's dancing partner returned her intact. He assured me that he would have asked for my permission, but I had left her alone for quite a while and it seemed a shame that this lovely woman should be sitting when such good music was playing. I agreed and thanked him for delivering her safely. I explained to Susana that Santiago was a former client. She understood, "*Pero...*But, now you owe me more than just *one* dance."

At that moment the band started a *merengue* and she grabbed my hand and led me to the dance floor. As I wrapped my arm around her waist, she pressed her body to mine and asked in my ear, "Does it bother you that I should take the initiative?" Her smile was the public, cool corona of an inner, intimate glow, the kind that comes with having consumed more than one glass of something alcoholic. I shook my head.

Our dance was smooth, calibrated, as if always having existed in nature. Our rhythmic bodies and entwined fingers became contact points through which we intuitively transmitted the telepathy to gyrate, turn, sway in unison in obeisance to the African Mother God who watches over every step in her temple *merengue*. But in the middle of this spinning pleasure trance I caught, in snippets, a commotion.

Heads were turning to the ballroom entrance back by the bar. George was on his feet on the stage, looking out past the dance floor and the tables. Members of George's family had left their tables. An elegant-looking old man with long white hair and black-rimmed glasses was standing at the ballroom entrance. I caught these glimpses while keeping in step until the *merengue* came to a flourishing end. Susana took the words out of my mouth about her: "You dance wonderfully!"

From the stage I took in the drama transpiring in the back, where three Skywalker men were blocking the passage into the hall of the old man distinctive with his white mane and equally rich white mustache, dressed in a white suit. He stood with the help of a black cane with a silver-bright handle and tip and appeared to pose no more threat than what he resembled, a chicken-frying southern colonel. He was accompanied by a black-haired young man wearing round wire-rim glasses and a beard, a stock Parisian revolutionary. He, like the old man, remained stoic before the commotion about them.

Mami Lalia trailed George to the scene, I guess to make sure he didn't do something stupid. Before they got to there apparently somebody compromised and the old man was being helped to a chair at an empty table in front of the bar. His revolutionary sidekick sat too. George started to address the old man, waving his fat, bandaged finger as if he were conducting a symphony. Rosy went over, and the old man chivalrously stood up with the help of his cane and gave her a kiss on the cheek. She helped him back into the chair. She tried to be as pleasant to the young French intellectual, who gave her a limp hand without a smile, then she practically bent George's arm to get him to leave them alone. George retreated taking glances back at the old man. Rosy held George firmly as the couple stopped at tables to greet and thank the guests, who handed them envelopes.

Mami Lalia returned to the stage, clutching her purse, trembling, because she had a premonition. She asked Susana if she was having a wonderful time, if her son was behaving like a gentleman. Susana smiled. Whether to soothe Mami Lalia's nerves or to give her a real woman-to-woman answer to the inquiry on my measuring up as gentleman, Susana invited her to the Ladies' Room. Confused, undecided, Mami Lalia looked at me but finally left with Susana.

Seeing me alone, Rosy left George greeting guests and came back to the stage. She leaned into my ear. "See that old man at that table by the bar?"

"I felt the tremors when he came in."

"Well, that's George's Great Uncle Mauricio Skywalker Monteagudo. He's a survivor of the failed revolution at Jayuya in 1950. Ironically, his great grandfather was the original American Coronel Joseph Skywalker, who came to fight the Spanish in 1898. Now his descendant is a Puerto Rican nationalist."

"No kidding?"

"He was the black sheep of the Skywalkers, as you can imagine. He *had* to be invited but because he never answered the invitation, everybody was relieved that he wouldn't be coming. That guy with him is George's second cousin, Ernesto, also a fire-breathing *independentista*. Everybody assumed they weren't going to show up at this wedding of a pro-statehood nut like George on the Fourth of July."

"So what's he doing here?"

"Nobody knows. That's why everybody's jittery. The old man is a Yankee hater from way back. I don't think he can stand George. I was surprised he was so nice to me. George's Lion brothers told him that the first thing he said when he walked in was, 'Take down that thieving flag, you ridiculous spick,' like that, in English. Listen to me, I gotta be quick because George is waving me over. Can you talk to Mauricio to try to keep things calm."

"What am *I* supposed to say?"

"I don't know. Introduce yourself. Maybe you can talk to Ernesto. He's maybe heard that you defend the poor in New York. Introduce yourself as a fellow nationalist leftist before something happens."

"*Independentistas* don't all believe that *newyoricans* can be fellow nationalists."

"Oh stop. You know what I mean. You know how to negotiate. George has a Fourth of July ceremony coming up and doesn't expect Mauricio to just sit back and enjoy it, so he wants his uncle to leave, which might start a war with our family's nationalist and commonwealth sympathizers." She started down the stage stairs, then turned around and whispered loudly "Do something. Please."

Ernesto and Mauricio happened to be sitting beside the bar, where I had planned to refresh our drinks. I tried to think of ways to introduce myself but on closer view Uncle Mauricio appeared none too pleased with the way his family had welcomed him, and his nephew Ernesto exhibited the unamused demeanor of a hit man. I picked up a pair of fresh drinks. Susana hadn't returned when I got back to the stage, just as another wave of glass-tapping by the audience forced Rosy and George, now together on the stage and huddled in discussion, to grin theatrically and perform a Broadway kiss.

Susana returned, first helping Mami Lalia to her chair. She related that in the Ladies' Room Mami Lalia told her why she was anxious: her own family's pro-independence and pro-commonwealth divide was kindling for Mauricio Skywalker's incendiary pro-independence position. With everything she had heard about Mauricio, Mami Lalia shuddered at the real possibility that his presence may ignite a melee.

Nero started the rock phase of his repertoire with Richie Valens' version of "La Bamba" and all the teens joined their parents on the dance floor. George had gone off to the side of the dance floor and was talking heatedly to a cluster of fellow Lions. Nero's "La Bamba" segued into Carlos Santana's electric guitar arrangement of Tito Puente's original "*Oye Como Va*." The dancers clapped to the cha-cha rhythm. Meanwhile, accompanied by Sammy Skywalker and Head Lion Flores, the tipsy Spanish priest in sunglasses was brought to Mauricio's table.

Sammy hugged his uncle, shook hands with Ernesto, and introduced the priest, who in those sunglasses completed a weird-looking trio. Behind them, an observing stocky woman with a large handbag hanging from her shoulder was jotting into a notepad. George angrily gestured at her with his arms apparently insisting she go away but she answered something not budging when something Ernesto said set off George again and Sammy had to physically restrain him.

"*¿Cuándo*...When are you leaving for New York?" Susana's question took me by surprise. I had abandoned her to the goings on again.

"*En*...In two days."

"I'm sorry. That was a dumb question. Rosy had already told me."

I didn't have a conversation and said nothing. My guard was still up after Martiza.

"Eddie, do you mind if I tell you what I'm thinking?"

"I don't know. Let me hear it."

"That you don't have the anger that I associate with someone from New York."

"So I'm an 'island man'?"

"No, you're not. Still I feel at home with you. Maybe your best side comes out here."

"Maybe it's not this place at all? Maybe it's just you." *I couldn't believe I said that.*

She was merciful, a pause her only reaction. "Have you ever considered living here?"

"Most of my life, until this place made it plain that I didn't belong anymore."

"You have a good reputation and you'd be respected. Besides, nobody lives in an entire country anyway. All you need is a home. You already have your family here, Lalia and Rosy. People who love you."

Nero went on a break. The guests mingled. My buffering of alcohol was wearing off. Susana had darkened my tropical lightness with the overcast of my real New York life. In a way, I was slumming with Susana as I had done with Yvette before I was forced to see her as real in our real lives. I imagined my bringing Yvette to this wedding.

"What are you thinking?"

Mami Lalia appeared, her anxiety heightened. "*Eddie, creo*...Eddie, I think there's going to be a problem." She pointed with puckered lips toward Sammy and George having a heated discussion with Ernesto, who vehemently shook his head. "The Fourth of July ceremony is scheduled to start now, before the cutting of the cake and the throwing of the garter, and George wants the old man to leave to avoid problems. The priest tried to persuade him sermonizing about the sanctity of a marriage but Mauricio is an atheist and that priest is too drunk to be taken seriously. George was also dumb enough to mention the patriotic celebration, and Mauricio just talked around the priest, daring George to celebrate the Fourth of July in his presence. And my brother, your brilliant uncle Homero, got into an argument with some Skywalker because he feels that old Mauricio should be allowed to stay because independence is always an option. Homero got it in his rum-filled head that if the Skywalkers kick out Mauricio, they were insulting the island's democratic Commonwealth status. Finally, to add to the shame, there's that society reporter, Anita Blanco Mann, taking everything down."

"So what do you want me to do?"

"I don't know. Homero has gotten our family worked up against those pro-statehood people, who are calling the Commonwealth a colony and not the ideal democratic model of autonomy that Homero believes. Oh, I hate this talk. Maybe *you* can convince Mauricio."

"Mami, look at that face." Still being talked to by the drunk priest, who from where I sat looked like a marionette. Mauricio was disregarding him, actually staring in our direction. "If the Marines didn't impress him, I certainly won't."

"George is angry and doesn't care whether Mauricio stays or goes. He just doesn't want anything to stop his Fourth of July celebration. His friends are holding him back from daring Mauricio to interfere, setting up a fight between George and Ernesto. Can't you just talk to the reporter and ask her not to write about this mess?"

"The last thing I want to do is identify myself to Anita Blanco Mann."

Just then, Mauricio positioned his cane and pushed himself erect. George tried to take hold of the cane and Ernesto grabbed him by his bandaged middle finger, causing George to let out a squeal. Nero and his band were just back from a break, and a magnetic cloud of tension soaked up all the noise in the hall as Mauricio walked with his cane in his distinguished elderly cadence across the dance floor to confer with Nero, who nodded.

Mauricio then turned, the entire hall's eyes following his slow steps. He proceeded in our direction, toward the stage. As the band played the first chords and Nero announced that the next number, by special request, would be a *danza*, Mauricio climbed up the three steps to the stage and came up behind Mami Lalia to request the next dance.

Flabbergasted, her eyes leapt at me and Susana, who nudged her to accept his invitation. She gave Mauricio her trembling hand and our family's side applauded wildly. As the couple slowly stepped down from the stage, Nero extended the *danza*'s prologue—during which the *damas* and *caballeros* normally parade ceremonially in a circle, giving bows and curtsies before commencing dance—until the star couple reached the dance floor when, adding surprise to surprise, the *danza* Nero started to play was "*La Borinqueña*," Puerto Rico's national anthem.

Our family burst into applause once again as George's tables remained silent. George, in another corner caucus with brother Lions, pointed to the dance floor and then to his watch. Otherwise, the hall's tension was relieved by the sight of the senior couple who were joined by other couples of their generation, all from our family. The video cameraman recorded Mauricio as he flirted with Lalia to the waltz-like *danza* steps of the schizoid "*La Borinqueña*" whose original lyrics were Lola Rodríguez de Tió's nineteenth-century poem that called patriots to battle, exhorting, in the final lines, to fire phallic cannons at Spain to win "*la libertad, la libertad*" but that under the U.S. were neutered to plug the island's being a great place to tan and surf: "*de mar y sol, de mar y sol.*"

Mami Lalia and Mauricio completed their *danza,* and he negotiated the three steps to the wedding party table to properly return her to the stage. He then proceeded a few chairs over and, to explosive applause from the Loperenas' Commonwealth-supporting tables, surprised Rosy with a kiss on the cheek. That's where Mauricio was standing, behind Rosy and before the Lion's huge American flag when, infuriated by this display of what he must have interpreted as gross nationalism, the playing of the *Borinqueña,* George took the microphone and loudly asked the veterans of Vietnam and of the 65th Infantry in Korea to rise.

Then, on George's cue, Nero played "The Stars and Stripes Forever" and, with batons twirling before the video camera, two rows of teenage Lion daughters, wearing one-piece bathing suits with sequined red, white, and blue broad stripes, marched into the hall as between the rows someone rolled out slowly—so the cameraman captured its splendor—a three-foot-high, rock-solid chocolate and vanilla ice cream sculpture of a bald eagle, to the standing applause of George's family and friends and a few of my family's tables. Anita Blanco Mann scribbled away. Ernesto calmly looked on, his chin resting on his fist. The baton girls then formed a chorus line to sing "It's a Grand Old Flag."

At that point, maybe because the "*Borinqueña*" had awakened an old seventies passion, and feeling inspired by Victor Lazlo in that scene from *Casablanca,* I went down to Uncle Homero's table and started singing "*Qué Bonita Bandera...*What a Beautiful Flag," a Pete Seeger favorite. Drunk Uncle Homero picked up on the idea and, moving his hands in reclined eights, conducted his table to sing in chorus. Ana Liza, whom I hadn't recognized after she changed from her bridesmaid's dress into a white seersucker suit, proudly stood up and sang loudest in her horrible voice. Finally, my Sumo-sized cousin Sweepea yelled out that *estadistas* shouldn't be allowed to take over Rosy's wedding. Entire tables on our family's side then rose to sing as George hollered into the microphone that they sit down and shut up as Nero continued playing and the teen chorus line continued singing "It's a Grand Old Flag."

The cacophony ended with a gun blast that produced a hall-wide scrambling under a table, every one left bare except for the flower centerpieces waving the two little flags. Crouched under Uncle Homero's table, I saw Mauricio standing alone in front of the huge Old Glory, leaning on his cane while holding a smoking pistol in the air. His eyes panned the disheveled hall. In the silence, his booming voice didn't need a microphone. "*Miren*...Look at those flags together on your tables. It's a disgrace. The flag of the country that sent our poor boys to get slaughtered in the front lines in Korea. The flag that sent them to die in Vietnam. The flag that experimented with birth control pills on our women before they let their own take the risk. The flag that keeps nuclear bombs around a defenseless population of two and half million people in three hundred square miles, something they don't dare even in their largest state. The flag that fried Pedro Albizu Campos with radiation in his jail cell because he possessed the magic tongue that could destroy their plans to swallow up our home, then spit us out." He fell silent, contemplative, shaking his head. "It's shameful, shameful..."

"*TÍO, POR FAVOR*...UNCLE, PLEASE..." George appealed into the microphone from under a table, his plea reverberating in the hushed hall. Patrol car alarms surrounded the building. Mauricio snickered and looked at the pistol. "This? This just has blanks." He tossed it onto the dance floor where it slid straight to the table under which Anita Blanco Mann, writing feverishly into her notepad, wiggled to avoid it, letting out a yelp.

Five carloads of SWAT-armored police officers in bullet-proof vests and armed with pump shotguns burst into the hall of unoccupied tables as guests started to get up from under them. Officers tried to understand everybody's talking at once and pointing fingers at either the gun on the floor or the old man. Meanwhile old Mauricio had stepped down from the stage. Disregarded as appearing to pose no threat to the police unable to decipher the collective chatter, he was able to reach the frozen ice cream bald eagle, and lifting his black cane, took a swipe that sent its rock solid vanilla bald head straight to George by Nero's microphone, who looked up just in time to spot it in flight and lay a perfect bunt with his middle finger.

George groaned with pain on one knee, prompting Rosy to run and give comfort while Mauricio, whose swing at the eagle came at the price of all his wind, teetered then lay collapsed. Ernesto was trying to revive him when Head Lion Flores insisted that the policemen remove them both as Rosy yelled at the video man to stop filming the riot squad and the collapsed old man. Mami Lalia stepped in and requested that Flores settle legal matters outside so the reception could continue.

Ernesto helped Mauricio out to the lobby, both flanked by Flores and the police sergeant, whose squad of officers followed. The wedding guests occupied their table once again. The decapitated eagle was sent back to the kitchen. Nero played a soothing "Some Enchanted Evening." At the mic Sammy apologized for the interruption and urged the hall to return to celebrating the joy of that day. The eagle started returning reduced to dessert portions alongside rows of toasting flutes. Sammy invited everyone to pick up a glass of champagne and a portion of the patriotic ice cream, which now seemed like taking communion. Nero started playing "*Solamente Una Vez*" when Flores requested that all raise their champagne glasses for a *brindis* to the newlyweds.

George and Rosy kissed and the room applauded. "*Ahora*...Now..." Sammy shouted into the microphone, "Let's get back to the real business of why we are here, to dance and have fun!" Nero played Hector Lavoe's up-tempo hit "*Panameña*" and the room came back to life. Susana and I were stepping down from the stage to dance when Rosy called us over to pose with her and George beside the wedding cake. But George wanted no part of that picture. His raised voice accused me of having instigated the ugly scene by building up that chorus of "¡*Qué Bonita Bandera!*", gesturing wildly with his bandaged finger, Rosy following it with her eyes as if ready to catch it in flight. George demanded that I leave the wedding that second, an order punctuated with a downward stab of his bandaged finger into the top tier of the cake before the video camera, an entire laughing hall, and the intense scribbling of Anita Blanco Mann.

Rosy was cleaning off his hand when Mami Lalia came up and requested a clarification on George's demand. Ana Liza and my cousin Sweepea accompanied her. To defuse the situation, they were asked by Mami Lalia to please return to their tables. Of the three, of course, none could be more formidable than the new mother-in-law, who requested to speak to both George and her son off to the side. We complied.

She first addressed George. Where did he procure the coco-nut-sized testicles to believe that he could dismiss her son from his sister's wedding? She thought it advisable that we begin this union of families harmoniously. Before George could answer, I stepped forward and explained that I did owe him an apology. I had started the chorus of singing not realizing it would stir such passions, "*Ya sabes, George...*You know, George, we newyoricans, never 'get' the island mind."

George respected Mami Lalia's request that he not answer as she gave me a look of being able to do quite well without my sarcasm. I then asked her if George and I could have a word alone. Her look was not approving, so to convince her I extended an honest apology to George for not respecting that this was his wedding to have as he saw fit. I extended my hand, which she begged George to take so the party may proceed. That done, she left us alone.

"Your friend Gilbert called. He told me what happened."

"About the car door?"

"About your bachelor-party date with Dina."

At my suggestion George personally intervened with the Lions and the police so that Mauricio could just go home. After that, the cake was finally cut, and Susana didn't catch the bouquet, and the garter didn't float anywhere near me. Susana suggested that we pass up the last hour of the reception. Mami Lalia and Rosy were not disappointed. In fact, they seemed to contain ecstasy. I kissed Rosy and wished her and George a fabulous honeymoon. On our way out Anita Blanco Mann pestered me for a brief statement, which I was in no mood to give.

Out in the parking lot Susana took a deep breath. "*¡Qué...*What a divine evening!" Inside, Nero's band was starting a *plena*.

"*Guelcome to de land of de pinga colada*," I quipped as I pulled out.

The tipsy Susana wreathed my neck with her perfume-scented arms. "*Eres...*You're crazy. You drive me crazy."

On the drive back to Susana's place, as the drinks wore off, I asked myself if her amorous excitement wasn't just a cultural vacation from "island men." Will she, like Maritza, come to her senses tomorrow, so despite my being a swell guy and a celebrity lawyer, she couldn't bring herself to be so crass as to shock her friends with the novelty of having taken for a mate a Rican from New York?

"*Dime...*Tell me more about yourself. Tell me about your life in New York."

"*¿Tenemos que...*Do we have to talk about that?"

"I'm sorry. You're leaving suddenly. As I told you at the reception, I can't imagine you in any picture we might have of Puerto Ricans in New York."

"Over there I'm a hotshot lawyer and here I'm a nobody Loperena, that's it. But to be frank, I am exactly what islanders think of when they say 'Nueva York' only I was lucky." *Not like Carlos.*

"So how did you turn out this way, so untypical?"

I paused.

"We don't have to talk about this. I just wanted to know more about you."

"My eighth-grade teacher recommended me for a minority scholarship to an exclusive boarding school and that led to my growing up away from that typical New York. I guess if I don't appear to be from there it's because I'm not really from anywhere."

"I see you belonging here. I see you as confident, even arrogant—I mean in a good way, in a way I like."

"When my parents took me from here, all I wanted was to come back. After I grew up and studied, I realized that my longing was not just to return geographically. Our people around me were acquiring a new identity, what I saw as our anger at being American minority nothing. When we aren't venting that anger, we're covering it up by boasting of being proud of being Puerto Rican, which was becoming more meaningless every day. We have to be 'proud' because we can't let *americanos* think they're so right and smug about themselves. I couldn't identify with that identity of not-being something, and never forgot when we were something with a clearer idea of what that was. And then our sixties consciousness of being social victims created an illusion of innocence, of our condition's not being to any extent our responsibility, of being childlike and not as complicated and flawed human adults to be measured against and compete with all other pathetic humans. I wanted to feel free to say, look, we're equal not because we're as good as they are. We're equal because we're as full of shit as they are."

Susana was at a loss for words.

I was disgusted with myself for allowing her to coax out of The Conversation.

"Now tell me about you, your parents." I needed to change the subject.

"My father mentally deteriorated shortly after my divorce. We found out he had Alzeimer's. He died just after I moved into my condo. My mother had died of breast cancer a year after I married. I was their only child."

"I'm sorry I made you bring up those sad things."

"Well, I was nosey about you, so..."

In the only available guest slot of the Caribbean Towers parking lot was a pile of horse manure.

"Oh God, how long must I bear this cross?" She looked around. "I'm certain he's patrolling... Just drop me off and go. I don't want you to pay for my mistakes." She pressed my hand under the dashboard. "I don't want to have to end it here."

She unlocked the door. I heard myself asking her to wait. She paused, and I just looked at her and she smiled, waiting for whatever I was supposed to say. I didn't know myself. "Tomorrow I have to see an ex-client out on the island. I know you have to work..." She would take a vacation day. To avoid "this, with Wáshington" she would meet me by the entrance of the Pueblo supermarket farther up the avenue.

Visiting the cooler mountains was the right move for that day, which by nine was sweltering with July humidity. Susana waited dressed in pink culottes, a pink and white cotton blouse and white sandals. Her hair was tightly sculpted into a thick braid, the sides held down behind her ears by gold-colored little butterfly hairpins that reflected the morning sun. Her slim body was not as sultry as Yvette's, but she was Susana. She hurriedly stepped into the car, and we started our trip, avoiding the highway with the threat of patrol cars by taking the older routes that were long and snaky, up and down rolling hills.

More scenic too, for stretches covered by overhanging branches of flaming Flamboyant trees that formed a glowing tunnel of blood-orange blossoms. It was also a route of abundant flavors. At a roadside shack we stopped for tamarind beverage. We stopped to pick up little yellow mangoes that were going to waste off the side of the road. At a place with a pig roasting over hot coals in front, we stopped for a snack of roast-pork bits with boiled green bananas. Between those pleasures, I told her about William Guzmán.

Chapter 24

Williams' story is really about his loyalty to his older brother Timoteo, whose problems began when he couldn't afford full-time study to avoid the draft. Under that threat, his part-time history and political science course at City College stoked his anger to question "the System" that used the poor as cannon fodder in Vietnam to perpetuate capitalism. Third World solidarity led to his identifying with the victims of Nixon's carpet bombings and fueled an increasing resentment of the American possession of Puerto Rico. Going to war to enrich his oppressors, wearing the oppressor's uniform, pledging allegiance to his oppressor's flag became inconceivable.

Arturo reminded him that he was receiving financial aid from his so-called oppressor. That's why military service was also his duty. "*Mi padre*...My father," Arturo lectured, "was a proud veteran who lost a tip of his frostbitten right pinky in Korea." To which Timoteo countered that Arturo's generation was a colonized herd in an island that went from kissing the hand of Mother Spain to kissing the ass of Uncle Sam.

For Timoteo, Vietnam's National Liberation Front and Puerto Rico's independence movement were but theaters of a single war, trying to achieve Fidel's breaking of the yoke of colonialism that he felt squeezed his neck as he sat on the stoop on 113th Street, or watched TV, or walked through Manhattan's rich East Side neighborhoods. Imperialist supremacy polluted the air he breathed since the very second he was conceived, and he felt the pain of the black Pedro Albizu Campos, who though a graduate of Harvard Law School was probably pushed aside by a drunk gringo sailor, in whose blond eyes the short Albizu was doubtless a little well-dressed nigger.

Timoteo grew a beard like Fidel's and Che Guevara's. He read and reread the poetry of Francisco "Pachín" Marin, who in the 19th century died to free Cuba so that it may save Puerto Rico because those two islands historically struggled against Spain as two parts of a whole. When his number in the draft lottery was called up, he disappeared.

The F.B.I. came to Arturo's door several times. They tried to find him through their offices in Puerto Rico. Months after his disappearance, one day the pastor at Arturo's Pentecostal church delivered an envelope that some mysterious person had left for him. The letter informed Arturo that Timoteo was safe and involved in serious work about which he should know nothing. The war ended the following year but Timoteo was still a wanted felon and poor Arturo was living with the consequences of that decision to escape the draft.

Explosions at Army and Marine recruitment centers were reported to be the work of a local Puerto Rican Independence organization and brought the F.B.I. to his door again because there was reason to believe that Timoteo was involved. Within weeks, "Timmy the Terrorist," as the N.Y. *Post* dubbed him, was making media threats: so long as Washington didn't move to give Puerto Rico self-determination, his organization The Pedro Albizu Campos Liberation Front declared war in the name of the oppressed around the world. The F.B.I. sent the press a background history on the Front, a young group inspired by predecessors who in the '50s shot up Congress.

"Timmy," with his beard and beret, briefly became a radical-chic hero. Arturo grieved that his son's anger toward this country had bent his son so unrecognizably out of shape. He prayed relentlessly for his boy's rehabilitation before he killed anybody or himself. He talked to his other son William, now a high school Spanish teacher and part-time graduate student, to please take heed from this lesson, to concentrate on his career, fuck around with as many women as he wanted, just not get caught up in this political violence. But unknown to Arturo, from almost the start his younger son had been in touch with his brother through their church, whose independence-committed ministers provided cover.

William was a key member of the Front and sworn to its goals. When the media finally tired of the Front and abided by Washington's request to downplay its cause, William was the one who urged on more serious actions, proposing the planting of a bomb in the Stock Market during trading hours or, in the tradition of Albizu's followers, to attack the Congress itself. The other movement members were not yet ready for such murderous acts, but William argued that the media would continue to deny newsworthiness to their cause until their retaliations were commensurate with how grievous they themselves saw the injustice they suffered.

That argument swayed the Front's majority to escalate, and its members agreed on bombing Fraunces Tavern, a landmark in the Wall Street area, where the founders of the United States raised their steins to the new Constitution of freedom for themselves at the expense of enslaved others and were already drawing blueprints for westward Euro-supremacist conquests. Their descendants, enriched by that history, were no innocents in this war, according to William. This vision kindled a renewed fire in Timmy, who volunteered to plant the bomb and prevent William's getting more deeply involved in the actual violence.

The bomb killed two people, wounding numerous others and, of course, could not be edited out of the day's important news. Timmy sent another communique on behalf of the Front taking credit for the act and blaming "the mainstream media for cooperating with Washington in downplaying and giving no exposure to their just cause: in Puerto Rico the United States continued committing the crime of colonialism against its international ban by the United Nations." Arturo was heartbroken, destroyed.

The following morning *The New York Post* published a profile of the "Communist criminal" Timoteo, whom Arturo Guzmán could not recognize as his son. William tried to console him, tried to persuade him to see Timmy's side, even though now that innocent people had died William himself was remorseful, having learned that between revolutionary talk and real revolutionary acts only one is just romance.

Timmy too was rocked by the grievous step he had taken as revolutionary but also realized that William was right in arguing that being taken seriously would only come about from becoming a serious threat. But the gravity of the experience also made Timmy more determined to discourage the involvement of his little brother, who henceforth was kept in the dark about plans to plant another bomb, ironically the one that would strike William.

Timmy had just finished building it in the abandoned building on Delancy Street facing the Williamsburg Bridge where he was hiding out. William entered the building and announced that he was coming up the stairs. Timmy hurriedly hid the bomb, disarmed he thought, under a pile of broken sheet rock on the floor under a window. Timmy opened the apartment door to let in William, who had come to tell him how their old man was feeling over the last bombing and express his own second thoughts about planting more bombs. To get William out of the building, Timmy agreed to discuss the matter in a coffee shop. The October day was chilly, so Timmy went to the apartment across the hall, where he actually lived, to get his jacket, leaving William alone in the room where the bomb was hidden. William, concerned that police might have trailed him, looked downstairs out the window of two without a pile of sheet rock before it. The bomb simply went off, catapulting him out and down to the top of a convertible, where he lay sprawled unconscious, his back ripped open on impact, his left leg broken from the blast.

Timmy ran, not sure if his brother was alive or dead. He almost made it to the subway several blocks away when his beard and desperate run provoked a pair of cops in a squad car to suspect his possible connection to the call they had just received about an explosion a block away. They chased him through streets and back alleys until, for some reason imagining an escape if he crossed the street, he was abruptly stopped by the grill of a passing car. Both he and William were taken to the same hospital. Williams' leg was set and eventually healed but was to remain partly paralyzed. The car that hit Timmy battered the right side of his face, fractured his right arm, and severed a thumb. I had recently opened my Bronx office and it was through Winston's left-wing connections that I was called to represent William alongside our comrade lawyer William Kunstler, who represented Timmy.

While in the custody of federal authorities, incredibly, he escaped. One can only still speculate that through some hospital maintenance connection that he used a literal "window of opportunity" at a certain time of day. Despite the intense security around his private room's door, with the right side of his face and his thumbless right hand bandaged, his right arm in a cast, he jumped out his sixth-floor room's window to land surely in great pain on some pre-arranged soft target, from where he was transported out of sight to this day. In time, with the help of an informant, the F.B.I convicted two Pentecostal ministers and four church members, who received sentences that ranged from ten to twenty five years to life. They never caught Timmy again.

Made fools of, the Feds were determined to charge his younger brother William even though according to Timmy's sworn statement William didn't know that he was interrupting the day's plan involving a bomb. He had showed up at the building to get Timmy to stop. So I was able to defend William as someone trying to end the violence and who was being railroaded by the government's vindictive and face-saving ethnic bias. When the jury returned its verdict, William walked, although limping from his fall, and I had defended the honor of an entire maligned Community.

After much physical therapy, William, dragged his bad leg to Puerto Rico to help out his father Arturo, who had inherited his brother's gamecock business. He settled into the land whose independence he felt worth fighting for after only spending two summers with his aunt when he was a child. He married once and fathered one child, divorced, then married again. Why he needed me now I was about to find out.

Chapter 25

"*William el Cojo* (William the Gimp)," as he was known in the town of Coamo, greeted us from the porch of his house on the leveled top of a hill. Paunchier than when I last saw him, his once black curly hair was salt and pepper and he now wore a mustache. "*¡Qué felicidad...!* What a pleasure to see you, my friend!" I introduced Susana. William introduced his wife Chichi. She was plump and busty and a soft golden tan brown all over with bright brown eyes and dirty blond hair. Old Arturo, taking a nap, would join us later.

Chichi seated us on the porch of their surprisingly large concrete house, the kind that *jíbaros* who once lived in wooden *bohíos* now enjoyed, the transformation my father never got to see. On a tray on a patio table was a large dish of hard salami slices on Ritz crackers. Chichi offered us beers then excused herself to get them.

From Williams's porch one could see only his own sloping property and the driveway descending down to the road beyond the ivy-covered fence that surrounded the house. There was a child's tricycle on the side of the driveway. "*¿Otro?*..Another one?"

"Oh yes, three years ago. Another little boy, Marco. He's at his godmother's being spoiled."

"How's Gerardo?"

"Grown up, being a pain in the ass. He's fifteen now, big man

225

with the ladies. He and Timmy's kid are staying in Santurce this week with Chichi's sister."

"Timmy had a kid?"

"Don't you remember? He had knocked up a minister's daughter. He's never seen his kid. He's thirteen. His name's Carlos. He's thirteen." The minister's daughter was flown to Puerto Rico when William's trial began, and I didn't hear again about what happened to her.

"So, Eddie, how did you celebrate the independence of your country? Did you have a patriotic cook-out?"

"My sister got married."

He chuckled, addressed Susana: "I owe this man so much."

Chichi returned with a tray bearing the beers in frosted mugs but still had work in the kitchen. William offered us the salami on crackers. "Susana, would you like to see my roosters? I myself had a lot to learn about this business, so I think you might be surprised."

Beers in hand we followed him behind the house to a large open-air shed lined with stacked cages of roosters plucked naked around their plump legs, giving them the appearance of bonzai-sized, sumo wrestlers. Their crests had been cropped and their regal tail plumage removed. Repeatedly, the crowing of one rooster was answered by others in a defiant chorus.

On the ground one blue-black, his crest and lower plumage intact, walked around chained to a pole. "This one doesn't fight." He pulled on the chain dragging the fluttering, protesting rooster toward him. Picked him up, grabbed a foot to exhibit. "See, he grows incredibly long and hard spurs. Prime stuff. These are cut off, polished and made needle sharp. If perfect, with no flaws, no cracks, they bring a good price."

We stopped before a large circular chicken-wire enclosure on the dirt floor. "Here I train them, like boxers. You prod them with a stick to make them run, build their stamina." I remembered Ray Cachola's basement cockfight arena. That night in Manhattan I found the experience fascinating, rebellious. Now those warrior roosters seemed no different than Timoteo and Carlos and even me pacing in our respective lives bred to claw and kill, to be pure anger.

Susana took my arm. "*Nunca*...I've never seen a cockfight."

"*No te..*You wouldn't like it," I whispered.

Back at the house Chichi had set the table for an early dinner. We sat on the porch and William asked us if we wanted another beer but we declined. William seemed to have run out of things to say. I signaled with my eyes to Susana, who caught on. "Let me help Chichi."

William waited. "Let's talk in English so Chichi won't understand. I appreciate so much you're coming to my house, bro."

"Better tell me quick."

"All the old man talks about is dying and never seeing Timmy again."

"What do you want from me?"

"The plan is to smuggle him to a safe house here. Everybody in this town will be told that Arturo was sent to New York for special medical treatment. A wealthy independence sympathizer will rent a sailboat supposedly for fishing. At the last minute, he'll have to back out but will leave the boat to his friends, who'll sail to where Timmy's going to be. Nothing will appear suspicious, a few men going on a fishing trip. If the Coast Guard searches the boat, all they'll find is a lot of fishing gear and a bunch of guys drinking beers. Tim will be wearing a designer bathing suit and jacket and will be carrying a U.S. passport. Timmy and I have really made it hard for *papi* and now he's in a bad way. He's got prostate cancer. He's diabetic. His bones are brittle. He's just going fast, man. And I know that Timmy wants to see Carlos. Y'know, that little kid had the worst luck in life..."

"Why do you need me?"

"Something can go wrong. Then Timmy would be sent to New York and we're going to need you. Would you be available right away?"

"William, I'm closing my practice. I can only promise that if something goes wrong, I'll get somebody good."

William heaved a sigh. "I know you'll try your best."

Susana and Chichi called us to the table set with food. William went to into another room. As Susana and I took our places at the table, William came out of the room assisting Arturo, who looked emaciated. Thick round glasses magnified his eyes that appeared to pop out of his head. His body shifted loosely in baggy cuffed pants. The short-sleeved light blue *guayabera* floated too large over his bird's body. He recognized me, gave me a warm *abrazo*, patting my back. "*Licenciado*...Counselor, how are you?"

William had placed me at one end of the rectangular table and now helped Arturo sit in the chair to my right and sat to his right. I introduced Susana facing him. By island habit, he asked what town she was from, and Susana told him she was born in San Juan. He smiled at me, pointing with his fork at Susana. "Counselor, you're not going to find a treasure like that back in New York."

Chichi served pork chops, red beans and white rice. They were delicious. For dessert she served coffee and a pineapple and coconut flan prepared for our visit. Throughout the dinner, conversation remained light until Arturo, who had not said a word, turned to me, "I see you, Counselor, and so many memories come back..." He started to weep. "I'll die with a broken heart...That country destroyed him...I couldn't talk to him. And that minister. Every night I pray for those innocent people my son killed and hurt." William helped him up and back into the bedroom. When he returned, we thanked him and Chichi for the dinner, explaining that we had to leave because I was flying to Miami in the morning. They saw us to Rosy's Mazda. William knew the avenues to reach me.

On the drive back to San Juan Susana asked if anything was wrong.

"*Pensaba en*...I was thinking over what I had discussed with William, which I can't talk about. I hope you can understand?"

She nodded.

"But I'm back now."

"You're back but leaving tomorrow. We only really know each other for two days. It feels like months, and the thought of your taking off is really getting stupidly hard." She took a strong, deep breath.

I couldn't feel free to let myself feel the same way.

Susana broke a long silence with a confession that she was not from the *campo* and Williams' world was strange to her. Simple women like Chichi she knew in passing as domestic help, as store clerks. Chichi told her of having been in San Juan just a couple of times. She described something that happened on the bus. Susana hadn't ridden a bus since she was a student.

"Well, Williams's world, as you call it, that's where my story began."

The sun was setting when we arrived at the Caribbean Towers. I wondered if the floating balloons of Susana's fantasy had all popped on the drive back. *Just as mine inevitably did with Yvette.* I pulled up to her condo's entrance. She asked me to park and come upstairs.

"What about Wáshington?"

"*No me importa....*I don't care. He might be out there in an unmarked car. I didn't want to trouble you with this situation, but he called this morning before I left. I told him that if he didn't stop pestering me I would call his new wife."

The birds on the balcony welcomed screeching hysterically. Susana covered their cages and asked me to wait, enjoy the glittering lights of distant San Juan harbor. She returned in a silky red night gown, bearing a tray with the unfinished bottle of white wine and two goblets. Her long braid was undone, her lipstick refreshed. She positioned her chair touching mine. We filled our goblets, tapped them, and sipped.

"You're leaving, Counselor, and I just met you yesterday. I know you've probably been with a lot of different women. Men have that advantage, but..." She sipped wine, and just smiled, her green eyes speaking for her. I took her hand. I wanted to believe that she was a life-size Tinker Bell whose pixie dust had given our meeting the magic of flight.

She looked away, out to San Juan harbor. "You must be far away. 'When someone leaves, it is because he has already left.' The Argentine Martínez Estrada wrote that."

I turned her face to me.

She took a deep breath. "It's obvious what I'm saying, isn't it." She put down her glass, leaned forward and stroked her lips against mine. Her silky thigh sidled beside mine, rubbing warm and frictionless.

We kissed, her mermaid hand unbuttoning my shirt, undulating over the coral reef of my ribs. Our weightless passage to her bedroom, our disrobing, our exploration of each other's body happened in slow motion, underwater.

In the morning she insisted on taking me to the airport forgetting that she didn't have a car. Rosy was not going to need her car while on her honeymoon, so I told her to use it and return it later. I returned to the house to pick up my things and say goodbye to Mami Lalia, who didn't seem to mind a bit that I hadn't returned last night. As I was putting my suitcase in the trunk, Mami Lalia whispered to me, "*Esa mujer...*That Maritza woman called again last night. I told her that you were leaving for Miami. She wants you to call her in New York."

At the airport Susana talked of parking to be with me however briefly before my flight, but I convinced her that it would be a futile inconvenience, her having to park and walk to the terminal, and arrive at work even later. I also needed to concentrate on carrying out what Sánchez O'Neil had scheduled for me at Miami and L.A. against my desire to just stay with her, which I also couldn't do, ironically because I had to protect myself from being exposed as a towering stereotype of a "street" *newyorican.*

I promised to call once I could, a rhetorical escape hatch, but the moment she pulled out my departure proved harder than I imagined. As if lifting a concrete block, I took out a calling card to get my messages. I had eight, all the same, "Socrates?" I boarded the plane annoyed that Timmy had knocked up that minister's daughter to father this luckless kid and that of all possible names his mother had christened him Carlos.

The takeoff was the wrenching I'd felt every time I returned to New York when I was a kid only worse. From my aisle seat I watched the island recede in the vast ocean until it disappeared. *Maritza wants me to call her in New York.* Would Susana too start an inner weighing of social pros and cons. Last night did she express a rebellion long harbored against "island men" and that *criollo* plane of Being on which she was expected to marry, raise children and live the island's idea of normal? If her parents were both alive and their feelings still mattered, would she be willing to displease them and marry someone with a nondescript lineage? Or was I simply back at Square One, deluded in infatuation, my leitmotiv since my heart was truly first broken by Dixie Culpepper?

Chapter 26

Dixie

In my senior year at Excalibur I was a full-fledged member of the artsy crowd, and Teddy Katsavos and I volunteered to serve as student hosts to welcome that year's incoming students, specifically the females. We took aim at two transfer students. A girl named Roberta stood out with a bra-size that bewitched Teddy instantly. I liked Dixie's long red hair. She introduced herself as being from Branford, Connecticut. She was sassy, blue eyes flashing as she boasted of having been expelled from two previous private schools for reasons that she didn't specify, finding the whole thing funny. We had just met and she said that she thought I was cool, and I also thought she was really cool, expressing her obvious disdain at the mostly square, non-artsy new students.

Teddy hit it off with Roberta, so we four planned to take the school weekend shuttle bus into Boston the next Saturday and see a movie. That agreement was made on a Wednesday, and the following day Teddy asked me where we should take the girls to eat after the movie. He suggested a Chinese restaurant. I hadn't thought about that. I could afford no more than the two movie tickets and something like a couple slices of pizza. Mami Lalia didn't give me much because my scholarship also paid for food, so I didn't have much spending money. I agonized over the dilemma until I finally told Teddy to take out Roberta by himself, lying that I really wasn't that much into Dixie.

Saturday morning I was crossing the grassy quadrangle to my dorm room from the cafeteria and bumped into Dixie, a late riser on her way to breakfast. She was wearing jeans and a black bomber jacket with a bright silver jet fighter over the front and a map of Vietnam on the back. It was really neat-looking and I asked her how she got it. "My father has all kinds of military friends." Dixie's father was a retired Navy Admiral and worked with a company that built submarines in Connecticut. "So we'll see each other later, right?"

I thought I'd have the courage to back out of our date but now the words remained lodged in my throat. I just stood there looking at her, having a meltdown.

"What is it?"

"I don't think I can take you out today."

She looked heartbroken. "Why? Did I say or do something to turn you off?"

"You're perfect. But I only have money for our movie tickets and Teddy wants us to go to a Chinese restaurant to impress you girls. I don't get much spending money from home." Imagining that admission would kill everything between us, I was about to say "See, ya. I'm sorry" and walk off.

"That's it? We can't be together because you don't have money? Don't be silly, baby." She grabbed my arm and, cuddling up to my body, warming me in the autumn wind, "I have enough or we can go Dutch. I want to be with you, so don't do that to me again."

My time with Dixie was the most glorious experience of my young life. She could talk about every book the artsy group assigned to ourselves. A folk singer and guitar player, Dixie could play and sing every song recorded by Joan Baez, who Dixie pointed out to me, was half-Mexican. Dixie was also politically "progressive"—the scintillating password that made one a true member of the under-ground crowd. Her eyes, like a *latina*'s, transmitted messages directly and at full blast. And she was blessed with a *latina*'s butt. The butt, she proudly claimed, came from her Italo-American mother. The red hair and eyes were her father's WASP-Northern Irish extraction.

September wasn't yet over when Dixie and I were walking around as if we were planning to be together forever. Dixie and I never went sexually "all the way," but she became my first sexual fantasy and muse, to whom I dedicated my first poems, like the one in which I described myself as "a dark planet Earth/ moon-bathed in your love," and to which she responded with a long letter like pages of a diary, revealing that she was convinced that "for the remainder of my life I would never feel the intense, encompassing caress that you give me in the form of your passion, and for this I send you my 360-degree rainbow of love, day and night." Armored by Dixie's love, I was impervious to what social snobbiness could gnaw at me at Excalibur,

After Christmas break we returned to be together as we had left off and made plans for the Spring Senior Day Outing, for the prom, and foreseen graduation parties. We even talked of trying to attend the same colleges as if I knew of getting a scholarship to make such plans. Our love seemed so durable that when Dixie's parents visited for the week preceding Easter Break, I figured the time had come for them to meet the intelligent young man with whom their daughter was going steady. I prepared myself for a weekend invitation to dine with Admiral Culpeper and his wife.

Her family came to Massachusetts on the Monday of that week but with a full social schedule that occupied every day. Evenings they would pick up Dixie to dine with them. On Thursday we happened to cross paths when we left our respective classes and I asked her if we could be together at any time before she would be leaving with her parents that Saturday. "My dad's really conservative, and he easily misinterprets. Can you understand?" Tomorrow night they will all be attending a catered wedding to which, Dixie explained, she couldn't just invite me. She hadn't packed but promised to see me before her parents took her to Connecticut.

I entered my dorm room and my then-roommate Jerry Bloom was at his desk finishing an overdue term paper. He looked up at me and asked who died. I had a bio exam scheduled for the next day but wasn't in the mood to do anything, so I went down to call from the public phone to tell Mami Lalia what train I was taking to the city on Saturday.

She deciphered something wrong from my tone. I couldn't contain my feelings and told her about having a girlfriend named Dixie, but that we had to separate for Easter Break.

"¿Cuando...When can I meet this Dixie?"

"Sus padres..Her parents won't let her come to the Bronx alone." I had meant to say "New York alone." I didn't mean to reveal the situation that clumsily.

Nevertheless, Mami Lalia got the point. "Oh, I see."

As I crossed the man road to the cafeteria for dinner, a dark green Continental passed by. Dixie was in the back seat. I ate dinner with Teddy, who was being picked up the next day. He and Roberta had decided they would be together after Easter, then after graduation, they would have to break up. She would be attending a summer language program in France and he would spend the summer with his parents in Greece before going to either Trinity or Amherst. I still hadn't heard from any colleges.

Back in my dorm, Jerry was still typing at his desk. I needed to study for that Bio exam but, exhausted in my sadness, plopped onto the bed, fell asleep, and had a dream version of a real gathering that took place in Teddy's dorm room. Dixie was talking about her parents to Roberta. I overheard her say that when Italians like her mother first came to New England her father's grandparents disapproved and also referred to their union as an "interracial couple, just like us" pointing to herself and to me. I awoke. Sitting on the side of my bed, I couldn't remember if Dixie actually said those words at the gathering in Teddy's room or if I only heard them in my dream. Somebody knocked on the door to tell me I had a call downstairs in the lobby phone. I thought it was really late but it was only 9:30.

The caller was Dixie. She had just returned from dinner with her parents and wanted to see me. Could I join her at the student snack bar? When I got there, she kissed me, squeezing me with all her might. "I love you. I'm sorry. I miss you."

But holding her didn't feel the same anymore. "Dixie, what do your parents think of interracial couples?"

Dixie remained silent for a long while. "Why is this important to you at this moment? Honey, they're not progressive. I didn't want you to get hurt. All Daddy talked about over dinner was how the minorities wanted to take over the country and how King really was a Commie."

I felt extremely tired again. At that moment I realized why I was so cool to Dixie, as cool as getting kicked out of school. I said something that might have been, "Okay, see you after the break," and got up from the table. Dixie might have sat there crying. I trekked across the campus to my dorm room and thought of calling Mami Lalia, to cry on her shoulder. But intuition told me that I'd get no sympathy from her, only laughter at this *americano* fuss over "color" and "interracial couple." I could hear her tell me, "Just because they're so stupid, you don't have to suffer their stupidity" and "All that matters is what she feels."

Chapter 27

At the Miami airport a short, fair, woman with her blond hair in a ponytail held up a sign that hollered out "LOPERENA." In a white blouse and dark-blue skirt, Gigi Ropanueva looked like a flight attendant. Thirty-something, her black eyebrows confirmed yet again that Cuban women had made Miami the Clairol capital of the world. She was Cubanly familiar, winning, and accelerated.

On the drive to the hotel I was informed of my Miami schedule: dinner that evening with the officers of the Miami Association of Spanish-Speakers of America (MASSA) and the following day a talk at the luncheon-general meeting of Cuban Americans for Democratic Action (CADA). MASSA was an initiative started by CADA, seeking to expand by uniting with every non-Cuban Latin American immigrant group amassing in Miami.

Unfortunately most immigrants were not yet ready to immerse themselves in local politics while the Cuban *exilio* didn't identify with the U.S. Hispanic community, explained Gigi, so except for the few liberal members of the older, Cuban-born generation—like their president and vice-president—the project still consists mainly of U.S-born members of Cuban Americans. "Different from the Republicans, our Democratic constituency has had to remain low key."

"Does that mean that you only meet on paper?"

"We do communicate but don't make a big splash. Our openness to dialogue with Cuba is unpopular. Our office has been broken into."

"In other words, you're not the Cubans we read about in New York."

"No, we're professionals born or raised in this country who want to understand our role as American *latinos*. That's why we look forward to hearing from you, one of Hispanic America's finest examples of leadership. Of course, we as Cubans and Puerto Ricans were already historically connected, 'Two wings of the same bird.'"

Geography, size, and sugar made Cuba a Caribbean focal point of intercourse, trade, and enterprise, a land of fast talkers. Small, insignificant Puerto Rico, after having retched up all its gold remained an ironically-named Rich Port inspiring no investments of any kind, including human effort. Colonial-era ships delivered mail once a month. Natural talents drained away in a society sclerotic with oligarchical privilege, a tradition strengthened by a nineteenth-century influx of Spaniards banished from newly independent countries.

In the nineteenth century *boricuas* fought and died to liberate Cuba as a first step to freeing their own *Borinquen*. That was when poet Lola Rodríguez de Tío, writing from the vantage of a more viable Cuba, immortalized the dually patriotic metaphor "two-wings of the same bird." In a poem that bird flies, but as wings go Puerto Rico is short, gliding, and metaphysical while Cuba is a long, ostentatious flapper, so if that mythical bird flew at all, it would only draw circles in the air, with the Cuban wing taking the credit for the illusion of the bird's going anywhere.

"By the way, Gus never confirmed the topic of your talk."

All I was prepared to expound on was how wonderful Susana writhed in the deepest throes of lovemaking. But when is our discourse anything but The Minority Conversation. "The title of my talk will be 'Hispanics at a Moment for Unity: A Call for a Congress.'"

In my hotel room Sánchez O'Neil called to be assured that things were going swimmingly. The Chicanos were ready for me too. Jackie Guadalupe Tynan, president of United Mexican-Americans and Chicanos (UMAC) will pick me up at Los Angeles. "I have to coach you a little on the Chicanos. But first, what are you going to talk about in Miami."

"What you wanted, Unity, 'Hispanics at a Moment for Unity: A Call for a Congress.'"

"Great. That'll go big in L.A. too. Just don't use the words *minority* and *of color* in Miami. They sound too niggerizing to Cubans. Stick to participation, the greatness of this country, its pluralistic traditions, stuff like that. Save those words for the Chicanos."

"No problem. Who are the people I'm having dinner with?"

"I really don't know. Probably the officers of MASSA. Just be nice, Eddie. The governor needs to see that you're a team player. He mentioned you and Constancia Vaselini again. Think of what you might lose out on. Oh, Marlboro isn't going to be charged with anything."

I remained silent.

"And something else." Long pause. *Something was wrong.*

"What?"

"Do you know a drug dealer named Carlos Benítez? They call him Big Carlos?"

"What's this about?"

"Detective Gerald Duffy, a detective at the 40th, who's has been leading the money-taking there, turned state's evidence to save his ass and is trying to convince the DA that somebody paid Esteban to kill that cop Callahan. Duffy says he knows who hired Esteban and that you know him too. This doesn't look good. This shit won't reach Miami or the West Coast anytime soon, but it's shit to deal with. So do you know this Carlos? Duffy says you've been pals since you were kids."

"Carlos was my best friend. Duffy, Carlos and I went to Saint Peter's together. Then I went to Excalibur and Carlos' life went in another direction. You know where I've been for the past ten years. Over twenty years ago I last talked to Carlos when I first came home from boarding school on a holiday break. He moved away after that. I have no idea what Duffy's trying to pull by linking me to him."

"You know the shit. The precinct is hot and the guys in blue are crawling out however they can. So Duffy wants to cash in on Carlos and, for some reason, on you. I'm sorry Eddie, but I'm not concerned with Carlos right now. I'm shitting a brick here because I don't know if I can believe what you're telling me about Carlos. Have you been seeing him? You didn't tell me that you ran into Duffy and Richard Bell."

"Look, Duffy, Bell, and I had an unexpected class reunion at the Danubio. I was there to see Yvette. We all went to St. Pete's and now Bell is Duffy's partner. They thought I was defending Esteban and the precinct didn't need more high profile. Out of nowhere Duffy throws in that I was lucky because I was recommended for that scholarship to Excalibur just because I was Puerto Rican. He's apparently still pissed off about that. Because Carlos and I were best friends, Duffy and Bell also had a hunch that I have been working with him. A hunch, just like that. So I guess Duffy's just getting even for that old pain about my scholarship."

Sánchez O'Neil sighed heavily. "Look, you're going to have to help me clear the air when you get back." *Either Duffy kept quiet about what he wanted from Carlos or Sánchez O'Neil was waiting to get more info from me. Unless Carlos betrayed me and lacking proof, Duffy's accusations would go nowhere.*

That evening the hotel lobby where I would be dining churned with events. Gussied-up Cuban couples proceeded to the rear, first-floor ballroom. Mainly women of all nationalities and racial types were filing up the carpeted stairs to the second floor after lining up at the foot of the stairs before a table beside a large cardboard cutout of the Ameriway logo, a huge blue "A" against a white background with a diagonal red stripe. A blond guy in a beige suit, friendly-looking and tough-bodied, sporting a crew cut, maybe an ex-marine turned salesman, checked off something on a pad, then handed some materials to each participant. The Spanish restaurant, *Capa y Toro*, where I had to be, was in the front lobby.

My party had gotten there earlier and was finishing pre-dinner drinks. Gigi introduced me and then introduced everybody at the

table. Enormous Ritchie "El Refrigerador" Amador and his small
blond wife, Alice Fayette. Ritchie used to play fullback for the Miami
Hurricanes but now worked in his father's printing business. Alice,
a nurse, spoke in a sweet, Southern low voice. Beside the Amadors
sat the large, black-haired Nubia Lezama de Caballero and her
tawny skinny lawyer husband Alonzo Caballero. Nubia introduced
herself as a "domestic engineer" but of late has replaced MASA's
secretary, who according to Sánchez O'Neil was a deeply troubled
woman who recently flew to Mexico and defected to Cuba. The
thin, mustached Alonzo wore thick, horn-rim glasses over a high-
cheeked, sucked in, stern face. He was the vice-president of MASA.
The president, Wally, was in bed with the flu.

Our waiter Reinaldo, a Spaniard gay in the proudly ostentatious
style of Figaro back at Westchester Avenue, recited the night's
specials. Nubia inquired in Spanish what province he was from.
La Coruña, he answered. Her grandparents, she noted, were from
there. Orders taken, Reinaldo left, and Ritchie changed to English
to welcome me on behalf of "our Cuban American generation just
beginning to make itself heard."

Alonzo excused himself to go outside to smoke.

"Exile is sexier than plain-Jane citizenship, and Castro is an act
too good to let go," Richie added.

"'Crucifixion, as all good Christians, know/ is the most sympathetic way to go,'" I added. "That comes from the play *Marat/Sade*."

"Oh, you got it," commented Nubia in her accented English,
"My father, just mention Castro's name and that would ruin the
conversation. 'Say tyrant,' my father would insist with *novela* dra-
matics. 'That man doesn't have another name.' For him, leaving
Cuba is on the level with the Holocaust."

Ritchie added: "Our local playwrights can't perform their works
if they show balance. I mean, I'm not a Communist. I'm not even
a Cuban, really, because I was born here, but if you're going to say
you believe in democracy, then it shouldn't just be words."

"I tell my friends..." Gigi spoke, "We live in another time. *Vaya*,
I try to communicate this to my parents but it's impossible." She had

changed to a black, one-piece dress and her hair was now woven into a braid wound in a bun.

I was hearing the Cuban American Conversation.

Reinaldo served the appetizers.

Nubia, whose pale chubby bare arms and hands emerged out of flowing sleeves and who seemed to conduct an orchestra as she spoke, excused herself for changing the subject for a minute. "Mr. Loperena, I notice that you don't wear a wedding band."

Gigi intervened in Spanish. "*Nubia, por favor...*"

The comment also froze Alice in the course of lifting a piece of Spanish potato appetizer with a fork. She raised her eyebrows before inserting the morsel in her mouth.

"It's okay. Nubia, I'm not married."

Alonzo returned as Reinaldo served the main course. He had ordered a grilled cod. Before cutting the first piece, he said in a modulated Spanish, "Don't all look at once, but over there are four men who trouble me. Two, the one in shorts and the one in a blazer, have car dealerships in Hialeah, but I know they have Colombian connections. I can't reveal how I know. The man in the white knit shirt is another Cuban businessman. But I don't know the one in the blue suit and sunglasses." Each of us took turns looking stealthily at nothing much to see, just four men talking.

Over entrees Gigi and Nubia exchanged some organizational scuttlebutt. Richie and I discussed the Yankees' poor performance that season. Alonzo remained silent, his demeanor of another time. Coffee and *tarta de queso* were being served when he cleared his throat to speak, and all prepared to listen. He observed that he read carefully the press kit that Sánchez O'Neil provided. He noted that if I had defended William Guzmán in Miami he doubted that I would be alive to be their guest. Everybody chuckled in agreement.

Alonzo cleared his throat again. "That table across the room imprints a negative image of *latinos* in this country, and this table is gathered to ennoble it. So I underscore the importance of a national movement that speaks as one voice of responsibility, and I say this especially about Cubans, who too often feel above the problems of other *latinos*. I am of that generation, but my wife is Cuban American and so are my children, and I am here for them. I see on the horizon a rash of Anglo ethnocentric hysteria. The English Only movement is only the beginning. These people are accustomed to buying up the property outright and *hispanos*, especially in the Southwest, are occupants who have had a bad experience with their new owners. Anglos live in denial that both they and our collective Hispanic cultures descend from deeper, common hemispheric American roots. But borders in the Americas are a chimera and continents always conquer armies. I don't worry about Cuba. I too love Cuba, and it will regenerate..."

The two car dealers got up from their table. The man in a blue suit and sunglasses, I was sure, was Juan Acosta, the "real" Puerto Rican who tried to convince Luz Vitali that I, New York Rican riffraff, could not speak for Puerto Ricans. That phony leftist honcho on campus got himself expelled, taking with him a poor New York Rican on a full scholarship who joined him in an occupation of the administration building in presumably their common cause of forcing the college to offer more minority scholarships and hiring more minority professors. The Rican brother wound up working for the U.S. Postal Service while Acosta just returned to his *papi*'s advertising agency in San Juan.

"...The United States is an American land, whether or not it understands what that means, and we *hispanos* were Americans a century before Anglo Saxons arrived to this hemisphere, and that history makes us destined to inform the American future of this country. In sum, as a disciple of Martí, I look forward to working toward Hispanic American unity and on behalf of MASA and its members I welcome our distinguished Puerto Rican guest." He raised his wine.

Alonzo's speech signaled the conclusion of our dinner. Gigi reminded all of their respective duties the following day. On departing each member wished me a good night. I asked Gigi if she had a few minutes. I wanted some feedback on the evening and an idea of what I could expect tomorrow. She sat again at the table. "*Creo que*...I think you came off very well with our group. Alonzo is our gauge. If he didn't like you, he would have passed the ball to Ritchie. You received full honors..."

"*Y mañana*..And tomorrow? More like Alonzo or more like Richie? I meant that Alonzo seemed still a lot more Cuban than American."

She switched to English. "Yes, that's true. Alonzo's really more Cuban, but, he feels that he's working for his children and grand-children. I consider myself American first but also in some ways Cuban. Does that make sense?"

"Does it ever."

"Sometimes I see myself all over the place. I started out with a loyalty to our parents' nostalgia for Cuba but I also grew up con-scious of being Cuban American, which we Cubans as Americans don't all understand in the same way. I tell my parents that we should identify with other *latinos*, and they answer that *hispanos* in this country are poor, so that makes them minority, so nobody cares what they think. She was really talking about Puerto Ricans. I tell her to appreciate that if it weren't for Puerto Ricans and Chicanos who fought in the sixties for civil rights the life of any future Latin Amer-ican immigrants would not be anything like it is today. *Cubanos* didn't figure in that formula because we cashed in on Cold War benefits so we don't feel we owe anything. Today I see *argentinos* and *venezolanos* come to Miami without confronting the hardships that I know *puertorriqueños* endured, so the newcomers can get right to business never thinking about how things got this way. Then they have an attitude toward *puertorriqueños*."

Gigi looked at her watch. "I've got to tell you this story before I go. I have a *puertorriqueña* friend who grew up in Brooklyn. She studied flamenco in Madrid, and I'm on her mailing list to receive notices of her performances. She was dancing at a Spanish restaurant near Wall Street when I happened to be in New York with one of my former girlfriends from my more 'conservative' days. I knew that we were on the right street but couldn't find the restaurant. I figured how many Spanish restaurants could there be in that dis-trict, so I stopped a carrot-top man in a suit. I asked if he knew of a

Spanish restaurant on this street and he said 'No I don't know of any Puerto Rican restaurants around here.' Wait, that's not the punch line. My friend didn't remark a thing. About three weeks later, back in Miami, I was having drinks at her house with her other friends and, as always happened, the conversation turned to politics, life in exile, etc. At some point she said, 'The one thing I really can't stand about *americanos* is that they can't tell silk from toilet paper. You ask for a Spanish restaurant and they think you mean a Puerto Rican one.' So you have that too. But then you have us." She stood and we exchanged a kiss on the cheek.

I accompanied her to the hotel entrance then walked back through the lobby filled with Latin music wafting from the rear ballroom. Waiting for the elevator, I looked at the Ameriway sign announcing their second-floor event. I got off at the second floor. At a table between a ballroom's two closed doors Ameriway credential verification was done by three middle-aged ladies, one black, one Asian, one white. I addressed all three. "My wife sells Ameriway products in Tampa but she's pregnant and wasn't feeling up to traveling. I'm staying in this hotel on business and just want to see if I spot any of her Ameriway buddies."

The white lady looked at the Asian, who spoke with a Spanish accent. "Well, why not wait until they come out? They'll be out soon."

"But I'm supposed to be at the function downstairs, and I took a break, leaving some people. Can't I just look around real quick."

"Well," said the black woman nodding to the other two, "This meeting is ending anyway."

Inside the ballroom a packed crowd cheered and whistled wildly for a short, brown woman running toward a raised platform where the ex-marine waited arms wide open beside a pyramid of Ameriway cleaning products—chemicals, brooms, cloths and sponges—before a huge splayed American flag. An ex-marine hug to more cheers, then the lady spoke into the mic with pulmonary strength in a thick Spanish accent, giving testimony to having arrived recently from Honduras with no husband and two children and being successful in selling Ameriway merchandise.

The audience punctuated her happy ending with a standing ovation, and Ex-Marine put an arm around her shoulder, conducting with his other hand a chanting of "I can do it." As the woman returned to her table, he celebrated, "Isn't this a wonderful country, isn't this the magic land where dreams do come true if you wish upon star and work hard." The audience cheered wildly. A recorded marching music signaled the end of the session. A tall middle-aged woman at the microphone reminded the exiting audience not to party too late and be fresh for the next morning's sales workshops. The exiting crowd bubbled and gushed in a common language, Ameriway.

Ameriway welcomes your tired, your weak, African, Asian, Aborigine, your Easter Islander, your Arab. Isn't capitalism the truest equality? In the offices of public school administrations somebody is calculating the allowable benign percentage of nonwhites in the educational system, but Ameriway would never. In Real Estate offices, skin tone and language may determine availability and market value, but Ameriway doesn't care about race or languages. Back in the countries of these new Ameriway citizens, the doors to the top are securely locked by lineage, race, and class, but in Ameriway they are equal citizens. So isn't Ameriway the promised land, the Magic Kingdom of Equality? Walking out among them, I was an Ameriway patriot. The three ladies had cleared out and the table was bare.

I was set to go upstairs and prepare my words for the next day when the voice of a male singer singing "*Mi Buenos Aires Querido*" in the lobby ballroom easily convinced me that it was too early to end the night. Across from the foot of the grand stairs, a banner above "Del Mar Ballroom" announced the Annual Dinner-Dance of the Archdiocese of Miami Boosters. At a long table between two doors sat two dark-haired elegantly dressed senior ladies and an even more senior gentleman. The thin, distinguished-looking gray-haired man, in a gray suit, smiled up at me. "*Caballero*...Sir, can I help you." *They will come no more,/ the old men with beautiful manners.* Inside the ballroom the singer announced that he would next sing "*la canción*...the song that honors the people from that beloved Isle of Enchantment."

"*¿Cuánto*...How much?"

"*Treinta*...Thirty, but it's so late now, only pay fifteen. You get one drink."

An enormous chandelier hung in the center of the large hall. The atmosphere was romantic and festive. I walked around the busy tables toward the bar, ordered a drink. The singer finished his tribute to San Juan and his final song would be "...a tribute to the suffering of a people that have waited many years to see democracy and freedom in their homeland." The first bars of "Cuando Salí de Cuba" were drowned out by applause. As couples stepped out on the dance floor, I was transported to Susana's arms as we danced at Rosy's wedding. But that romantic moment abruptly popped on seeing among the couples swirling on the dance floor, now without sunglasses, Juan Acosta.

His partner was a finely attired blond woman, who could have been his wife. Unlike Carlos, Juan Acosta attended church dances and boosted the Miami Archdiocese. But I didn't want to get myself in a funk over Carlos. Or over Sánchez O'Neil's inevitable questions about Carlos in messages that I knew I was postponing from having to confront by coming down to this ballroom. I chugged the drink and ordered another. Tonight the world was on its own.

Eventually I confronted the dark of my room. The red message light might as well have been on the hood of a patrol car. I disregarded it and called my office:.. *beep...beep*..."Bonino, here. That guy Upton Wane said that you recommended me. I'm a science fiction writer, you know that."...*beep*..."Hola...Hi, Susana. I know you're still away, and I understand you're probably too busy to call. Just wanted to tell you that our meeting was like a beautiful fantasy. I was just wondering if maybe it can also be real. Ciao."...*beep*..."Hi, Eddie, it's Gerry, Gerry Duffy, just wanted to see if you was there so we could talk about some things being said around. I'll catch you later."...*beep...beep*..."Socrates, you there? We need to talk. Important, really important."...*beep*...

I awoke with the energy to finally listen to Sánchez O'Neil's messages. I expected the worst, but the first message was just making sure that I had arrived and a second message spoke exhilarated over Gigi's report on how the talk went, "...Frankly, this good news about you was something I needed to hear after yesterday with this Carlos business. But we'll get to that. Give a good talk and have a good flight to L.A."

Only the mystery of the cauliflower brain can explain how, in the maelstrom of a pounding headache and practically no sleep, I awoke hearing the cadence of the first words I would deliver. I scribbled an introduction and then an outline from which to improvise. I was mentally expanding on the body and conclusion when Gigi phoned my room. I was frank with her on needing a little time to prepare, and she told me to relax, that I was scheduled to speak after the lunch, which I could skip.

The same Del Mar ballroom that held the Miami Boosters dance last night had been divided, the Cuban Democrats only needing half the space without the chandelier, and that space wasn't filled to capacity. Maybe thirty people, their lunch dishes being cleared. Ritchie and Nubia came from their tables to greet me. Alonzo followed. Gigi introduced the photographer René from *The Miami Herald*, who took a group shot. Wally was still sick so Alonzo would introduce me. I followed him onto a platform to sit on a folding chair while he opened the meeting with a summary of the organization's recent activities.

Then he commenced an anecdote of an experience with his little girl on their way to Walt Disney World when they stopped at a Wiggly Dixie supermarket, where "At the cash register a black woman wore an English Only button. I was offended that an employee should be wearing this button and asked the manager, also a black man, who listened to me respectfully. When I finished, he inquired if the woman had refused to take care of me, or did she say something to me or my little girl that offended us. The woman indeed had not, but I answered she had no right to wear the button on her uniform, not if she is representing a company that does profitable business with Spanish-speakers throughout South Florida. The man then pointed out that the woman wore the button on her own blouse and not on the store's red blazer. The problem here was one of bad faith. This kind of litigation mentality misses the point..."

His voice erupted slowly, a rising lava of philosophical indignation. "If you fire the gun from three miles out on the sea and it kills a person on the shore, no murder was committed? English Only is veiled bigotry, and bigotry is just a euphemism for supremacy, which must be declawed because of its tacit immorality, its own groundlessness in the metaphysical scheme..." And so forth in verbiage so dense he seemed in danger of gagging. In that thicket I waited and finally heard him pronounce my name as his hand swerved back toward me.

I had already removed from my attaché a legal pad with the outline on the first page, and at the lectern, waited a few seconds then leaned into the microphone and began: "Today we speak up to defend our right to simple historical truth. Spanish predates English in this hemisphere by almost a century, and yet we are being painted as cultural invaders. We are asked to see ourselves as past immigrants from Europe when Our Old Country is America itself. We cannot tolerate a Manifest Destiny of Ignorance. For English Only is simply that, an imposition of mythology against history. Anglo Americans must accept the consequence of being the most powerful in a continent with over four hundred years of Spanish roots, and as my friend Alonzo put it so poetically, 'continents conquer armies' and what conquers is history." Long applause.

"This audience before me is America. We are part of the real United States, the great multilingual theater. Then there is the false America, in which our children are taught to know Shakespeare but kept ignorant of Cervantes. That false America, a celebration of patriotically customized ignorance of America itself is what English Only wants to impose on our children. For advocates of English Only, America signifies the S-O-M-E of its parts; for us America is the S-U-M of its parts. From pole to shining pole, the U.S. feeds from America, thrives strong and nourished by its robust spirit, whose mother's milk rises up from mountains and plains from the

Patagonia to the Canadian Artic. Along with our native brothers and sisters, with their ancient and mingled American roots, we make the United States American, not the other way around."

The entire hall rose to applaud that collage from my college political poems and seventies conversations at Smith Wesson. Alonzo gave me a bear-strength *abrazo* then held up my hand before René, the *Herald* photographer. Gigi invited me to stay for a drink with her and Alonzo, but relieved of the pressure of having to give a talk, I suddenly felt exhausted, surrendering to my lack of sleep, from which I hoped to recover on my flight to LA that afternoon. I did recover a couple of hours but only after being kept awake for half the flight by Sánchez O'Neil's parting reference to that "Carlos business."

Chapter 28

At the LA airport not Jackie Guadalupe Tynan but a big-eared, mustached, black-haired little man in a black suit holding up "LOPE-RENA" on glossy cardboard was to whom I identified myself. "Hello, Mr. Loperena," he extended his hand. "Miguel Maus. Very honored to meet you. You were expecting Jackie, but she was tied up and I was able to unburden myself of obligations. Jackie will drive you to tonight's reception." His grin leveled his thin, downy mustache. He insisted on carrying my suitcase.

Sánchez O'Neil, he said, had forwarded news of my success in Miami to the Angelenos. "Gigi faxed us your picture in the Spanish version of this morning's *Miami Herald*, the one in which Alonzo is holding up your hand." In the parking lot, he pointed at the round logo on the doors of the white station wagon, a circle of words— United Mexican-Americans and Chicanos (UMAC)—enclosing the crossed flags of Mexico and the U.S. "Not all of us like to use 'Chicano,' but our organization is about unity." He lay my suitcase on the back seat.

In the car Maus talked a blue streak. "We Mexican-Americans believe that only through English will we make the American Dream a reality. The Chicanos disagree. They insist that we live on a mythical land called *Atzlán*, which predates the Anglos. We Mexican-Americans, on the other hand, believe that we are all *hermanos de La Raza*, of course, *hispanos* in blood and soul, and we encourage Spanish as a second language but this is our country, so English should come first. They expect that Spanish will be an official language of the United States. At least that's how I see it. But we both agree that Hispanics have a right to speak whatever language we please in private because, after all, this is America and..."

He finally came to the day's agenda: "We have included you in a lunch that we are hosting for directors of important Southwest Hispanic arts and cultural organizations, who are in the city for a conference. I thought it would be a good idea to recruit them to promote the National Hispanic Conference, which a vocal group of Chicanos is now insisting it be called the National Latino Conference. Gus suggested that you be at this lunch so you can a get a sense of the national Hispanic consensus and also because he told us you are a first-rate poet and so it is fitting that you should be there. Tonight we'll have drinks at the home of John Anthony Shadow. He's, of course, the former actor who is our new L.A. school superintendent. There you will be introduced to our Los Angeles community leaders, the ones who will also be hearing you at tomorrow's meeting."

The lunch was at Los Ranchos Lindos in Downtown L.A., a restaurant beautifully designed in red adobe clay decorated with blue and white porcelain tiles with lapis lazuli flower designs. The place, patently a site for Chicanada power lunches, was packed. At the door to the room reserved for our gathering stood a woman holding a clipboard. Maus introduced me to Jackie Guadalupe Tynan. She was tall, slender, and high-cheek-boned, with a clay-smooth complexion and caramel-colored, shoulder-length hair. Under her short-sleeved, loose dark blue dress Jackie seemed to be, although not very noticeably, pregnant. She greeted me with a half-smile, and immediately informed me that Sánchez O'Neil had left word that it was important that I call him as soon as I arrived. *Trouble already?*

She guided me to the public phone. *Long distance, had to dig out a calling card.* In moderate heels Jackie was an inch or two taller than me, exuding a powerful something that kept me struggling

not to peek sideways at her. "I'll wait for you at the dining room."
She said this pointing in its direction with her smooth-clay bare left
arm decorated with an Aztec-design silver bracelet and on whose
hand glistened a couple of torquoise and silver rings but no wedding
band. Sánchez O'Neil's secretary told me to hold then he came on.
"Hi, is everything okay out there?"

"I just got to an L.A. restaurant."

"Okay. Listen, I know you too long, and I respect you too
much to hand you shit and believe shit about you. Gerry Duffy
may be doing whatever asshole thing but if we don't confront it
right now, it might work. I'm going to see what I can do. Lucky
for us you're in L.A. right now. Change of subject. What do you
think of Jackie Tynan? Classy isn't she? She was married to a major
Democratic Party donor in L.A. The guy was on the board of several
corporations, not quite sure where he made his bucks. Big divorce
settlement, that's all I know. But she's free now."

"She may be free but she's pregnant."

"Oh, too bad."

"No wedding ring though."

"Hmmm, don't know what to tell you, buddy. But I gotta run,
so let's make this fast. Gigi called again to tell me that you were
outstanding. Cuomo was told about the Cubans' reaction and after
the Gerry Duffy bullshit that good news couldn't come at a better
time. You know, the governor's drooling over your getting exposure
and the possibility of attracting Hispanic recognition that can help
him both in New York and with the Democrats beyond. But be
careful with the Chicanos. They're another thing altogether and I
know you might confront some things that will set you off."

"Like what?"

"Listen to me carefully, they deal with this country a little different than we do. Their history is different and they have issues
with whites, with each other, with Mexico, with I don't know what
else. Look at Mickey Maus, who I heard picked you up at LAX.
He's giant-size, no, make that industrial-size bullshit in a pair of
pants. He came over here to pick fruit when he was nineteen and

when the Civil Rights Movement hit, he intercepted that ball and ran like a motherfucker. I know your first instinct will be to get out your machete and cut off his hypocritical balls, but calm down. Just play with it. You fuck them over and the first fax I'll get here will be complaining that New York has sent this smooth Rican to run down the Chicanos, and the national conference will not take off."

"Who's John Anthony Shadow? I know he was an actor who is now the Superintendent of Schools."

"Okay, another kind of Chicano. Check that, he prefers Mexican-American. Don't you remember that Hispanic Heritage Month event you couldn't attend because you were in the middle of the William Guzmán trial. I told you that I was introduced to this former actor nobody knew was a Mexican American. After Anthony Quinn felt free to reveal that he was Mexican, Shadow came out. He, like all of us, jumped on the Civil Rights elevator. But he made it to the penthouse. Just remember that this Shadow is on his way even further up, so be extra careful. Reagan loves him, a white Hispanic role model."

"I remember him now, just forgot his name. Yeah I read his whole story."

The luncheon room was colorful with the same lapis lazuli motifs as the main dining area, its large windows well-appointed with burlap shades. On my entering, Jackie took me to an empty chair diametrically distant from where she was sitting and to the left of Maus, who popped up from his chair and tapped his water glass, "Excuse me, if I can have your attention." The table complied.

"Now I have the pleasure of formally introducing Eduardo Loperena, lawyer extraordinaire from New York, who will be the keynote speaker to tomorrow's planning meeting of community leaders. I will now introduce all of you to him..."

Cuaotemoc Paniagua, Field Representative of the Ford Foundation, whom I knew from other reunions with funding sources for culture organizations that Winston and I represented; Frank Houghton, a pale and slender balding man who represented the National Endowment for the Arts; Drew Calaveras, the paunchy

Coordinator of the Arizona-New Mexico Cultural Restoration Initiative (CANCRI); Monique, the retired blond screen actress, who starred as a femme fatale Greek spy in the Oscar-nominated *The Umbrellas of Bulgaria*, and whom nobody knew was Mexican-American until 1971 when she agreed to appear at a fundraiser for the Medical Fund to Save Border Children (now almost seventy, she still looked striking, with blue eyes twinkling across a veil of her own exhaled puff of cigarette smoke); Mrs. Maus, Minerva Hoyo de Maus, diminutive and peppery-looking, a high school principal in Downtown L.A.; Marta Cisneros (Matty), the President of the Texas-based Mexican-American Council on Arts and Culture (MACAC), a heavy, brown woman who, seated to *my* left, offered me a limp, spongy hand, greeting without a smile, and last Jackie, whom Maus praised "as our L.A. community's Muse or goddess, I'm not sure which," to which the table laughed in unison. Paniagua stood, raising his glass, and on behalf of the table, "Allow me to welcome one of the Puerto Rican community's shining stars, whom I read about for many years and whose work has helped the broader Hispanic population in ways for which we are all grateful." Others raised a glass except Matty Cisneros, who looked plumb bored. I ordered chicken enchiladas from a brief menu and was served a goblet of sangría. The table returned to conversations that my arrival had interrupted.

Maus to my right, who apparently had no agenda of his own, threw in empty questions: "How are those after-school painters producing?...So will our culture survive this Ice Age, hombre...Did you finally get in touch with the Provost? I told him you needed to talk to him." In between these outbursts, Maus rambled on in my ear about the need to uplift Hispanic culture and cultural works. Matty Cisneros to my left, paying me no mind, chatted with Monique. The food arrived and, after a lull for eating, the conversations picked up again.

I thought about Timmy, whose bombs killed people because he wanted to be free in some idealized, liberated perfection of Puerto Rico as our own free country. If he had only realized that if independence ever came, it would be at the right cocktail reception and to the advantage of the likes of Maritza and Juan Acosta. And so what if independence came? Poverty would keep My People in the U.S., like these Chicanos with a free Mexico under California. Which is worse? Hispanic class oppression and dysfunction or the better-paid and more efficient treadmill of Anglo American bullshit toward an elusive American equality?

Here at least we meet the enemy on the field of wine goblets and fresh tortillas, victories tallied as budget allotments for Monique's community art and film projects, Drew Calaveras's art therapy classes and poetry writing programs, Matty Cisnero's heritage enrichment seminars and free Spanish literacy programs. For the sake of the next funding of these noble and righteous causes, its advocates were now becoming bloated with abstractions, verbiage, gestures, enchiladas and wine. On both sides of the border one crashes into human nature. Lost in those thoughts I didn't realize that I had been staring at Jackie, who caught me looking and smiled.

Over coffee Maus stood up, tapped on his water glass again. "Before we conclude our lunch, I want to reiterate a southwestern welcome to our visitors from the east, Mr. Houghton and Mr. Paniaga and, of course, Mr. Loperena. It is our pleasure to share with you our southwestern culture and heritage." Drew Calaveras, who sported a wealth of black, Indian hair and prominent front teeth, applauded, "Allow me to second that." Everybody else applauded.

Maus remained standing. "This is how our organizations defend one another: *unidos*, politicians and culture, leaders and heritage, power accessible to the people."

"*Así mismo.* That's right," Matty said, swallowing her last bite of cheesecake, "In our Spanish workshops, we put our money where our mouth is."

Maus continued. "The reason we are so tightly knit is because even our *políticos* are keenly sensitive to the cultural situation of Mexican-Americans. As children of the Southwest, we know what a struggle it is to keep our culture from disappearing. We must work hard to conserve our *identidad* in danger of disappearing in Anglo culture and through your leadership our children will understand what it means to be a Mexican-American." Lifting his water glass, "¡*Viva La Raza!*" The table toasted in unison, and I joined in, enjoying the sight of The National Endowment's and Ford Foundation's toasting to La Raza's demand of contrition because Anglo America has historically tried to rub out Maus' culture.

When I put down my sangría, my line of sight crossed Jackie's again. She got up and came around behind Maus to whisper something in his ear. Maus nodded. Jackie walked away from the table and out the room. Maus tapped on his water glass again. "Earlier I introduced you to Mr. Loperena as our keynote speaker for tomorrow's planning meeting, but you should also know that he was also invited to have lunch with us today because like José Martí, he is also a soldier-poet, one of those *puertorriqueños románticos* and therefore also a model of the kind of relationship of art, culture and political leadership that Hispanic communities enjoy."

Drew Calaveras started a round of applause.

"Unfortunately he doesn't have the time to read for us from his beautiful work, and Jackie has the car in front ready to take him to his hotel."

I broadcast my pleasure of having met all present, privately looking forward to being driven to the hotel by Jackie. Maus saw me out to the hotel entrance, where Jackie waited in the UMAC station wagon with my suitcase still on the back seat. We pulled out.

"Mr. Loperena, the hotel where you're staying is just as few minutes from here, and the Community Center where you'll be speaking tomorrow is also here in downtown. John Shadow's place for tonight's reception is in Pasadena."

"Please call me Eddie. Mike said you'll be taking me to that reception."

She smiled. "No. I'm sorry. I had to back out. My sister's in from San Diego."

I contained my disappointment. "When's the baby due?"

She looked down as if reminded that she was pregnant. "In January."

Neither of us had anything to add.

"Mr. Loperena, can I ask you a question?"

"Sure, but please call me Eddie."

"Yes. Eddie. Well, it's not really a question. More like an observation. You don't seem to fit in this scene. You're not looking for the same things they are. It's just a first impression."

Jackie penetrated into that part of me that I had felt in the presence of Louise Hobson. I stared out the car window. "What do you think I'm looking for?" *If you could answer that you would be helping me so much.*

"I don't know. I was observing you at the lunch. I don't really know why I said what I just said. I'm sorry."

More seconds of silence.

"Can I ask an impertinent question?"

"Maybe I can answer it before you ask: no, I'm not married. You were pretty obvious when you fixed your eyes on my hand. You can understand why I won't be there tonight. My sister is visiting, as I said, but this is also a very complicated time in my life, and after a certain hour I get exhausted. I have to get up early to work with Mike to setup tomorrow's meeting. Mike is my right hand, but except for my small staff, I run this organization and have to remain fresh and alert. I'll probably call in the morning before I leave to pick you up. Mike and Minerva will take you to Shadow's house tonight."

In my hotel room the telephone's message light was already blinking. I asked myself what I was thinking with Jackie when I hadn't resolved anything with Susana. But that conversation with Jackie left me wondering if I was the right fit for Susana.

Chapter 29

The L.A. Superintendent of Schools John Anthony Shadow—originally Wenceslao Muñoz—was just another modestly successful Anglo actor when "Roots" became the rage. His coming out as a Mexican-American suddenly made him valuable as emblem of Hollywood diversity, and Actor's Equity invited him to work on committees. From there, President Johnson invited him to serve with other minority artists on a national cultural and arts Heritage Restoration Project of the National Endowment. The press progressively pumped him up from the "well-known," to the "respected," and at some point the "great" former Mexican-American actor when in reality he had worked in only seven B movies.

His work in Washington fueled a political career in California, where he ascended on the scales of appointed, high-profile positions, including a statewide panel assessing the California school system. Being a high-profile Hispanic somehow also made him naturally expert on the education of Chicano children. That "expertise," reaffirmed by his successful participation on many education panels, eventually filled out a resume that sustained the logic of his being named L.A.'s home-bred school superintendent.

Later, as the nation moved to the Right, he became a vocal moderate Mexican-American who argued that, while heritage was important, bilingual education should take a back seat to the education of Mexican immigrant children in English. Talk had it that Reagan might appoint him the U.S. Ambassador in Mexico although a counter-rumor ran that when word of that possible appointment reached the ears of Mexico's President Salinas, Reagan heard it whispered straight from *el presidente* that he shouldn't even think of appointing a greaser, especially one who couldn't speak Spanish, although doubtless phrased in more stately and diplomatic diction.

On the way to Shadow's house, Mike Maus and Minerva mercifully talked mainly to each other. Numerous cars were already parked on the property surrounding the large ranch house. Maus deposited me and Minerva in front then looked for a place to park. Someone dressed as a butler opened and Shadow came quickly to the door to greet Minerva and his New York guest. He welcomed me to his ample living room.

Shadow was a striking figure who seemed genetically hardwired to act in movies. Conceived in Technicolor, his almost hairless facial skin was a very light bronze, his eyes gray, and his lips a naturally bright pink. He was also appointed with an intact head of hair (now salt-and-pepper) parted down the middle, high cheeks, an aquiline, razor sharp nose, and perfect white teeth. In stagy total command he gave me a firm *abrazo* and asked the butler to bring me a cocktail—scotch is it? He still had to attend to some arrangements before formally introducing me. Meanwhile, he left me in the care of a trio of men in dark suits.

Cronies of Sánchez O'Neil, they were anxious to hear what I knew about their friend's aspirations' to land in Congress. I avoided confirming anything, not knowing with whom I was talking. Sánchez O'Neil must have really sold me, judging from the attention I was getting. I tried to follow his first lesson when he was a City Councilman and attended the open house that Winston and I hosted to inaugurate our office in the Bronx, "Eddie, make people feel important. Never forget to ask for their name and never forget a face." I asked for names that I almost immediately forgot.

Jackie's absence made this experience unbearable. With just a few words she had made me see that my even pretending to cast myself in the role of a politician was absurd. Outwardly my face smiled while inside I called out to her as if only she knew, somehow, what I was supposed to do next: everyone around me heard the distinguished guest, the prominent New York Puerto Rican lawyer, but I didn't know who he was. I clung to the scotch in my hand.

"But how does your community feel about the decision to cut Title Three and Seven funding in the event that a tax bill isn't passed in this session of Congress." "Can you speak for your community on whether mainland Puerto Ricans should be allowed to vote on any referendum to change the island's political status?" "How is your community confronting the English-Only backlash, which has us divided here?" I managed to answer each question evasively, with variations on "It's really too early to tell." On a relaxing wave of a circulating second scotch, Eduardo emerged.

Shadow and Mike Maus were listening to Minerva explain the implications to a school like hers of making English the official national language. Mike wore a face of listening intensely to Minerva's words that he must have heard ad nauseam. She spoke in a mild, sweet voice. She was fairer than Mike, her hair and eyes glittering crow-black. "Ninety six percent of my kids live in Spanish-speaking homes. Forty three point two percent of my students are in bilingual programs. Spanish is the language through which my students receive maternal love. And that is what those English Only people are trying to deny American citizens." *The Conversation.*

"Well said, Minerva, bravo, bravo," Shadow praised in an amplified professional actor's voice that arrested the room's attention. Holding a glass of white wine in one hand, he gently tugged at my elbow to guide me away from the Mauses to the center of his living room. "Excuse me, ladies and gentlemen. I want to welcome our special guest, Mr. Eduardo Loperena, whom I know among such a well-informed crowd needs no real introduction. So to you..." He raised the wine, "Welcome and thank you for your advocacy of our Hispanic causes." A sip, and he continued. "Now, *he* has been formally introduced but left at the disadvantage of not really knowing who *we* are. So I thought it would be appropriate that we identify ourselves individually."

A handsome, middle-aged woman with black hair descended the stairs behind Shadow, who turned. "Ah, Bonnie, yes, perfect timing." His theatrical hand reached out to Bonnie. "You all know my wife Bonnie, but our guest of honor does not. Mr. Loperena, this gorgeous woman is my wife. Bonnie, this dashing paladin of a lawyer is Eduardo Loperena, our keynote speaker for tomorrow's regional meeting. Bonnie, I must add, is more than my wife—we must learn to watch out for these oversights. *Doctora* Haydée García Shadow heads an outreach program of the Psychotherapeutic Support Unit of Downtown Social Services."

I extended my hand, which she pressed.

"And now, please, if the organizational leaders could line up and identify themselves."

The men left their wives in a side cluster to form a line that covered Shadow's wide scenic window to a lighted kidney-shaped swimming pool. Except for the hostess Mrs. Shadow, among the spouses of the nine leaders about to introduce themselves only one appeared to be Chicana. On Shadow's cue, the first leader on the left gave his oral professional bio. To Eduardo the presentation reeked of a pride in each leader's accomplishment at having "made it" despite being that pathetic thing implicitly understood to be a *real* Chicano, like the *vato* serving them their drinks at the bar. (Shadow had been quick to let his guests know, *sotto voce*, that he frequently gives part-time and domestic work to *vatos* from prison halfway houses). I struggled to restrain Eduardo's artsy snootiness and tried to listen with the proper courtesy at what he kept perceiving as an anal oral presentation, a choreography of servitude and denial, an homage to the color and culture pecking order of Gringolandia.

After each resume of titles, roles, positions, the leader pointed to his mate, a sweet Anglo spouse in the crowd, who waved to me, Loperena, whom after my third scotch Eduardo had pushed aside altogether, and he was not catching any names or titles and obstructing my retaining any except for the name of the last presenter, a Something Gonzalez.

The only male with wavy hair, the tawny, handsome Gonzalez with a mustache prefaced his introduction with the baritone statement that he was not Mexican American, "and I am not going to say what I am," his brazen shyness igniting a profound silence that he himself broke. "I'll just say that I am the President of the Consortium of Inner City Minorities Youth Councils in the Greater Los Angeles Area." He proudly introduced his "better half," the only Chicana, who waved giving a cutesy smile. *Gonzalez, maybe from Louisiana?*

"Well now," Shadow summarized, "leaders like these have changed the face of our community. I remember when I was a child how our parents walked meekly, afraid to make waves, always asking for handouts…"

I struggled to remind myself that *I*, not Eduardo, was the one being addressed, but Jackie ambled across my mind, that strange temple of amalgamated genealogies and interacting spirits: that soft clay skin, that honey-colored hair falling to her shoulders, that fine dress over her maybe three-month belly, that ghostly, weightless walk and that confident smile, that sense of inner *aristos* emanating like a fragrance. And the way she simply reached into my soul and unfurled it in front of me—

"…Now we have come to represent ourselves according to our numbers. We're no longer invisible but highly present, and we don't ask, we demand."

To those words, incorrigibly, through the sheen of my stupid, scotch-enhanced smile, in a manner that I cannot explain how or even why such a nonsensical utterance could rise up my throat and float past my lips, Eduardo remarked: "Excuse me, but I fail to discern the difference between begging with a hat and begging with a gun."

Sánchez O'Neil felt the aftershock by fax and telephone and his phone call awoke me at dawn. "You don't seem to get it. This guy Shadow is on his way up, very high. I had to tell him you get that way when you drink, that I keep you away from liquor for that very reason, that it was my fault for not warning them."

I was on the hotel bed barely awake, the phone against my ear.

"Eddie, you there?"

"Same place."

"Look, the best thing is to not give it a thought. Shake his hand this morning as if nothing had happened, give your speech. The same one that everybody loved in Miami."

"Okay, I'll try."

"What do you mean, you'll try?"

"I didn't write it all out, Gus."

"Oh Christ. Ed, don't make me look bad. I'm your biggest fan, you know that. Don't do anything ridiculous for which I'm going to get the arrows. Look, even if you plan to drop out later, just follow through with this as a favor to me, okay? You'll be at the caucus, right? "

"I will."

"And you won't fuck up? You'll just talk about Hispanic unity. Just try to remember exactly what you said in Miami. Okay?"

I didn't really want to fuck up. While showering and preparing myself for the day, I came to a decision. I tried to reach Jackie through the UMAC number. She was at the Community Center auditorium. I was given that number. After three people put me on hold, Jackie picked up, catching her breath. "Mr. Loperena, I'm sorry you had to wait so long. Is there a problem?"

"Call me Eddie, please. Well, yes, there is. I'm not feeling myself."
Actually, my problem was that I was.

"Oh no. This is terrible." Jackie's disappointment made me feel stupid and mousey, behaving like a prima donna. I also suddenly remembered what, immersed in my egoistic drama, I completely forgot: my giving the talk offered the fringe benefit of seeing her again.

"Jackie, I'll try to make it. But I have to speak with you first. Is that possible? Just a few minutes." I didn't intend for this request to sound like a hard bargain.

Jackie's pause was long. "I'll leave right now, and we can talk at your hotel's coffee shop."

We met in the lobby. She was wearing a comely blue and beige dress and although in low-heeled shoes, she was still a bit taller than me. In the coffee shop Jackie ordered an herbal tea. I ordered a coffee. "Your wisecrack last night at John Shadow's house was all Mike talked about this morning. What did John say to you?"

"He just stared back incredulous then smiled it off. But he didn't pay me attention for the rest of the night. Nobody did. After I stood around alone for a while, Mike asked if I wanted to be taken to the hotel. He got Minerva and we just slipped out. Even Mike said practically nothing on the way, so that's saying a lot. After I thought about it all night I came to the conclusion that the remark was pretty clever."

For the first time she gave me a full smile, an event more important than the political forest fire we were discussing. "Crazy too. You're closing doors."

Does she find me cool like Dixie or crazy like Susana?

"Is Shadow what you wanted to talk to me about?"

"No I needed to talk to you about what you said in the car yesterday, I mean that you could see..."

"Jackie!" somebody interrupted, "what a great surprise!" A short man in a gray suit wearing a Pancho Villa mustache, came over and planted a kiss on her cheek. Behind him waited a thin, freckled young woman with round black glasses, carrying a briefcase. She wore a gray skirt and a Burberry blazer.

"Eddie, I'd like you to meet Arnaldo Ribera, the talk show host. Arnie, this is Eduardo Loperena. He's the New York..."

The waitress brought the tea and coffee.

"I know who he is. Do you mind if I join you two," Arnaldo said already sitting down. "Lore and I..." He looked over his shoulder. "Oh this is my producer Loretta Casey Cotton. Pull up a chair, Lore. We've been researching the brouhaha over the English Only referendum and bilingual education and *his* name came up. Just yesterday Lore and I were discussing the possibility of a show on this language issue. She just mentioned it again to me in the car. What a coincidence!"

Jackie intervened: "Yes, he's supposed to give the talk in an hour, that's why we have to leave." She glanced at her watch.

"Well, now that we've met, Eddie, I'd like to talk over some program ideas with you. Lore can set up a meeting. In New York, in L.A., wherever you say. I'll tell you what. I've got to be here another day. Why don't I invite you to dinner. I'm really impressed by the things I've read and heard about you in New York and would like some time for us to get to know each other. I mean, it's great to meet a fellow talented New York Rican."

Before Arnaldo's blitzkrieg I looked for guidance from Jackie, who fixed her eyes on her tea.

"We'll be in touch." Arnaldo got up, followed by Lore, who handed me a calling card. "Jackie, if you need anything, anything at all, let me know." He squeezed both her shoulders to give her a kiss on the cheek.

Arnaldo and Lore were gone in a whirlwind.

Jackie looked at her watch. "We have to rush."

On the drive to the Community Center, I broke the silence. "What's with you and Arnaldo?"

She took a deep breath. "I needed somebody after my divorce and he was there."

We were only minutes away from my scheduled talk and I hadn't given a second's thought to what I was going to say.

The Community Center was on the fringes of downtown L.A., the meeting to be held in the ground floor auditorium. I shook hands with two other speakers seated in a row of chairs behind a podium, where Mike Maus was extending a huge *abrazo* to, alternately, "Mi Gente," "La Comunidad, "La Raza" and "los hijos norteños de los hijos de la Chingada." The audience seemed grouped with the younger, most radical in the back, a middle sector of thirty-something professionals, and the VIP front rows made up of businessmen and the leaders from the previous night.

Maus was introducing a representative of the United Farm Workers, Marco Antonio Vargas, while I attempted to jot some notes on my legal pad for an improvised speech against my intuition that back in New York my name was sliding down a steep ceramic hole. Jackie materialized in front of me and handed me a slip of paper.

Arnaldo was inviting me to dinner in Anaheim. A limo would pick me up. As Vargas stepped up to the podium, I scribbled on the legal pad, "Will you have dinner with me tonight?" She shook her head. I returned the slip, nodding. She turned and left the hall.

Vargas was delivering his speech in Spanish, defending "*los pobres...*the working people exploited by greedy farmers...." and was interrupted several times by cheers and raised left fists from the younger people in the back and most of the thirty-something crowd in the middle-rows. The front-row hearts of the business leaders seemed less touched, either finding the speech too radical or not following its Spanish.

Next Maus introduced the bearded President of the Nuevos Hijos de Atzlán, a sort of revolutionary satyr, his bottom half in fatigue pants and combat boots, his upper half in a shirt, tie and blue blazer with brass buttons. His speech was also eclectic, in both English and Spanish, as he defended the transnationalism of border culture. "... The border is *una invención* of European dudes who still think they can tell *Madre* Earth what's up and what's down. Our *hermanos de la Raza cruzamos el* border *cuando* we decide to come up *Norte*. They're just following the trail of *nuestros espíritus ancestrales*. What bullshit border are we talking about? After thousands of years some gringos come and say, 'here, right here, from this point on is Los Estados Unidos.' We say, 'We'll see about that down the road, amigo. In the meantime, Welcome to Atzlán.'"

The middle rows reacted half-heartedly while the youthful sector in the back rows cheered wildly, with no response from the front-row suits.

Finally, John Anthony Shadow stepped up to the podium to a standing ovation from the front rows. In theatrical, near-British English, he defended both the rights of the Mexican-American's cultural heritage and the need to teach Mexican-American children bilingually. "But our communities need to recognize that they belong to this country, America..." (A youthful voice in the back heckled: "The United States") "...whose first language is English." Front row cheers and applause clashed with some middle and many back-row catcalls and boos. Shadow paused, waited out the interruption.

"I know that we have differing views on this subject but we all agree that the national Hispanic communities must unite to confront the English Only backlash, which is really about more than just language. So we are here to formalize a Southwest consensus to send its voice to the Hispanic Unity conference in Chicago next year. And as gesture of that unity," he paused, perhaps to bite his tongue, "we…are fortunate…to have a speaker from our…Puerto Rican cousins in New York, the lawyer Eduardo Loperena."

While Shadow spoke, owing to a convergence of distractions—dredging up what I was going to say, Jackie's words, what Sánchez O'Neil really knew about Carlos and me, the class and culture conflicts in the hall—for a moment I forgot where I was, so it took me seconds to connect the applause with Shadow's dull buildup followed by a hand gesturing back to me as the guest speaker. I approached the podium, where I lifted the legal pad's vinyl cover to the first page, presumably of my talk, but actually to blank pages. I kept my eyes on the page as if reading.

"As you all know, the purpose of this meeting is to unify us into one national Hispanic voice to confront this latest backlash against bilingual education by a campaign to make English the United States' official language. The divergence of views that preceded me at this podium give us a clear appreciation of our collective complexity, whether we call ourselves Hispanic Americans, *hispanos*, or *latinos*, and in your specific context, Chicanos or Mexican-Americans. Spanish for our communities, of course, is a not a choice, or an ethnic symbolism. Like any language, it comes from a spiritual center, it translates the soul."

Scattered applause, strong from the middle, moderate from the more youthful back rows, dull from the front.

"And it isn't a foreign language but our American language, spoken in this part of America since Europe discovered there was an America. Our English too is American and properly ours, and in the Southwest English is customized bilingually into a unique voice. For many in this region, then, Spanish is important collaterally with English, a necessary complement to a complex dual cultural personality." Great applause from the rear and the middle rows, moderate from the first rows.

"But still for others, Spanish is simply a political or cultural symbol of a past to be exchanged for greater participation in American culture. A great number have no practical use for Spanish at all. For some of these, Spanish is even the language of shame. They say, like my former classmate at Harvard Law School Raymond Reyes in his recently published book, *Memory from Hunger: The Education of Raymond Reyes*, why bother? Why not use the language of power and cast off the language of failure?"

Applause from the front rows and even middle rows against loud boos from the back.

Jackie returned.

I looked down under the lectern platform to sip water from the glass provided and felt that the hall was rotating. When I straightened up, I paused to look out at the silent faces awaiting my next words, presumably on my legal pad, which I no longer bothered to look at. "So I can only offer for your collective thought the words of my own perceptions." I paused again to formulate those perceptions, reaching back into my entire life story. "English's new apologists argue that bilingual education deprives a generation of children their rightful place in American society. They decry the cultural fragmentation of America. Surprising that line of argument because fragmentation and marginalization have been the substance of our American identity. We call it minority."

The young radicals and the moderates interrupted with a standing ovation. Front-row suits turned to wave at them to sit down.

"For two centuries the words of the Constitution were disregarded, and we the minorities have been expected to continue as the repository of national hope so that someday the country lives by its Constitutional words literally. We are the caretakers of American dreams so the white mainstream doesn't have to worry itself about their input in keeping alive an ideal America."

Both the young back rows and the moderate middle rows cheered. The suits sat with arms crossed.

"We, who have picked fruit, sacrificed son's lives in wars, built railroads, have been usurped from native lands to expand white United States as our down payment toward making the Dreamed America a reality, we want to know when the Anglo will picket and protest toward creating that dream country. We shouldn't surrender our collective past, our cultural sense of worth in exchange for just a civil American citizenship with no true cultural membership."

The radical middle and youthful back rows jumped to their feet, applauding wildly as, on *their* feet, the rows of suits jeered both me and those behind them.

Shadow grabbed the microphone from its fixed base and firmly but coolly pleaded for a civility in the name of La Raza. With hands extended palms-down, he gestured as if by this Herculean theatrical effort he could stuff the people back into their seats. Jackie masked with her hand what appeared to be laughter. Once the crowd composed itself, Shadow covered the microphone and snapped at me, "Look, I don't know who the hell you are or where you're going with this but end it soon." He affixed the microphone onto its stand.

Shadow had addressed me, but I wasn't the speaker. Eduardo had taken control. He took a deep breath, and proceeded: "It's time for us to grow up, encourage our young people to reach beyond aspiring to be 'community harmony representatives,' or 'racial relations officers,' or 'social outreach experts.'"

The radicals cheered.

"Why are we constantly suing in courts just to be liked or recognized? Why do our children waste precious time trying to figure out their confused minority existence rather than just aim to achieve and become self-sustaining. That's the advantage Latin American immigrants have over us: they don't have this ridiculous relationship with American culture and aren't mentally muddled by the junk we grow up with, the pathetic self-doubts and the chronic anger that has been our American identity.

"If this ridiculous conversation is all this country has to offer, then we should become citizens of a wider world. That's why I propose that we master Spanish, become proficient, literate in Spanish and master English, become proficient and literate in it. Not to appease or make stupid political or ethnic statements but to compete effectively in the wider world. True literacy in both languages will permit our youth to do business with and in other countries, not rely on hiring quotas. American culture consecrates ignorance as patriotism. Don't learn Spanish. Don't learn history. Just jump through the hoops. That limiting American culture has made itself the last thing to which you should pay attention in determining your life. A new country is waiting to be discovered in which we are all part of the majority. Tie your children to English Only and you yoke them to this minority-making racket run by carpetbagging dream merchants."

Pandemonium broke out as the radical middle and the entire youthful rear sector stood on their chairs to hoot and cheer while the suits in the front booed violently, stomping on the floor, provoking the radicals to throw their balled-up programs like grenades at the front rows. Mike Maus ran up to the microphone and elbowed Eduardo aside. "We're Americans first!" He urged his sympathizers to stand up and chant. "Americans first!"

From the back arose the cry, "*¡Viva la Raza! ¡Viva Atzlán!*"
Did they hear what I meant to say?

Shadow wrestled the microphone from Maus, then with arms in the air, Charlton Heston as Moses before the people of Israel, he yelled to the top of his thespian lungs to "Please, please, please calm down, brothers and sisters, La Raza should respect diverse views," his voice either successful at invoking reason or arriving when the energy of the outbreak had fizzed out. Slowly the people took their seats. Shadow covered the microphone and told the guest speaker, "That's it. Sit down."

But Eduardo, having vented all he had to say, put away his legal pad and shut his attaché. His walking off the platform prompted more applause, whistles and boos.

Out in the corridor I gave no comments to the pursuing reporter

271

from a cable community news station, who followed me out to the Center's front lobby. I was opening the door to exit when I heard Jackie call.

"Eddie, wait." She tried to contain laughter. "I can't talk right now. At four Arnaldo will be sending a limo to your hotel. Look—you'll get a lot of information from him about me that I would rather tell you myself. Here's my number. One of our drivers will return you to the hotel. Just wait right outside."

"I'll walk. I need fresh air." *After that self-injected massive dose of our Conversation.*

Chapter 30

Downtown L.A. evoked its history: Chicanos, Mexicans, Anglos, Blacks, Asians, banks with the names Federal Western and Wells Fargo, movie houses with the names Teatro Azteca and Teatro Rex. Aromas from a parked mobile *taquería*. I requested two *carnitas* tacos and a bottle of water from the smiling, puff-cheeked *mejicana*. Eating from the provided ledge, I remembered Brother Al's lessons in California history, how Anglo thugs invented a Bear Republic to steal Mexican property. Tacos consumed, I kept walking, seeing the Los Angeles I first saw as filmed for *The Mickey Mouse Club*, circumventing the Mexican imagery, inventing an all-blond California. I reached the hotel.

I disregarded the blinking red message light. With a couple of hours to nap, shower and start refreshed for my date with Arnaldo, I called the desk to be awakened in an hour, then I took off my suit, stretched out. But even though exhausted, I couldn't drift off, picturing myself a Chinese juggler who has been keeping so many plates spinning on top of rods and now they were all teetering, about to crash. I finally did nod off only to be awakened by the front desk feeling as if only minutes had passed. I showered, changed shirts, and put on the same suit, ready for my evening with Arnaldo. At the hotel entrance awaited a gray Continental limousine.

The Bella Tuscana Restaurant where I was taken was in Anaheim.

The maitre'd led me to Arnaldo's table. He got up, shook my hand. "Great you could make it." He called over the waiter, Dominic.

Our ordering drinks and his suggesting entrees out of the way, we got down to business.

Arnaldo thought that conservatives' wanting to overhaul Affirmative Action called for a show that displays its outstanding results. Our meeting gave him an idea for a show on success stories of Affirmative Action deserving of higher profile on a national level. What did I think? "Is Affirmative Action Reverse Discrimination or Pro-Active Equality?"

"How can you tell that I earned my career through Affirmative Action?" I smiled.

"Well, my research shows you jumping from the South Bronx to places like Smith Wesson and Harvard in the seventies. Rocket science?"

Dominic brought a romaine lettuce salad and snail appetizer.

"Do you mind if I interview *you* for a bit?"

The question caught Arnaldo by surprise.

"Are you and Jackie seeing each other?"

"Oh, Jackie's the magic word."

Dominic brought Arnaldo a telephone. "Oh, hello. You just happen to be the main course of our conversation." Enjoying the irony obscenely, his thick mustache stretched over his smile. "Okay, don't worry. Well, why don't you tell him yourself."

I took the phone.

"Well, Eddie, several of Shadow's people didn't speak well of you. Are you proud of yourself?"

"Well, only if *you* think that's bad, that's all that counts."

"Now that you caused a seismic tremor, what do you do?"

I preferred to have this conversation with her alone. "Can I answer that in person?"

"Well, I was hoping to speak with you and explain some other things, but maybe it won't be necessary. I'm sorry tell you now that I can't take you to the airport tomorrow morning, and I believe that Mike will not be disposed. We'll send a cab."

"You didn't answer my request."

"I don't think that'll be possible. Call me later."

I returned the telephone to Dominic.

Arnaldo smiled and nodded. "You've impressed her, I can tell that."

A pair of bus boys rolled in the platters. Arnaldo had ordered us a veal entree that smelled out of this world. Dominic, thin with a bald plate and a skinny mustache, deftly served portions. "So, what did you want to know about Jackie and me? We're close friends. We used to be an item."

"She's pregnant."

"You noticed."

"Is it yours?"

"Well, yes and no. Jackie broke up with Tynan because he refused to have a kid with her. He had kids from a previous marriage and— you know the story. Anyway, she was desperate, her biological clock. We both realized that our relationship was a rebound thing. One day she asked me if I would be the contributor of sperm, promising to make no demands and not even telling the kid unless I later consented. I do think she's a great person, so I agreed to do it. That's essentially it. I confess I don't know if I can keep away from my own blood. I don't think this new science is for us Latins, and I'm planning on getting married again. But you and I are here to discuss the possibility of making *you* the star! I think you have a lot to contribute as exemplary of positive things that Affirmative Action brought about. There are people who see the educational opportunities that you received as a form of social injustice to white youth who never get those chances. You can answer them!"

Gerry Duffy saw my being selected for Excalibur as an injustice and now wants to get even.

I nodded.

"What are you doing tonight?"

"Unless Jackie comes through later on, I'm going back to the hotel."

"Well, I'll let you in on a secret. She was supposed to be my date at a party near here but she just canceled. You can be my date. The hosts are a weird pair. I'll fill you in on the way." We went in his car. He told the limo chauffeur to chill out for a few hours, then show up at ten at the address he gave.

Arnaldo's hosts were a film-producing couple, Peter and Rosette Stone, who started out in children's television, branched out into television miniseries and full-length features and most recently, in Sweden, opened a porno factory specializing in, according to their logo, "kinky adult films in good taste." They were celebrating the tenth anniversary of the founding of their Dog Bite Productions. Inside their spacious split-level house, wall-to-wall people while strains of a piano played a melody vaguely audible. Young handsome shirtless men in black vests and wearing little plastic bow ties meandered through the crowd bearing trays.

Arnaldo was well-received by every person he passed. He especially attracted beautiful women generous with hugs and kisses. At each stop I was introduced as one of the history-making lawyers in New York, responsible for major civil rights victories. We each picked up a glass of champagne as Arnaldo led me through the crowd until he called out, "Peter." Peter Stone was a short, brown Chicano, with a full head of graying hair. He wore gold frame glasses and his face seemed inflated, choked by a black-tie bib.

"I want you to meet Eddie Loperena, a *paisan* New York Rican lawyer who's worked on some high profile cases—and he started out as a poet."

Peter moved a martini glass to his left hand to extend his right hand and greeted me with a squeaky voice. "All right, glad to meet you. You know, I'm a true L.A. *vato*, man, so we're like *hermanos*. It's good to see a *boricua* doing good stuff. In fact, we're just gearing up to hit the Spanish TV and film markets. Oh, Rudy, Rudy! I want you to meet somebody." Peter garnered the attention of all within hearing range, curious to see who was being fussed over.

Rosette Stone née Uberheer, rail thin and gaunt, had disproportionately large breasts. Her mane of bright springing red curls down to her shoulders accented a sallow complexion and washed-denim eyes. She moved blithely in a blue sequined minidress, towering more than a foot over Peter. According to Arnaldo, her parents were Nazis who hid out in Chile. In their dotage she handed them to Nazi hunters. Arnaldo guessed that her half in Stone's business came from gold bars that used to be her parent's. Peter, Arnaldo knew for a fact, had been a street hustler whose money blossomed from the same trees that produced his chronic sniffing and gave him that voice.

"Rudy doll, this is somebody we have to talk to. A hero Puerto Rican lawyer and a writer, from New York. The guy we've been looking for."

"Eddie, my wife Rudy."

She spoke to Arnaldo in a hoarse voice. "And I assume you're going to use him for some show."

Arnaldo smiled.

Her hand hung straight out in front of my lips. Unsure whether to take it or kiss it, I took it.

"So, when can we talk, Mr. Loperena?"

"Anytime," Arnaldo broke in. "But let him enjoy himself first."

"Oh, I'll make certain of that. There are women all over this place who can use a handsome toy." Rudy curled her long left arm around my shoulders and proceeded to steer me through the crowd, first stopping to exchange our now empty champagne glasses with brimming ones. Under Rudy's arm and with champagne already circulating my system, I allowed myself to be moved about, her camcorder.

She introduced me to a middle-aged, bearded plastic surgeon with his much younger looking, surely surgically-rejuvenated wife. An artist with the scalpel, Rudy testified, her right hand lifting as exhibit one of her breasts. Next she pinched the behind of her male graying hairdresser, who had cornered a younger man. Next she pointed to a couple of attractive blonds. "Look at them. What would you say, Bryn Mawr, Mount Holyoke? They're our latest porno stars. There's nothing these girl's won't do, but with such taste and style." Blond Greta of the big tits was Dutch and Blond Toni of the big tits was German. I, of course, was glad to meet them all. "If you want to see more, we can go to the screening room." The girls laughed at the suggestion as Rudy rolled away her camcorder.

"Why aren't men swarming?"

"Everybody knows they're lovers."

As another tray of champagne came around, we picked up refills then Rudy steered me, videotape rolling, past more smiles, quips, comments, toward the door then outside to a figure-8 swimming pool, to its far end where under the night sky a couple frolicked in an illuminated Jacuzzi.

Rudy greeted the couple as they climbed out of the bubbling water, informing me that they were two of their production studio's emerging actors. Fabulous-looking, the dripping pair proceeded to grab towels at one of two poolside tables: he black, muscular, wearing a front-bulging, for-him bikini, and she long-haired Asian with a smooth, proportioned body in a wisp of a bikini. Once dry, the couple put on their shoes and returned to the party, waving at us. They passed Peter, who came out to the pool to call Rudy over. She excused herself. Both laughed about whatever it was. They gave each other a peck on the lips, and he returned into the house.

Her curls bounced to her returning gait. When she reached me, the light coming through her living room window shone through her hair. Peter had just reminded her to run past me that idea they both had for a dramatic television series about a lawyer. "Not a big-bucks lawyer, but a real crusader. The show is about two characters, a Latino Perry Mason who works with a black dick, I mean whose partner is a black private eye, whose clients are from the inner city. Two really smart cookies." Arnie, she quickly added, didn't know about this idea when he happened to bring me to the party. "And when he said that you're also a writer, well that's all Peter had to hear..."

Through my alcohol haze I didn't recall being introduced as "writer" but fortune is fortune.

"We still have to flesh out the concept, but your lawyer experiences should provide some terrific ideas. What do you say?"

Couldn't say no to nothing yet. "Sure."

That was all Rudy needed and instantly switched back to play mode, "Oh, Peter just told me that Arnaldo had to leave, that the limo will take you wherever you want." *Arnaldo playing Cupid.* She spoke undressing. "Doesn't that Jacuzzi look tempting?" She stripped completely. Her tits were enormous and her muff red. Her back was covered with freckles. She slid smoothly into the churning, illuminated water. "Why don't you join me. It's rich."

Chapter 31

The limo swerved a bit too fast out the Stone's driveway, making my head spin more than it already was. *Champ pain, too much champ pain*, and in my brain's fuzzy acoustics Ismael Rivera singing with Rafael Cortijo's combo the refrain about the black guy murdered for having big lips. *Mataron al negro bembón./Mataron al negro bembón.* Rudy in the Jacuzzi was hard to resist but I couldn't keep up my impulse or my dick when my mind was on Jackie.

Submerged in the Jacuzzi, Rudy untied the laces of my left shoe. Alcoholically remote, I also watched her untie the lace of my right shoe. "My husband makes porno movies because he is a liberated and happily married man. Why do you think that is?" I put on my best rakish face, kneeled and softly coddled one of her breasts in the water, but begged her forgiveness because the limo was actually waiting to take me to a late date I had made in Hollywood with a former woman client. I framed it as business turned into pleasure so Rudy could forgive me for declining her beautiful offer for a dignified reason. If not my male image, I hoped to have salvaged my nascent television writer's career. I kissed her wet hand.

Her tone became fully professional, "If we follow through with the television series, we'll be in touch through Arnaldo." Then, mutely excusing me from her presence, she leaned her head back against the edge of the Jacuzzi and closed her eyes. Like the klutzy, clean-cut suitor played by somebody like Jimmy Stewart, I walked the length of the pool, my shoelaces flapping. *Champ pain, champ pain.* A lark with Rudy was worth its own weight in existential pleasure but I intensely wanted to speak to Jackie and there wasn't enough champagne to help me enjoy the moment with abandon.

I plopped into the limo to confront the remainder of my life. After instructing the driver to take me back to my hotel, I called Jackie on the car phone. She had just gotten off the phone with Arnaldo. "You two seem to have really hit it off."

"Any chance we can see each other tonight?"

"Eddie, you are flying off tomorrow morning."

"I don't *have* to go anywhere, tomorrow morning, or anytime."

She sighed. "I'm going to be more frank than I should. I wanted to see you but my feeling this way about you scares me. I see you, as you say, inside, and its chaotic in there. I need to find peace in my life, and you...upset things. I can't join you on your roller coaster, not with this baby coming. The timing's all wrong. I wish you happiness and direction, Eddie. Good night."

The emptiness felt vast, a thick inner asphalt extending for several exits, among them the one to Disneyland in one mile, which in my state reminded me that Graziela had died. I told the driver to take the next exit. "The park's about to close soon," he advised, but we rolled up to the park's entrance. A security person believed my story that I had visited Disneyland yesterday but had forgotten to pick up requested souvenirs for my kids. A lone man in a business suit arriving in a limo at that hour didn't look like someone there to stiff Uncle Walt's Company. On the other hand, the limo probably gave me a privilege the guard would have denied. But the lie was too painfully close to what ruined our day at Disneyland, *a possible kid.* The guard gave the driver instructions where to maneuver toward the parking lot. At that hour no amplified music welcomed me past the ticket booths as it played when Graziela and I entered the park, on that day for me The Least Happy Place on Earth.

Nobody we knew cared to visit this original Disney park. The big deal had become the new one in Orlando. But for both of us as kids Disneyland was that magical place indistinguishable from our dream of California, celebrated every weekday afternoon on *The Mickey Mouse Club*. Disguised as a kid's show, it was a half-hour infomercial on the futuristic park being built in California, America's original Tomorrowland. Carlos and I watched *The Mickey Mouse Club* every afternoon religiously. Graziela watched too and shared the dream of seeing The Golden State.

Our drive across the country was to be our second honeymoon, the restart of our marriage, rocky after I had announced that I was ready to start a family. We visited Amish Pennsylvania, Ohio corn fields. We saw the St. Louis arch, ate Texas steaks, purchased Navajo jewelry in New Mexico, photographed mesas and the red desert. Being so far from our New York seemed to give Graziela and our marriage a new life. She even got affectionate.

But in Las Vegas her period was late, and her reaction informed me to know better than to fool myself that skies were only cloudless blue ahead. Two days later, as we lined up to purchase our tickets to Disneyland, the antics of anxious children visibly disturbed her. Now on Main Street so late at night, few children dotted the crowds and mostly adults and teenage couples strolled along this replica of a bygone U.S.A. I headed toward Pirates of the Caribbean in Adventureland, what Graziela wanted to see first.

No long lines were waiting to enter *Lafitte's Landing*. I boarded a passing boat and, to the recorded singing, rode down the bayou not entertained by pirate episodes on the way to the Spanish Main whose Caribbean port Graziela found so romantically reproduced. Under the crossfire of cannons, I relived her huddle against me and my delusion that maybe she was feeling a genuine honeymoon desire to start over. But her mood changed again, brought on by her period, and she disappeared into herself.

Out in Adventureland night, the steamboat's whistle signaled the last departure. I hurried in time to board it, not the red-haired and freckled Huck Finn that Graziela would have preferred but me, the mustached riverboat gambler. Why is Huck the American icon when the gambler was as also a pure a product of America? Why is innocence the national myth when sweet guys like Bill, Jack and Rob live up to those names in raking in the lion's share of the globe's natural resources? The practically empty river boat sounded its steam whistle and pulled away from the pier.

On the sunny morning that we sailed, Graziela and I were leaning on the rail taking in the sights when a young Asian mother tapped her shoulder, "Take picture, please." Behind the woman waited an entire family arranged by height in three rows, in front a tiny grandma and three small children wearing mouse caps with ears. The family was part of a larger group that had occupied the steamboat, all wearing a green T-shirt identifying them as Korean Methodists. The children waved "Hi." Grace was really good at taking pictures, but she walked away, "You do it." I took the camera and aimed it encompassing Cinderella Castle as we passed it in the background. Camera flash in bright sun. The young mother raised her index finger, "One more, please." Graziela might have behaved differently had we taken this boat at night. No children, only a handful of people trickled out.

I was heading toward Main Street but cut through to Fantasyland, which I barely got to see because of the serious mistake I made after Graziela came out of that Women's Room in Adventureland. She hadn't fully recovered from the scare of her late period and I should have thought better about where I wanted us to go next, Fantasyland: it was full of little children. I tried to distract her by making known that my favorite Disney animation movie when I as a kid was *Peter Pan*. Graziela at first agreed to join me on the Peter Pan ride, then backed out after finding herself on a long line with so many little kids. She had had enough of Fantasyland. I never got to go on the ride.

No children were lined up now, the Peter Pan pirate ships automatically passing for no riders. I zigzagged through the empty queue lanes and hopped on a ship that swept me off into the English night. London shrank below as I flew off to hover across the entire story: Our picking up the Darling children, the arrival at Never-Neverland, the Lost Boys, Captain Hook, the Crocodile, the threatening Indians, the escape from the clutches of the pirates and finally the return home to London. I got off the ride thinking about Captain Hook. The hook that disfigured his body disfigured his life, epitomized in that ever grimacing face. He lived enslaved to avenging his loss.

Loudspeakers announced that Disneyland's grand closing parade was about to begin.

The last steam engine train to Main Street waited. I jumped into the empty rear of a car on whose front benches sat parents with three children, a little boy about four, a girl about six and a baby that the mother cradled while the seated father held a folded stroller. The older children argued over who would hold a stuffed Mickey until the mother, who had been warning them to stop, grabbed the Mickey and planted it between her and her husband, ending the debate. The station conductor came up beside me, looking to the front and rear of the train, and waved to the engineer. The train pulled out.

When Graziela and I took this train the slow summer sun was beginning to set. We were sitting, as I was now, on a car's rear bench with the train filling up. In the front bench a mother leading a little girl of about four by the hand practically threw her onto the bench. Mom was a burly, haggard-looking blond. Behind her a Man-Mountain papa, potbellied, bearded, in blue overalls, with long brown hair held down with a red, railroad-worker bandanna was holding a little boy of about six by the hand. In a voice heard throughout the station he scolded his wife for tossing his little girl into the seat. She waved him off. "Don't you wave that hand at me," he roared. The little girl began to cry. The mother stood up, confronting her husband nose to nose, and responded in a voice as if amplified by the speakers on Main Street, "FUCK YOU. FUCK YOU. FUCK YOURSELF A MILLION TIMES."

Train speakers requested that passengers "please sit down so the train can leave the station." The husband grabbed his wife by the throat, reprimanding her for using language that was not a good example for his children. "Do you understand me? Do you? Say it." His wife gagged out something that convinced him to release her just as five uniformed security personnel materialized. They requested that the family please get off the train and go with them. The huge father ordered his wife and children to stay put, positioning himself between the Disney personnel and his family. One security person extended his hand around the man's girth to coax the boy off the train, and the father kicked him in the shin. "Keep your hands off my kid, you Mexican greaseball."

The five piled on the Mountain Man, who threw them all off as the Keystone Cops from Main Street appeared accompanied by six state troopers, to the rest of the train's applause. The troopers finally handcuffed the man, who was whisked with his family through a camouflaged exit. The conductor apologized on behalf of Walt Disney, then the train rolled out.

Trembling Graziela curled in my arms. I tried to convince her that, all in all, it had been a wonderful day, which she had enjoyed despite that last-minute horror show, that such things could happen anywhere, saying cheery things I did not myself believe, not only about that day but about the illusion of our ever really communicating and having a real marriage.

On this night, the champagne got the better of me as the train left the station. As the night breeze lulled, my eyelids fell. The conductor awoke me to exploding fireworks and whistling rockets that shot into the night sky then burst into globes of shimmering pink and blue particles that descended on both sides of Cinderella Castle. The night's parade had begun and I arrived at Main Street just in time to see Mickey Mouse pass by, scepter in hand, leading the electrically-decorated floats.

Country Bears, Queens and Maidens, Mermaids. A float of King Neptune carried a bounty of illuminated sunken treasure chests, presumably Spanish treasure chests. From one open chest a mustached pirate pulled up and let cascade fistfuls of doubloons. *Carlos.* On the float that followed, Peter Pan led Wendy and the children in flight out a Victorian house window. An amplified voice announced that the parade's theme that season was "It's a Wonderful World."

I followed the floats toward the park exit, deciding to bury

ıere in Disneyland, the parade her funeral procession. On
l site she could purge her sense of stigma of being born
ɘr people, on a meager land with a meager legacy. Poor
Graziela was no match for the psychological press kit that came
with our unsolicited citizenship in 1917 to this wonderful, egalitarian land in which she wanted to be perfectly equal. Something
drove her away from our peculiarly dysfunctional island origins to
an Anglo America that also daily broke her heart. Unable to think
a happy thought, her pixie dust failed her on her flight out the
window. For the first time, I wept for her. I didn't want to be in
Disneyland anymore, suddenly afraid, as I had written in my poem,
that I might die here.

The parade's grand finale continued behind me as I outpaced it
toward the parking lot, toward Realityland. My shutting the limo's
rear door awoke the driver.

Of course, the hotel's phone message light blinked furiously.
Maybe Jackie called, a stupid thought because our lives were exactly
as she had laid them bare. Susana was the one I should be thinking
about if I believed that she were possible. But to invite her as well
to join my messed-up life? Maybe Susana was better off if she came
to her senses as Maritza was able to do.

I disregarded my messages, not needing to hear Sánchez O'Neil
render the prognosis that I had no political future, and then the
kiss off of our friendship because he discovered something more
about me and Carlos. I will land in New York with only the legal
commitment to save myself. I asked the front desk to wake me up
at six, then drifted off into a deep sleep that was interrupted by the
ringing phone. I thought it was my wake-up call but the clock radio
said four. Had to be urgent, so I picked up.

"Eddie, sorry to wake you up so early but I couldn't wait because
I have a lot to do today and have people waiting. First thing, Shadow
called me steaming mad. This can't go on, buddy. Man, you've left
those people in total disunity."

"I know, but I couldn't continue blowing out rhetorical diarrhea."

"Very deep, Eddie, but we're not ready for that yet. I guess I've gone as far as I can with you. You're not with my campaign any-more, I'm sorry. But we're still friends, I hope. I can use you in the background, like before. Maybe that's best."

Are you so sure? I'm just as toxic in the background. Just wait.

"But that's not why I called you so early. We have a real problem having to do with your old friend Carlos. I'm getting beeped right now. Listen to my message so we can talk when you get back. Have a good flight." He hung up.

There was no way I could sleep after that. I sat up, took a deep breath to actually wake up, and listened to his message.

"Eddie, Carlos Benítez got collared yesterday and last night he was found hanging from a prison pipe. They're calling it a suicide. There's more I can't go into now. Carlos wrote something the *News* published that touched the community, especially after a guy locked up in Riker's, the son of a woman in my district, told his mother that he saw Carlos being taken out of his cell. She called *El Diario*. Now people are hurling garbage cans at patrol cars. I have to get out there and cool tempers. I'm planning a rally in Manhattan tomorrow morning and here's where you come in. We've got to move the Mayor to..."

On the red-eye, in the jet's dimly lit steady roar, I sat at the window seat in a cabin of passengers all catching up on their sleep, what I couldn't do because a huge painful church bell in my gut had been tolling the loss of Carlos. Over the tolling I kept hearing repeatedly the words of his letter urging me to inherit his dream and escape for the both of us from our New York Rican lives, hear-ing him as the man but seeing him as the boy, my "big brother," growing up with me on 136th Street.

I finally drifted into a half sleep in which I thought back to when our separation really began with my new life, the year before I left for Excalibur, at the end of our sixth grade. Carlos was put in the smarter A seventh grade, to which I wasn't assigned even though we had the same grades. Mami Lalia believed that I was kept in the B class because I was born in Puerto Rico and not in New York like Carlos. Maybe the school thought I still had more English to learn. That was when I started to lose Carlos because the school was about to do me a favor, although not actually the school but Brother Albert, who made all the difference.

Chapter 32
Brother Albert

A new teacher would be teaching the B seventh, returning to the classroom after working that summer in the South with Dr. Martin Luther King, Jr. He was young, black Irish, and exuded energy. He had recently marched on Washington and arrived charged up to share the experience in teaching us Current Events. He taught us what Negro people endured in the segregated South and about our Catholic duty to support their struggle, a lesson needed in the still mostly Shanty Irish neighborhood: Richard Bell was the only black kid in our class. Brother Albert also taught both sides of the Cold War, of a war going on in Vietnam and about revolutions in the world.

To teach us that our lives were determined by Current Events, every day he read to us from either *The Daily News*, *The New York Post*, or *The New York Times*, an activity that for some reason excited me. After school I started picking up one of the only two newspapers the bodega sold, *The News* or *The Post* and read it completely using a dictionary. The bodega owner Rubén was so impressed by my diligence that he started saving me the copy of what paper he had read. My contributions to the class discussion clearly made Brother Albert proud of me.

But I seemed to be the only person in the entire school who liked him. Whenever he stepped out of the room, the Irish kids would warn us that their parents said that Albert was teaching us "Commie" thinking. One Sunday after mass the Irish parents marched into the Monsignor's office and demanded that Brother Albert be removed. Monsignor lamented that he couldn't get another teacher overnight but that the diocese had promised to reassign him. Brother Al stopped bringing in newspapers and cut short his lessons on Current Events. The class lost its excitement but the Irish kids still kept demonizing him. At the end of the year he said he wasn't sure if he'd see us again but that he had enjoyed being our teacher. The Irish kids were gleeful that their parents had gotten their way.

But no parish wanted his radicalism, and being short on teachers, St. Pete's couldn't unload him. The Monsignor quelled Irish angers by bumping all the Irish students to the "A" eighth grade while containing Al's "Commie" poison to the boys of recently arrived Polish, Hungarian, Italian, and Puerto Rican parents, who did not communicate with each other or that well in English. Being his favorite student, I had been recommended by Al for the "A" eighth grade, where I should have been in class with Carlos. But I was glad to have Albert as teacher again.

Over the summer Al regained his old courage. One day he explained that some years back President Johnson had started a War on Poverty, giving opportunities to poor people. He said this looking in my direction. Poor people needed food to eat and clothes to wear and a place to sleep. Poor people lived in the Congo and in India. Poor people were helped by the nickels that we slipped into the little cardboard box for donations to the missions, our penalty for doing some dumb thing in class. I slept at home with my mother and swam in St. Mary's Park pool. In the summer I was in Puerto Rico where my cousins were lawyers and doctors and our family rented buses to take family outings to the beach. We didn't yet own a TV set in New York and Mami Lalia worked every day, but up until Brother Albert looked at me I had never thought of us as poor.

I didn't connect the Current Events of Johnson's War on Poverty to me until after we got back from Christmas Break, all of us anxious to graduate that spring. Carlos' mom warned that if she lost her job, he'd have to attend a public high school, but Mami Lalia had marshaled her better-off sisters to continue helping so I could attend St. Dominic's High on the Grand Concourse. Then a week after we started the new semester, Brother Albert asked me to stay after class. His request scared me and he quickly added, "we're going to the rectory for some really good news that Monsignor wanted to give you personally."

I couldn't associate the white-haired Monsignor O'Hara with "good news." Tall in his black cassock lined with red, he was the ultimate, frightening school authority. Thankfully, Brother Albert accompanied me. We entered the Monsignor's large office and he greeted me and pointed to the chair directly in front of his desk. He cleared his throat. "Mr. Loperena, in the spirit of our times, an exclusive, private boarding school is offering scholarships to students of color from impoverished backgrounds." He cleared his throat again. "After careful consideration, your teacher, Brother Albert here, has concluded that even though the section-A eighth grade had a couple of Irish and Italian kids with better grades, your grades, Mr. Loperena, were computed to be higher, factoring in your B-group environment, which excelled over those of other students who also belonged to the qualifying socio-racio-cultural target population." He looked at Al, "I'm sorry. I just felt morally compelled to throw that in." Speaking directly to me, "You understand that a boarding school is a place where you live and study there, in this case near Boston?"

I nodded, even though through my fear of the monsignor I didn't really understand.

Brother Albert, he went on, heard about this program and nominated me in the name of St. Peter's School, so "the one to thank here is your teacher, who thinks highly of you. Nothing is certain until that school interviews you with your mother. Brother Albert will be visiting your mother tonight to explain the details. Will she be available?" I nodded. When we left the office, Brother Al explained that he had recommended me for a full scholarship to a private school where I would have to live on a campus, like a college student, and I finally understood.

That night when Mami Lalia got home I told her that my teacher was coming to speak to her and she thought I had done something so horrible. I talked fast to convey the possibility of my getting a scholarship to a really nice private school. Elated, she quickly touched up the apartment, changed from her house dress. I was afraid to hear her reaction when she heard it was a boarding school. Brother Al arrived at around 8:00. Mami Lalia sat him on our sofa and offered him juice. He had just finished dinner. Rosy came out of the bedroom and was introduced. Al commented that maybe she'll be attending St. Pete's next year. And Rosy looked up at Mami Lalia. He asked me if I had given the good news. She answered "Oh, yes."

"That private school practically guarantees Eduardo entry into a good college and a scholarship. But you do understand that this opportunity comes at a cost of seeing your son leave home."

"Why?"

"Oh, I thought Eddie told you. This is a boarding school near Boston, a school where he goes to live."

Mami Lali looked sick.

"This is a rare opportunity."

She promised to think it over.

"I must hear from you soon because they have a deadline."

"Of course."

Al was already up and by the door. He congratulated me again before leaving.

Mami Lalia had promised to think it over but once the door closed behind Al she began to cry and begged me to forgive her because she couldn't allow it. Rosy started crying too. Mami Lalia never told me that she had planned to send Rosy to school in Puerto Rico, so letting me go away to that school would be a pain too hard to bear. The following morning I passed on the bad news to Brother Al. That afternoon Monsignor O'Hara sent a letter for me to take home. It invited Mami Lalia and me to the rectory after the Monsignor said Sunday mass.

Rosy and I sat outside his office as he spoke to Mami Lalia. I was trying to listen to their conversation while Rosy insisted on telling me about a kid in her kindergarten class who ate his snot. I told her to shut up. The Monsignor was detailing for Mami Lalia what it could mean for her son to attend one of the country's most prestigious schools. It hurt her to deny me this opportunity, but she was afraid of losing me to influences away from parental discipline. That was when the Monsignor said he was going to speak to her very candidly.

"I myself am concerned because this isn't a Catholic school. But I must say this, and I don't mean to sound disrespectful. From the looks of things, Mrs. Loperena, St. Peter's parish and the school are due for a change. More people are coming every day, from your country, as you yourself have noticed, from very poor backgrounds, and the stronger danger exists that, in your situation, Eddie will not be able to escape from what this city's streets will be offering him every day of his still young life."

His frankness touched a very sensitive button in Mami Lalia, who had been complaining that the neighborhood was getting worse with riffraff *jíbaros*. She said she knew that possibility and had arranged to send Rosy to be raised in Puerto Rico. Mami Lalia whispered something I couldn't hear and the next thing the Monsignor opened his office door and called us both in.

He addressed me sternly. "I'll be notifying you through Brother Albert on the day and hour when the school representatives will come to interview you and your mother. You will be representing St. Peter's and our Catholic values. Do you feel that you can do that, represent our moral values, both at the interview and then at their school if you leave us?"

I, of course, said yes.

Two weeks later, the private school's representatives met us around dinnertime in the Monsignor's office. Mami Lalia took off from work half a day to go to the beauty parlor. She appeared at the school in black high heels and a blue dress with black lace trimming, looking ready to go dancing. (Years later I would conclude that my mother's colorful folksiness probably secured my getting the scholarship.) Luckily her coat covered everything until we got to the rectory. Rosy was dressed to look as she were going to a party too. I, of course, wore my school uniform, khaki pants, white shirt and blue school tie.

One interviewer, a Latin guy, introduced himself as David Rivera, and the other was a black woman with an Afro, her name Geraldine Jones. They asked questions about my hobbies, my after-school activities, my ambitions. I told her I read a lot, hung out with my friend Carlos, couldn't do much after school while my mother was working. She wanted me home. Mami Lalia was asked about her work, about where she grew up, and her feelings about her son's living so far away. Geraldine Jones understood the hardship of being a single mom as she was also raising two children alone. When the interview was over, David Rivera revealed with a sense of moment that the school in question was The Excalibur Academy. That the name meant nothing to us disappointed them.

Rivera described Excalibur as one of the country's most exclusive schools. He elaborated on its national reputation, exhibiting a special pride in their scholarship program, "which addresses the special considerations of qualified students from communities of color." Mami Lalia showed no reaction just then, and I hoped she hadn't caught the interviewer's actual words. But back home when Rosy was in bed, she asked me to clarify. "*¿Ese hombre...*Did that man say that the school was looking for good students 'of color'?" I shrugged, as if I hadn't paid attention, hoping she wouldn't cancel our scheduled visit to the campus the following weekend. She didn't say any more on that subject although to visit the Excalibur campus she combed out her wavy hair straight back.

Spring hadn't yet warmed up and it was freezing on that Saturday when the scholarship students were invited to see their new school for the first time. Everywhere was still white from old snowfalls, so the green bucolic scenes on the glossy brochure was not what welcomed us. Nevertheless, the elegant campus and its orderly dormitories made a deep impression on Mami Lalia. My future looked promising until we arrived at the welcoming reception for the new scholarship students, when I sensed her reaction and waited for the other shoe to fall.

A battery of teachers had described their respective curricula, and the Headmaster was stepping up to conclude the formalities when Mami Lalia couldn't contain what she had been thinking as she constantly looked around the room. "Of the fifteen scholarship recipients," she whispered in my ear, "one other was *hispano* and the rest *morenos*." Lucky for me the graciousness of her hosts and the administrators' pitch on Excalibur's proven record of producing successful young men and women otherwise had kept her distracted with positives.

On the train back to Grand Central she remained silent as I read *Mutiny on the Bounty*, dreaming that I was Fletcher Christian in love with a beautiful Tahitian girl. I was also hoping that, seeing me read, Mami Lalia would be discouraged from interrupting. She closed her eyes and fell asleep for most of the ride, not waking up until we entered New York from Connecticut. By then I was looking out at sections of the city I hadn't seen before when she spoke as if I had asked for her impression of the school. "*Me gusta...*I liked the clean campus and the school's obvious attention to rounding out a young person's education. I like the new life that it offers you."

The train was crossing Harlem in the setting sun. I opened the novel, hoping that my reading would work a second time, but she continued, not about the school but about Rosy, who was left with our neighbor Gertrudis. "*Rosy tiene que...*Rosy must go back to Puerto Rico, where she'll grow up to be a proper woman. For the same reason, I'm allowing you to attend Excalibur, and that is the only reason why I am consenting." She said nothing more as the train descended into its city tunnel toward Grand Central Station. When the train stopped, we shuffled behind exiting passengers on the platform. We were approaching the stairs when she stopped and said, "*No puedo creer...*I can't believe that they're giving you this scholarship because they think that you are black."

I laughed off her racist island ways just then but overtime realized that my life was about to change profoundly only because all our lives had already changed. We were no longer the people we wanted to think we were, which was differently inaccurate from the people we now were perceived by others as being. Back then, I only intuited that confusion, which in time I would realize was my American identity. My ability to eventually articulate the confusion I traced to my leaving home for Excalibur. So the more immediate credit for this new life I had to give to Brother Albert.

At the graduation ceremony, I felt bad that I wouldn't see him again. Mami Lalia and I thanked him for all he had done. I shared my excitement of looking forward to that boarding school and said that I didn't know how to thank him enough. His answer stayed with me and guided me since then: "If you want to thank me, remain committed to justice."

PART FIVE

TOMORROWLAND

Chapter 33

I had prepared myself for whatever surprise awaited in my apartment. But Duffy apparently hadn't figured out that I lived where the official renter was still Bonino Feliz: the suitcases were still in my closet.

I sat on the sofa, a chess piece threatened by any move. I screened an incoming call, Sánchez O'Neil against a background of bull-horn-amplified rallying cries. "Eddie? I'm in front of Gracie Mansion where we're protesting the killing of Carlos Benítez. I'm ready to resign because Mayor Koch is dragging his ass."

"I'm here. Just came in."

"Did you hear what I said?"

"Most of it. Who arrested Carlos?"

"Duffy's partner Bell got a tip and they grabbed him at a phone booth while trying to make a call. That precinct's been shaking Carlos down for some time. A while back he got in trouble with his own guys and almost got killed. He offered to become an informant if the cops would help him get out of the business. Duffy got rid of his enemies but made sure Carlos stayed in the business to get a cut. So Carlos made his own plans. Some money that cops were supposed to receive as evidence and that they were probably going to take for themselves disappeared with Carlos. Then your Esteban stepped into the shit. The D.A. thought Esteban was involved because Callahan was Duffy's contact with Carlos. Anyway, Carlos knew once they arrested him he was dead, whether or not he gave up anything, so he wrote a letter that he got to Mike Vega, the columnist at the *Daily News*. Vega wrote his own bio of Carlos, which put a different spin on this supposed suicide. He studied at St. Peter's School, went to St. Dominic's High for a year, then something went wrong. Later he was sent to Nam, got wounded and came back to the business. Vega showed that Carlos was a kid the Bronx just ate up and that the cops now just killed."

Yeah the whole sociological, ethnic, politically interesting story, but besides that Carlos had big muscles and a big heart, and I never saw his grandmother ever hug him.

"You still there?"

"Don't tell media people about my being his best friend as kids. I don't want to get personally caught up in this."

"Well, I can't gag Gerry Duffy, who has it out for you. Look, we have to get the Mayor to act fast on investigating his death. You may be a political flop, but now you can do for us what you've always done for us in court. Don't forget your people need you, and both of us are a really from the streets." He dropped a quarter in the pay phone.

I envisioned my life having never met Brother Al and growing up loyally beside Carlos, maybe after a certain point not seeing any hope or any opportunity to achieve the lives that we saw people enjoy on television. I imagined myself making some good money fast and locked up in Riker's Island that night with Carlos. And then I imagined the biography that Eduardo often dreamed of. If only my father had been lucky enough to find a job in one of the new factories and moved his family into our house in P.R. so I would have attended a Catholic grammar school, then a Catholic high school, then the University of Puerto Rico, where maybe I would have met Susana...

"What does that mean, Gus, from the streets?"

"You know what I mean. You're a kid from the Bronx. You kept saying that even after your snobby education. I thought about you all night. You're just a Bronx kid who got lucky, and it was only because of your community, the people you came from, that you qualified and received all the breaks that came down the pike. So now it needs you..."

It was always going to need me, Captain Hook always staring at his hook. But when was my debt paid up? When was I to become Everyman who stares into the universal dark and not just at our streets.

"Eddie, you gotta call Mayor Koch. He respects you and knows you carry clout with the community at election time. He wants us to swallow that Carlos killed himself..."

"I was just about to book a flight to P.R," I thought I said.

"...What the heck, another spick dead in this city is just one less headache, isn't it, shit. I believe his letter, and he wanted out..."

Maybe I only thought I said I was flying to Puerto Rico. But would Susana walk with me down my South Bronx even if the buildings were engulfed in flames, or walk arm in arm down her island world with a flaming New York Rican social stigma? Is this crisis after crisis what I had to offer? And how long will that life last if anybody finds out the person Carlos was trying to reach on that pay phone was me?

"So this is the crap we're facing, the same old battle, buddy..."

From Susana's balcony I'm looking at the harbor lights of San Juan bay. Holding the receiver in one hand, Susana brings me the phone, tells me that somebody named Carlos Benítez had been killed and Sánchez O'Neil needs you in New York to file some legal motions. She isn't happy. I promise her this would be the last time. She starts walking toward me, holding out the receiver but with every step she recedes, shrinking. She becomes the permanently smiling Mickey Mouse.

"Eddie, Eddie, you still there?"

"Still here."

"Look," Gus sighed, coming to the end of his rope with me, and as was his gift, detecting something wrong, "we'll be meeting with the Mayor at three. If you're still one of us, you're there." He hung up.

Two minutes later the phone rang again. Sánchez O'Neil recorded: "I hope you're not answering means you're on your way. Mike Vega came down to report and just told me that somebody shot your Yvette. They hit her in the thigh. She's at Lincoln Hospital.

I guess you'd want to go straight there but she's going to be okay and we really need you here. I sent Isela to see her."

Yvette was probably shot to bring me out to where Duffy's lions could tear me limb from limb. I wanted very much to see her. Yvette deserved that and more. But Esteban would probably be at her side, with a greater right. I looked up Lincoln Hospital's number. The operator connected me to the room where a nurse answered that Yvette was still under sedation. I left the message that I was glad to hear she'll be okay. *I had to let her go with my New York life on my way to...*

I confronted my choices. Carlos was gone, and now I had no option with his "valuable papers." Handing them into any authority will incriminate me, prove Gerry's accusations right. Throwing the suitcases into the East River or burying them in a landfill would gain me nothing. Gerry's boys will never believe that I didn't keep them. *Do it for you and for me*. Carlos' dying wish that one of us fulfill a dream. Do I disappoint him again? *Take yourself home to the Puerto Rico you always talked to me about when you came back every summer...you go home for me, for me, your big brother. Then go kick ass. Tell'em all to go fuck themselves because they can't touch you. Do it for you and for me*. But our "home" no longer existed—if it ever existed.

I thought of that day in the hills with Susana when we rode in the green brilliance on our way to William Guzman. In my desperation, just then I imagined her as a window from which I could leap and actually fly. Susana answered her office phone. I apologized for not calling sooner. I confessed to being afraid that, after that day, the fantasy would lose its glow. She tried to speak but I begged her to let me finish. I acknowledged that this moment was not the best to consider our getting together, but that I needed to leave New York and hide out for a while, why I would explain later. For all I knew, I said frankly, I only needed to use her, because I didn't want to escape alone.

"*Te pido*...I don't want you to talk that way. Don't be afraid of anything, especially of me. I want to use you too."

Eastern airlines only had stand-by flights available. American had nothing. Finally, I booked on Pan American for that evening. I called back Susana, who refused to be deterred from picking me up at the airport at whatever hour.

I emptied my attaché of everything except for two legal pads, some pens. Then from their shadow vault, I removed the suitcase numbered "1," following Carlos' instructions, opened it on the bed. I stuffed batches of Carlos' "papers" in my suit pockets. In moving around the batches, I discovered a buried thick manila envelope. Inside were a batch of photographs and a small, black and white school notebook. The photographs were of Carlos handing an envelope to men in fancy brass-button uniforms, not regular cops. I thumbed through the notebook, a log with names and dates and amounts.

I put everything back in the envelope, threw it in my attaché, along with a change of underclothes, a pair of socks, a shirt and a pair of jeans. I locked the suitcase and was about to shut the attaché when I remembered that I was embarking on the beginning of my new life and so I crammed in the first chapter I had written of my "minority story." I carried the attaché and suitcases to the elevator and down to the garage to my car. I opened the trunk and removed the carpeting, a fiberboard covering, and the spare tire. I filled the spare tire bucket with Carlos' "papers," then covered them with the fiberboard and the carpeting, throwing the spare tire on top. I locked the trunk. In a dumpster next to the garage door, I deposited the suitcases. Bonino had a key to the garage and a spare valet key. He could park the car in my spot behind the deli where Duffy would never look. By the garage door I waited for the car service to pick me up.

The four hours before flying were safely spent at J.F.K. at a terminal bar. I finally boarded the jet, still in my suit since L.A., looking like a businessman with a purpose among tourists and My People. I was assigned an aisle seat beside a woman whose little boy sat by the window. I asked her if the boy was going to spend the summer on the island. She nodded. She only has a two-week vacation and so her sister cares for him summers so he doesn't have to spend entire days alone in their apartment. "*Nueva York es*...New

York is dangerous." I asked if her boy still spoke Spanish. "*Poco.*" The jet engines were revving up for the take off.

By now I too should have grown up a proper citizen as that kid will be, a monolingual English speaker deserving of the American Dream. If I had customized my ignorance and no longer spoken my parents' language or entertained any curiosity about their history or identified with their ancestry, I would have been living way out on Long Island or north of Westchester with a *guerita* and spending my nights drinking with fellow Americans whom the American Story claims all loyally performed the same patriotic ceremony. Despite so many opportunities, I failed to improve on my inferior origins.

I should have also been marching with Sánchez O'Neil before the Mayor's mansion, performing my role of defender of the equality and worth My People in the name of centuries of oppression of people of color, demanding municipal contrition for the NYPD's murder of a Puerto Rican boy that the Bronx had chewed up. By my accusation I would have honored my Constitutional freedom to litigate and exact financial retribution from a just society that, when brought before the courts, really did not diminish the value of human life. And the crime would have behooved me to exact even more payment having all the signs of a racially-motivated crime, committed on the sinful assumption that Carlos' colored life was disposable.

Instead I was *in flight*, also failing Brother Albert. His truly American spirit inspired me to confront un-American injustice, to demonstrate in his name that in a grand Hollywood finale the better angels of American nature would triumph. One day I tried to find Al's whereabouts, and a priest told me that he had left the brotherhood and married a former nun. Did Al, like Winston, bailout of the shot-down seventies? Would he understand why his favorite student was in flight, fleeing from his promise to fight for social justice?

The jet was lifting the weight of my history into the sky, and I was again in the air, as in all my life. In the little window receded glittering New York, a Nova in infinite space. This moving jet, according to international conventions, was U.S. territory, not unlike Puerto Rico, a conceptual extension of a disconnected geography. In physical reality, Puerto Rico is commanded by ocean and climate, like it this jet was in fact traveling through the Cosmos, strictly speaking, Nowhere. I thought of Carlos' idea of traveling from place to place like the character in that old TV program, *The Man without a Country*. Carlos, I realized just then, had really called my office to tell me that he too was tired of his American anger and wanted to be home if he could find it.

I shut my eyes wanting to sleep, but despite the two scotches at the terminal bar, I couldn't nod off. Once we reached cruising altitude, a woman flight attendant came down the aisle offering headsets for the movie followed by another attendant offering refreshments. The boy by the window took the earphones and a ginger ale with a bag of peanuts. The movie started playing on the monitor.

Some boys hiked in a woods, reminding me of a hike I took with some Excalibur classmates. We were working as a group for a science class, gathering leaves and moss. The leaves had turned colors and it was chilly. On the way to the spot we were told provided the best samples, a classmate named Julian Foster told us about his having gone that summer to Disneyland. It was my first semester at the school, the year before I roomed with Teddy Katsavos and made real friends with his "artsy" crowd, so being with those guys I still felt like an outsider. But when Julian started telling us about Disneyland, about which everybody knew every detail from *The Mickey Mouse Club*, we were briefly all real pals. In the movie, the boys in the woods discover a human finger.

I shut my eyes, and this time finally dozed off until roused by the plane's bouncing preamble to landing. The male flight attendant reviewed that seat belts were affixed and trays up as the jet dropped down altitudes, leveled out, and then dropped down more altitudes, repeating the pattern until, in the window a glitter of another Nova's lights came into view. At that moment I willed this flight to be the fantasy escape to our beginning that Carlos believed possible, our leaving behind our American anger to return home where all unhappiness is cured and we as a people sing as we walked politically independent and without fear of want on our tropical green Paradise. The landing gear grumbled as it extended, and suddenly my hand was no longer a hook as a flashing Tinker Bell led our way. Carlos and I were free of The Conversation forever as our flying pirate ship descended into the post–industrial lights of Never Never Land.

Chapter 34

Nowhere, Two Years Later

The exhilaration of my fantasy-landing in Carlos' name was quickly extinguished by the reality of my still being tethered to New York, where I still existed in blooming narratives. A columnist from *The New York Post* commented on how my sudden disappearance seemed to support Gerry Duffy's accusations of ties to a drug dealer. He ascribed my reputed absconding to my having grown up bonded by our shared street culture to this Big Carlos that The Community was now defending. Objectively and articulately the writer argued that Eduardo Loperena fell into disgrace because you can take the Puerto Rican out of the Bronx but you can't take the Puerto Rican out of the Puerto Rican.

I was also tethered across the Atlantic through messages left on my office answering machine by Sánchez O'Neil, Yvette, Bonino. William Guzmán left me several, but given the dirigible of suspicion floating over my sudden disappearance, I couldn't engage in a chat possibly monitored by the F.B.I. Either the plan to smuggle in Timmy was ditched or it succeeded in reuniting him with Arturo and he finally got to see his son Carlos. Timmy's arrest would have overloaded the news wires.

A week had passed and I had yet to notify Mami Lalia where I was. She left me a message in my Bronx office worried because Luis had called her after someone just back from New York had told him the news of my disappearance and its being reported as linked to some drug business and some missing money. I called Mami Lalia to explain that Luis was repeating baseless rumors about nefarious connections, that I had left New York to return to Susana, and to induce even more secretions of calming dopamine, I described our passionate reunion as a soap opera that needed to be continued after our first meeting on Rosy's wedding day. Mami Lalia, of course, had foreseen this climax.

Thanks to Susana's cable service that provided New York TV channels, two days after I got here I learned that Duffy was indicted. The following day six more cops handed in their badges, among them Richard Bell.

I felt bad about waiting that long to contact Sánchez O'Neil after he counted on me to confront Mayor Koch. Late into the night that I disappeared he left me the message, "Okay, Eddie. This is a tough one. I guess you're not with us anymore." In the morning, his throat hoarse, he expressed fear that whoever shot Yvette had killed me: "Call me, Eddie, at least let me know you're still alive."

Once out of danger I called his personal line at an hour when he was most likely tied up, so I could fully articulate my rationale that Yvette's shooting was a message that I interpreted as a death threat, forcing me to vanish until the arrest of Duffy's gang. I left him Susana's number. He didn't return my call. Three days later I called again. Several days passed before he called, cordial if distant. He had been very busy.

I asked about Yvette. He said that he visited her at the hospital, introduced himself as being there on my behalf, apologizing that I couldn't show up. "Of course, for you, she understood. I asked if she knew who could have shot her. She shook her head then thought out loud, 'maybe one of those two who on the night that Eddie...' Then she stopped, just looked at me. Esteban showed up, so that was that. Clearly something was going on I didn't know about. Frankly, I don't know if I want to know, and that's not why I'm calling."

After his building me up as his campaign manager, the ugly rumors surrounding my disappearance were poisoning his run for Congress. Both his Democratic primary opponent, the Barrio-bred Richard Fonseca, a labor lawyer who worked for Local 1199 Service Employees International Union, and his rival Republican running for the same East Harlem congressional seat, Mario Marcantonio, a dentist whose practice was above Patsy's Pizzeria, a vestige of Italian Harlem on Pleasant Street, were portraying him as my crone covering up for my being a longtime secret partner of Big Carlos. *Marcantonio's great great grandfather was the legendary socialist New Deal Congressman Vito Marcantonio, so poor Vito must daily spin in his grave.*

"I don't believe Gerry's trash talk and how I feel right now, don't know if I believe you either but you gotta get back here and undo what damage has been done to my campaign. And if helping me isn't a reason enough to get your ass back here..." He paused. "Gerry's jerked off that Oreo DA Johnson about your taking off with drug money so now *he's* horny to fuck you good. He's already interviewed everybody who knows you, including me."

Sánchez O'Neil tried to cover for me before Johnson, vouching for knowing my every move because I was his point-to legal advisor. He cited the shooting of Yvette as one of many death threats, ginning up my cause with my being burned out after years of social struggle while enduring an unhappy marriage, invoking Graziela's well-reported death. "Johnson didn't swoon at the end of that love story, so if you don't clear up this shit, you can kiss your new love and say goodbye for several years, *compa'.*"

I agreed to perform the necessary cosmetic surgery on our public images by meeting with Johnson.

"But before you talk to him, I need to have some questions answered, face to face."

Susana understood the danger Johnson posed and I promised her to be back in two days. I scheduled an appointment with Johnson for Monday morning, flying out on Sunday morning, leaving that evening to mend things with Sánchez O'Neil. We met away from

The Community's eyes, at Lanza's in the East Village. Our effort to be characteristically jovial was strained. I described Susana and my plans to stay with her after surviving this business with Johnson.

"You're sure you can hack it down there."

"I don't see myself as being down there or anywhere, just with Susana. I can now write as I had wanted and when I get sick of being there, we'll come to my apartment, which I still sublease from Bonino."

"What do you plan to do to make a living?"

"Don't know yet."

"I can use your help in Washington every so often."

"Sounds right."

He looked at me and grinned. Took a sip of Chianti. *He was being patient.* Our entrees arrived. I described the madness of my sister's wedding, my brother-in-law's pro-statehood fanaticism. My storytelling was intended to postpone business in the hope that the bottle of Chianti we were knocking off might soften what suspicion he withheld in reserve behind his crafty loyal pose that made no mention of the real business at hand. He had eaten most of his Italian cheesecake dessert and was finishing his cappuccino when, the bottle empty, I thought the moment right. "Gus, I have another story to tell you, the one you've been waiting for."

He nodded, wiping his lips.

"I hadn't heard from Carlos in more than twenty years. He was in deep trouble and needed to travel light, so he asked me to hold two suitcases of his personal possessions..." I conveyed the guilt I had harbored because I left Carlos behind in the Bronx, "He didn't have an island family, no one to support him in New York, no role models of our own culture that wasn't the narrow, *jíbaro* world of our South Bronx. The scholarship luck that tapped my shoulder never tapped his. The year I left for Excalibur, Carlos had to attend a public high school, made different friends. At a party he met an older woman who made a living selling cocaine. My mother heard of Carlos' new ways and insisted that I sever our friendship. I did but through the years I wondered if I had not left him behind maybe I could have influenced his choices. When he called me, I couldn't abandon him again. So I agreed to hold his suitcases, which he promised to recover soon. No drugs, just papers, some photographs. When he died, I was trapped. My connection to him in any way, once revealed, would instantly incriminate me. Anybody could invent any duration for my involvement with him and claim whatever of the contents of those suitcases. Gerry got it in his head that Carlos had left me some cash that they were expecting to get and, because he never got over my receiving that scholarship to Excalibur, broadcast that story about my secret partnership. You can't count on two hands the assistant D.A.'s who after feeling shat on by me in court wouldn't send out invitations to festively barbecue me."

He nodded, chuckling. *His gaze was steady, a veneer of loyal appreciation coated a core of unenchanted scepticism.* "But Carlos did get in touch. And what did the suitcases contain?"

"As I said, personal things, photographs, a diary he kept, important papers. But just the fact that I once knew Big Carlos feeds any good imagination."

I opened my attaché on my lap and removed a manila envelope. Holding it up, I explained as Carlos explained to me in a note he left with the photographs: "To protect his ass from never coming out of some basement alive, Carlos insisted that pay-offs always be made in public spaces. Cops in undercover would either go through a garbage bin or pick up a paper bag from under a park bench. Lower-level guys like Duffy and Bell did that, but nobody's seen hard evidence of rumored higher officials. Those guys got their cash hand-delivered by Carlos himself in remote areas at odd times, such as early morning in the Bronx park surrounding The Botanical Gardens. Very stately, gold-buttoned uniforms arrived looking dapper for the photographs Carlos paid someone to take with a telescopic lens." I handed him the envelope. "These are duplicates. Look at them so nobody near can see them."

Sánchez O'Neil held the envelope close to his chest like a poker player. He displayed random combinations of eyes widening, eyebrows arching and nostrils flaring. I then handed him another envelope with copies of the backs of the original photos, on which Carlos handwrote the name of the recipient, the date, the place, and the amount. He perused them, chuckled again, handed everything back.

"The court can verify that those pictures weren't doctored and can professionally compare the handwriting on the log Carlos kept with the handwriting on the back of the photos and with the letter that Carlos handwrote to Mike Vega at the *News*."

An ice skater's spin couldn't have been smoother than the Deputy Mayor's reversal of attitude. He became once more the old prankster Sanchez O'Neil. Not just, I figured, because he wanted to purge this rancid issue adulterating his campaign but because I knew he had some issue with Johnson he never made clear although I suspected it had something to do with the woman he brought to Father Steven's fundraiser. Getting Sánchez O'Neil drunk, if not on Chianti, on the power he could exercise over Johnson was also key to my strategy to divert his attention from a more itemized inventory of Carlos' personal possessions.

He begged for the pleasure of delivering the evidence as my representative, and I took advantage of his exuberance to get his guarantee that he wouldn't pass on this material to a sycophant journalist on the prowl for a scoop. He beamed at that good idea but agreed. I then handed him another manila envelope of photos, this batch with the faces cut out. Those puzzle pieces I had put into a business envelope along with the copies of the backs of the originals. I suggested that he present the faceless photos first and invite Johnson to actually see faces and names. He could decide to become an accessory if he didn't follow through. Gus giggled, loved it. I called for the check, paid the tab, my gesture imposing a conclusion to the evening, an inertia against backtracking to remember that we really hadn't exhausted an explanation of the contents of Carlos' suitcases, the agenda having moved on to the following day.

Sánchez O'Neil had his fun as I waited parked by a fire hydrant in front of the D.A.'s Bronx office near Yankee Stadium. He had left me copies of the three newspapers he read every morning, but I never got past a couple of *Times* stories when he was back. "At first he said the faceless photos don't prove anything, and I said, 'Yeah but they do with the faces and names.' Would you like to take a look? They're in this envelope, along with a handwritten record of names, dates, places, and amounts. Johnson grabbed the second envelope but didn't open it. He asked me to leave the material as he was going to investigate thoroughly this serious allegation. I advised him that these were all copies, of course, and that to start his investigation properly he should clean the slate and publicly exonerate my campaign manager from Duffy's accusations because money has obviously also disappeared thanks to the sleight of hand of the NYPD. Man, we couldn't get luckier. Duffy is going down making accusations that brass was taking a slice of his pie and here I walk in with proof. Johnson doesn't have the *cojones* to touch this shit. Love it."

Sánchez O'Neil had earned lunch, which I enjoyed with a qualified relief, suspecting that he remained loyal by suspending judgment of me, between a rock and a place not exactly as hard and maybe even awfully cushy. That night I flew back to Susana.

The next day Sánchez O'Neil called me to tell me that that morning he would be giving a press conference to broadcast the D.A.'s press release that I had been cleared of any wrongdoing. The following day I watched on cable the local CBS New York news report that over two million in cash had been found stuffed in the back seat of a minivan garaged at the home of Carlos' arresting detective, Richard Bell. The news video showed piles of bills, citing a police spokesperson that the money was believed to have been taken at the time of the arrest of the dealer known as Big Carlos. Bell was the collaring cop of record and owner of that minivan containing the money. Those photographed brass buttons were spared years of shameful oxidation.

Two years have passed, but Sánchez O'Neil tells me in a light-hearted yet suspiciously skeptical way that, despite my being legally exonerated, Rican political leaders still smirk every time my name comes up. And not just leaders, The Community still spreads the joke. Six months after I came down here, Mami Lalia whispered to me that her Dominican neighbor heard from Bronx relatives that the word going around has me vanishing from New York with a shitload of drug money. Of course, she assured me that she never gave gossip a second of her valuable time, especially not Dominican *chisme* that maligned her son. For nothing could shake her conviction that I would do nothing wrong and that my returning to be with Susana was actually the handiwork of San Judas Tadeo, who paid her the ultimate dividend when, the month before, Susana and I eloped and spent our honeymoon on St. Thomas. Tadeo, in fact, was coming through a second time because on last Lincoln's birthday Rosy gave birth to my nephew Abraham, blessing George beyond words.

Susana and I planned to have a family soon, given our ages, and she's expecting in seven months, another almost-American citizen. She sold her condo, and we now live with her birds in a house she had always dreamed of, a sugarcane plantation's main house facing the Sea of Nowhere. A mansion of another time raised on wood pillars, with a new metal roof of wave-molded zinc slabs painted green, refurbished with a modern interior. This house is on a private acre moated by the reality of our love against any delusions about My People or the defunct Paradise to which all my life I had dreamed of returning.

It's easy to confuse my lost Paradise with this place, my Nowhere. The sizzling sun's the same over the same emerald landscape. The same coconut palm trees line resort-quality beaches. The same floppy plantain fronds glisten green along its central mountain range. The same red-orange Flamboyant trees flame amid the green hillsides. The same clean highways all lead to sprawling, traffic-congested San Juan. In other words, this place identically resembles that floating factory that mass-produces inhabitants who simultaneously pursue their cultural independence and their *Jíbaro* American Dream, industrious their schizoid frolic on a long, colonial leash.

For my part, I am separately decolonized, a citizen of politically independent Nowhere with a pied-a-terre in the Bronx, where Susana and I spend long weekends and vacations. In my free country

I keep up with New York developments good and bad. Figaro, for example, last year felt the first symptoms of AIDS. He held on with drugs and moved to New Jersey, where his sister cared for him. He died a few months later. On the same sad note, last year the poet and playwright Usmail Rufo died of an overdose of heroin. I attended a memorial ceremony at the Simpson Street Community Center, invited at the urgency of Bonino Feliz.

On our occasional trips, while Susana shops or visits a friend, I take Samson out for lunch, leaving him a little something he can spend. Susana and I attended the wedding of Abigail Gainsay at the Puck Building. The Gainsay's faith in me can resist a nuclear explosion. Other developments: Esteban and Yvette married six months after I came down, and she recently had another baby girl. Arnaldo Ribera, the TV reporter, never did get back to me. Neither did the *vato* Peter Stone call from Los Angeles. I presume that both Arnaldo's interest in me and my possible television writer's career with Stone blew up in the same explosion of my scandalous disappearance. At least one writer did well: Bonino Feliz had a moderate best seller last year, another science fiction novel under his pen name Felix Goode. Finally, the cherry on top: Buzz Tencuidao worked successfully as Gus's campaign manager, and now I regularly do legal work for Congressman Sánchez O'Neil, which requires that I fly to Washington. He says that anonymously I've been a greater asset to My People than I was as an activist lawyer.

Sometimes New York visits me. After the last elections, the now thrice re-elected City Councilwoman Isela García Chase flew down for the closing of a condo she purchased in Isla Verde. She never re-married and instead of running for a fourth term is preparing for her retirement in her enduring illusion of Paradise. She's gotten chunkier. She said I looked happier than I had ever looked, a hard admission because Graziela was her good friend. She fell in love with Susana. We went to see her huge condo, fifteen floors up in Hato Rey. I advised her not to unpack at least one bag because we Ricans live in a braid of our mainland and island worlds. She said the island had never stopped feeling like home but I took skeptically the thought of her readjusting to how it had changed, perhaps because the weekend before Susana and I were dining at an Italian restaurant in the Condado and bumped into Martiza Islas.

Luis had told me that she had married some island Somebody. Last year she landed a tenured position at the University of Puerto Rico's Río Piedras campus, an appointment riddled with the finger-prints of local *Senador* Juan Acosta, who now sponsors a Draconian initiative against drugs, a project that recently segued into another. Talk of testicles larger than NBA hoops, Acosta invited the fresh-man Congressman Gustavo Sánchez O'Neil for a weekend at the Dorado Beach Hotel to discuss channeling federal money to his anti-drug measures—milking The Community's mainland nostalgia for kindredness. Over a drink with real friends, he will surely laugh at his taking for a fool a *newyorican* who fantasizes that he's Puerto Rican while Sánchez O'Neil will have widened his power base in Washington by tightening the webbing between the mainland and a congressionally impotent and needy island.

Sánchez O'Neil reserved his free Sunday afternoon for *piña coladas* with us. Susana looked great in a white flaring dress with a royal blue flower-print sash around her waist, with her long hair hanging loose, showcasing her equally beautiful personality that incited the *caballero* in the Congressman, who let her know in his *jíbaro* Spanish that I was one lucky man. She thanked him for that complement in English, settling him into his more mellifluous linguistic comfort zone, where we stayed.

Sánchez O'Neil shared with us the challenges of a freshman congressman, knowing whom to help from the long line of suppli-cants, sycophants, and lobbyists, such as Acosta with his anti-drug program. He brushed off my reminder that Acostas pissed on me and mainland Ricans at Smith Wesson: "He's a local senator of Podunk. I'm a Congressman of the United States."

I heard in his answer Susana's wisdom that now that I had stepped out of the American Conversation, I also had to liberate myself from the Boricua Conversation and not flatter Acosta with anger nor empower any other Acosta who would rankle me. "*Solo disfruta...*

Just enjoy your life with me and write. That's all that matters. You know what you are and I know what you are and that's enough." In other words, I was reminded that I was indeed one lucky man.

Here I come to the end of my book, not the minority story that Louise Hobson encouraged me to write to kick off my writer's career, of me as a metaphor of American promise. Instead I wrote to dispel rumors that would bury in public palaver the sincere years that I devoted to defending The Community. I had to explain, knowing that my decision could undo everything I had achieved, why I did not abandon Carlos again. I started out convinced that I fully understood my motivations for that decision. But as I wrote, more sharply I came to understand that decision as the consequence of the toppling of a domino in my life by a preceding domino fallen by a prior one, on and on, my present under the weight of my past, my decision the ineluctable consequence of my American life.

Finally, I cannot end without acknowledging my debt in completing this book to the impassioned madness of Bonino Feliz, whom I may have portrayed less respectfully than the stern editor who emerged to rescue it. Bonino interpreted my fall from celebrity grace as the self-immolation of an angry New York Rican who emerged from the flames with his middle finger upright, telling American culture to speak with one tongue or sit on it. Bonino inspired me to complete this book after I began to doubt its value or sense. For I set out pretending to write not as a whining minority but as Everyman driven by greater ideas, and in the end, because that is how our American lives are rigged, I only produced another elaborate session of our pathetic Minority Conversation. I shared my state of mind with Bonino in a letter that accompanied my first draft.

His response: his edits of the manuscript arrived with a videocassette of the original 1958 black-and-white version of *Invasion of the Body Snatchers*. Human-like aliens land on earth, farm plants that grow pods full of a sap that, when the pod is placed beside a sleeping human, gels into a vegetal clone "advanced" in lacking feelings and therefore pain—or joy or love—usurping the life and identity of the sleeper. The newborn clone then disposes of the now useless donor body. I had seen the 1978 remake also about modern dehumanization. But while viewing this original version my thoughts drifted to how much easier my life would have been if I had slept beside an American pod and awakened to do the American thing, worked for a Manhattan law firm, raked in the big bucks that my Harvard crown was worth, having evolved not to be distracted by impractical feelings.

Bonino saw the same imagery differently, and fearing that I would miss his point, he followed up the video with the letter: "I sent you that video because I see its metaphors as central to you and your book, the *boricua* humanistic soul snatched by vegetal passionless, dehumanized *americano*. But you refused to fall asleep so a two-dimensional double could dispose of your three human dimensions. Our history is not epic, our geography is small, so we must measure ourselves by our capacity not to be defeated. An imprisoned inner self screams to be cleansed of a pathetic colonial history whose latest chapter is our crippling American identity, which must be rebuilt again from scratch, on equal terms. From the "bad" Agüeybaná, the brother *cacique* who never believed that those stinking iron-clad bearded white men descended from heaven, to our *criollo* ancestors who spat at Spain's divine right to rule, who sharpened machetes and leveled musket balls against it, and whose descendants later shot up the U.S. Congress and in desperation placed bombs in New York, something in us refuses to capitulate to others' insistence that we be small. Your story is not just about you and changes our culture even if our own people don't read your book or don't understand what you are getting at. I see you as our Don Quixote who can say what he said after failing at his ramshackle errantry, 'Nobody can deny the nobility of my effort.'"

Heroic Bonino and Isela García and Sánchez O'Neil, towering minority repositories of American hope, pushing their elephantine country toward true color-blind and unethnocentric equality, armed only with their mutilated national membership and fueled by their American anger. Graziela and Carlos rebelled against the worlds to which they were sentenced and found an escape that killed them.

We all sought the same redemption but I was the least heroic and the squanderer of the most opportunities.

For despite being passed the mantle of Brother Al and Nicholas Gainsay, who both envisioned in a chamber of Jefferson's heart a perfected democracy like a distant galaxy to be reached someday. Despite being compensated for my patience with my equalizing education, I couldn't endure the uphill struggle to belong experienced as a lifelong really-not-belonging, an identity of perpetual exoticism, perpetual aspiration, passed on to my children and grandchildren, doled-out glimpses of hope from the manipulative largesse of supremacy. I could not. I could not. I could not. And nobody can deny the nobility of my failure.

yes! the rebellion of the educated hyphenated man